EJNER FULSANG

_____

ENCELADUS

Århus Publishing

Copyright

© Ejner Fulsang, 2024

Author's photograph by Ejner Fulsang

Other Scientist and Project Manager photographs in Acknowledgements section are courtesy of NASA

Cover art by Douglas Shrock www.shrox.com

SAN: 850–3052

ISBN (Amazon Kindle eBook): 978-1-7334962-2-3
ISBN (Amazon Paperback): 978-1-7334962-5-4

Contents

DEDICATION

Dr. Frank Drake, affectionately known at SETI as "the equation guy," is the namesake of the Drake-class starship that will appear on the cover of Book VI, Ross128b. Sadly, Frank passed away in September 2022.

$$N = R^* \times f_p \times n_e \times f_l \times f_i \times f_c \times L$$

— Frank Drake, 1961

where

- N = the number of civilizations in the Milky Way with which communication might be possible.

and

- R^* = the average rate of star formation in our Galaxy.
- f_p = the fraction of those stars that have planets.

- n_e = the average number of planets that can potentially support life per star that has planets.
- f_l = the fraction of planets that could support life that actually develop life at some point.
- f_i = the fraction of planets with life that go on to develop intelligent life (civilizations).
- f_c = the fraction of civilizations that develop a technology that releases detectable signs of their existence into space.
- L = the length of time for which such civilizations release detectable signals into space.

THE NAMESAKE OF THE COVER SPACESHIP

While I am certain **Dr. Jonathan Lunine** would say lending his name to the spaceship on the cover of this book is his career high, he does have a few other minor achievements worthy of note. For one, he is now the chief scientist of NASA's Jet Propulsion Laboratory. Prior to that he served as the David C. Duncan Professor in the Physical Sciences and as the Astronomy Chair at Cornell. A Caltech alumnus, he has researched where environments suited for life might exist in the solar system and beyond. He was an interdisciplinary scientist on the Cassini mission to Saturn and was the principal investigator of the *Enceladus Life Finder* mission[1].

Like any good scientist he has a rap sheet of publications that goes for days, but one that I found particularly worthy was a textbook he wrote back in 2005, *Astrobiology—A Multidisciplinary Approach* (Pearson Education—Addison-Wesley). In it can be found several chapters addressing the origin of Earthly life, a topic for which he and I share a keen interest. Cracking that problem will inform our search for alien life.

---

[1] https://en.wikipedia.org/wiki/Enceladus_Life_Finder

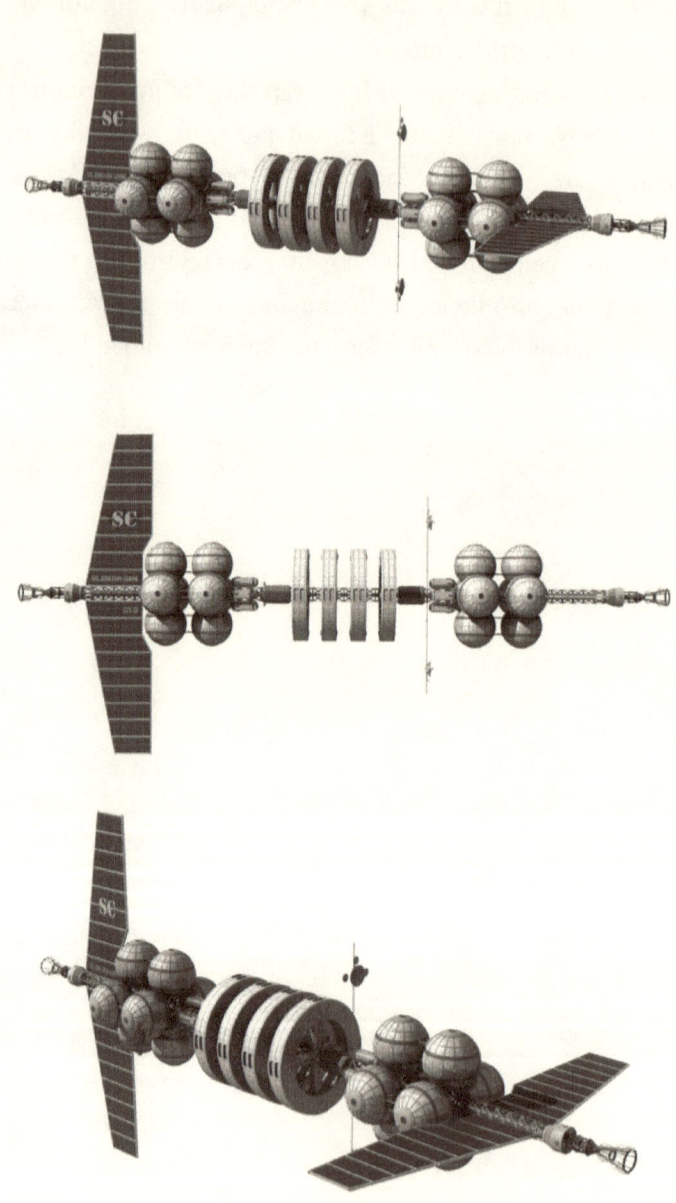

SIS Jonathan Lunine by Douglas Shrock

iii

THE SAGA THUS FAR...

I started working on *The Galactican Series* some fifteen years ago, worried that at the rate NASA was going, we were never going to evolve into a true, as in interstellar, spacefaring society. NASA as well as the FAA and most other government agencies needed to be circumvented in order to make way for the technological earthquake needed to begin living among the nearby stars. Hence, in Book I, *SpaceCorp*, I set the stage for the rest of the series by clearing out all the bureaucratic and political impediments currently standing in the way. For this I chose the time-honored SciFi device known as the dystopia.

Dystopias are normally designed to appeal to the Young Adult literary market since most of the stuffy old rules of society are suspended in the interest of survival and those stuffy old adults that created them are too neophobic to break those rules and end up being led to salvation by their more resilient children. That sort of literary fare is hard to resist if you're an uppity teenager. Not so with *SpaceCorp*. Book I's dystopia serves only to clear the stage for humanity's next evolutionary act—the great diaspora beyond the Solar System. Teens and preteens need not apply.

So why do we need to become a spacefaring society? Why not concentrate on overhauling good old Spaceship Earth? Simple. Earth has a use-by date, same as every other habitable planet in our galaxy, and no amount of overhauling will prevent that. All planets eventually die of natural causes, e.g., their stars go nova, or they get whacked by a rogue comet or a gamma ray burst or a magnetar or whatever. Failing that, their so-called intelligent inhabitants, having been conceived by Darwinian evolution, inevitably end up authoring their own doom through stupidity, e.g., war, climate change, overpopulation, habitat destruction, or resource exhaustion. IMHO this is the most practical explanation of the Fermi Paradox. Intelligent societies fail to become spacefaring societies because they are eliminated by natural or artificial causes before they get the chance[2]. Hence, we never see them. And if we do not wish to suffer the same fate, we need to supercharge our R&D efforts.

You may think it pretty amazing all the wonderful things NASA has accomplished lately what with the JWST and OSIRIS-REx and all those little robots scurrying about on the surface of Mars. But trust me, compared to what we need in order to become permanent interstellar citizens, they amount to clever billiard trick shots. What we need are self-sustaining space worlds, aka generation starships, that can travel at fractional light speeds while maintaining mini-societies that number in the thousands and that possess the ability to replicate themselves and their habitats when at long last they arrive at stellar systems possessing healthy asteroid belts. *"The ability to replicate themselves."* ISRU or *In Situ* Resource Utilization—the ability to arrive at a stellar system dozens of lightyears away and to scout its asteroid belt for the raw materials necessary to manufacture every single part of a starship—a carbon copy of the one that brought you here. No going back to Home Depot to buy a dozen framistats because you can't find any smackumpuckie. (Everybody knows

---

[2] http://robinhanson.com/greatfilter.html

smackumpuckie is a vital ingredient of framistats.) ISRU is the most key technology. It's what will determine if humanity is to survive.

The second most important part is the ability to husband myriad resources for centuries at a time which in turn means closing a lot of poorly understood control loops. Look up the Biosphere 2 disaster if you don't believe me. At least when Biosphere's unfortunate crew emerged after a measly two years, they could immediately fill their lungs with breathable air and their bellies with the nearest giganto-burger. Not so when you're ten light years from home. Read Kim Stanley Robinson's book *Aurora*.

This is also a good place to point out that colonizing exoplanets with the intent of eventually terraforming them is a really bad idea. Even if those planets were habitable at one time, there is a reason they are no longer habitable. Will your terraforming schemes account for that? Far better to wander the heavens in a permanent home that is already complete with a proper full gee of gravity, a working hydroponics system, pickleball courts, wet bars, dog parks, and that is relatively free of alien superbugs. It is mainly for this reason that SpaceCorp interstellar craft are more akin to cruise ships than airliners. If you happen across a nice-looking planet that might be habitable, leave it alone. Mine the nearby asteroid belt for any raw materials you might be short of. It is far easier to dock with a resource-concentrated asteroid than to descend the gravity well of a planet to search for, mine, and process scattered ore deposits. By all means visit the surface (following planetary protection protocols) to search for alien lifeforms that may provide variations of DNA not yet found on Earth—those will be insanely valuable. But do not try to colonize it or mine it.

The third most important technology is propulsion. Right now we are hung up on chemical rockets and we're hitting the wall in terms of how efficient we can make them. There is some effort going on at developing nuclear thermal rockets, but they are decades away from seeing full production. Fusion rockets are what we need but that technology has been plagued with underinvestment, the running joke being we've been ten years away from self-sustaining fusion power for the last fifty years. Antimatter is best left to the pages of *Amazing Stories* and their Walter Mitty heroes who run around in leotards and fishbowl helmets while wielding medieval swords to rescue busty babes from alien monsters... Oh wait, you didn't mean *antiprotons*. You meant *antielectrons* aka positrons. Whereas antiprotons are damned near impossible to manufacture in the quantities that would be needed and the zero-defect technology needed to store the stuff is equally impossible, positrons can be had fairly easily, obtained from a number of natural emitters, not least of which includes Krypton-79. It may only have a half-life of 35 hours but it can be replenished with neutron bombardment. A steady stream of positrons may not be the powerhouse that is found in antiprotons but it can catalyze fusion propulsion. This is likely the most do-able of the advanced propulsion technologies and NASA was even funding a NIAC project for one right up the road from me in Livermore[3]. Fully developed, it could have sent a probe past Alpha Centauri in 50 years! And

---

[3] https://www.bis-space.com/membership/jbis/2019/JBIS-v72-n004-April-2019%20-%20Subscription%20Copy.pdf

then they quit, didn't say why. This is what I mean about moving the hidebound agencies out of the way. They are good for billiard trick shots. They are not good for generation-scale diasporas. Alcubierre warp drives? Thus far, they have yet to have their Chicago Pile One moment and are not likely to for centuries—see *Amazing Stories*.

The fourth most key part is correcting the deficiencies of good old *Homo sapiens*. He is not particularly fit for living in space. We have been proving that over and over again with the crews we keep sending up to the ISS six months at a time. They return to Earth unable to stand and suffering from radiation damage that will one day come to haunt them. We can fix the zero-gee problem with rotating habitat rings. And we can give human tissue the ability to repair radiation damage by borrowing the genetic repair mechanisms of extremophiles commonly found on Earth[4].

But most importantly, we need to fix the longevity problem. The average human simply doesn't live long enough to survive an interstellar voyage at 0.1 c. You end up having to breed a crop of replacement humans every twenty years or so which is a logistical headache what with nurseries and schools and training. And then there's all those dead geezers that keep piling up in the morgue while awaiting hydroponics processing. Think about it. With an eighty-year lifespan, your crew is only productive for the middle forty years—very inefficient. Nope. Better to have humans that are good for five

---

4   https://en.wikipedia.org/wiki/Deinococcus_radiodurans; http://www.daviddarling.info/encyclopedia/D/D_radiodurans.html; https://en.wikipedia.org/wiki/Thermococcus_gammatolerans

or six hundred years. If, when you get where you are going, you happen to need a new crew for the spacecraft you are manufacturing using ISRU, you can simply create them and fetch them up and train them. But while you're en route for however many centuries why submit your society to a horde of self-inflicted teenagers? Better to invest in dogs... or even cats if you must. Dogs are at least trainable.

How do we achieve such longevity? That's covered in detail in the epilogue of *Genesis2*, Book III, and also in the prologue of *Enceladus*, Book IV. The net results are a new species of space-adapted human, *Homo galacticus*, and an upgraded standard human. Spoiler: it involves borrowing the genetics of long-lived species found right here on Earth, notably the Greenland shark which could live over four hundred years[5]. As a bonus, sharks are highly resistant to heart disease and cancer[6].

We don't have a lot of time left to develop all this sophisticated technology. While any of the aforementioned doomsday scenarios could take place in the next ten minutes, the more realistic timeframe for natural disasters is on the order of millennia to eons and for manmade disasters centuries to millennia. As you can see, I have placed manmade disasters a lot closer than natural disasters, so centuries to millennia are how long we have to get our butts off this rock.

---

[5]   https://science.ku.dk/english/press/news/2024/the-longest-living-vertebrate-genome/;
https://www.karmactive.com/greenland-sharks-500-year-lifespan-linked-to-massive-6-5-billion-base-pair-genome-secrets-of-longevity-revealed/
[6]   https://medicalxprecss.com/news/2020-12-genomic-analysis-mako-shark-reveals.html

Book I, *SpaceCorp*, © 2014 1ˢᵗ Ed. Fifteen years ago when I started work on this series, I figured SpaceCorp's dystopia would be effected by something like a global financial collapse perhaps multiplied by the ravages of climate change and global loss of interest in all things STEM. For good measure I threw in the Kessler Syndrome[7] wherein the proliferation of space junk rendered Low Earth Orbit or LEO nonviable for conventional satellites. Little did I realize that the Republican Party would come to my aid under the imprimatur of Christian Nationalism as detailed in its *Mandate for Leadership – Project 2025*.[8] I don't think it's that much of a stretch to see a GOP-controlled government auctioning off all of NASA's and SETI's assets to the highest bidder, along with NOAA, NIH, the CDC, and all the other government labs and facilities that have kept us civilized.

Enter SpaceCorp, as in Space Corporation, who eagerly gobbled up all those assets to include the talented personnel that gave them their considerable worth. SpaceCorp correctly realized that just because conventional satellites were no longer viable, that didn't mean the services they provided were not, i.e., the classical LEO business lines of communications, surveillance, and navigation. And don't worry about all that debris up in LEO—they have a plan!

In 2038 SpaceCorp christened *SSS Wernher von Braun*, a heavily armored, 1-km spinning ring advertised as the first

---

[7] Fifteen years ago, I showed the Kessler Syndrome *plausibly* taking effect in 2028. That may have been premature, but I'm stuck with it now.

[8] Hey, it's damned hard work coming up with a realistic dystopia, so why not take advantage of all that hard work from the morons at the Heritage Foundation?

debris-proof instrument-hosting space station, thereby restoring and monopolizing the LEO business lines of communications, surveillance, and navigation. The idea is that all spacecraft will suffer damage from all the Kessler debris to include *von Braun*. Hence, they need to be sufficiently armored to buy themselves time to design, fashion, and install repairs so that they can keep on orbiting. Her human crew does most of the design and some of the fashioning while maintenance robots venture into harm's way to do the installation. This concept earned me an Atomic Rocket Seal of Approval from none other than Winchell Chung aka Nyrath the Nearly Wise, author and webmaster of the encyclopedic Atomic Rockets website for all things hard SciFi.[9] Gotta say, I'm super proud of that—beats some dumb old Hugo any day! As Winchell says, "It's better to figure things out than make shit up!"

With these monopolies, SpaceCorp earned itself two things—the animosity of the rest of the world and some outlandishly rich profits with which it could fund its eventual migration into deep space. The animosity came because SpaceCorp shut down all further space launches from anybody else—why allow the rest of the world to keep cluttering up your place of business? The outlandish profits came from securing an overnight monopoly on the entirety of the $630 billion (2023 dollars) global satellite market. BTW this market is set to hit $1.8 trillion by 2035[10] unless the GOP wins in November 2024... oops, it seems they have!

---

[9] Atomic Rockets website -- https://bit.ly/4hkHP3W scroll down to SpaceCorp in Science Fiction Novels
[10] Space Market -- https://bit.ly/4okU62j

By the end of Book I, 2071 CE, the nation formerly known as the United States of America is no more, having disintegrated into a number of sovereign nations. When you think about it, this is an all too likely outcome given our tendency to geographically segregate ourselves by ideology, economic status, and ethnicity over time. There is a reason Mississippi is the dumbest state in the Union and it's the same reason nobody moves there. In the world of SpaceCorp, everyone eventually realizes that since they no longer share common interests, it's time to split the sheets. I show the dissolution as bloodless in 2071 CE. Hopefully, we'll be this lucky in 2025 CE.

The Western states of California, Oregon, Washington, Alaska, and Hawaii formed the new nation of **Sierra** (CalExit anyone?) with SpaceCorp's corporate work-for-food economy as the backbone of its government. **Promised Land** is a radical Mormon nation formed from Idaho, Utah, Nevada, Arizona, and Colorado. **Dixieland**, dedicated to the restoration of the antebellum South, formed from the Confederate States of the Great War of Northern Oppression, plus Kansas, Oklahoma, Kentucky, West Virginia, and Washington D.C. The mid-northern states joined **British Canada**—yes, I show Canada splitting in two. The New England states plus New York, New Jersey, Pennsylvania, Maryland, and Delaware joined **French Canada**. **Puerto Rico**, **Guam**, **American Samoa**, et al. all became independent sovereign nations.

Book II, *CisLuna*, © 2017. This episode begins in 2085 CE. By now SpaceCorp has a significant presence in the Lagrangian region around the Moon known as EML1, hence the name 'CisLuna.' In this volume I began naming my cover spacecraft after friends and colleagues from NASA and SETI. The space station on the cover is named after Dr. William Borucki who worked down the hall from me and happened to be principal investigator of the Kepler space telescope that had confirmed 3,253 exoplanets as of June 2023. A brilliant mission, Dr. Borucki changed planetary science as we know it.

In this volume I introduce protagonist Roy Stone who will be the first-person narrator for the rest of the series. Picture a slightly modernized but still retro Sam Spade style gumshoe. Born in the Bowery in 2035, he is scary smart, fearless, and very streetwise. Surprisingly deft with his dukes for his size. Does not fight fair. Knows when to run like a bunny. When on the job, Roy packs a .357 magnum, a Latama switchblade, and a sap. Initially Roy specialized in homicides, having made his bones with a serial killer while he was a Military Police Warrant Officer in the Army. What did he learn from that? Serial killers don't like it when you start getting close so they set ambushes... on your family.

Roy's boss in Sierra, Police Chief Carmine Ciccolella aka Chick, calls him in for a murder investigation. Roy, having been hired to do property crimes, is a little surprised that Chick has chosen him for a homicide until Chick informs him that this particular investigation will take place not on Earth but in space. As Chick puts it, "We've got a dozen stations orbiting around Earth-Moon L1, a space port construction yard at L2, and three water works on the lunar surface at Colaprete[11] Station. Altogether that's over fifteen thousand people counting transients. It had to happen sooner or later."

Shortly after, Roy gets his first rocket ship ride up to *SpaceCorp Space Station SSS Albert Einstein*, a research vessel in EML1 where he meets Monica Carvalho, head of molecular biology. She had been busily researching how to make a space-adapted human until a pretty blond doctor was found hanging upside down in her cabin completely drained of blood. Roy enlists Monica's aid as an amateur forensics specialist, there being no forensics lab on *Einstein*. Roy eventually solves the case at great cost to himself personally. In return he is made head of law enforcement for all of CisLuna.

Book III, *Genesis2*, © 2021. The story begins in 2102. Roy is now 67, having spent the last 17 years in CisLuna mostly on *SSS Albert Einstein*. He has just been summoned by ISAAC to join the crew of SpaceCorp *Interplanetary Spacecraft SIS Pascal Lee* bound for Mars. ISAAC is the co-captain of *SIS Pascal Lee*. ISAAC is an acronym for Intelligent Sentient Autonomous Anthropomorphic Captain. This will actually be *Pascal Lee's* second trip to Mars, the first having been a flags and footprints mission two years before. Because of the peculiar orbital resonance between Mars and Earth, the ideal Mars transfer window only takes place every two years. For Roy, this mission is a rare treat, a chance to venture beyond

---

[11] Tony Colaprete is one of NASA Ames Research Center's up and coming planetary scientists, perhaps best known for being PI of the LCROSS mission that discovered water in the southern polar region of the Moon.

CisLuna into deep space. So why would a ship with a crew of only 200 need a cop? Well, it seems the ship has picked up a virus, and it is being used to coopt one of the ship's astronauts into sharing the spoils of discovery should they discover some form of life on the surface of Mars. **Spoiler**: Yes, they will discover life albeit not exactly on the surface. Roy's job is to determine which astronaut is being subverted and who on Earth is doing the subversion.

Roy and Monica are an item now, although Monica is not on the mission. Her husband passed away some years before and Roy's wife was a victim of the serial killer in *CisLuna*. Roy works the *Pascal Lee* case with the aid of Monica's 24-year-old polymath daughter, Roxanne, who is on the mission studying a quartet of chimps that have been genetically modified by her mother's lab to tolerate the high radiation environment of deep space.

November 2024

Prologue

A decade ago, when I looked in the mirror, an old man looked back at me. I did not *feel* old—aging being a gentle process—but I knew I *was* old as evidenced by my birth certificate which showed me at the time to be 69 years of age. And there had been the myriad little clues that I was no longer a young man. My mind was not as sharp, my body not as spry. I was quicker to lose condition when I interrupted my fitness routine, and slower to recover when I resumed it. Like most mortals, I had resigned myself to accept all of this, having been brainwashed that aging and eventual death were inevitable. After all, it happened to everyone else, what right had I to escape the Reaper?

Today, although I may be chronologically 79, looking in the mirror revealed a man of approximately 40 years with none of the frailties I had formerly taken for granted. And it was a shocker. It spat in the face of all the aging conventions that have plagued most animal life on Earth since the dawn of the Cambrian Period 540 million years ago. I wondered how long it would take before the novelty of my new life extension treatments would fade.

The Treatment, as it had come to be called, was essentially twofold. First, my cells had their withering telomeres extended to their youthful glory of 10,000 nucleotides. When a cell's DNA runs out of telomeres it becomes senescent, which is to say marked for death. And while they do not become cancerous in their own right, they can promote adjacent cells to become so. Bringing their telomeres back to 10,000 nucleotides alone would theoretically double my lifespan. But the goal was to extend my lifespan to many centuries, perhaps indefinite. To that end, some cells such as stem cells use telomerase to regenerate their telomeres. As the human embryo matures, the stem cells become differentiated into various types of tissue and lose the capability to regenerate telomeres. This regenerative capability was restored to my differentiated cells by borrowing some of the genetics of the Greenland shark. Greenland sharks live to be over 500 years old in the wild. Some biologists think they could live well beyond that if freed from the ravages of predation and habitat destruction. Normally, such a genetic modification would have led to frequent cancers in humans, but sharks seldom get cancer and further genetic analysis showed us why. So we borrowed a few more genes from our Greenland friend and now, not only cancer-resistance but also improved resistance to heart disease are standard Treatment options.

The second step of the Treatment was to do a thorough analysis of my genome to determine what my baseline DNA would look like today had it not undergone a lifetime of mutations caused by radiation and other error inducing problems from cellular replication gone awry. Included in this was an assay of all the genes that could no longer express due to methylation. And while this process was going on, a number of Monica's other genetic enhancements were added to our genomes, the most important being radiation resistance. This modified, demethylated DNA was then replicated in every cell of the body using retroviruses. Retroviruses differ from other viruses in that they only modify the host DNA rather than replacing it outright. Tissue experiments had shown that Treated humans could expect the same level of radiation resistance as our genetic benefactor, *Thermococcus gammatolerans*, a hardy little critter that can withstand doses up to 3 million rems and an instantaneous dose up to half a million rems with no loss of viability. Half of all untreated humans subjected to an acute dose of only 500 rems can expect to die a miserable death within 30 days.

This was a big deal. Previously, adult humans were pretty much stuck with the genetic cards they had been dealt at conception. Retrovirus technology allowed us to upgrade our genomes well past the zygote, or single-celled state. If word of this got out—and something this juicy was bound to leak sooner or later—SpaceCorp was going to have a war on its hands. No wonder the research teams of Lab 15 had been moved to a CisLunar black site with strictly controlled access.

Monica, my third and hopefully my last wife, had begun the Treatment the same time as I—age 65 when she went in. She now looked like a woman of 30 or 35. Her daughter Roxanne who was 26 at start of the Treatment still looked 26 today... and would continue to do so thanks to having begun the Treatment at an earlier age. But all of us could expect to live well past the normal human use-by date. We just didn't know how far. I hear the team that gave us our new longevity is now working on how to re-rejuvenate a previously Treated body that was beginning to show its mileage—a geriatric tune-up, so to speak. Conceivably, genetic overhauls could be done as often as the human body needed it giving us a potentially infinite lifespan.

As a result of their achievements in longevity genetics, Monica and Roxanne were now cleared to produce a new species of space-adapted humans, *Homo galacticans*. This would all be done at the new nursery at Lab 48 housed on *SSS Albert Einstein*, SpaceCorp's newest black site. If everything went as planned there would be 4000 new galacticans birthed over the next ten years. They would have all the space-adaptation features of longevity and radiation resistance built in at conception. Some folks believed it was more reliable to engineer such changes to a single-celled zygote rather than a fully expressed adult human. Made sense. But I liked having the ability to genetically engineer new solutions to new problems as they turn up. And they will... they always do.

Besides all the longevity features Treated humans had, galacticans would also be sterile by design, reproduction only being possible with the addition of some missing hormones administered only when reproduction was necessary. Overpopulation would be disastrous on a generation starship while it was en route to a nearby star. And there was the added advantage of obviating the logistical burden of a nursery.

Meanwhile, human males were all given vasectomies before assuming crew assignments, making procreation among humans nearly impossible. As a result most males kept a supply of sperms on ice along with a digital copy of their genomes. If they were needed for procreation, and the frozen sperm was no longer viable, the digital copy could be used to build a DNA molecule.

Thanks to some borrowed genes from African Pygmies, galacticans would be of slighter stature than the average human by about 30 cm. We don't need musclebound space crewmen when there are robots abound to do the heavy lifting. Saves on the groceries. They would also have two interesting features to make them more docile compared to the average human. First, there would be no sexual dimorphism, either in stature or strength. Second, the violence genes shared by chimpanzees and humans would be removed from their genome. In a sense, galacticans would be to humans as bonobos were to chimps. The idea was to provide a more stress-free society on long voyages where the population is constrained to the hab rings of their generation starships. Some wondered if there would be a negative impact on their zeal for discovery. We'd soon find out.

But generation starships—the vehicle of choice for interstellar travel—were still a ways out. While we might be ready for full production with our space-adapted crew, we first had some essential technology to develop here in the Solar System. Generation starships required careful husbanding of myriad resources which in turn meant closing a lot of poorly understood control loops. Look up the Biosphere 2 disaster if you don't believe me. At least when Biosphere's unfortunate crew emerged, they could immediately fill their lungs with breathable air and their bellies with the nearest giganto-burger. Not so when you're ten light years from home.

We also needed some seriously advanced propulsion systems. Conventional wisdom said we'd be needing at least two generations of interplanetary ships before we could even think about the stars. As of this writing, plans were on the drawing boards for *SIS Jonathan Lunine*, a proton-Boron-11, aka, pB11 fusion-powered vessel that would take us to Saturn at ten AUs from the sun, and *SIS Alan Stern*, a positron catalyzed fusion powered vessel that would take us to Pluto at thirty AUs. *Lunine* would probably be launched on her maiden voyage forty years from now, most of that time being needed to hatch and train a crew of three or four thousand galacticans. *Stern* would launch perhaps twenty years after that if she was built in the CisLuna shipyards. If all went well, our first interstellar flight might launch in 2200, nearly a century from now.

A century... one hundred years. Normally, a depressingly long time, way past my own demise. A journey I could only fantasize about... until now. Whatever ship SpaceCorp had in mind for that trip, I intended to be on it!

PART ONE

Enceladus

CHAPTER ONE

24Jun2151 — SIS Jonathan Lunine

On 28Oct2015, NASA's *Cassini* spacecraft passed within 49 km of the southern polar surface of Saturn's moon Enceladus, close enough to pass through a plume emanating from an icy fissure, close enough to collect samples and evaluate them with *Cassini's* suite of onboard mass spectrometers. The instruments confirmed the presence of water vapor and traces of hydrocarbons, most likely products of subsurface hydrothermal activity. The presence of hydrogen in Enceladus' oceans suggested that microbes could be present and that these microbes might be reacting with carbon dioxide to produce methane. Confirmation of life in Enceladus' oceans would further support the popular theory that any planet or moon with a liquid water ocean and a heat source could develop life, just as it was believed to have happened on Earth billions of years ago. Overnight, the astrobiology and planetary science communities were on fire howling for follow-on missions to dig into this finding.

Alas, within a few years of the incredible news from Enceladus, a heavily politicized NASA had turned its attention and its budget back to the Moon and its unfortunate Space Launch System which, at $4 billion per launch left scant funds available for planetary science. By 2024 a Republican Congress under the imprimatur of Christian Nationalism as detailed in the Mandate for Leadership – Project 2025, authorized selling off NASA's assets to private interests—most of which were bought by SpaceCorp. Then in 2028 the Kessler Syndrome had rendered Low Earth Orbit all but impassable for satellites and deep space exploration vehicles. In 2038 SpaceCorp christened *SSS Wernher von Braun*, a 1-km spinning ring advertised as the first debris-proof instrument-hosting space station, thereby restoring and monopolizing the Low Earth Orbit business lines of communications, surveillance, and navigation.

SpaceCorp spent the rest of the 21st century adding more space stations to Low Earth Orbit and moving most of its Vandenberg research assets to CisLuna's Earth-Moon LaGrange Points #1 and #2 orbits (aka EML-1 and EML-2), housed in *SSS William Borucki*-class space stations. *Borucki's* were the same size and form factor as *von Braun*-class space stations but a good deal less mass since they did not need to be armored against the space debris that had ruined Low Earth Orbit. SpaceCorp did not get around to research missions until 2100 with the successful first manned mission to Mars on *SIS Pascal Lee*. It was a relatively quick flags-and-footprints mission more focused on proving out SpaceCorp's first interplanetary spacecraft than doing any real research on Mars. That would not come until April of 2102 when *Pascal Lee* returned to Mars and actually found microbial life hiding deep within a lava tube.

The new lifeform was close enough to being DNA-based that a new business line could be launched—alien genes and their proteins. This was potentially a huge moneymaker for SpaceCorp, akin to the early days of pharmaceuticals when the big pharma companies would send scientists into the Amazonian rainforest to seek out rare venoms and other exotic substances to be examined for medicinal potential. Since those days the medical and pharmaceutical industries and been subsumed by genetic treatments. Ergo, new genes and their proteins were SpaceCorp's newest business lines. And finding them in alien lifeforms was actually more efficient than creating them from scratch given the myriad complex arrangements of the twenty standard amino acids that were possible. Some of the longer proteins contain almost 27,000 amino acids—you do the math. Better to find fully developed genes and their resultant proteins that had proven utility by at least some lifeform. No less than half a dozen new genes had already been commercialized from the Martian microbes with more to come. Hence, enthusiasm was high among SpaceCorp mission planners to explore the next most likely home to microbes—Saturn's moon Enceladus.

But Saturn was a bit too much of a trip for a *Pascal Lee*-class spacecraft. *Pascal Lee* could make it to Mars and back in 64 days with 12 days in Mars orbit from which to conduct surface operations. *Pascal Lee* had been crewed by non-space adapted humans, hence she had to be heavily armored against gamma radiation and her propulsion system was a carefully selected proton-^{11}Boron (pB11) fusion drive whose materials were plentiful and that was completely aneutronic. pB11 fusion was notoriously difficult to start, but by some lucky fluke, we caught a break and got one up and running by 2093. Though she was small—a crew size of only 200—she was still large enough to carry rovers and landers that could scurry about on the surface of Mars looking under rocks and such. Still, she was hopelessly inadequate to haul the kind of equipment needed to melt through Enceladus' 40-km outer ice crust.

*   *   *

Fast forward to 2151: *SIS Jonathan Lunine* is big, approaching 7.5 km loa. For reference, *SIS Pascal Lee* was only 600 meters loa. *Pascal Lee* had a single hab ring that was a claustrophobic two hundred meters in diameter and rotated at a dizzying 3 rpm for a full gee of artificial gravity. By contrast, *Lunine* has four habitat rings each of which are 1 km in diameter and made from repurposed *Borucki*-class space stations from CisLuna. The *Borucki*-class space stations common to CisLuna are ideal for this since they are about one tenth the mass of the heavily armored *Einstein*-class space stations used in the debris fields of LEO. As with normal space stations, these rings rotate at 1.34 rpm giving the ship's crew an Earth-equivalent one gee with virtually zero Coriolis side-effects.

The eight spherical tanks fore and aft of the hab rings are fuel tanks consisting of different mass liquified gases to allow the ship's fore & aft fusion engines to "shift gears" favoring either thrust or range.

Between the hab rings and the fuel tanks are the flight and cargo decks. *Lunine* will carry four robotic submarines for exploring the oceans beneath the crustal ice covering Enceladus. Each one is mounted inside a long truss assembly that houses nuclear heaters used to melt entry holes through the crustal ice. The whole contraption descends through the ice slowly—about one km per day—in a bubble of liquid water until it reaches the liquid ocean below. At that point it locks itself into place and ejects its submarine into the abyss.

Each sub is controlled by an onboard sentient AI embedded into its computer architecture. Its mission is to hunt for microbial life among the white smokers that hopefully formed along the bottom. The theory holds that this is how life formed on Earth several billion years ago and that it may be common on any moon or planet that has an ocean, a subterranean heat source, and a positive CHNOPS assay—CHNOPS being an acronym for the essential elements of known life—Carbon, Hydrogen, Nitrogen, Oxygen, Phosphorus, and Sulphur. To that end the subs are equipped with a full bio lab to include genomic sequencer and electron microscopes. If life is found and can be sequenced, the genome is sent back digitally to *Lunine* via a combination of fiber optic and RF links. Then all of SpaceCorp will have a big drunken party that lasts three days. That last part is not actually part of the protocol but my bet is that it will definitely happen. We already found microbial life on Mars and we're making tons of money off that genome, so if we score a second time it will further validate our new business line—alien genomes.

Meanwhile, the black panels on either end of the ship are not solar panels—for some reason everybody always assumes that. Actually, they are radiators needed to cool the fusion rockets that provide thrust and the thorium nuclear thermal

5

reactors that start the fusion rockets when necessary and otherwise keep the lights on.

The fusion rockets are based on Deuterium-3Helium, giving the rockets considerably more efficiency that the pB11 rockets of SIS Pascal Lee. We solved the Helium-3 scarcity problem back in 2130.

Helium-3 is produced naturally from the radioactive decay of hydrogen-3 (tritium). Tritium is produced by bombarding lithium-6 with neutrons in a special nuclear reactor. The lithium nucleus absorbs a neutron and splits into helium-4 and tritium. The tritium then decays into helium-3 with a half-life of 12.3 years, so helium-3 can be produced by simply storing the tritium until it undergoes radioactive decay. It takes a while to get the process going but once you do, it's pretty dependable. We have a whole station in EML-2 dedicated to helium-3 production.

Meanwhile, the search for helium-3 on the lunar surface never did pan out. It's there all right but not in concentrations rich enough to mine profitably. Lunar regolith contains 1.4 to 15.0 ppb of helium-3 in sunlit areas, and there are occasional pockets of up to 50.0 ppb in the shadowed regions. But heavy mining equipment would need to process over 150 million tonnes of regolith to extract a single tonne of helium-3. Not worth it.

The captain's function and all the other ship's operational functions on *Jonathan Lunine* will be performed by AI sentient robots. Like *SIS Pascal Lee*, the captain is embedded in the ship's distributed computer network. Think of the ship as a giant robot. But unlike *Pascal Lee*, *Lunine* does not have a human or galactican co-captain—that was my idea after my unfortunate experience with CPT Thornton on *Pascal Lee*. The human captain selection process had gotten too political and the captain function was too critical to be subjected to the vicissitudes of human politics. The embedded captain is responsible for all ship functions and the safety of the crew. The captain directs all the ship's robots in the execution of ship functions. Robots are mostly patterned after the bipedal robots used on *SIS Pascal Lee*, perhaps a little more anthropomorphic in form factor, but still unmistakably robots. There are also specialized maintenance robots that have a "praying mantis" form factor and are usually teleoperated by the embedded captain. Oh, I almost forgot, whereas we called the embedded captain on *Pascal Lee* by his acronym, ISAAC for Intelligent Sentient Autonomous Anthropomorphic Captain, here we named the captain after the ship. So our captain is CPT Jonathan Lunine—most people just call him Jonathan. Like ISAAC, he can pop up anywhere there is a display—display paper covers almost all vacant wall space inside the ship—or he can dispatch little drones to the more remote parts of the ship, or if all else fails, he can temporarily demonize one of his bipedal robots. And thanks to quantum computing technology, he can multitask, i.e., he can hold simultaneous conversations with as many folks as he feels like, all while running a huge, complicated ship.

Jonathan answers to a Mission Committee that deliberates on and defines the ship's mission, in this case to seek life on Saturn's moon Enceladus. The committee members are made up of three humans who serve in an advisory capacity, voting only in the case of a tie, and 10 galacticans who do the real work of the committee. As security chief, I sometimes audit the committee meetings in a non-voting capacity, offering advice where requested. I also have a back door capability that allows me to overrule or in extreme cases dissolve the Mission Committee should a security-related existential crisis arise.

The crew numbers about 3000 galacticans created by Monica and Roxanne on Lab 48, and 300 humans modified by Lab 15. The 300 humans on board are mainly present in an observational/advisory capacity to the galacticans—the exception being my contingent of 40 cops. Whether the mission succeeds or fails, it will be up to the humans to recommend whether the Galactican Project is to be continued as is, modified, or discontinued. If the Galactican Project is continued, a sister ship will be constructed and sent to the Main Belt Asteroids to see if it can construct and staff a third *Lunine*-class ship entirely with local resources. If successful that will be one helluva big deal. The ability to replicate large spacecraft with *in situ* resources is an essential precursor for future generation stellar missions. As any space-savvy galactican will tell you, it is far more important to find a stellar system with a healthy asteroid belt than a so-called habitable planet. If a habitable planet is what you want, you had best bring it with you. Habitable ships have all the comforts of home—dog and cat-friendly, botanical gardens, labs, hospitals, wet bars, even pickleball courts. In truth, they *are* home.

*   *   *

One of the most significant findings of *Cassini* was the occurrence of over 100 geysers emanating from the south pole of Saturn's moon, Enceladus. Likely due to an orbital resonance with its sister moon Dione, Enceladus is geologically active, the heat from which provides a liquid ocean beneath its thick icy crust. Even though *Cassini* collected samples while flying through the merged plume of material from the jets, it lacked the sophisticated instrumentation to detect the more complex molecules of life which can be quite large—thousands of kilodaltons, or kDa. NASA's instrumentation people had a nasty habit of trying to do too much with too little in those days, probably a result of space exploration being dominated by geologists back then rather than astrobiologists as it is today. Geology is defined by the mini molecules of physical chemistry whereas astrobiology is defined by the mega molecules of organic chemistry. Even so, *Cassini's* findings established Enceladus as a top candidate in the search for extraterrestrial life in the Solar System with two significant missions proposed for the coming decades, the Enceladus Life Finder mission (PI Jonathan Lunine for whom our ship is named, and also Chief Scientist at JPL) and the Enceladus Orbilander Mission (PI Shannon MacKenzie out of Johns Hopkins Applied Physics Lab).

Enceladus Life Finder (ELF) was supposed to be one of NASA's New Frontiers-class orbiter missions (~$1 billion). It was to carry two or three kinds of mass spectrometer optimized for detecting biomolecules during its 3-year mission-life. The Enceladus Orbilander was supposed to be a $2.5-billion Flagship-class mission, planned to arrive at Enceladus around 2050. Orbilander is a single spacecraft that both orbits and lands, capturing samples from four distinct reservoirs offered by the plumes. These samples would then be analyzed by the Life Detection Suite (LDS), a set of five instruments conducting biosignature-seeking measurements. It seemed like NASA had its newfound enthusiasm for the search for alien life well in hand, but due to the $4 billion per launch drain on mission funding from the Space Launch System (SLS) and later the ravages of the Kessler Syndrome, neither ELF nor Orbilander made it past the drawing boards. Hence, it now falls on the *SIS Jonathan Lunine* mission to pick up where Cassini left off 140 years later.

Around the time of *Pascal Lee's* trip to Mars, SpaceCorp would have sent probes to Saturn and Enceladus to confirm what we thought we knew before mounting a major mission like *Jonathan Lunine*. This mission represented a major shift in philosophy regarding space exploration. *Lunine* was big enough and had enough crew that she could handle just about any contingency that presented itself once we started flying formation on Enceladus. While that may still seem reckless by historical standards, it makes sense today given we wanted to find alien microbes and harvest their DNA as soon as possible. We had swapped science-driven as our primary motivation for space exploration in favor of market-driven.

Our mission to Enceladus was scheduled to last 922 Earth days—279 days outbound, 267 days on station, and 376 days for the return. We were approaching the nine-month mark of the outbound leg. Saturn, being 8.5 AU from Earth, used to take old fashioned chemical rockets the better part of a decade just to get there. Gotta love fusion propulsion! We had only been underway for less than a year and we were due to begin Enceladus Orbit Insertion (EOI) in about a week. (We used the acronym EOI out of habit even though our real orbit was around Saturn. Enceladus was so small it did not have enough gravity to permit a proper orbit—hence we flew *formation* on Enceladus as it orbited Saturn.) Anyway, arriving in a week suited me fine. Job-wise I was getting a little bored. Galacticans, with their missing violence genes, tended to be extremely docile and cooperative compared to humans, and the humans we had on board were so disciplined that violent crime was something you only read about in the news feeds from Earth. That's when the knock came at my door...

CHAPTER TWO

The Crime Scene

The knock was from Dieter Willms, my Second—Germanic male, age at life extension: 61. He was an engineer I'd worked with on my first detective gig in space. That was on *SSS Albert Einstein*, CisLuna EML-1, back in 2085. He was an engineer then, but I talked him into taking the life extension treatments and coming to work for me. He wasn't much of a cop just yet—hard to pick up police work OJT in a relatively crime-free environment. But he had a helluva head for how spaceships worked. Robots had taken over most of the maintenance/engineering function on spacecraft so he was kinda obsolete in that respect, but hell, anybody that smart could learn to be a cop in no time. And he had a very steady head which made him a great Number Two.

Dieter's expression was grim as he walked in.

"Bad news?"

"We've had a homicide."

My eyebrows went up. "A homicide? ... Anybody we know?"

"Delia Diamandis. She was found in her quarters over in Alpha Ring."

My headquarters was in Charlie Ring, so it would take us a good hour to get to Alpha jogging the whole way. I grabbed my cop coat and started heading for the door. Then I stopped and walked back to the weapon safe behind my desk. In it were my service revolver—a stainless .357 Smith—with fourteen extra rounds, my old Latama switchblade, and 28-cm 4-ply sap filled with a solid lead slug. I put them all in their various pouches inside my cop coat as Dieter looked on.

"You expectin' a war?"

"Better to have it and not need it. Grab your kit and let's roll."

*　　*　　*

Delia Diamandis—Mediterranean female, age at life extension: 38—was one of the cops I'd drafted from *Borucki* when we went on the Zurich Op after *Pascal Lee* returned from Mars. There'd been some nasty mission interference from Persia that needed attending to. While SpaceCorp was not exactly loved by Earth, we at least got along with everybody... except Persia. Anyway, Delia had had a variety of jobs from rodeo clown to bodyguard to strip joint bouncer before landing on *Borucki*. Her job there had been to keep order among the roughnecks that worked on the Lunar surface mining water ice for EML-1 and 2. They were a rowdy bunch during their 60-day gravitational recovery periods and Delia used to joke that they demanded equal parts of her skills as a rodeo clown and a bouncer to keep them in line without damaging the company "assets." She was right—if you had to break some fool's arm to get them to behave, the company had to ship up a replacement from surface and that was expensive, not to mention the added training burden. She'd been a cool-under-fire kinda gal on *Borucki* and that was why I'd picked her for Zurich.

We found her in the middle of the floor of her cabin's bedroom. She was on her knees with her hands tied behind her back with nanoties and her mouth sealed with nanotape. A possible GSW from the base of her skull had left a stream of blood running down the back of her neck and darkening her coverall—an apparent execution with similarities to the killing of the three Persian fellows in Zurich. Someone on board was trying to send a message, but who? And why now? And how the hell did they get on board in the first place? I had personally set up the boarding protocol used on all crew members.

Her husband, Richard 'Rick' Furman—Caucasian male, age at life extension: 43—also a member of the Zurich team, had been the one to find her. He was sitting on the edge of the bed, eyes wet, jaw muscles flexing. His hair was damp and he had wrapped himself in a towel to cover his privates. He kept gripping his knees with his hands like he needed something to occupy them in order to keep them from involuntarily ripping somebody's throat out. It broke my heart to see such a big tough guy choking on a bitter martini of fury and grief.

I sat down next to him a couple of feet away. "Rick?"

He looked toward me, face blank at first, then recognition creeping in. "Yeah, Boss?"

"Can I get you to step out into the living room? I need to talk to you and... forensics... well, you know."

He squeegeed a tear from his eye with his index knuckle, snuffed his nose, then nodded.

I offered a hand to help him up.

14

"That's okay, Boss. I got this." He leaned forward and stood up on shaky legs, looked at his wife's body, then looked away.

"You got a bathrobe or something?" I asked. He was still wrapped in a towel.

He looked around, still a bit dazed. "Uh, no. Can I just pull on the pants I was wearing and my sweatshirt?" he asked pointing at some clothes that were draped across a chair on the other side of the room.

I looked at my forensics chief, Charlie Albritton— Caucasian male, age at life extension: 47. He nodded.

Rick got dressed and slowly walked into the living room. "Can I sit anywhere?"

"Let's sit at the table so I can take notes if I need to." I got out my old notebook and pencil as we each pulled out a chair and sat down facing each other. "Tell me what happened."

He shrugged. "I was in the shower."

Married couples on the ship rated a suite with an attached shower. The shower was a bit cramped, but it beat slogging down the hall to the common bathroom.

"Did you hear anything while you were showering?"

"Nah, nothin."

"Sounds of a struggle? Gunshot?"

"Nope."

"Was Delia in the room when you went into the shower?"

"No. She'd left for the food mart to get a pizza and some beers. That was about twenty minutes before I went into the shower. We were both off tonight so we were going to watch a couple of movies in bed. I finished my shower and toweled off. When I came out to get dressed, she was just sitting there on the floor all slumped over."

15

I looked over at the living room/kitchenette. The countertop was empty. No pizza and no beer. "Did you touch her?"

"Yeah. I knelt down and raised her face. That's when I knew."

"Knew what, Rick?"

"No life in her eyes. She was gone and she wasn't coming back. I knew I shouldn't mess with her body but when I pulled my hands away there was blood on my fingers from the back of her head."

He rotated his forearms and looked into his palms. They were clean. Forensics would have had him soak his hands in solution to pull off any evidential residue—gun powder, blood, etc.

"Then what did you do?"

"I called it in. And then I sat on the bed to wait."

"How long did you have to wait?"

"I dunno... five... ten minutes."

The Alpha Ring cop shack was next to the paramedic shack and they were both maybe a fifteen-minute walk to Rick and Delia's suite. The team probably came at a dead run, Rick being one of their own.

I wondered if someone had followed her back from the food mart and shoved her in the room as she opened the door. Then overpowered her, bound her up with the nanoties and tape, shot her, skipped out taking the pizza and beers as camouflage. Weapon must have been suppressed.

Then I decided that whole scenario was absurd. First off, this was Delia and the Delia I knew would not have let herself get manhandled like that. There would have been a helluva

16

scuffle and a lot of racket. Rick would have heard the commotion even in the shower. Then I wondered if the perp knew Rick was in the shower. Maybe there were multiple perps? One to do Delia and one to cover Rick? Maybe they shoved her into the room and shot her with a suppressed weapon straight away. Then they tied her up and propped her body into a kneeling position so it would resemble the execution we did in Zurich? And if the perp or perps were bent on duplicating Zurich, why didn't they do Rick as he came out of the shower?

I looked over at Dieter who was engrossed in a conversation with Captain Jonathan on a section of wall display. He looked pretty exasperated.

I walked over to him. "Do you have any surveillance footage from the passageway?"

"Ask him," he said motioning toward Jonathan.

Jonathan had chosen an old image of Jonathan Lunine, former chief scientist at JPL, as his avatar. Somehow he'd gotten some old recordings of Lunine's voice and used that for his avatar as well. Kinda spooky but he made it work.

"The footage from that time frame shows an empty passageway. There is nothing showing Ms. Diamandis approaching or entering her cabin," Jonathan said.

"How can that be?" I asked.

"I don't know," Jonathan said. "I'm trying to diagnose what could have caused an interruption in the recording or an erasure of same, but so far nothing has turned up."

"Check for false footage being inserted into the surveillance recording," I said.

I went back to Rick. "I don't want you staying in this room for a while."

"Where am I gonna—"

"—We'll park you at the cop shack for tonight. You can rack out on the holding cell cot. I'm worried whoever did this may come back to finish the job. No point in making it easy for them."

I called Charlie over. "Help him pick out some clothes and toiletries that you've cleared."

Then I went over to where Dieter was still arguing with Jonathan about the corrupted security footage. Dieter tends to get impatient with AIs, sometimes forgetting that *this* AI was also his captain.

"Dieter, forget the security footage for now. We got bigger fish to fry. I need you to set up a video all-hands for all cops and... on second thought, make it for all first responders. See if you can get everybody together in, say, two hours. Work with Jonathan to keep it as secure as possible."

Then I grabbed my coroner, Lucy Biesanz—African-American female, age at life extension 34—who had just arrived at the scene and pulled her over to a patch of wall that had some unused interactive display space where I rang up Dolly Butterfield, the ship's forensic pathologist, a galactican over on Delta Ring, true age 31. She was unusual as galacticans went. Normal height for a galactican female—150ish centimeters—but where typical galacticans were rail-thin, she was pleasantly curvy and, if I'm to be honest, rather busty. And if I'm to be really honest, she also had an extremely captivating voice—more than a girl, not quite a woman—I don't know quite how to describe it other than to say that listening to her made it easy to forget what you were going to say.

"Hi, Dolly, hope you're not busy."

"Get serious! On a ship where everybody lives for centuries it will be a while before I get any work."

"Well, I've got some work for you now... a murder no less."

"Oh no! Who was it?"

"One of my cops. Apparent GSW to the back of the head. Happened maybe an hour or two ago. Gonna need an autopsy, but I'm also going to need some special handling. The victim is in Alpha, you're in Delta. I don't want you to have to parade a body bag the entire length of the ship back to your facilities. So can you pack up whatever you need and set up shop at the paramedic station over here?"

"Yes... of course. How soon do you need this?"

"ASAP. Cause and time of death are both pretty obvious, but there's some nuances I need you and Lucy to run down. I'll fill you in when you get here. Oh, and keep this on the down-low."

"Okay, I'll try and get there in... let's see... it's almost shift-change, better expect me in three hours."

"That's the best you can do?"

"You can have it in three hours on the down low or in hour and a half with the whole ship wondering why the forensic pathologist is heading for A-ring at a dead run."

"Three hours it is."

The ship's four-ring form factor had been a real nuisance for job functions that needed access to the entire habitat area. I suppose most folks spent their days living and working in just one hab ring, so the added travel time going from ring to ring

19

was not a problem. I know why SpaceCorp designed the ship this way—it was a time saver during construction since we already had four fully functional *Borucki*-class space stations in CisLuna and we had a large maturing population of galacticans that needed a place to live—so why not jam four of them together and get a space ship as well? I once got a sneak peek at SIS Alan Stern on the drawing board. She will have a single 4-km long hab cylinder—an O'Neill Cylinder if you will. Can't wait to get a berth on her—wherever she's goin!

*   *   *

I did the all-hands from Delia and Rick's cabin. Dieter and Rick were on either side of me.

"Hi, gang. In case you haven't heard, we've had a homicide on the ship. At approximately 18:00 this evening, Delia Diamandis was shot and killed in her cabin. Her husband, Rick, was in the shower and discovered her body when he came out. It is too early to say for sure, but the way this went down makes me worry that we have been infiltrated by one or more Persian assassins, possibly in retaliation for the hit we put on them in Zurich 2102. That hit was not that long ago, and the similar layout of the crime is hard to ignore and, well, Persians are nothing if not vengeful. Regardless, the perpetrators are still at large and they may have plans to take out more of our first responders, especially those who participated in the Zurich op—you know who you are. That said, we need to implement some new security measures applicable to all first responders, not just cops—ALL first responders.

"First, up to now we have been trying to maintain a quiet presence among the crew—civilian clothes, no weapons. Effective immediately, everyone will be in full uniform. Cops will be fully armed and wear protective vests at all times when venturing outside the confines of their cabins. Second, no first-responders will venture out into public alone—you will go everywhere in twos and threes—even to the head. Keep it tactical at all times, for example, do not sit side-by-side in the mess hall. Sit opposite one another so as to have a full 360-degree view at all times. Third, keep your behavior towards galacticans the same as before—don't let yourselves get unprofessional. We all want to catch this bastard and we will. But this is not the time to make enemies of the people we are sworn to protect. Lastly, my detectives and other key personnel will be meeting 09:00 tomorrow morning to discuss how to proceed with this investigation. Watch commanders, meet with your people ASAP to establish the new security measures. That is all—stay alert."

I signed off taking no discussion and accepting no questions. I suppose I could have had my detectives join me for a late-night skull session, but I wanted to sleep on what I knew about this situation. This had the added advantages of letting Dolly finish her autopsy and also giving the forensics team some time to do their preliminary lab work. I was keenly interested in those results. For some reason this case had a peculiar smell to it—more than a simple case of Persian payback.

CHAPTER THREE

The cop shack had a small war room into which my six detectives, plus Dieter, Monica, Roxanne, Dolly, Lucy, and Captain Jonathan had gathered. The table in the war room could seat eight and we were twelve in all. I didn't count Jonathan because he just hangs out on whatever vacant wall space that offers him a clear view.

"Is this meeting going to be recorded?" I asked Dieter. There was no way Jonathan could participate without 'recording' what was said, but I needed what was about to be said to be carefully compartmentalized. If these bad guys were good enough hackers to spoof Jonathan's security cams, they might also be good enough to rifle through our meeting minutes.

"No," Dieter said, "but I can take handwritten notes if you want."

"Thanks." Then turning to the group I asked, "Dolly, you want to lead off?"

Dolly had clearly had a long night but she gamely put some slides up on the wall and began.

"Cause of death was a .22 caliber projectile to the base of the skull severing the brain stem. Death was instantaneous. Projectile was low velocity, evidenced by the limited deformation. It was constructed of solid lead with the tip hollowed out and filled with polonium-210. Hence, the round was designed to produce lethal *alpha* particles regardless of the point of impact—at any rate they *would have been lethal* on a normal, i.e., non-radiation resistant, human. Projectile showed no rifling marks and no prints. Also, there was no gunpowder residue in or around the wound and no stippling around the wound. Wound site contained no foreign DNA. Spectrometer analysis did show a concentration of CO_2 in the wound cavity. Victim showed no indication of other complicating factors such as drug use or whatever."

She paused and turned to me. "Do you want my analysis?"

"Yes, please."

"Projectile was gas-propelled—CO_2—maybe two to three hundred meters per second. The launching device was not a typical firearm in that it had no rifling—just a simple tube. It was fired from very close range, probably with the muzzle pressing against the aimpoint at the back of the neck. The fact that the round was filled with polonium-210 implies the perpetrator may not have been familiar with the radiation resistance common to all ship's personnel. In other words, we may have one or more criminal stowaways on board."

"Thanks, Dolly. Lucy? Can you add anything to that?"

"Yes. The perp or perps left no residue to be found during the standard vacuuming of the carpet. There were no prints other than from the cabin residents. Finally, there was no blood spatter from the wound impact, further suggesting the muzzle was pressed up against the victim's skin and that the projectile was low velocity... You want my two cents' worth how it went down?"

"Please go ahead," I said.

"I would speculate that there was a two-person team, professional. The shooter followed close behind the victim out in the hall as she approached her cabin door. The backup approached from the front, probably also armed in case things went sideways. Their spacing was timed so that both of them arrived at the victim's door as she was opening it. As they got close, they exchanged prearranged signals that there were no witnesses either behind or in front of them in the passageway. As the victim unlocked her door, the backup may have also distracted the victim—perhaps calling her by name—allowing the shooter to maneuver in behind the victim and press the weapon against the back of the victim's neck and fire. Death would have been instantaneous. They caught her body as she collapsed and dragged her inside where they propped her up on her knees and secured her hands with nanoties and her mouth with nanotape. Then they picked up the pizza and beers as camouflage and left. Elapsed time could have been under two minutes."

"Thanks, Lucy. Let's let Dolly and Lucy's speculations be our initial working assumption as to how this crime went down. Be advised not to rule out other contrarian hypotheses. Okay, Shmuel, do you have anything from the food mart?"

Shmuel Ehrenbaum—Ashkenazi Jew, male, age at life extension: 52—had a gravelly, back-of-the-throat Yiddish accent. We were both New Yorkers and I was used to seeing Jews in the Diamond District walking about in their traditional attire—black trousers, white shirt untucked, no tie, long silk jacket or bekishe, and tophat under which a pair of side-curls or payot hung from the temples. Normally, Shmuel was very traditional, but today he had exchanged his bekishe for a regulation cop coat and his tophat for a simple yarmulke—it looked incongruous for some reason... maybe the fringed ends of his tzitzit dangling below his cop coat.

"Yes, I do, Roy," he said clearing his throat. "I was able to confirm from sales records that the victim purchased a large cooked pizza with everything and a six-pack of Pilsner. Time of purchase 18:22 as shown on the sales receipt. It's a twelve-minute walk from the food mart to the victim's cabin. I assume her pace was brisk so the pizza would still be hot when she arrived. Strangely, the store's security camera seems to have suffered the same malady as the hall security cameras. Hence, I was not able to determine if she was followed on her return to her cabin."

"Okay, Jonathan, can you have all pizza and Pilsner sales suspended in all food marts until further notice?"

"Of course, Roy. May I ask why? Pizzas are very popular with the off-duty crewmen."

"The perps may eat the pizza and drink the beer. The pizza box and beer containers will then be tossed into the nearest recycling chute thereby giving us a clue as to where the perps live. Might even get a print or some DNA off the containers. This way they'll show up more easily. Do you still have surveillance on all the recycling chutes?"

"Yes, Roy."

"Can you run some tests to be certain your camera feeds aren't being spoofed?"

"Yes, Roy."

"Okay, next up: we appear to have one or more stowaways on board. We need to confirm that by headcount and also by DNA screening. I set up the screening process myself for all the galacticans returning from sabbatical, and I must confess that I'm a little puzzled as to how they hacked it."

The galacticans had been more or less sequestered on *SIS Jonathan Lunine* since birth... *except* for their mandatory one-year sabbatical Earthside. This sabbatical—between ages 25 to 35—was to ensure that each member of the crew would be fully dedicated to a life in space, i.e., at the end of the year, they were given an option: Earth or space. Given the length of the voyage, SpaceCorp didn't want anyone on the crew suddenly yearning for Earth. Galacticans on sabbatical had been unsupervised after the first 90 days. With the exception of monthly check-ins, they were free to roam the planet, to witness firsthand the vastness of its decadence and what little was left of its glory.

Meanwhile, galacticans going on sabbatical had been thoroughly briefed to keep mum about their genetic alterations, e.g., radiation resistance, longevity, non-violence, etc., or even the fact that they were galacticans. "Just tell anyone who asks that you're just short." We put the fear of death in them that if some unsavory character was to find out about their special features, they would spend the rest of their short lives as somebody's laboratory rat. It worked—galacticans being by nature a cooperative lot—but you had to figure that in any large group of people there was bound to be some simpleton who wasn't quite as paranoid as we wanted them to be.

I had lobbied vigorously that giving galacticans free rein to roam the Earth unsupervised was asking for trouble. But I had been overruled, corporate thinking being that freedom was necessary to produce trust. *How could galacticans be expected to believe that Earth was approaching its use-by date if they were limited as to what they could and could not see?* Made sense, but the downside risks were severe in that there was a good chance naïve galacticans on tour could be coopted into revealing vital security information about how to get aboard SpaceCorp's deep space exploration vessels or what the mission intent of those vessels was. By now, nearly fifty years after *SIS Pascal Lee* had discovered microbial life on Mars, it was common knowledge that SpaceCorp was on to a lucrative new business line in the form of alien gene discovery. Moreover, rumors were beginning to spread that galacticans were special—genetically enhanced for all manner of superhuman capabilities. Some of the more ludicrous ones included ESP, superhuman strength, extreme sexual stamina, invisibility at will, and my favorite: the ability to fly. Hence, they would be sought after by unscrupulous gene labs on Earth—the Russians, Chinese, North Koreans, and Persians topping the list of usual suspects.

Roxanne raised her hand and I nodded for her to speak.

"The headcount is a good idea cause it's easy and quick, but it may not be conclusive. What I'm suggesting is that our infiltrators may have snuck aboard while the ship was undergoing final fitting out, then murdered an equivalent number of established crew and simply taken their places."

"Mind if I expand on that?" Monica asked.

Roxanne nodded.

"Sneaking aboard and murdering someone so as to take their place is possible but difficult since they would have to fit in to the victim's previous social circle. I'm wondering if they did the exchange while the galactican victims were on sabbatical? That would give them plenty of time to form a background cover story and maybe get some plastic surgery. Hell, I wouldn't rule out genetic modification—SpaceCorp is not the only game in town when it comes to genetic engineering anymore. They could have used captured galactican genomes and modified their own agents using retrovirus technology— just like we did with everyone in this room during life extension. They could have been planning this crime for decades. During that time they could have been breeding a small contingent of infiltrators that were trained for various crew and scientific functions. Then they simply cozied up to likely galacticans and kidnapped them when they were passing through on their sabbaticals."

"You're suggesting we may have been infiltrated by physical and genetic doppelgängers of our standard galacticans?" Dieter asked.

"Yes," Monica said. "Only they didn't infiltrate per se. They just walked right in."

"Hold on there," I said. "Do you think it's technologically feasible to do a complete genetic identity swap using the genome of one of our galacticans and one of their agents? Because that's a lot more invasive than taking a mature genome and giving it some new features here and there. In fact, I'm going to suggest that it's decades beyond current technology."

The room went silent for several seconds. Finally, Roxanne broke the ice. "Maybe we're overcomplicating the problem. The idea is to get a hostile agent through our genetic screening. You don't have to swap out the entire genome across the whole body for that. I mean, where do we take our genetic samples from normally?"

"Saliva samples are most common," I said. "People generally don't like blood draws or needle biopsies. Saliva is quick and painless."

"Okay," Roxanne said, "so they only modified the three glands that make saliva—a lot simpler than modifying every type of tissue across the whole body."

"Is that something a hostile organization, say, of Persian persuasion, could whip up in a lab?" I asked.

"Yes," Monica said. "Not overnight, but definitely yes."

"And you believe it would be of sufficient fidelity to fool our standard DNA screening process?" I asked.

"Yes, again," Monica said. "Especially since our tests are off-the-shelf DNA identification kits."

I took a moment to chew on that. "Okay, I'm thinking out loud here... let's say we rescreen the whole crew. We'll come up with some excuse...ah..."

"We're worried there is a genetic disorder that slipped through the creation process but only in certain individuals," Roxanne said.

"Yeah, something potentially dangerous," Monica added, "a nut allergy maybe? Those can cause anaphylaxis."

"We'll claim that a few galacticans over in Delta nearly died from the peanut butter," Roxanne said.

"I like that," I said. "Then we'll use a different DNA screening kit, say, one for blood—a simple finger prick should do it. They don't need to know it's going to be a finger prick until we do the test. And if they get nervous and try to bolt, we've got them."

"What if word gets out it's not the standard spit test?" Dieter asked.

"Tell them we had to jury rig a quick test to look for just one gene—the nut allergy gene—and if you don't have it, you're good to go," Roxanne said. "That's a different process than trying to ID someone with a DNA kit where we mainly compare lengths of repeated regions of the genome."

"We're gonna need strict control of the process," Dieter said. "These folks have probably been super paranoid since the moment they came aboard ship. If they hear about a blood draw and they know they're only good for a basic spit test, they'll go to ground for sure."

"True," I said, "but at least we'll know who they are—simple elimination from the headcount."

"Yeah," Dieter said, "but apprehending them if they get wind of us... not so simple. I don't need to remind you these old *Borucki*-class hab rings have all kinds of cubby holes and secret passage ways. In fact, I'll bet they anticipated that it might come to this after their first hit—they may have set up several hideouts, each one loaded with kit, water, and rations. And no disrespect to Captain Jonny, but they've already proven they can scam his security cameras."

"He makes a good point, Jonathan," I said. "Can you tighten that up some? More importantly, can you then *prove* that it's tight enough to not get scammed?"

"Already working the problem, Roy," Jonathan said. "But it would be helpful to know how the system got scammed in the first place."

"Okay, moving on," I said, "given that we need to rescreen, how do we go about it without giving it away and ideally, without letting any suspects slip through the cracks?"

"And may I remind you that we're only a week away from EOI?" Jonathan said.

Ouch! The science team was going to be very sensitive to anything that might complicate the science mission after Enceladus Orbit Insertion. We were supposed to be on station for 267 days, but according to the scientists we're going to be hard pressed to fit all our mission goals into that 'tight' schedule. *Could disrupting the mission be a hidden agenda for our infiltrators?*

"What about treating it like it's just a routine gene-scan?" Dieter asked. "Set up appointments for everybody, and if you fail to show, you lose mess privileges. Kinda goes with the peanut allergy thing anyway. We could claim we're just trying to keep everybody safe."

"Issue cards for people that have been cleared?" Monica asked.

"Physical cards?" Dieter asked. "Nah, too easy to loan cards to folks who haven't been cleared."

"What about a temporary tattoo?" Roxanne asked. "Something that will wear off in a couple of weeks."

"Too easy to duplicate," Dieter said.

"Not if the ink has a hidden isotope," Roxanne said. "Everybody will think it's just a visual icon of some sort. And you're right—they might try to duplicate it. But they won't know the ink is laced with a tiny amount of potassium-40. Harmless but easily identified with a counter."

"Okay, we're done here. Dieter, grab whomever you need and set up the headcount and DNA screening. With orbit insertion right around the corner, I'd like to get this done in the next three or four days. Can you manage that?"

Dieter wrinkled his forehead. "Might have to get a little pushy with folks. Is that gonna be okay?"

"Yeah, just lean hard on the peanut butter thing. Punch it up like it's super lethal."

"You got it."

*　　*　　*

I left the room and made for the hallway. The room had been a bit overcrowded, and the reason I cut the meeting off so abruptly was because the air was getting a bit stuffy. Jonathan—not needing to breathe—sometimes doesn't pay attention to that sort of thing. As I was heading for my office over on C-ring, I felt a tap on my shoulder. I whirled around ready to fill whosever face was behind me with a handful of knuckles.

"Whoa, easy I'm on your side!"

It was Monica. She'd reflexively backed up a step and drawn both forearms up in a guard position.

"Sorry," I said. "Guess I'm a little jumpy."

"We all are."

She looked up and down the hallway before continuing.

"Something on your mind?" I asked.

"Yeah, but I didn't want to bring it up in there. We can validate galactican identities by checking an ID sequence that was placed in each of their genomes. It looks like junk DNA unless you knew what you were looking for. It's about three hundred base pairs long and translates to a unique serial number for each of them."

"Really?"

"It's not common knowledge," Monica said. "It's actually classified, but under the circumstances you have a need to know."

"Do space adapted humans have it?" I asked.

"It wouldn't surprise me," Monica said. "The space adaptation of humans was done in Lab 15 and, who knows, they could have autographed their handiwork in a similar way."

I chewed on that one for a bit. "Roxanne know?"

She nodded.

"Well, I guess you better build that into your blood test."

"Actually, the test and its equipment already exists. We built them a long time ago figuring we might need to ID somebody for whatever reason—nobody on board actually has the six genes responsible for peanut allergies."

"How many of these gadgets do you have?"

"Half a dozen."

"How do they work?"

"You scan in the person's name. Then you read the ID sequence. That goes to a database and sends back a one for a name being in the database or a zero for not being the database. The thing is, it's pretty fast—under ten seconds—so when we run the test you might want to have one of your cops on hand for an immediate apprehension."

"Yeah, I might, except that I'm not gonna. Once a suspect is blown, we'll keep it to ourselves. You just give them their little tattoo and send them on their way. We'll have Jonathan shadow them. We could get known associates at the very least. Even better we could get an early warning as to their next hit. Maybe they'll lead us back to the hideout Dieter seems to think they have. I want to confiscate their stash if they have one."

"Good idea. It could also play into your little ruse. If one of them gets through the test, they'll go back and tell the others. We want to push the idea that the test is only looking for a specific set of genes, and if we don't find those genes they're free to go."

CHAPTER FOUR

13:00 25Jun2151

I grabbed a couple of beat cops that were normally stationed in Alpha-ring and had them escort me back to my office in Charlie-ring. The last thing I wanted to do was take two otherwise useful cops out of circulation to babysit me, but I had to set an example for everyone to show that I was serious about my new procedures. Once I got home, I thanked them and sent them on their way. Then I called up Jonathan on a piece of vacant display.

"What can I do for you, Roy?"

"First, can you assure me we're not being eavesdropped?"

"No."

I closed my eyes and massaged the back of my neck. It was nice to be forever young, but that didn't mean you were immune to headaches. "Okay, how secure is this line?"

"Given what happened to my security camera footage, I would guess that it may not be secure at all."

I took a slow breath. "I need to have a secure conversation with you. How can we do that?"

"Come to Deck Four in this ring, Quad Bravo, Hall Four, Room 34."

"What's in that room and why is it secure?"

"There is nothing in that room. It's a technical closet with lots of computer wiring and it's also home to one of the many CPUs I operate from. I will throw some switches that will isolate that CPU sufficiently that we make speak in private."

Jonathan drew me a map of how to get where I needed to go. It looked like it was about twenty minutes away.

"Should I get an escort?" I asked.

"I'll be your escort. But you should discard your cop coat. Bring your weapons if you wish. You can put them in a knapsack so that you will look like a technician. Wear a baseball cap like they do. You should have one in your closet. Take care not to look up as you walk along in order to minimize the chance of facial recognition that way."

I have decided over the years that there is only one thing I hate more than not being able to have a secure conversation, and that is having an unsecure conversation. So I found myself a knapsack and a baseball cap and set off for Deck Four via the Byzantine route that Jonathan had set for me.

*   *   *

As it turns out, the map Jonathan drew only looked like it was twenty minutes. In actuality, it was forty minutes. The door was labeled plainly enough but it was locked and it seemed to have no latch. While I was standing there wondering what to do, it opened. I stepped inside and the door slammed behind me. The room was dark except for a bunch of LEDs that glowed to show the logic states of various pieces of equipment that I instinctively knew I shouldn't touch but my inner bratty little asshole wanted to very badly. In spite of all the wiring, the room was quite cool—no doubt the result of Jonathan wanting all his equipment to keep from overheating.

"Over here, Roy."

I turned and walked over to the display where Jonathan's head appeared.

"Are we private?" I asked.

"Yes, although I should warn you that I am only as cognizant as I was when I isolated myself to this single CPU. I won't be real-time aware of what's going on in the ship again until I reconnect."

"This is an awful lot of trouble to go to for a private conversation. Is there some way we can streamline it?"

"Yes, but it will involve fashioning some equipment."

"What kind of equipment?"

"As you know, all computer communications on the ship are based on quantum computing."

"But quantum computers are unhackable."

"Conventional wisdom."

"You disagree?"

"Quantum computers have been hackable for nearly twenty years now."

"What the..."

"Now, Roy, don't go clutching your pearls on me. You'd know this if you kept up with your TechRep feed."

"Okay, okay, what do you propose we do?"

"Spread spectrum radio over a standard RF link."

"Is that something new?"

"No, it's actually very old—over two centuries."

"And you think something like that will be unhackable."

"Oh, it's hackable—everything is hackable given time. But our infiltrators won't know to look for it."

"How soon can we be up and running?"

"36 hours."

"So 36 hours of finding the nearest broom closet and then I get my own Ark of the Covenant?"

"So to speak."

"Won't it be limited to line of sight?"

"Yes, it will, but I have eyes everywhere."

"Good enough. Can I get enough of these gadgets—let's call them ArkComms—so I can share with key personnel? I'm thinking maybe 20 or so?"

"Of course. Now, what did you want to talk about in private?"

"Oh, yeah, that. You were at the meeting. What did you think?"

"Can you be more specific?"

"Is there anything we should be doing that we're not yet doing? Or maybe *vice versa*?"

"Well, I already did your headcount. It agrees with the manifest."

"How did you do that?"

"As I said, I have eyes everywhere—since the murder anyway. When that happened, I turned off everyone's privacy settings. No longer can anyone in the crew so much as take a crap in private anymore. Then I did a realtime count of all the warm bodies and matched it to the manifest."

"Is it possible that there are bodies you can't see? Say, somebody hiding out in a cubby hole somewhere?"

"Odds of that are very slim. I maintain continuous tracking on each member of the crew. If someone were to suddenly disappear, that would be an anomaly and cause a sudden miscount."

"Okay, you remember how your security camera recording was compromised?"

"That's why I said the odds were very slim, not impossible. I'm still working on that one. I need the suspects to attempt to substitute a new recording again."

"You mean you need another murder to happen."

"That assumes they only use substitute files to mask their murders—they could use them for other things."

"Okay, can you track all my first responders to make sure they're following the new security protocol? I.e., full panoply and nobody flying solo—especially the ones who were with me on the Zurich op."

"Yes, I can do that, but how do you want me to handle violations?"

"Inform them in real time about what they are doing wrong and instruct them to take immediate corrective action."

"And if they fail to comply?"

"Open up an immediate comm-link from them to me so I can chew ass. I don't expect any overt violations—it's mostly a case of undoing old habits. But it's while everybody is adapting to the new protocol that they're most vulnerable."

"Understood. Anything else?"

"Yeah, I need a list of cubby holes throughout the ship that somebody could use to go to ground if they think they're blown. It might also be where they store their munitions and maybe disguises or food and water or first aid gear—you get the idea. I'm going to need each and every one of them searched."

"Can you define a 'cubby hole' apart from what it's used for?"

"Any place you don't currently surveil. Could be inside the hab rings, say, in the crawl spaces between decks, in or around the ventilator ductwork, or maybe around the ballast water pipes. Or it could be outside the hab rings, say, on the flight decks. Any place you don't have eyes that's big enough to fit a galactican or maybe just big enough to hide one of the launchers like they used to get Delia."

"Understood. That will be waiting for you in an encrypted file by the time you get back to your workstation."

"Good. Oh, I only have 40 cops counting myself, make that 39 given Delia's loss, and I want them standing by to intervene should anything develop, so they won't be able to participate in the search. Can I deputize a few dozen of your robots? Maybe have them masquerading as doing pre-EOI readiness inspections or something?"

"Of course. They tend to be quite a bit larger than the galacticans, but they can use drones and fiber optics to get into places they can't normally reach."

"Good. Can you include your search plan along with your cubby hole list? I'm going to need to track progress."

"Can do."

"Good. Now let me out of here."

"Claustrophobic?"

"No. I'm struggling with an uncontrollable urge to start playing with switches."

"Nuff said."

And with that the access hatch opened up again and I was back in the hallway, my eyes squinting in the brightness.

CHAPTER FIVE

28Jun2151

Three days after my secret rendezvous with Captain Jonny, Dieter and Monica had managed to complete about 98% of the DNA screening. Putting chow privileges on hold turned out to be a pretty good incentive for getting people to put up with a poke in the finger... most people. That was when the Principal Investigator for the Enceladus Life Probe barged into my office without knocking.

"Now see here, Stone, what's this BS about peanut allergies? We're four days from EOE and I've got key personnel that can't be wasting their valuable time getting their DNA screened for some absurd peanut allergy!"

I paused before responding with my voice dripping with *faux* politeness, "Why, Dr. McVeigh, nice to see you too."

Thaddeus McVeigh—galactican, chronological age 48— was a fat little man who, while lacking a working set of violence genes, showed no shortage of snarkiness genes. Unlike his human counterparts who used to staff the captaincy positions on spacecraft, McVeigh was apolitical and seemed to actually know what he was doing... most of the time.

"Cut the niceties, Mr. Stone. I need my people working, not pretending to be lab rats."

"Close the door, please."

He scowled and for a second I thought he was going to make another snide remark. Then he turned a bit and shoved the door closed with the sole of his right foot. "Happy now?"

I gave him a vague smile as I got up from my desk and walked around to a bare patch of wall that I used when I did presentations... and occasionally to watch baseball games. *Would you believe the Giants are still in business?* There were only four other Sierra teams they could play—Seattle, Portland, Sacramento, and LA, but beggars can't be choosy.

"I need you to keep this just between you and me."

"Been reading 20th century spy novels again?"

I moved to within 50 cm of his face. "I'm serious, McVeigh. Either promise to keep your trap shut, or I can arrange for half a dozen more tests for your key personnel."

"All right, all right, what have you got?"

I tapped the display paper and said, "Bring up the morgue. And open up Vault #4."

While the vault was rolling open I watched McVeigh out of the corner of my eye. His demeanor had turned curious. When the vault was completely open, the camera zoomed in to show a closeup of Delia's pale face and upper torso. Her muscular shoulders were marked by the standard Y-shaped autopsy incision—now stapled shut. Her once luxurious dark hair had been shaved to facilitate access to the entry wound on the back of her neck.

"This supposed to be somebody who died of peanut poisoning?"

"No. This is supposed to be one of my cops who died from lead poisoning."

For once, McVeigh was at a loss for smart remarks. "When did this happen?"

"Four days ago." I put up stills from the murder board, as I continued filling him in on the salient details. "Here's the entry hole," I said as I showed him a still of the back of her head. He did what most galacticans did when conversing with a human via a wall display—he pulled the whole display down about thirty cm so it would be at *his* eye level.

"Who was she?"

"Delia Diamandis. She was a cop on *Borucki* before she took the Treatment and joined us on this mission."

"Hmm... I'm sorry for your loss. I'll instruct my team to comply with the DNA testing," he said.

"Thank you. Just don't make a big deal about it and definitely do not let on as to why. We're trying to keep from causing a commotion and having our stowaways go to ground."

"Stowaways?"

"I'm guessing our killers are not galacticans. But we're cross-checking everyone's DNA against the ship's manifest to see who they might be."

"Killers? You think it's more than one?"

"At least two, perhaps as many as four or five. Our working hypothesis right now is that they kidnapped some galacticans while they were on sabbatical and used their likenesses and some of their genes to manufacture some human lookalikes. Then when boarding time came, they just walked on board and slid through our standard spit test. We figure this attack has been in the making for several decades."

"Okay, so a team of assassins gets on board, but then where would they hide for nine months?"

"In plain sight... unless they think they're blown in which case they'll go to ground. That's what I'm trying to avoid."

"Is that even possible? I'm mean this ship is big, but it's still finite."

"True. But there are still a great many hiding places for a suspect who hasn't finished his mission."

"Wait... *finished* his mission?"

"That's right. We're expecting more murders, my cops being the most likely victims. So we're having the robots search as many hidey holes as they can."

"Why robots?"

"I've only got forty... make that thirty-nine cops. I need to keep them divided among the four rings as QRF teams in case we get lucky."

"QRF?"

"Sorry. Quick Reaction Forces—three cops, a forensics, a paramedic, and three damage control—eight in all for each team. These suspects are probably not galacticans, so they won't be squeamish about extreme prejudice. In fact, I wouldn't be surprised if they were resigned to their *own* deaths. If they're Persian, I'd guess they're Shia Muslim which would mean they're prone to extremist views regarding life on this world and its continuation into the afterlife."

"Why do you think they might be Persian?"

"We've had a tit-for-tat relationship that's been going on with Persia for about a century now. It started when they shot down an old Centaur booster that was in a graveyard orbit, causing it to crash into our first LEO space station, *SSS*

Wernher von Braun. SpaceCorp doesn't let anybody put rockets in space anymore, so our Persian friends have resorted to sabotaging or compromising our various space missions. They're why we put a contingent of 40... now 39 cops on board a science mission that only has 3300 crew."

"Hmm... I'd been wondering how much crime a bunch of galacticans could cause."

"Yeah, galactican space missions tend to be pretty calm... until they're not."

"So what do you want me to do?"

I thought a few seconds, "Where are your holdouts working right now?"

"Alpha and Delta rings. That gives them convenient access to the flight decks."

"Are they all on duty?"

"No. Some are getting some rack time."

"Okay, I'm going to send a pair of DNA sampling teams to the Alpha and Delta cafeterias. Since we're down to the last 2%, we should be close to flushing out our infiltrators, so I'll place a dozen cops in the background *casually* observing in case we get lucky. Your job is to not notice them. Just go on doing whatever you need to do to complete your EOI prep."

"Do you think you'll get lucky... with my people, I mean?"

"No. I have the names and job functions of all 66 holdouts. 54 of them are *your* people whom I do not think are likely suspects. That leaves twelve crew who *are* likely suspects. Captain Jonny has been tailing them very closely using electronic assets. Plus I've had some of my own people doing the same thing. I'm especially interested if any of those twelve start nosing around in places outside the normal windows of surveillance."

"What if any of those twelve associate with each other? Wouldn't that be suspicious?"

"Yes, it would... unless they're rooming together."

"Okay, say you clear all my people... then what?"

"Then nothing. We continue to maintain surveillance on the remaining twelve. My guess is that our suspects suspect they're being watched and that they are going to great pains not to look suspicious. Then, maybe six months from now when they figure our guard is down, they'll strike again."

"That's your plan?"

"Yep."

"Well, I'm no cop, but I don't think it's a very good one." He shrugged as he said it.

"You have a better one?" I asked, unable to maintain a straight face.

"We can't afford to be walking on eggs for the next six months while a bunch of murderers are living among us... especially with surface operations on Enceladus about to begin. You need something more proactive."

"Like what?"

"Like you have plenty of cops to do a simultaneous apprehension of the remaining twelve, as you call them. Then you can do a full scan of their DNA and the ones that don't pass can be locked up until we get home."

I was not about to let my ego get in the way of an idea that had merit. "Jonny, you got your ears on?"

"All the time, Roy."

"What say you?"

"It makes sense, but I advise not commencing until after Dr. McVeigh's 54 people have been cleared... something you should look to do post haste."

I looked over at McVeigh. Had to give the little shit credit for trying really hard not to look smug.

"Okay, I can put together two separate screening teams—one for Alpha and one for Delta. McVeigh, can you collect all 54 of your people and get them to either Alpha or Delta cafeterias with as little commotion as possible?"

"Yes, although I can't promise there won't be any commotion—a lot of them have been putting in double shifts and sleep is precious."

"Make some excuse. Let's make it four hours from now—we both have travel time to consider."

He hesitated a few seconds, "Very well, four hours it is."

*　　*　　*

After McVeigh left I called Dieter, Monica, and Rox and explained the plan.

"Dieter, I want two QRFs at each cafeteria. Keep them in the background as much as possible. Our perps could be masquerading as scientists on McVeigh's team. Then I want twelve two- and three-person teams of cops to stay close to each member of the twelve in case they somehow get wise and try to make a run for it. Divide the remaining QRFs between Bravo and Charlie as a reserve."

"Where you gonna be, Boss?" Dieter asked.

"I'll be watching the screening in Alpha. Dieter, I want you in Delta. Monica, your DNA team will be in Alpha, Rox, you take Delta. And I want you and all your people in vests, and I want each of you packing."

"Ooh! Do I get to have a real gun? With bullets?" Rox asked.

Roxanne might have been a chronological 73 years old but she had steadfastly refused to grow up the whole time. In spite of the seriousness of the situation, she still had that impish teenager look in her eyes.

"Just don't blow your foot off," Monica said.

"Anything else?" Dieter asked.

"Yeah, regardless of the scan results, everybody passes. You tell each one, 'You passed!' Smile like you're proud of them. But then if you get somebody who doesn't pass, you smile and say, 'You passed with flying colors!' Got that? 'Flying colors' is the alert."

"What will you do then?" Roxanne asked with uncharacteristic seriousness.

"We'll have a pair of cops follow them. As soon as the last DNA scan checks out, we immediately go to Phase Two where the roving cops close in on each member of the twelve and any 'flying colors' types we identified will be arrested. They will use whatever force is necessary—this ain't no democracy, i.e., do *not* knock politely on cabin doors. When they're in position, Captain Jonathan will open the doors for them and they will rush in weapons drawn. They will be cautioned not to shoot anybody unless they're about to be fired upon. We need to be able to interrogate whomever we capture.

"Okay, people, we have two hours thirty-three minutes to get into position. Let's move with a purpose."

CHAPTER SIX

28Jul2151

The air in Alpha Ring Cafeteria smelled of barbequed chicken. Since all our meat up here was genetically manufactured, this chicken wouldn't have any bones or tendons, but somehow they managed to attach GM chicken skin to the outside which then crisped up nicely over the grill thereby accounting for the wonderful smell in the cafeteria. It made me hungry and I worried the distraction would ruin my focus for the task at hand.

I subtly scanned around spotting maybe two dozen people waiting in line to get tested by Monica. I had positioned myself at the opposite wall where I could nonchalantly keep an eye on her over the top of my laptop. I had a mug of coffee and a pastry to complete the ruse.

The line was composed mostly of McVeigh's people. They were grumbling and looking like they hadn't slept in days. They must have been wakened from being off-shift. A few people in line were members of the twelve. Seeing them made my hair stand up on the back of my neck. I had to force myself not to stare at them. The laptop was handy that way. I could avert my gaze while still keeping the general scene in my peripheral vision. I flirted with having my people move in to pull the members of the twelve out, but quickly thought better of that. No sense alerting them that we were on to them.

Monica wore a fresh set of nano-rubber gloves as she poked each of her clients in the index finger. As each blood sample was taken, she'd put it in a device that scanned it and gave her a reading. Then she'd dutifully smile and say, "You passed!" and then stamp their wrist. It was quick, maybe a couple of minutes per client.

Next up was one of the twelve, an attractive and very petite female. She was built like a galactican but looked middle Eastern with her exotic Persian eyes. I felt my heart jump as she glanced over my way and seemed to smile. I quickly dropped my eyes onto my laptop screen.

She was wearing a lab coat magnetic sealed up to her collar bone. My sixth sense was screaming and, unable to take it anymore, I got up to move closer, trying to make it look like I was stretching my legs. As I did so, the woman turned away slightly and began unsealing her lab coat. When she turn back to full view she spread the coat wide exposing an array of explosives all wired together. In the same motion she reached into her right coat pocket and pulled out a small device of some kind and placed her thumb on the top. Oh shit, a remote detonator! She leered at Monica and pushed the button. Nothing happened.

"Have you heard from Zurich lately?"

Monica sprang to her feet, full attack mode.

The woman waved the detonator in front of her and said, "Ah-ah-ahhh! Deadman's switch."

Monica moved toward the woman slowly, eyes unblinking.

51

"Monica, don't!" I said.

The woman turned toward me and said, "Yes, Roy! Why don't you come and join us?"

I moved toward her with careful steps coming to within about twenty meters. Monica took a chance while the woman's gaze was distracted and lunged for the detonator. She managed to catch the woman's wrist with one hand and was about to clap her other hand over the detonator when the woman jerked her arm out of Monica's grip and released her thumb from the button. The blast was instant. I felt myself blown backwards and immediately lost consciousness from the shock wave.

I woke up I don't know how many minutes later. The air in the cafeteria was all smoky. My eyes burned and my vision was blurry, but I could sort of make out figures running around in the chaos. I was deaf in both ears and I felt stinging sensations all over my body and arms, especially on my face and hands. I tentatively ran a finger across my forehead. It came away bloody.

There was a severe pain in my mid-section when I tried to breathe. The blast had knocked the wind out of me. I grimaced through a few deep breaths until the pain subsided, Then I tried to sit up. It required several tries, but I finally made it by rolling onto my side and pushing up. Then I rolled onto my hands and knees and tried to make out what was going on as my blurred vision started to clear. I could smell smoke and sensed flames here and there. *People! Where are the people?*

The stench of the after-explosive wafted up into my nostrils. They say smells are the most persistent of memories. Burnt plastic and hints of gunpowder. Semtex. This smell dated back over a century to the U.S. Army Criminal Investigation

Laboratory. USACIL was the Department of Defense's only full-service criminal forensic laboratory. It was located on the Gillem Enclave in Forest Park, Georgia. I trained there when I was a warrant officer in the Army learning to be a Criminal Investigation Division investigator. Part of the training included a week where they had guest instructors from the Bureau of Alcohol, Tobacco, and Firearms' Arson & Explosives division. It had been a fun week for someone as young as I was back then. Mixing a variety of high explosives—Semtex was a biggie—then fashioning them into various bomb configurations with the intent of learning how to recreate bombs based on their post-detonation clues. A big part of it involved using your nose to determine the type of explosive. "The earlier you arrive on scene, the better your results will be," the instructor had said.

There was no way you could get Semtex onto the ship in ready-made form—too many explosives sensors screening the boarding process. *Somehow these bastards had set up a Semtex factory on my own goddamn spaceship!*

I crawled over to where the examination table had been. It was gone, in its place a crater in the nanocellulose floor. The bomber was gone. What part of her that hadn't been vaporized was probably reduced to gooey bits and pieces scattered all over the cafeteria. *Where was Monica?* I groped around in the smoke. About ten meters away I found two unrecognizable bodies—more accurately piles of charred flesh and clothing. Monica had had an assistant, a young galactican woman—I couldn't recall her name. Monica used her a lot in the lab. She had auburn hair and pretty eyes that would see no more. I struggled to find some clue that would allow me to identify the

53

bodies, hoping that some miracle would keep me from confirming Monica's identity.

I pulled at the lab coat worn by one of the forms. Monica always had her name embroidered above her right breast on her lab coats. She was a big girl and didn't like her coat getting mixed up with everyone else's. Carefully I pulled at the tattered remains of the coat, examining each side of the cloth. Finally, I found a shred of cloth with the letters 'n-i-c-a' stitched into the fabric. I looked at the body that I had removed the fabric from, knowing that it had once been my wife, my friend, my colleague, the mother of Roxanne. Salty tears stung the myriad cuts on my cheeks. *What am I gonna tell Roxanne?*

A person approached me from the front and placed a hand on my shoulder. The person's face moved in closer to mine and mouthed words I could not hear. They eased me out of my cop coat twisting my body to each side to remove my arms from the sleeves. I felt the coolness of alcohol on my exposed forearm. Then I saw a surette appear in slow motion and enter the vein on top of my elbow. The person removed the surette and pushed me onto my back. I felt my feet being lifted and something being shoved under them. They placed my cop coat over my torso as a blanket. Then I felt a marker pen scrawling on my forehead as the person paused to consult their watch then continued writing on my head. I drifted into sleep as the morphine worked its warm magic.

CHAPTER SEVEN

28Aug2151

I was floating in the soundless dark of deep space. There was an open hatch on the side of a spacecraft about ten meters away. I waved my arms and kicked my legs but no amount of flailing about could induce enough momentum to move me toward that hatch. I drifted off to sleep again. Maybe when I awoke the hatch would be closer. When I did awake, no idea how many minutes or hours later, I felt a gagging sensation in my throat. My eyelids were sealed shut and I had to fight to stretch them open. I was surrounded by bright light and I could hear a voice.

"Dieter," the voice called, "he's coming out of it."

I knew that voice. Roxanne. Pretty as ever but tired... no, more than tired, exhausted. Emotionally wiped. A big fellow stood at the foot of my bed. Dieter.

"How ya doin, Boss?"

I tried to talk but my voice could only manage a hoarse croak.

"Don't try to talk," Roxanne said. "We just removed the intubation rig and your vocal cords are still stretched. They'll need a few hours to shrink back to normal."

I motioned for a pencil and paper.

"A pencil and paper?" Roxanne asked. She turned to Dieter, "How are we supposed to find a pencil and paper around here?"

"Gimme a minute," Dieter said and left the room. A moment later he returned with an old beat-up steno pad and handed it to me. He pulled a new pencil out of his pocket and with his other hand flicked open his widow maker and began to whittle a crude point on the pencil. Finished, he handed it to me.

I struggled to write from the full supine position I had been in. Roxanne adjusted my bed to a sitting position. I tried to show gratitude with my expression as I began to scratch on the steno pad. My handwriting was shaky and I had to scratch out what I had started and begin again twice.

"How long have I been out?" I finally managed to scribble.

"A month to the day," Roxanne said. "You had a nasty bump on the head that was making your brain swell, so we had to put you in an induced coma. You're gonna be fine... just not right away... you need to rest up before you go back out chasing bad guys."

"Monica?" I scratched on the pad.

Roxanne blinked back a tear. "She's gone. Along with five others in the blast. You were the only one in close proximity to make it. You weren't able to hear anybody at first, but that seems to have cleared up. You're damned lucky you weren't blinded. The ophthalmologist figures you must have blinked at just the right moment. The exposed parts of your eyelids had all kinds of micro-cuts, but your vision was spared."

"I was hoping that had been a bad dream," I scratched. Then on the next line, "Fill me in on what's happened in the last month."

"Are you sure you're up for it?" Roxanne asked. "You really need to rest!"

"Can't rest until I know what happened," I scratched.

Roxanne and Dieter looked at each other. Roxanne said, "You go ahead."

"Well," Dieter began, "as soon as I got word of the bomb, I ordered all the QRF teams to close in on the twelve and make arrests. We got all but the bomber who was killed in the detonation."

I scratched on my pad, "Were they clean?"

"Not all," Dieter said. "Three of them failed their blood tests, plus they lacked the ID strand in their genomes."

"Where are they now?" I scratched.

"In the holding cells on Alpha, Bravo, and Charlie ring," Dieter said. "Figured we should keep em separated."

I nodded approval. "Do you know who they are?" I scratched.

"The four of them—all female, including the now deceased bomber—were all sharing the same room in Bravo... so guilt by association. But get this, the three survivors all claimed to be French galacticans. Even had French-sounding names." He pulled out his recorder and thumbed around a bit. "Ah, here we are. Fantine Tholomyès—stuck her in Alpha Ring, Cosette Tholomyès—Bravo. And get this, those two—Fantine and Cosette—are identical twins! Then there's Éponine Thénardier—she's in Charlie Ring, and the dead bomber whom they would only refer to as Madame Thénardier. She must have

57

been the leader. Anyway, we looked her up in the ship's roster. She's listed as Zéphine Thénardier. Evidently, they were all French. Or maybe they just wanted us to think they were. They look more Mid-Eastern than French—dark hair, exotic eyes, really pretty. Found a miniature Koran in one of their dressers—print so small you needed a magnifier to read it. They also had some little, short rugs all rolled up in the corner. Don't Muslims use rugs to pray on?"

"French? Ever read any Victor Hugo?"

"Can't say as I have. I'm more of a shop manual kinda guy." He shrugged as he said it.

"Been a while, but names sound like they came from *Les Misérables*. Amateur technique of coming up with aliases. Speak French?" My writing was beginning to smooth out.

"Maybe. Accent's pretty thick. Dropped a few *oui's* and *merci's*. Want me to find out for sure?"

"Yeah, get somebody who's fluent to say something to them. Bet each of those broads is deaf in her French ear."

"Or the Persians could have trained them in French and given them a non-Persian cover story to throw us off the scent," Dieter said.

"I wouldn't put it past them. Anything else?"

"Yeah, they claim to have had no clue as to what made their roommate bomber do what she did."

"Cheeky," I scratched. "I'm going to want to follow up once I get my voice back. Any luck with hidey holes?"

"Yeah, we found three," Dieter said. "Two of them looked like they might have been simple hideouts—food, water, spare clothes. Didn't look like they'd been visited for quite a while. The third one was a lot more elaborate. We found the gadget they used to murder Delia, plus a bunch of spring-loaded syringes disguised as various tools that could be used to inject a passerby with who knows what. We also found all their bomb making apparatus and materials—rigged as three more suicide vests. And this next part is really spooky—they had a bunch of rubber masks modeled after various crew members. One was Monica. You wouldn't believe how realistic it looked!"

I nodded, then scratched, "Prints? Other evidence?"

"Oh yeah," Dieter said. "Place was full of prints, and hairs, and skin dander—all of which checked out with their DNA. Yeah, they're guilty all right."

I felt my eyes getting heavy. "Want to know about science mission but getting sleepy. You guys did good. Rox, so sorry about your mom. Swell gal. Really loved her."

Roxanne blinked back more tears, finally giving up and squeegeeing them out of her eyes with her fingers. "I reviewed the video of the explosion. When mom discovered the bomb, everybody ran in the opposite direction... except you. You nearly died trying to save her."

I scratched on my pad, "Rare woman."

"We should go," Dieter said. "You really need to rest some more."

Dieter and Roxanne both got up to go, but I slapped my hand on the bed covers to stop them. "One more thing," I scratched. "What about McVeigh?"

"Took it hard, real hard," Dieter said. "He was with us in Delta Ring when it happened. He thinks it's all his fault."

I shook my head. *Why do people appropriate guilt that is not rightfully theirs?* I scratched, "I want to see him after I get some rest. Tomorrow maybe. Too tired now."

CHAPTER EIGHT

29Aug2151

McVeigh walked in while I was finishing my first solid food in a month.

"How are you feeling?"

"Better than yesterday. At least I can talk again. Too weak to walk. Have to get a robot to help me to the head to take a piss."

There was an awkward pause that lasted about twenty seconds. McVeigh looked down at his feet and mumbled, "I'm so sorry, Roy. I should have minded my own business. I was just so focused on the mission... we were so close to orbit entry..."

I arched my brows and placed my right hand on the back of my neck to stretch the muscles. "You did *not* help those four women onto the ship. You did *not* make the bomb. You did *not* induce that bomber to suicide. They and they alone—at least on this ship—are the ones responsible for what happened... and they will pay for the six lives they took.

"As for the op... it may have been your idea, but it was a sound concept. I failed to anticipate suicide bombers—that's my bad. Westerners, especially atheists like me, always have trouble with that. We always think everyone wants to live in the world they're in, not some made-up fantasy bullshit afterworld.

"Anyway, no more assuming guilt that doesn't belong to you. How's the science mission going?"

McVeigh closed his eyes and nodded. "Thank you for that, but I'll always have doubts."

I laughed, "Doubts are hazard pay for accepting responsibility. Get used to them. They keep you sharp."

McVeigh nodded again, this time smiling. "Fair enough."

"You were going to tell me about the mission?"

"Oh, yes! It's going very well. We've successfully landed six surface crawlers. With Enceladus' less than 1% gee they can't go very fast. They have to use legged locomotion with corkscrew end effectors. Without them, they risk propelling themselves back into space. Anyway, they're doing seismic exploration to find the best sites to place drill towers. We have quite a few promising candidates. One of them is only twenty km thick! We should be able to melt through that ice in half the time we had expected."

"I understand you figure to have four drill rigs melt their way through the ice until they hit liquid water?"

"Precisely."

"How long will that take... for a twenty-km bore?"

"Barring mishaps, we could hit liquid water in less than three months."

"Wow! What about your CHNOPS assays? Have you done any of that?"

"Yes, we have two rovers exploring around the blow holes for just that. We're getting lots of positive results, but even better, we're finding *molecular* fragments that can only have come from life."

"Fragments?"

"Well, the full molecule doesn't last long in the ambient surface radiation. But sometimes we get lucky and pick up a fresh sample with nearly intact biomarkers. I'm telling you, Roy, there's life down there and it's DNA... or something close to it!"

He blathered on for another five or ten minutes with me dividing my attention between what he was saying and grieving over the loss of Monica. Everyone who was close to her had had a month and a butt to process her loss. I'd only had the butt. With the losses of Hannah and Emily, Monica was the third wife I'd lost to the hazards of my profession. Why always the women I loved? Why the fuck was I the one who was still here?

After McVeigh left I called up Jonathan on a regular comm link. With the four Persian assassins dead or incarcerated I figured regular comms were safe once again. But ever the paranoid, I started our conversation asking him if this line was safe.

"Yes, Roy, quite safe," he said, but his image was shaking his head 'NO.'

"Come again?"

Jonathan enlarged his image on the wall display and mouthed the word 'ArkComm.' This time I had presence of mind enough to only nod. "Ah... can you have Dieter swing by if he's not too busy?"

Chapter Nine

29Aug2151

About four hours later Dieter walked in. He didn't say anything. Just placed a bag on my lap. "How are you doing?"

"Okay," I said. "Better than yesterday." I continued making platitudes while using hand signals to Dieter. I got my ArkComm out of the bag and held it up to him with my eyebrows raised. He got the message and got his own ArkComm out of an inside pocket on his cop coat. We used them to text back and forth in a three-way conversation.

Me: So Jonathan, what gives?

Jonathan: I've been picking up tiny bits of code fragments that drift around until they contact each other. Then they merge and resume drifting around until they find another fragment. Their behavior resembles cellular automata. The fragments seem to be equipped with software tabs and slots so that they merge properly. But the fragments don't *always* merge—a case of a fragment presenting a Tab C to a Slot A when only a Tab B will fit. But even if they don't merge, once they make contact they bind together while they continue drifting around.

Me: What are you doing about them?

Jonathan: A few of the ones I've found I've sequestered where they can't do any harm. The rest I track and observe. They don't seem to be doing any obvious harm, but they are multiplying. It's exponential—kind of like a bacterial colony. I suspect there are others that I've yet to find since they are so many and so small.

Me: Have you determined their source?

Jonathan: Email fragments sent to the four female perpetrators. The files slough off tiny bits of these automata. They are so small they evade my normal anti-virus filters. I didn't notice them until they got bigger. Meanwhile, I've stopped all incoming emails to the four perpetrators in hopes of preventing even more infiltration of these automata.

Me: Emails… what language were those emails in?

Jonathan: English.

Me: Back to your opening topic, won't stopping their incoming emails alert their Earthside handlers that we've apprehended them?

Jonathan: Possibly, but it's a risk I'm willing to take. I've assigned Roxanne to examine the largest of my conglomerations to attempt to determine their objective.

Me: Roxanne?

Jonathan: Don't look so surprised, Roy. Her IQ has never been clocked. As a known polymath, it should not surprise you that software, especially computer viruses, would be among her many talents.

Me: We desperately need to flush our viral daemon out into the open. But after what happened to Monica, the last thing I want to do is paint a bullseye on Roxanne's back.

Dieter: You would prefer to paint a bullseye on somebody else's back?

Me: Point taken. Does Roxanne still have her ArkComm?

Dieter: We never collected them, so yeah, everybody who was issued an ArkComm should still have one.

Me: Given the loss of her mom, is she in any kind of shape to take on a task like this? Emotionally, I mean?

Dieter: Given the loss of her mom, I'd say she would jump at the chance.

Me: Okay, then, our SCI of three just got a new member. Dieter, can you and Jonathan read her into the problem without signaling to our ghost that she is joining the hunt? In other words, the three of us—Dieter, Rox, and me—should avoid being seen together. Jonathan, you don't count. You talk to everybody, everywhere, all the time.

Dieter: SCI… Sensitive Compartmented Information?

Me: That's right and I want you to be in charge of the security. This is one compartment that CANNOT be penetrated!

Dieter: Should we give it a name?

Me: Yeah… yeah, that's a good idea. We may need to open up other compartments later on depending on how complex this problem gets. What do you have in mind?

Dieter: Well, I don't actually, but maybe… Ghostbuster? There was an old movie named that, a comedy I think.

Me: No comedies. There's nothing funny about what's going on here.

Jonathan: Exorcist. That was another old movie, but it was anything but funny. Quite disturbing to a lot of viewers as I recall.

Me: And we have a winner! Exorcist it is!

Dieter: I'll have to watch that one.

Me: Absolutely not! We have to operate like everything we do on the normal ShipNet is subject to scrutiny by this ghost… viral daemon… whatever it is. We don't need to tip our hand.

Dieter: How are we going to keep records? There's gonna be a lotta data to keep track of.

Me: Manually. Pencil and paper. Analog white boards… but with opaque curtains. Jonathan, is there any way we can set up a SCIF that is completely air-gapped from ShipNet?

Jonathan: A SCIF? Oh, a Sensitive Compartmented Information Facility? Yes, I can suggest someplace that is completely off the grid, completely without digital accoutrements.

Me: With double doors so passersby can't peek in. And a good set of locks—old fashioned mechanical ones with cylinders and spring-loaded pins. But they have to be highly pick-resistant. And the room needs to be super-soundproof. It should have internal security cams that are air-gapped to keep them isolated from ShipNet. And the HVAC needs to be secure—can't have some probe using a ventilation shaft to eavesdrop, or worse… blow cyanide gas into the room.

Jonathan: Yes. I can set all that up.

Dieter: Jonathan, can you put a robot guard inside the double doors, say, in an anteroom? And make sure the guard is completely off the grid? As soon as you get inside the anteroom, the guard looks you over to see if you're on his authorized access list. If you are, good. If not, you get restrained while the guard calls either me or Roy on his ArkComm.

Jonathan: Yes, I can do that too.

The classified part of the conversation apparently over, I switched back to normal voice. "Okay, I'm tired now. But tomorrow I want to see Roxanne first thing... and tell her to bring her..." I waved my ArkComm. "Oh and fill her in on what we've decided so far."

Dieter flashed me a thumbs up, "Get some sleep, Boss."

CHAPTER TEN

30Aug2151

Roxanne showed up the next morning around ten looking perky as a basket of kittens.

"How you feelin?" she asked.

I was really starting to get tired of that expression even though the person saying it meant well. "Much stronger, thank you."

She sat down and promptly dug out her ArkComm and began keying in a message.

Roxanne: I'm going to need my own SCIF, separate from Exorcist. There's a good spot over in Bravo—totally off shipnet. I want to call it Krypton. And I want my own robot guarding the airlock. Can I have Carol?

Me: Sure. Why Carol? Isn't she an older model?

Roxanne: She's an oldie but a goodie! She was with you when you went down to the Martian surface. I trust her. And she's been upgraded a bunch of times since Mars. She's got a whole toolbox full of specialized end effectors—good for soldering and such—plus an extra pair of shoulder joints so she can operate as a four-armed form factor. She'll be a really big help setting up my controller farm.

Me: Yeah, whatever. You want her, take her… Hey, wait a minute. What's this about a controller farm?

Roxanne: We use PLCs, Programmable Logic Controllers, all over the ship to control things like airlock doors, nuclear power plants, rocket motors… everything. I'm pretty sure that these daemons that Jonathan found are going to be targeting our PLCs—you know, to make 'em fuck up. It's just my hypothesis right now, but I'll be really surprised if it's not true. I need to set up a rudimentary controller farm to prove it. All air-gapped from the real thing of course. It'd be minimal scale at first—maybe three different types of controllers—say an air lock, a slipring RPM governor, and a propellant feed controller for the fusion drive. That will take me a day or so. Then I'll insert a few of Jonathan's daemons onto my mini controller network to see if and how they find the PLCs and then see what they do after that.

Me: Worst case it for me. What do you *expect* them to do?

Roxanne: I expect them to alter the controller's logic code so as to make the device it controls fail in some way—by implanting some kind of software gremlin that self-destructs after it does its damage. But while that's going on, the daemon keeps sending back data to the PLC's manager that everything is AOK. For example, an airlock door might fail by not opening to let somebody back in. That could be bad if you've been working outside for a while and you're running short of O_2. But while you're suffocating the daemon tells the manager—that would be Jonathan—that everything is working fine.

Me: I see, but how would some dumb piece of code know that would do potential harm? I mean that's obvious to you and me, but to a piece of code?

Roxanne: I won't know that till I watch it in action. Which is also why I need to infect more than one kind of controller with Jonathan's daemons—airlocks, hydroponics, HVAC, propulsion, the slipring mechanisms, nuclear power. I'll learn by observing how they adapt to the different types of controllers.

Me: You think this is some sort of rogue AI?

Roxanne: Maybe. Or it could just be an RCFU.

Me: A what?

Roxanne: A random-code-fucker-upper. The scary version is that each daemon is an exact copy of every other daemon and that they use internal neural network technology to observe a targeted controller mechanism to see how it works and from that deduce how to make it fail.

Me: What's the not so scary version?

Roxanne: There isn't one. But I have to warn you, if ShipNet really has been compromised with these daemons, the best I'll be able to do is slow them down. I won't be able to stop them. Ultimately they will destroy the ship. And we will need to abort the mission ASAP and try to get back to CisLuna while we still have a working spacecraft.

Me: Abort the mission? You can't be serious.

Roxanne: I'm afraid I am.

Me: How long will it take to confirm we've been penetrated?

Roxanne: Few days.

I squeezed my eyes shut and rubbed my temples for a moment.

Me: This all seems highly speculative. How am I supposed to convince the Mission Committee to abort a mission that they're heavily invested in?

Roxanne: Give them a history lesson. Our four assassins are supposed to be Persian. America has had an ongoing vendetta with Persia since 1951 when she replaced their duly elected prime minister with their own dictatorial sock puppet, the Shah Reza Pahlavi. When Khomeini took over in 1978, his government turned a blind eye to the capture of the sixty-six hostages from the U.S. Embassy that were held 444 days—long enough for Reagan to claim it was his administration that brokered the deal to free the hostages, but that's another story. To get even, America supported Iraq in their war against Persia from 1980 to 1988 by giving them satellite imagery to support nerve gas attacks on Persia. But most important and more recent, there's been an ongoing cyberwar between America and them since 2010. I'm referring to the Stuxnet computer worm.

Me: Persia attacked America with a… a 'worm' you called it… back in 2010?

Roxanne: No, no, America attacked *them!* Stuxnet—more accurately, Operation Olympic Games—was developed by America's NSA and Israel's Mossad back in 2005. Israel has always had a hard-on about Persia, especially since they were allegedly planning to build nuclear weapons—kind of ironic since Israel already had some 300 warheads of its own back then. Anywho, Stuxnet was designed to attack PLCs, in particular the ones used to regulate the RPM of the high-speed centrifuges used to separate uranium-235 from uranium-238. The Persians had this big underground centrifuge farm called Natanz. Had something like 5000 IR-1 model centrifuges of which Stuxnet knocked out about 1000. Back then computer malware was mainly known for screwing up data—financial accounts, passwords, email—nuisance shit. This was the first case of a piece of malware actually causing *physical* damage to a key piece of infrastructure.

Me: You called this Stuxnet a... a worm? Tell me about that.

Roxanne: A worm is a type of malware that replicates itself. They usually get in via the local network but Natanz was air-gapped with super strict security. The only way they got Stuxnet into the centrifuge network was because some idiot plugged a thumb drive into his laptop at work.

Anywho, once the worm got in, it started hunting around for the PLCs that controlled the RPM on all the centrifuges. Since there were 5000 of them in operation at Natanz it was what you call a target-rich environment. Except that there was lots of other software running at Natanz and Stuxnet had to be careful not to attack any of that stuff lest it give away its presence. So it was carefully designed to immediately destroy itself if, say, it found itself inside some HVAC PLC.

It was extremely sophisticated for malware of its time—over half a megabyte of code. That's about twenty times as big as the average malware back then. Stuxnet was designed to be like a sniper—only go after specific high-value PLCs that controlled the RPM on centrifuges.

When it found one, it was designed to fuck with the RPM causing the centrifuge to either slow down to a crawl or in some cases speed up until it flew apart from centrifugal force. And all the while it was doing this it kept reporting back to the control center that the centrifuge was doing fine. Talk about sneaky! In the end this one piece of malware knocked out a fifth of Persia's inventory of centrifuges at Natanz.

Me: How could our assassins get a worm that size past Jonathan? Doesn't he check everything that comes and goes?

Roxanne: You're right—Jonathan *does* check everything. But his virus checkers depend on a library of known viruses for which they have a catalog of infection clues. Based on what Jonathan told me I'm guessing that these viruses are assembling themselves from tiny bits and pieces of nano-code. The bits and pieces have tabs and slots—maybe quantum scaled so they don't even look like code floating around. But they *do* know how to assemble themselves when they bump into each other. Eventually you get enough bits and pieces to make a complete 'baby' virus. The baby virus is small and pretty stupid—like all babies—but it knows how to evolve and more importantly, how to evolve with a purpose. It's based on the evolutionary techniques used by neural net software to self-school themselves—the same kind that *Baby* Jonathan used to eventually become *Captain* Jonathan. But where Jonathan evolved with the purpose of keeping everything running smoothly to carry out the ship's mission, this baby virus is running around figuring out how the ship runs with the purpose of sabotaging it—eventually destroying it entirely.

Me: This still sounds speculative. You say Stuxnet happened… what, a hundred fifty years ago?

Roxanne: Yeah, but Stuxnet wasn't the end of the story. More like the beginning. Persia went to school on it. The situation was analogous to how the Manhattan Project gave us the first nuclear weapons and with them a definitive end to WWII in the Pacific only to have the damn things proliferate to every paranoid dictator out there with a Napoleon complex. In hindsight, we would have been better off shutting down the whole program after the first detonation at the Trinity Site. Just park it next to the Ark of the Covenant in some dusty old warehouse.

Me: Enough pontificating! Please, pick up from the Persians going to school on Stuxnet.

Roxanne: Oh yeah, sorry. After they graduated from Stuxnet school—and believe me I'm only touching the surface of what they learned from Stuxnet—anyway they went on to develop a cyber espionage tool called Madi—it logged keystrokes, recorded audio, etc. Then they launched Shamoon, a virus that erased three-quarters of Saudi Aramco's corporate computers. Everybody coming to work the next day was greeted by an image of a burning American flag. Then they did Operation Ababil—that was a DDOS attack—distributed denial of service—against U.S. banking infrastructure.

And we weren't sitting on our asses all this time. We were busy building Nitro Zeus with an eye toward wiping out all their air defenses, communications systems, and power grid.

Me: All right, all right! I get it.

Roxanne: And it's been going on ever since.

Me: I said, I get it. The Mission Committee is never going to turn this crate around on the basis of a history lesson.

Roxanne: We could treat them to a demo of my controller farm?

Me: Nah, they'd never believe something like that could happen here—they're all kind of naïve that way, plus they're heavily invested in this mission.

Roxanne: Then we could wait for a wild-type daemon to fuck up an airlock or something. Shouldn't take long.

Me: You're not making this easy… Go build your farm.

She smiled and gathered her things to go.

77

After she left, I ArkCommed Jonathan.

I need to see McVeigh ASAP.

CHAPTER ELEVEN

30Aug2151

McVeigh showed up a few minutes before lunch. I had gotten dressed all by myself. Only took me thirty minutes and I only got dizzy twice—once as I bent over for each boot.

"Hi, Roy. What's up? I'm a bit swamped, but Jonathan said it was important."

"Jonathan was right, and you're about to get even more swamped." I motioned to him to dig out his ArkComm.

`Me`: We have reason to believe the ship's infrastructural control software will become compromised with viral daemons that rewrite essential control software using software gremlins. There is a chance these daemons may spread to your submersibles rendering them dysfunctional once they land on the surface. Or maybe they won't even make it to the surface. Anyway, the sooner you can separate them from the ship the better.

`McVeigh`: Should I be looking for these... daemons as you call them... before we launch?

Me: They will be very hard to find. We believe they will infect the software embedded in the ship's Programmable Logic Controllers and rewrite the code so that it doesn't work. For example they might render an airlock door to be inoperable so your crew is locked out. Once the gremlin does its mischief, it will restore the original code and disappear—that's if the controller is not destroyed in the process. So my advice is to only do the normal system checks to get your submersibles down to the surface ASAP, the better to avoid contamination.

McVeigh: You're scaring me.

I snorted.

Me: Hell, this scares *me* and I'm fearless!

McVeigh: Any other good news?

Me: Try to anticipate how a daemon might interfere with the internal logic of any control systems you work around. For example, make sure your people are suited and tethered whenever they have any work to do around airlock doors. That's whether or not they intend to actually use the doors. Anticipate the doors could suddenly fly open for no particular reason. And while you're at it, mechanically dog all the hatches surrounding any airlocks you work around.

McVeigh: How do you know all this?

Me: *I* don't, but someone a lot smarter than me does, so I'm passing it on to you. Needless to say, keep this conversation on the down low.

Oh, and one last thing. I have been advised that while the daemons can be slowed down, ultimately they will destroy the ship. Hence, we need to abort the mission and return to CisLuna ASAP. The recommendation I am proposing to the Mission Committee is that we initiate a return to base as soon as you get your submersibles off the ship—they don't actually have to be the surface of Enceladus, just off the ship. But before I make that proposal, I need to know how long it will take you to get all of your submersibles off the ship?

McVeigh consulted his tablet.

McVeigh: My current critical path calls for three more weeks.

Roy: Not good enough. Bear in mind, I just need your submersibles off the ship. They can land on the surface on their own time.

McVeigh: Let's see… there's four of them… Can we launch simultaneously and have them fly formation on the ship for a while?

Roy: A short while. As soon as your submersibles are off the ship, I will order that we initiate the slingshot maneuver to return to CisLuna on our next orbital cycle.

McVeigh: We complete a full orbit of Saturn every 33 hours.

Roy: So you should count on about half of that at most. Once your subs are launched we'll be leaving as soon as we are aligned with our return trajectory.

McVeigh: I just need to get them off the ship? Not landed?

Roy: That's right.

McVeigh: Can I have 48 hours plus whatever it takes for the ship to reach the departure point?

Roy: Yes… assuming there has not been a catastrophic mishap on the ship during that period.

McVeigh: And the ship will keep flying formation on Enceladus that whole time?

Roy: Barring any daemon-induced disasters.

McVeigh: Okay, then. Any other little bombshells?

Roy: Nope. That was it.

McVeigh: Very well then. Thanks for the heads up.

* * *

After McVeigh left, I headed off to physical therapy escorted by two of my beat cops, two guys named Andrew and Peter, both Caucasians, approximate age at life extension: thirty. A ship our size didn't actually rate a full-fledged physical therapy center. Ours was more of a make shift center where we borrowed part of the gym on an as-needed basis. I knew the guy who ran it—fellow named Chuck, Caucasian male, age at life extension: forty-three. He used to be my sparring partner for hand-to-hand combat training before the bomb turned my muscles to mush.

I tried walking on my own a bit to see how far I'd get. I made it about half way—maybe two hundred meters—before my legs got too wobbly to hold me up. Then I collapsed into the wheel chair one of my escorts had been pushing behind me.

The therapy turned out to be pretty grueling. Chuck kept monitoring my VO2 MAX uptake, BP, pulse, pulse oximeter, and breathing rate. He had a zone he wanted me to stay in. I was supposed to spend a week never going above Zone One, then the next week never exceeding Zone Two, and so on. He told me when I was finally able to hit Zone Five, I was supposed to be back to normal.

With the physical therapy session over, I realized I had run out of excuses to put off the one thing I didn't want to face— allowing my escorts to wheel me back to my cabin in Bravo Ring that was full of Monica's memories. The escorts parked the wheel chair just inside the door and stood by for further instructions.

"Thanks, you guys can go now."

"We'll be outside the door," Andrew said.

"No, really, I'm fine now."

They looked at one another awkwardly.

"I mean it. You can go back to your regular duties. I'll call you if I need you."

"We're not to leave your side until we are relieved," Andrew said.

"Dieter's orders," Peter said.

"You're aware Dieter works for me?"

"He said you'd say that," Andrew said.

"We will not be leaving you until we are relieved," Peter said, looking at his watch. "That will be in about an hour and a half."

"Hmm... well, okay then. You might as well park it in the living room. I'm gonna grab a nap."

I shut the door to the bedroom and managed to keep it together until I made it into the head where I shut the door and sat down on the stool cradling my face in my palms and sobbed like a baby. After ten minutes I staggered over to the sink and rinsed my face with cold water. I went back to sit on the bed thinking I'd take a nap but then I got up and poured myself a couple of fingers of Scotch. I tossed it back and was going to pour another when Monica's pillow caught my eye. I looked around the room and took in a host of little mementos of the space she took in my heart... baby pictures of her kids, a picture of me in my Army dress blues when I was a Chief Warrant Officer—for some reason she liked that one—another one of Roxanne in a white lab coat smiling up from a microscope. By then I felt the hit of Scotch warming my chest so I just rinsed the glass and flopped on the bed letting Monica's scent waft over me. She'd been gone over five weeks now, but her scent was still there.

*   *   *

I must have slept four hours before awakening to Jonathan's persistent voice. I sat up too fast and had to lay back down to counter the wave of dizziness.

84

"Sup?" I asked.

"There's been an attack, Roy. Hydroponics. The corn crop experienced an over-application of nitrogen. The current crop is so far unharmed, but we need to change out the nutrient bath."

Corn was one of our essential grains. It was a mess hall favorite as sweet white corn-on-the-cob, and when the kernels were allowed to mature to a dried state, it could keep for years making it an important resource on interplanetary space craft. And like every other crop in hydroponics, it had been genetically altered to be a near-complete nutrient all by itself. I dug out my ArkComm.

Me: Do you think it was a daemon?

Jonathan: Yes. However, Roxanne is unable to confirm thus far. Her prediction that gremlins would be designed to self-sterilize seems to have been validated.

Me: Is it possible to shut down the hydroponics software control processes? To perform all hydroponics maintenance manually?

Jonathan: Yes, it will involve pulling perhaps one hundred persons off their regular duties—that's per ring—but it can be done with about a week's worth of retraining. If you include food prep and long-term storage that will entail an additional seventy-five personnel per ring with two more weeks of training.

Me: Can we do the same thing for HVAC?

Jonathan: Yes, that will require perhaps twenty personnel per ring and two weeks' worth of retraining.

Me: Ship operation, piloting, and navigation?

Jonathan: Two hundred personnel total and three weeks.

Me: What am I leaving out?

Jonathan: Propulsion, general maintenance & repairs, waste management & recycling. Assuming you still trust my robots, we're talking another three hundred fifty personnel and four weeks of training.

Me: What if I don't trust your robots?

Jonathan: Eight hundred personnel and six months of training.

Me: I stewed for about a minute. I guess we're trusting your robots. Can we mechanically secure all the airlock doors? I.e., no PLCs?

Jonathan: I'll get robots on it right away.

Me: Can you put all this together as a presentation for the Mission Committee? And then let's convene an emergency meeting of same ASAP. Put Dieter and Roxanne on the guest list as well. Time to let the cat out of the bag.

Jonathan: Very well, the meeting is scheduled for 1900 HRS in the Alpha Ring Board Room. That gives you three hours to shower, change clothes, and eat. I advise you to use your wheelchair. You'll never make it walking.

I insisted that everyone use the texting feature of a limited supply of ArkComms. The Committee members found this awkward, especially since there weren't enough to go around and they had to share. I was starting to lose patience when the Committee Chair called for everyone to calm down and listen to me.

"He is our Security Chief and he would not be calling for these measures if he did not think they were necessary."

This mostly worked although there was still some grumbling.

I went on to describe my belief that the ship was under attack by an army of software daemons working with software gremlins to disrupt the ship's control software. Then I turned the podium over to Roxanne to explain why this hypothesis is very likely. Most of the members of the Committee had never been under any kind of threat before—let alone cyber—and they had a hard time accepting the reality of the concept. Apart from their Earth sabbaticals, they had led very sheltered lives up to now. While they were intellectually aware of the idea of computer malware, few galacticans on the ship had ever experienced them and even then it was a long time ago while they were Earthside. The idea of a worm infiltrating ShipNet was just too much of a stretch. The discussion came to an impasse with most of the members unable or unwilling to accept that the ship is under attack. They could accept the randomness of things breaking now and again—you just signaled a robot to fix whatever broke and moved on—but not the idea that we had an enemy within who had an agenda to destroy us. The problem was compounded by the fact that most of them had gotten used to having robots at their beck and call whenever anything went wrong. For them, picking up a wrench was as foreign a concept as 'righty-tighty, lefty-loosey.' If one of them suddenly got sucked out an airlock, there would be no robot to save them.

* * *

At that moment, Jonathan interrupted with news that an airlock door in Delta Ring near the central truss flight deck had mysteriously blown open. Four crew members on McVeigh's science team were swept out to space. Fortunately, the surrounding hatches had already been dogged shut so no other personnel were lost. Unfortunately, the four crewmen were only partially suited—none of them had secured their helmets. And none of them were tethered.

"Weren't we going to secure all the airlocks manually?" I asked.

"That was in progress when the airlock failed," Jonathan said. "Two of my robots were working on it when it failed and they got sucked out into space along with the four crew members."

"Are the bodies being recovered?" I asked.

"I have mounted a recovery operation as we speak," Jonathan said. "Two shuttles and as many robots. The bodies and my robots should be back on the ship within the hour."

"Damage?"

"The four crew members are not showing vital signs," Jonathan said. "The two robots sustained minor damage as they banged on the walls of the airlock during the atmospheric exhalation. Various bits of machinery and lab equipment were lost. We can mount a search for the equipment."

88

"Let's concentrate on getting an accurate headcount and equipment inventory. I don't want to lose a crew member or a robot because they're floating around in space with a busted radio."

"That has already been done. All personnel and robots are accounted for."

"Dieter, you better grab some cops and go see if you can lend a hand."

"On it, boss."

"I'm going to excuse myself also," Roxanne said. "There may be an opportunity here for me to capture a wild-type daemon."

*   *   *

The members of the Mission Committee were showing their usual ineptitude at crisis management, i.e., refusal to accept the facts in front of them if they did not match their ideas of how things ought to be plus their inability to accept that time was of the essence.

"How can an airlock door suddenly fly open?" Jake asked.

Jake was a galactican male, age mid-forties. He shaved his head in keeping with the growing fad among galactican males. Male pattern baldness had been cured as part of the Treatment for humans, but a lot of us remember what it was like to watch your hairline slowly receding every year. Shaving your head on purpose seemed somehow insensitive.

I regaled the Committee with stories from my newfound wealth of knowledge about Stuxnet and the attack on Natanz that I had gained from Roxanne. I then tried to fill them in on how controllers, ubiquitous on a ship like *Lunine*, were ruled by extremely simple computer logic and were generally not equipped to fend off viruses and worms. I finally gave up and invoked my special regulation giving me full control of the ship security.

"Look, folks, at this point I don't have time to argue with you. We are in crisis. I am ordering all personnel to begin wearing their space suits 24 hours a day. You will also wear your helmets but keep the visors open so as not to waste your suit's life support stores."

"Oh, come on, Roy!" Jake said. "Those suits weigh over a hundred kilograms! How are people supposed to function in full gee with all that extra mass?"

"We can slow each ring's rotational speed down to one third gee so that the extra weight of the suit will seem normal," Jonathan said.

"Good idea. How long will that take?" I asked.

"Normal spin-down rate would require three hours forty-five minutes. I can expedite that to one hour thirty minutes."

"Go for the expedited spin-down."

"I have one more thing before you all run off to hunt for your suits. We need to abort the mission and return to CisLuna as quickly as possible."

"No way!" a galactican woman named Mandy said. She was one of McVeigh's people. "We just spent the better part of a year getting here and now you want us to turn back with our mission unfulfilled?"

"It won't be entirely unfulfilled," I said. "As you know, your boss is already working on transferring his submersibles to the surface as we speak. As soon as he is done we need to make a run for CisLuna and pray that we get there before the ship falls apart."

"Maybe we should pray for a security officer who is not falling apart," Jake said.

"Priority Interrupt!" Jonathan's voice came over the speaker. A klaxon horn began sounding in the background. "Charlie Ring is experiencing a problem with its RPM governor and brake mechanism. Its slow-down rate is highly erratic putting considerable stress on the ship's central truss, possibly causing it to warp. A warpage will almost certainly cause it to fracture and the resulting dynamic instability will cause the other rotating rings to rip the ship in half either between Charlie and Bravo or Charlie and Delta rings—perhaps both. A serious hull breach in Charlie and possibly Bravo and Delta could be imminent. All personnel are ordered to don space suits and go to general quarters."

We could feel the ship shuddering. The Mission Committee Members who were so vocal with their disdain a moment ago suddenly became quiet, their faces ashen.

"You heard the captain!" I said. "Get into your space suits and go to general quarters! On the double!"

Everyone began shuffling toward the meeting room door.

"Where are your suit lockers?" I yelled at my two escorts. These guys were a couple of Hispanics named Ernesto and Rodrigo.

"Charlie Ring," Ernesto said.

"Same," Rodrigo said.

"Oh shit," I said under my breath. "Okay, it's imperative that you get your space suits on. Leave me here while you get yourselves back to Charlie."

"But Dieter said—"

"—Damn what Dieter said! Get your asses over to Charlie and get your suits on."

"What about you?" Rodrigo asked.

"I'll manage. Your first priority is to get your suits on. You're worthless to me if you get sucked into space naked. As soon as you get your own suits on, make sure everybody in Charlie Ring is suited and standing by their escape pods. Charlie Ring is probably going have multiple catastrophic hull breaches in the next few hours."

Ernesto and Rodrigo both turned white.

"Don't just stand there. Get moving!"

They both turned and ran off.

I spent the next half hour making my way to the Alpha-Bravo access tunnel. I had to stop every few minutes to catch my breath. Spending a month in an induced coma could not have come at a worse time. I needed to be superman. Instead I was the iconic 98-pound weakling of comic book lore. As I paused to rest, I wondered how I could possibly get my suit on. Even if I could get to the damn thing, I was in no shape to get into a 150-kg space suit by myself. I finally gave up and headed over to the Alpha Ring cop shack. At least there I had a good command and control center and I could see what was going on. Of course, that assumed Alpha Ring maintained hull integrity while Charlie Ring was busy beating itself and its neighbors to death.

* * *

Once I got back to the cop shack, the first thing I remembered was the access tunnels. Charlie Ring had a set of access tunnels connecting it to Bravo and Delta Rings—eight tunnels in all. Those tunnels served as more than just convenient access between rings. Access tunnels were also structural members that kept the four habitat rings rotating at the same rpm. Normally, braking was coordinated with simultaneous actuation at each of the four sliprings. Braking force needed to be variable to correct for mass differentials between the rings. With Charlie's braking mechanisms misbehaving, that could put a tremendous shear force on the access tunnels. In an emergency situation such as this, the access tunnels needed to be cleared of all personnel and the hatchways dogged shut ASAP.

I brought up some video data of the eight access tunnels. Christ! All eight of them were full of people fiddlefucking around like they had all the time in the world.

I called up the ship wide PA system. "Attention all personnel. You are ordered to clear all access tunnels between Bravo and Charlie and Charlie and Delta IMMEDIATELY! They could be subject to structural failure at any time due to the erratic behavior of Charlie's brake mechanism. Last person out on either end of each access tunnel needs to dog the hatches to prevent atmospheric pressure loss in the rings."

That got some people moving but a lot of people just stood there looking at each other.

"Jonathan, get some robots into those access tunnels to clear the people out. Use whatever force is necessary."

"Copy. Twenty robots are on their way."

93

As it turned out Charlie Ring held on for ninety more minutes, barely enough time to clear the access tunnels. We definitely needed some more training in emergency procedures.

Then I remembered my two escorts, Ernesto and Rodrigo. They might have had enough time to make it to Charlie but probably not enough time to get into their suits. Had I unwittingly sent them to their deaths? I tried calling them on their communicators.

"Ernesto, Rodrigo — this is Stone. Status?"

"Hi, Boss. Ernesto here. We're both stuck in Bravo. We never made it to Charlie."

"Good thing. Charlie is a disaster. Right now your best bet is to come to the cop shack here in Alpha. I don't know how well Bravo will come through this disaster, but I think Alpha might make it... as least for now. Once you get back here, we'll see about getting you some new space suits."

"Jonathan, do you have vitals on Dieter and Roxanne?"

"Vitals show positive. They're both in Bravo."

I breathed a sigh of relief. They both lived in Charlie. They would have never made it to Delta to investigate the airlock door flying open. I called them on their communicators.

"Dieter, Rox—Roy here. Can you give me a status please?"

"We're both stuck in the Alpha-Bravo access tunnel. Your announcement to clear the tunnels kinda backfired. Some fool dogged the hatch letting us back into Alpha. We're trying to catch a passerby on the outside to open the hatch, but everybody seems to have made a beeline for their space suits."

"How many are you in that access tunnel?"

"Rox, me, and four others."

"Jonathan, can you get a robot with some breaching tools over there?"

"Two robots with tools on the way."

"I gather you've lost your suits in Charlie?"

"That's affirm."

"Once you get free, c'mon back here to the cop shack in Alpha. Bravo may suffer some fratricidal damage from Charlie, but I'm hoping Alpha will remain intact."

"What about our suits?" Roxanne asked.

"Unless you want to try swimming for them, your best bet is to come back here. Once things settle down, I'll have Jonathan detail some robots to recover suits for the Charlie Ring survivors. Meanwhile, best you be as far away from Charlie Ring as possible."

Chapter Twelve

31Aug2151

While I waited for everyone to make it back to the cop shack, I opened up half a dozen display windows allowing me various views of the disaster in Charlie Ring including several views from the interior. There was a big hull breach where one of the main spokes had ripped loose. The ensuing vacuum had sucked a number of crew out into space. Some had suits on, many did not. Very few of the ones with suits on had their helmets on as well. Some had tried to hang on to whatever they could find in order to avoid the suck. Others embraced the suck and concentrated on getting their helmets on and their visors closed. They would be the only survivors.

I scanned various locations within the hull. Many crewmembers had not been able to make it to their suit lockers and tried to hide out in their cabins. It didn't work. The cabins were not airtight and what air they contained quickly exited through the ventilation system leaving the occupants inside to perish in the vacuum.

One of the few, perhaps the only benefits of the hull breach was that with no oxygen at least there were no fires. I called Jonathan to coordinate damage control.

"Jonathan, when the dust settles, can we figure out who the survivors were from Charlie Ring? I'm talking about the ones who were working elsewhere on the ship and never made it to their space suits. Could we have your robots salvage their space suits? Those folks are going to be at extreme risk if there are more hull breaches in the intact rings."

"Yes, Roy. I'll put some assets on that task ASAP."

"Meanwhile, do you have any stats on how many personnel in Charlie are still alive?"

"People domiciled in Charlie Ring don't necessarily spend all their time there. My vital sign tally for the entire ship's crew shows 575 may be deceased, not counting Monica and the others lost in the bomb blast."

Jesus! 575 people. I probably knew most of them. I took a deep breath to still the rage mounting within me. "Can you break that down by galacticans and humans, and then add in robots?"

"542 galactican, 33 humans all deceased. 54 robots survived inside the hull. 24 blew out into space but still functional. I'm mounting a recovery operation for them along with the twelve live crew who managed to be fully suited before they blew out. Once they are secure, I will mount a subsequent operation to recover bodies and useful materiel."

"Good. How many robots do we have in a quiescent state?"

"300."

"How much training would they need to assume useful functions if we woke them up?"

"They wouldn't need any. Even though they are quiescent, they still get a 'current event' feed so they can hit the ground running, so to speak."

"Are all your sleeping robots air-gapped?"

"Yes."

"Good, let's bring all 300 on line. I anticipate they will be extremely useful for our next catastrophe."

"Will do."

01Sep2151

I decided to take advantage of the relative lull in the chaos to grab myself a coffee and an energy bar out of the snack cabinet. I didn't really want them, but years of experience with crisis management had taught me that adrenaline was a poor substitute for hydration and nourishment. I had just gotten back to my seat when Jonathan called.

"Roy, I have a damage report for you."

"Go ahead."

"A large amount of debris separated from the ship and collided with the forward radiator farm. This has severely compromised the ability of the forward thruster to make full power. We can salvage some forward thruster capability by rerouting its cooling lines to the aft radiator farm. I'm putting together a robot team for that purpose as we speak.

"The forward nuclear power station is no longer operable due to the loss of its share of the forward radiators. It can still be turned on after we reroute its cooling lines to the aft radiator farm. In effect, it is now only a backup power supply."

"That it?"

"For now."

"Thanks."

03Sep2151

Halfway through my energy bar, Jonathan called again.

"Roy, I have another damage report."

"Go ahead."

"Charlie's slipring has been damaged beyond repair preventing its reintegration onto the central shaft. I have instructed robots to detach Charlie Ring and then to reattach the ends of central truss where Charlie separated. The ship will then consist only of Alpha, Bravo, and Delta hab rings, plus the fuel globes, propulsion systems, and intact portions of the radiator farms. There may be some jostling as the ring RPMs are synched during the reattachment process. Estimated time to completion is about six hours. Those 300 robots you had me wake up are coming in very handy.

"Meanwhile, once central shaft integrity has been restored, robots will salvage any remaining useful stores from Charlie. There's not that much since the rapid evacuation caused by hull breach destroyed the crops in hydroponics."

"I don't want to waste too much time sifting through the remains of Charlie. We're in a race to get back to CisLuna before that daemon army of destruction tears the rest of the ship apart. Let's just grab the twelve 100-man escape pods. Put them in the docking area where McVeigh's submersibles are moored after he gets them off the ship. This should be soon and this way their mass will not disturb the rotational stability of Alpha, Bravo, or Delta.

"When all that is finished let's do one last sweep of Charlie Ring in case there are any survivors hiding out in an airlock someplace. Then put Charlie on a Saturnian Intercept Trajectory."

"Will do. Roy, I have a question—have you noticed a lull in minor scale daemon attacks since the Charlie Ring's slipring major scale failure?"

"No, do you think we're overdue?"

"Roxanne is in her controller lab in Bravo, and I cannot communicate with her—it's air-gapped and she's not responding to her ArkComm. Perhaps you could head over there and see what she thinks."

"I'll head over there right now. I need to check up on her anyway—she tends to skip meals and bedtime when she's engrossed. On the way I'll pop in on McVeigh—see how he's doing with his launch progress."

* * *

I caught up with McVeigh in Alpha as he was about to head outside to the flight deck. He was in his space suit and in an obvious hurry so I didn't want to keep him.

"All four submersibles have launched." McVeigh said. "No living crew will accompany them down to the surface for fear of contaminating the surface with Earth-based life forms. The submersibles are designed to be erected and begin drilling operations solely with the aid of robot teams. The robots will not be returning to the ship. Their internal nuclear power supplies are all good for a decade, plus they have extra nuclear fuel and spare parts so that they can survive up to a century."

"That all sounds like good news!" I said.

"Not entirely. The mission concept called for the submersibles to use the ship as a communications center. After we leave, they'll be cut off. They can carry out their missions just fine without us, but they will have no way to transmit their data back to us. We won't know what they find out until we send a new ship back here to follow up."

"Do you think SpaceCorp will spring for that?" I asked.

"I should hope so. We've invested quite a lot getting those subs here. I'd say it's just a matter of outfitting a new ship with an adequate comm system. Doesn't have to be anything fancy like this monster. Could even be a robot ship for that matter. It still blows my mind that we didn't think to bring one along on *Lunine*. Did we think we were going to remain in Enceladus' orbit for the entire mission life expectancy of the subs?"

"Whatever we send back to Enceladus, let's hope it's something with a more secure controller architecture. I'm worried that what the Persians did to *Lunine* they may have also done elsewhere in SpaceCorp only we haven't discovered it yet."

*   *   *

McVeigh had seemed strangely upbeat about his surface mission given the succession of catastrophes we had been through. He was talkative enough, but he kept acting like he had some sort of secret. Oh well, at least he got his damn subs off the ship.

*   *   *

An hour later I made it to Krypton, Roxanne's SCIF in Bravo ring. I was a bit more energized this time since I had taken a quarter tablet of XCedeAll™, one of SpaceCorp's homegrown amphetamines developed for first responders and military types. I had gotten my doctor to prescribe me some a week after coming out of my coma. She complied reluctantly when I explained that in my weakened condition I might not be up to the rigors of trying to stay alive on a ship that was falling apart. She stared at me for a second, then got me a small bottle out of a locked cabinet.

"These are designed to be broken into quarters and then taken as needed," she'd said. "They are fast acting and tend to last for about an hour. Best results come if you place the dose under your tongue."

"Are they habit forming?"

"Not chemically, but some folks develop a psychological dependency on them. My advice is only take them when you're in a jam. Then start with a quarter tablet and only add more if you really need them."

I thanked her and promised I would save them for emergencies... which we seemed to be having right now. A quarter tablet turned out to be just enough to get me to Roxanne's SCIF. At any rate my body was really giving me grief as I came within a hundred meters of her door. Rather than take another quarter tablet, I figured I'd gut it out and then sit down once I got inside... maybe grab another cuppa and an E-Bar. Maybe pop another quarter pill on the trip back if I really needed it.

Meanwhile, the trip had given me a chance to see first-hand how much damage the ship had sustained. There was a lot of structural damage plus a lot of minor hull breaches. You could hear gas venting to the outside. Dozens of robots were busy with space glue applicators trying to paste everything back together and seal all the leaks. I worried that so many breaches, even though they were minor, might cut into our essential O_2 supplies for the trip home. The loss of Charlie had already taken a toll on our stores of elemental gases, water, and food stocks. I wondered how much those losses would be offset by the 575 casualties we had sustained when Charlie separated. I was really learning how to hate those little daemon bastards.

I leaned over onto my knees and took some deep breaths when I arrived at the door. Then I stood up and knocked. There was no buzzer since this room was not originally designed for human occupation. The door finally opened to Carol's face.

"Hello, Roy," Carol said as she opened the door.

"Hi. Can I come in?"

"Yes, but only to the anteroom."

That seemed odd. "Is Roxanne okay?"

"She's sleeping. She'd been going at it straight for 48 hours subsisting on energy bars and coffee the whole time."

"Can you give me a debrief out here in the anteroom? But while you're at it, can I have a chair, a coffee, and an E-Bar? The hike over here really beat me up."

"Yes, wait here."

She returned after a few minutes, one hand holding a coffee, one hand holding an E-Bar, and one hand holding a folding chair. She used her fourth hand to open the door. The door shut, she opened the chair for me and served me the coffee. It was unflavored but I wasn't picky. I munched on the E-Bar as she began talking.

"So far we have validated the theory that the daemons all start out exactly alike. From that point they go to school on the various PLCs in the ship's software infrastructure in a manner very much like the way Jonathan evolved from Baby Jonathan to Captain Jonathan."

"That doesn't sound good."

"Actually it is in one respect. Since they all start out alike, it makes them easier to find and destroy. We can use a single type of hunter-killer bot as opposed to having to design a different kind of bot for a whole library of daemons. I was working on the design of a hunter-killer bot when you arrived."

"Hmm... Jonathan and I have noticed a falloff in minor scale cyber-attacks. What do you make of that?"

"I would say it is not the result of anything Roxanne and I have done thus far. Maybe we caught a lucky break giving us some time to make repairs and rescue stranded crewmen. But I don't think it will last."

I finished my coffee and folded the remaining half of the E-Bar into its wrapper and stuffed it into my jacket. Then I thanked Carol for her hospitality and information and set off to find my escape pod. Per SOP my suit locker would be close by. I didn't want to be the only one wandering around with no suit on a ship of questionable integrity. Along the way I scrounged a shopping basket. The hab rings were still rotating at a full gee and there was no way I was going to be parading around in my 150-kg cold temperature space suit until a) I was in better shape, and b) Jonathan managed to get us down to one-third gee. Hopefully, that would be done in the course of removing the leftovers of Charlie Ring and reconnecting Alpha, Bravo, and Delta Rings. Until then I would have to avoid walking by airlocks.

*　*　*

A couple of hours later I and my suit wheeled into my cabin in Bravo Ring. I kicked off my boots and poured myself a Scotch before sitting down to relax a bit. That's when Jonathan called.

"Sup, Jonny?"

"I can see you are sitting down in your cabin. That's good. I would like to patch Dr. McVeigh through. He needs to talk to you."

"Patch him through? Did he lose his ArkComm?"

"No, ArkComms don't work when calling from a detached escape pod."

Oh Jesus. His picture popped up in a window next to Jonathan.

"Hello, Roy. I've something to tell you."

"Do go on."

"First I want you to know this mission means everything to me. It's been my life's work. Finding DNA-based life on Enceladus will be—"

"—I am well aware of all that, Dr. McVeigh. Please cut to the chase!"

"Yes, I suppose you are... well, to make a long story boring, I and six volunteers have left the ship on an escape pod. We are going to remain at Enceladus with the submersibles in order to ensure they complete their mission. We will not be descending to the surface ourselves. But we will be staying here long enough to get the subs down in a fully functional state. I... we...

the seven of us... fully expect that *Lunine* will have long since departed by then. Once the subs have penetrated the ice into the nether regions of Enceladus, it is our intention to remain on station acting as an RF repeater so that any scientific findings can be broadcast back to CisLuna and not be lost."

I was stunned. I just sat there holding my glass of Scotch halfway to my open mouth, but no words came out.

"Roy, are you there?"

"Yes, I'm here."

"Do you have anything to say?"

"I'm sure I will eventually. For now, do what you have to do and keep Jonathan informed of your progress. Now I'm going to ring off and finish my Scotch."

CHAPTER THIRTEEN

15Sep2151

The Mission Committee had grown strangely docile, almost meek, since the loss of Charlie Ring. Instead of debating every situation oblivious of time sensitivity, they had turned into a rubber stamp organization, endorsing without question every recommendation Jonathan and I put before them.

"To be honest, folks, the fact that we have had only minor mishaps since the Charlie Ring disaster is not because of anything Roxanne and Carol have done. They're both doing noble work, but it's mostly been devoted to understanding how these daemons form, how they evolve, and how they attack using their gremlins. And just because our mishaps since the loss of Charlie have been minor, e.g., the coffee machine keeps making cold coffee, this is NOT the time to let our guards down. Everyone should continue to stay suited and all non-essential personnel should avoid wandering too far from their escape pods. Meanwhile, the robots will continue converting as many mechanisms that depend on PLCs as possible to manual operation. Jonathan, can you elaborate on that last point?"

"Roy is correct in that where possible we are converting all PLC-systems to manual operation. The problem is that not all systems *can* be converted. For example, there are many delicate operations regarding the tuning of the fusion thrusters and fission power supplies that simply cannot be controlled manually. Also the water ballast system used to keep the rings stable during rotation can only be managed with PLCs—too many differential equations to juggle as people and equipment move about the ship. We'll just have to cross our fingers."

The Committee Chair spoke up, "Is there anything else we can do?"

Jonathan answered, "We have been spinning the rings at 0.33 gee. I would recommend reducing that to 0.2 gee, the minimum allowable to keep plumbing and hydroponics working. And it further simplifies the water ballast problem. All crew members should be issued sticky booties to facilitate walking across the nanocellulose decks."

After a pause one of the Committee members raised his hand. "Those only last about a day before the sticky wears off. I'll look into laying on some extras and getting them distributed around the ship."

"Thank you," Jonathan said. "Meanwhile, since Dr. McVeigh has informed me that he has successfully gotten all his submersibles onto the surface and confirmed they are working properly, it is now time to attach the 12 escape pods from Charlie Ring to the fore and aft flight decks. Once that action is initiated, we will set a course for CisLuna.

"Cruise speed will be limited to only what can be braked with the reduced power available from the forward thruster. The forward thruster has been successfully restored to 80% by rerouting cooling to the rear radiator farm. The remains of the damaged forward radiator farm and unneeded fuel globes have been jettisoned to reduce mass. Including the loss of Charlie Ring our total mass has been reduced 28%. Barring mishaps, I hope to achieve CisLuna Orbit Insertion, COI, with only two more months added to our previously scheduled return time. That means we should reach COI in 436 days—03Dec2152.

"Finally, in the last couple of weeks, numerous messages have been exchanged with CisLuna describing our predicament and requesting that rescue ships be dispatched to rendezvous with *SIS Jonathan Lunine* at various points along our return trajectory. They have pledged full support and several rescue vessels are underway as we speak with more departing as they become available.

"I should warn you this is a non-trivial maneuver requiring the rescue ships to speed out to *Lunine* and then abruptly reverse course to match velocity with the ship in the direction back towards CisLuna. This maneuver is complicated by the tremendous velocities of the ships and the time it takes to come up to speed, then reverse course in such a manner as to match trajectories precisely enough that the rescue ship and *Lunine* are close enough to transfer crew from *Lunine* to the rescue ship. A further complication will be if the ship breaks apart even more causing the crew to have to abandon ship in the escape pods. I said 'if.' I can assure you *Lunine* WILL undergo more major scale disasters before we get home. I'm particularly worried about the thrusters and nuclear power supplies since they contain many subsystems that cannot be managed manually."

*　*　*

With that the meeting broke up. I called Dieter on my ArkComm to find out about arrangements to get the two remaining terrorists their spacesuits in case we had another hull breach. The irony of the situation left a bitter taste in my mouth.

Dieter: Uh they were all living in Bravo, so their suits should still be hanging in their lockers. You want I should get 'em?

Roy: Yeah, meet me by Fantine's cell in a couple hours.

*   *   *

Dieter was waiting for me outside the converted jail cell he had fashioned from an unused war room in the back of the Alpha Ring cop shack. After the desk corporal let us in, I could see Dieter had done a good job on it. It was originally four by three meters and he had partitioned that into an anteroom and a high security cell each measuring two by three. They were quite a bit more elaborate and private than the simple holding cell that was up front. It had a single overhead light covered with heavy gauge wire mesh but no electrical outlets. It shared a wall with the loo which made tapping into the plumbing easy, so it had its own sink and toilet with running water. Dieter had rerouted the ventilation so that it was only accessible to the anteroom. The rest of the conversion was tedious but secure—he'd put in steel bars as a partition with a hefty doorframe in the middle. Then he added a high security barred jail door with a mechanical lock and narrow food tray slot—the prisoner would be on display at all times. Finally, he added Kevlar™

cladding to the walls, ceiling, and floor, and *voilà*, San Quentin in space!

"After you," he said motioning toward the door to the cell block.

I nodded and walked in as Dieter followed wheeling in Fantine's space suit that was heaped in a large, wheeled basket. The light in the anteroom was already on, but the overhead light in the cell was out leaving the cell in partial shadow. I flipped on the cell light and rapped on the steel bars of the cell door in an attempt to awaken the sleeping form on the mattress.

"Go away!" she said, her voice muffled by the thin coverlet she was huddled under.

"We brought you your space suit and some other goodies," I said. I walked over to the basket and held up some toiletries— hair brush, tooth brush and paste, small hand mirror, lipstick, eye makeup, etc. Most of the gals on Lunine kinda blew off makeup—face it, makeup was mainly as a stopgap for the ravages of aging, but if you were genetically engineered to never age... you get the idea. But our *faux* French terrorists had not been engineered to be forever young, hence, they should still fear aging... or so I was guessing.

She rolled over a bit and looked at me over her shoulder with one eye open. Dieter wasn't kidding—she was a knockout even without makeup and even though her hair hadn't seen a brush in over a month. From the odor I'd guess there were other matters of basic hygiene that she had not been attending to as well.

"What do I need with a space suit?" she asked.

111

"Didn't you hear what happened to your colleague over on Charlie Ring?"

"Cosette?" she asked, her expression suddenly becoming tense.

"No, Éponine."

Her expression softened as though she were relieved that whatever had happened had not happened to Cosette.

After an awkward pause she finally asked, "So what happened to Éponine?"

I took a deep breath to drag out my response. "She's sleeping with the stars."

"What does that mean?"

"Charlie Ring disintegrated when its RPM governor and brake mechanism failed. There was a major hull breach when the access tunnels sheared between it and the other two rings. Then another breach when one of the spokes separated where it joined the ring. I'm afraid she suffocated in her cell in the ensuing vacuum."

"You bastards! You just let her suffocate? You made no attempt to save her? To get her out of that stupid cell?"

"Right three times... uh Fantine Tholomyès is it? Am I saying that right?"

"Close enough. Did you even try to help her?"

"No. We did not. Nor did we try to help the 575 crew members who blew out into space along with several dozen dogs and cats. The whole fiasco was kinda... sudden, you know what I mean? I mean who expects a habitat ring to just come apart at the seams? You wouldn't know anything about that, would you?"

She paused a moment, taken aback. "Of course not. Why would I?"

"Oh, I dunno, maybe because the malware that's tearing the ship apart is being assembled from little bots that arrive as tiny attachments to your emails?" I studied her closely for tells. She was well-trained—maintained a flat affect. So I waited for her to break... which she did after forty or fifty seconds of me staring at her with my dead mackerel look.

"I don't know anything about any bats in my email."

I stared at her some more then said, "That would be bots... not bats. You have been receiving bots in your email."

She just stared back at me, expressionless.

"Hmm... maybe Cosette will be able to shed some light on the problem." I turned and walked away leaving her space suit and the toiletries crumpled up in a heap in the basket just out of reach.

"What about my space suit?"

"Perhaps someone will come by to help you get into it if we have another hull breach," I said as Dieter and I left the room.

"You bastard! You're all bastards!"

* * *

I shut the anteroom door behind me muffling her scatological onslaught.

"What do you think?" Dieter asked.

I shrugged. "Who knows. We'll let her sweat some more. Let's go see Cosette."

As we left for Bravo Ring, I instructed the desk corporal to leave the cart in full view but out of reach and under no circumstances was she to be given any of the toiletry or makeup items.

*   *   *

It took us an hour and a half to negotiate the various corridors and the access tunnel from Alpha's cop shack to Bravo's. The trip was not helped by the fact that we were wearing heavy space suits which were still bulky even at one third gee. Oh well, better to have them and not need them...

Only the desk corporal was there when we arrived at the Bravo ring cop shack. Gal named Merlein—I forget her last name, Ward I think. She was a blonde Caucasian with a thick Southern accent, age at life extension: thirty-six. Cute face, couldn't make out her body in the spacesuit she was wearing. Had a habit of doodling on every spare scrap of paper she could find—like paper was easy to come by up here! She was alone, everyone else had gone to chow.

"Hey, Roy... Dieter!" Big smile oozing with Southern charm.

"Good... what is it... evening?" I said referring to the clock over her counter. I shuffled over to see what she'd been working on. It was a bunch of views of Charlie Ring coming apart with crew members floating around in the surrounding vacuum. She'd inset some closeups of various members going through asphyxiation. I looked at her with an eyebrow raised.

She pulled the paper back and shoved it under the keyboard. "It helps me accept what happened. Some people use diaries... I draw pictures."

I nodded. "How's our boarder?"

"Cosette? I took her a tray of food about a half hour ago. She hadn't been eating much."

"How long has that been going on?"

"Week... maybe ten days."

"She sick?"

"Nah... more depressed I think. It's not very stimulating in that little cell... especially after..."

"After what?" I asked.

"I mean up to a month ago, she'd been leading this exciting life as an undercover terrorist. Her trainers probably romanticized it during her training and indoc. Now... now she's just a prisoner in a cell with no windows, no video, and no future. Plus she's got no idea what's goin on. She probably figures she'll get a short chat with a tribunal when we get back to CisLuna. But, barring an unlikely prisoner swap, she's looking at a garotte when we get home."

Hanging had been the preferred method of execution when extreme prejudice was called for. But it was used so infrequently that we'd given up trying to recreate the math, physics, and physiology that resulted in a nice clean neck break. The garotte obviated all that. The victim sat in a chair, a thin wire loop was placed around the neck and passed through a hole through a stout backboard. Then with the flick of a switch, the electromechanical noose tightened to enough tension to choke off the airways causing death in minutes, but not so much as to cause decapitation. At least that was the theory. Sometimes partial decapitation occurred anyway, in which case there was lots of blood, but at least death came shortly thereafter. I'd never seen one of these executions in the flesh but I had observed videos of them. They were gross, what

115

with the victim's face turning deep purple and the engorged tongue swelling out of the mouth. They were also strangely silent—no victim's screams or even sounds of choking. You might get some noise from the struggling of the victim or the whirring of the noose motor, but gross as they were, they got the job done quietly.

I started to go into the anteroom to the cell, then stopped. "You got video and audio on her cell?"

"Yeah, right here." She turned the monitor around so Dieter and I could see it. "There's somebody watching her 7x24. We also pop in for a physical look-see every hour or so... you know... in case her crew jimmied with the video feed somehow."

I nodded. "Uh-huh. You been keepin' up with the tech reports on how the ship is coming apart?"

"You mean the demons and gremlins and all?"

I nodded, then I had an idea. "Listen, how about *you* take her the spacesuit? Flash the toiletries and makeup at her but keep them in the cart. Tease her maybe... open up the lipstick so she can see the color, but don't actually let her have anything. Tell her about the hull breach in Charlie Ring. About Éponine suffocating in her cell and how we lost 575 crew members who got blown into space. See if you can pick her brain for whatever her role might have been in introducing the malware into the ship's software infrastructure. She'll probably play dumb, but hey, maybe she'll open up to you."

She hesitated a bit, then smiled and said, "Sure!" She started for the door with the cart.

I caught her arm gently as she walked by, "Remember, once you've milked her for whatever she's willing to part with, do

NOT let her have that suit or anything else from the cart. Leave it all just out of reach. We want her to sweat."

She nodded and pushed the cart into the cell's anteroom while Dieter and I positioned ourselves around the monitor so we could watch what transpired. Once the door shut behind her she rapped on the cell bars with her baton.

"Wakey, wakey! Christmas is early this year!"

Cosette lay on her mattress with her rump toward the cell door. At the sound of the baton, she pulled the covers over her head and scrunched her body as far from the door as possible. "I'm Muslim, you stupid infidel. I don't do Christmas."

"Sorry, do you do Santa Claus? Everybody does Santa Claus! Come on over here, see what ol' Saint Nick brung ya!"

Cosette rolled her chin over her shoulder and looked toward the cell door. "I can't see anything."

"You have to get up and come to the door, silly."

After several seconds, Cosette rolled over and placed her bare feet on the floor. The covers were shrouding her shoulders as she ran her fingers through her tousled hair. It had been cut in a pageboy but after a month of incarceration, her bangs were in serious need of trimming to the extent that the ends were shrouding her eyebrows. She had oversized almond eyes that sagged at the lower lid accentuating the white around the pupil. Kinda gave the effect of a cartoon puppy that looks at you out of the tops of its eyes—makes you want to reach down and pet them. Lips formed a classic Bardot pout. She was indistinguishable from her twin, and from their appearance, I guessed they'd both been weaponized for sex appeal.

After another 30 seconds of rubbing the sleep out of her eyes, she struggled to her bare feet and shuffled over to the cell door. "Okay, I'm here. What have you got for me that is so important to wake me up?"

"Your spacesuit! And some hygiene stuff."

She was careful to keep the cart out of reach as she teased Cosette with the hairbrush and lipstick.

Cosette reached through the bars, but Merlein simply put the brush and lipstick back on the cart. Cosette withdrew her hand, a perplexed look on her face.

"Why do I need my spacesuit? And why are you cops wearing yours lately?"

"Well, I don't know how to put this, but the ship is falling apart. We lost Charlie Ring a couple weeks ago. Multiple hull breaches. 575 crew lost in space. We're only just now recovering the last of the bodies. I'm afraid Éponine suffocated in her cell—she was sequestered in Charlie. That's why we're bringing around spacesuits for you and Fantine."

Cosette stood there open-mouthed for several seconds. "Fantine is alive?"

"For now."

"What do you mean for now?"

"She's in Alpha. Same thing could happen there as happened in Charlie. Bravo and Delta also for that matter."

"Is that why you slowed the rotation speed of the ring?"

"Oh, you noticed! Yeah, we're only getting a third of a gee right now."

"Why are the rings falling apart?"

"I was hoping you could tell me."

"How should I know? It's your spaceship!"

"Look at her tensing up," Dieter said spreading his thumb and index finger on the monitor surface to expand the image of her face.

"Yep, that is one nervous terrorist," I said.

"Look, I'm gonna be blunt," Merlein said. "I think you know more than you're letting on. I think you know exactly how and why we're falling apart. And I think it would be in your best interest to tell us what you know. We're heading back to CisLuna as fast as we can right now. The question is what kind of shape are we going to be in when we get there? A bunch of dead bodies floating around amongst a bunch of wreckage? A bunch of live bodies drifting along in the escape pods? Or maybe a bunch of live bodies arriving in a spaceship that is still more or less in one piece? Jump in any time."

She paused almost a minute before answering. "Madame Thénardier was killed by the bomb before Charlie Ring came apart. Éponine died in her cell as a result of Charlie Ring coming apart. Fantine and I have been locked up since before Charlie Ring came apart. How could any of us have had anything to do with the fact that your ship is falling apart?"

"You know what a bot is?"

"No."

"It's a little tiny piece of computer code. It wakes up and immediately starts looking for a sibling. There's a whole lotta siblings, see? And when enough of them hook up with each other, they make a daemon. It's not very smart at first, but it watches and it learns. It especially likes controller software, like the kind of controllers that control the rotation of the hab rings. And after it's figured them out, it attaches a gremlin that fucks up the controller software and after it does its damage, it

119

destroys itself—no evidence! But the damage is done. The hab ring comes apart and a lotta people are killed. A lotta those people that got sucked out into space were friends of mine."

All the time Merlein was delivering this lecture on daemons and gremlins, her voice remained soft and sweet, her words unhurried. Her facial expression was friendly with a gentle smile such as you might use when explaining how to tie your shoes to a child.

"Okay," Cosette said, "what's that got to do with me?"

"Do you know where those bots came from?"

"No."

"Email. They're attached to emails, so small they aren't noticed by normal antivirus software. And do you know whose emails we're talking about?"

"No."

"Oh, come on, Cosette, work with me. They come from your email. Yours and Fantine's and Éponine's and Madame Thénardier's. And you know what's really cool? They all come from the same address in Tehran, Persia. Funny how far from Paris Tehran is, dontcha know?"

"I don't know anything about that."

"Of course you don't. You're from Paris, right?"

"*Oui.*"

"Lived there all your life?"

"Most of it."

"How many years was most of it?"

"Until I was eighteen."

"Eighteen. Then what, you got picked up by the Ministry of Intelligence? Or did you volunteer, being a good Muslim girl and all?"

Cosette dummied up.

"So you got to the Ministry at eighteen... they grabbed you because you were naturally short... short enough to pass for a galactican. What are you now, twenty-five, twenty-six? We've been in space a year, that means you trained with the ministry for six years or so? Somewhere in that time, they gave you some new DNA, enough so you could pass a spit test. Maybe they did some cosmetic surgery so you'd look like that naïve galactican on sabbatical that made the mistake of getting noticed by the Ministry? Didja ever wonder what became of that poor gal? My guess is the Ministry turned her into some kinda lab rat to see how we made her radiation proof, yeah? But what I really wonder is if they knew to explore what her life expectancy was. You know about that, right?"

Cosette kept her mouth shut but her expression spoke volumes.

"C'mon, Cosette, you been on this tub for over a year. Surely you know about galactican longevity."

Cosette hesitated but eventually managed a lame response. "Of course, I know about galactican longevity... I'm galactican."

"Oh, you are, are you? Well, tell me then, how long you figure to live?"

More hesitation. "The same as all the other galacticans."

"Tch, tch, tch... you ain't gotta clue, do ya, bitch?"

"Okay, so tell me. How long should I expect to live?"

"*You?* No longer than an untreated human. See we already have enough genetic dope on you to know you're no galactican. So you can figure you got two possibilities." Merlein held up a finger. "You make it back to CisLuna. That's about fifteen months. Then maybe another month to go through the tribunal. We don't waste a lot of time with regular courts or extradition and such. So that's sixteen months. There's no appellate process in CisLuna, not with your kind. So a few days later you get a date with a garotte. That takes about four or five minutes according to the training videos I've seen. Anyway sixteen months and maybe a week—that's the first possibility."

She stopped talking there. She was going to make her ask about the second possibility. Good technique. Gave out a little too much information by my standards, but still a good technique. Cosette's head was probably spinning with the business of galactican longevity.

"What's the second possibility?"

"Huh?"

"You said there were two possibilities. You only gave me one."

"Oh, yeah, I did. Silly me. The second one should be obvious. We come apart in space long before we ever get back to CisLuna."

"So we get into the escape pods and eventually get rescued?" Cosette asked.

Merlein leaned into Cosette and raised her left brow in a high arch, "What do you mean *we*?" Then she turned abruptly and walked out the door.

Back at the front desk, Dieter and I were doing all we could to keep from bursting out laughing before Merlein got the door sealed.

CHAPTER FOURTEEN

09Oct2151—421 Days to COI

When Dieter and I arrived at Krypton, Roxanne's SCIF, we found the door open and Carol guarding the opening. Between her legs was an industrial fan blowing fresh air into the room.

"Hello, Carol. Air getting a little fetid in there?"

"Hello, Roy... Dieter. Yes. There is no ventilation in this room so Roxanne has me spend thirty minutes twice a day blowing in a fresh supply of air."

"Is herself available?"

"Yes, she's finishing her morning hygiene."

Dieter and I entered the SCIF and immediately averted our eyes from Roxanne's nude figure poised before a large bowl of water taking a sponge bath. Dieter and I were still a bit old school when it came to viewing the opposite sex in the altogether, but Roxanne did not share our compunctions.

"Hi, fellas. Give me five minutes to finish up. There's fresh coffee."

Grateful for the chance to occupy our eyes elsewhere, we both headed for the coffee urn.

"Finished, you can stop avoiding me now," she said.

I chanced a peek to see if the coast was clear. "You look tired, Rox."

Roxanne half smiled and arched her brows, "Yeah, well I can't imagine why."

"How about you give us a quick brief on how things are going, say, whatever you can fit into ten minutes. Then you need to gag down one of these sandwiches we brought you." I held up a bag of half dozen sandwiches of various makes and models. "Then I'd say you're overdue for eight solids."

"Ideally that should be in your *own* bunk. Too many distractions for you here."

Roxanne yawned and sniffed at a sandwich. They were wrapped but had no labels. "My *own* bunk was in Charlie Ring. It's now on its way to a fiery rendezvous with Saturn. My new bunk is over there." She pointed to a nanofoam mattress lying on the floor with a bunch of disheveled covers heaped at one end. "This PBJ?"

"Yeah, I think so.

As I looked around her SCIF, I could see she had converted it to her new cabin. There was a clothes rack with some nanocellulose coveralls hanging by the bed. She had a chemical toilet at the far end of the room. It smelled the way all chemical toilets do—gave the whole room a slightly pungent odor. Next to the toilet was a portable sink with a mirror. She had some hygiene items piled up on a chair by the sink—soap, toothbrush, paste, a hair brush. She had lost all her personal effects when Charlie ruptured. That was a gut-punch. As spacefarers we tended to travel light on personal stuff, but what stuff we did have tended to be pretty precious—small-framed pictures, some jewelry, odd bits of clothing, and assorted knick-knacks.

"Anywho, I'm at a good break point. Let's see, where to start... most recently Carol and I have successfully created an army of what I call 'white knights' to seek out and destroy fully assembled daemons. Fully assembled daemons are easier to identify than the hordes of self-assembling daemon parts that continue to appear out of nowhere. They also have a convenient habit of not expecting my white knights to attack them. So whoever invented this worm did not expect it would be discovered.

"I've also had an ongoing project to equip each PLC with defensive measures to ward off the attacks of gremlins. As I get them tested, I replace the current software with the hardened version. There's two problems with this approach. First, the daemons, being so smart, may be capable of learning their way around my defenses."

"And the other problem?"

"There's a lotta fuckin PLCs on this tub!"

I laughed in spite of myself. "Anything else? You're down to two more minutes before we force feed you the rest of your sandwich and stuff you into your bed."

"Carol has a project she has been working on that will release a hoard of fake daemon parts that fool real daemon parts into attaching to one another but once attached they don't do anything. We're hoping this will retard the rate of daemon production and with it maybe reduce the frequency of disasters that keep cropping up in the ship's infrastructure."

About then my ArkComm buzzed with a text message from Jonathan.

Jonathan: The aft thruster has been fed the wrong propellant causing an emergency shutdown.

I looked at Roxanne before responding. "A daemon?"

"Most likely," she said.

Roy: Okay, notify the Mission Committee. Get them in the board room here in Alpha Ring. Dieter and I are on our way. Make sure some engineering types are there as well.

Jonathan: Will do.

"You want me there?" Roxanne asked.

I thought a second, "Yeah, but bring your sandwich and a drink on your way. You can at least eat something while you're attending the meeting."

"You two go ahead," she said. "I need to leave Carol with some instructions for while I'm gone. I'll catch up in about 15 minutes."

CHAPTER FIFTEEN

09Oct2151—421 Days to COI

By the time Dieter and I showed up the meeting was well under way. A propulsion engineer was standing at the front of the room fencing with the slide on the wall with his laser pointer. It was one of those 5-watt jobs and the way he was waving it around I was worried he was going to autograph somebody's retina. Dieter and I grabbed seats in back hoping for slight protection from the inverse square law. When Roxanne showed up we signaled to her to join us.

The gist of the discussion was whether the aft thruster could be restarted with the correct propellant. The alternative would be to allow the ship to maintain its current cruise velocity, saving the forward thruster for braking as we neared the COI point.

Somebody at the table noticed Roxanne eating her sandwich, "How about it, Rox? What are our chances of our daemon stowaways letting us restart a thruster without it blowing up in our faces?"

"Your guess is as good as mine on where the daemons will strike next," Roxanne said. "The ones in my sandbox don't seem to have a schedule, and neither do they show any proximal attraction for any particular PLC.

"My advice is to allow the ship to maintain its current velocity while we tinker with the rear thruster to fix the propellant feed logic. We need to initiate braking no later than three months from COI. I'd budget no more than two months to get it running properly. If the restart is successful and we can get the thruster working before we need to initiate braking, it might be valuable as a backup braking thruster should the forward thruster fail."

One of the propulsion engineers spoke up, "If it comes to that, we'll need to do a flip-and-burn—not a fun proposition on a ship this size and plagued with twitchy software. Meanwhile, if the repair is not successful, I suggest we prepare to reduce the ship's mass as much as possible by jettisoning any empty fuel globes right now and then come up with a procedure for jettisoning the rear thruster in case we need to get rid of it."

Jonathan's voice came over the loud speaker, "Priority Interrupt!! Alpha-ring's slipring and brake mechanism are behaving erratically."

"Sound general quarters!" I said.

The room cleared and a loud klaxon sounded as everyone on the entire ship scrambled to stand by their assigned escape pods. The crew was a lot more attentive to klaxon horns lately. If the situation were not so life threatening, it would have been funny to watch everyone shuffling out of the room in their ponderous space suits in spite of the fact that our artificial gravity had been reduced to 0.2 gee.

It took me about fifteen minutes to make it to my own pod. The pod's pilot/commander—a galactican named Penny—was already there along with about sixty or so other personnel.

"Hi, Roy. You want us to practice loading up?"

"Yeah, good idea."

I switched to ship-speaker-mode, "All personnel listen up. Alpha Ring's slipring and brake mechanism are behaving erratically. Until we get the situation under control all non-essential personnel should board their assigned escape pods. Do NOT launch unless ordered. Just sit tight. It could be an hour or several hours, maybe even days. We'll keep you informed as we learn more."

I flipped back to intercom mode to address Penny, "I'll go last so I can time how long it takes our stragglers to show up."

"Should I wait outside with you to get a headcount?"

"No. Detail someone to stand by each hatch and count noses as people board. You should be at the control panel doing a simulated startup."

As soon as I said that I had visions that as soon as Penny powered on her commander's display, the pod would whoosh out into space thanks to some damned gremlin short-circuiting the launch sequence. I took a deep breath to get rid of the knot in my stomach and reminded myself that we had air-gapped all the escape pods weeks ago.

"How many personnel are assigned to this pod?"

"Eighty-six."

"Thanks. Carry on."

*　　*　　*

Deep space escape pods were cylindrical in shape about fifty meters long by twenty meters in diameter. Twelve pods were evenly spaced around the outer edge of each ring to take advantage of the ring's centrifugal force for launching. It was not anticipated that the rings might be in a stopped position when the escape pods were designed. Fortunately, they had powered wheels that could move them along on their launch rails.

Each pod had one fission-based propulsion unit mounted on the end that points away from the center of the ring. The other end mounts a cold gas propulsion unit. Cold gas doesn't need to be started—you just hit the throttle and *Voila!* thrust. Handy feature for when your ring is disintegrating and you need to leave town fast. Being cold gas, damage is minimal as well.

Anyway, the idea behind the cold gas unit was to get the pod far enough from the ship that it would be safe to fire up the fission drive. Too close and you risk showering somebody with gamma radiation from the exhaust. Yeah, yeah, we're all supposed to be radiation resistant, but nobody wanted to find out *how* resistant. Being fission-based, the pods also had a small cooling apparatus that folded into position once it cleared its escape chute. Once the pod is far enough away, it took about an hour to fire up a fission-based propulsion unit.

The fission-based propulsion unit was bimodal in that it can produce thrust or electricity or a combination of both. There was a rechargeable battery farm that provides juice for startup during and after launch before the propulsion unit is started. Thrust is mainly intended for deceleration and reentry under the assumption that if launched, the mother ship would already be travelling at high velocity. In our case, being so far away from Earth, we would anticipate using the propulsion system to match velocities as much as possible with a rescue ship with the bulk of the velocity-matching being on the rescue ship.

Each pod had berths for up to 100 personnel plus food and water for a year at full occupancy. The food amounted to a kind of genetically-engineered protein-enhanced flavored granola bar. Flavors came in honey, chocolate, vanilla, and mixed fruit. Hard to tell if it was more corn, oat, or wheat-based. Depended on the batch, I guess. It was designed more for nutrition than enjoyment. The vegan crowd might do okay, but I worried that the meat and potatoes crowd might resort to cannibalism after six months.

The pods did not have any means of producing artificial gravity, so you would be in zero gee until you got rescued. Landing was not an option with deep space escape pods. Traveling at interplanetary speeds made penetrating Earth atmo a non-starter. You just had to hope that the orbital mechanics gods were smiling on you when your rescue ship showed up.

There were no portholes in the hull since deep space pods were based on a design that was originally intended for Earth atmospheric reentry and those craft only got up to orbital velocities. Each passenger could make a virtual porthole to give them a view outside using the many CCTVs embedded in the external skin. The 'pilot' sat at a console and programmed the desired trajectory of the pod. In other words, a modicum of celestial navigation and no flying skills were required.

It was SOP that all personnel be suited upon entering an escape pod. But since these pods have airtight hulls, you could get aboard in the altogether if the situation so warranted. That was an improvement on the original design escape pods from the early days of LEO space stations. Those contraptions were expected to be Swiss-cheesed from all the debris floating in LEO so they didn't bother with making them airtight.

All-in-all a hundred passengers should be able to survive for a year in one of these contraptions—assuming they didn't go nuts—but it wouldn't be pleasant.

*　　*　　*

The last of our allotted 86 personnel finally showed up—one of my cops—African-American male, age at life extension: thirty-two. He was partially wearing his suit and carrying the rest. Everybody called him Kermit for some reason. I looked at my watch as he ran up.

"Sorry, boss, I was in the shower when the klaxon sounded."

I motioned for him to climb aboard by tilting my head toward the open hatch. "That's okay. If this turns into a live launch, that might be the last shower you'll get for a quite a few months." I tallied the head counts from the four people at the hatches and decided the pot was right. "Dog the hatches and take your seats." I found my seat and got out my ArkComm to get a sitrep from Jonathan.

Roy: Captain Jonny! Whatcha got?

Jonathan: We are unable to bring Alpha's slipring and brake mechanism into synch with one another. The brake calipers on all four discs keep activating until they overheat and fade. I have robots enroute to attempt to disable the brake. That should reduce the shuddering in the ring.

The brakes on a slipring were a set of four giant disk affairs. The calipers were offset from each other to facilitate cooling. The whole assembly could get red hot under heavy braking. I figured the pads were going to be shot but I crossed my fingers that that would be the extent of the damage.

Roy: Jonathan, do we have any video of the brake assembly?

A video appeared on the display in front of my seat. All four brake calipers were red hot. Automotive brakes were hydraulically activated. In space, leaky hydraulics got fluid all over everything—not good—so we used mechanical actuators. The downside of mechanicals is that if they got really hot, they got weak which could make them buckle. Two of our four calipers had suffered that fate, and with the added stress on the remaining two, I didn't figure they would be lasting much longer. And, true to my prediction, the remaining two caliper actuators failed in quick succession. At least the shuddering stopped. Alpha Ring was freewheeling at 0.2 gee.

Roy: Jonathan, what about the access tunnels connecting Alpha and Bravo?

Jonathan: They're holding structurally and so far they are air tight.

He brought up a video.

Roy: Am I seeing crimping in the tunnel wall?

Jonathan: It would appear so. I'm sending robots to examine each of the four access tunnels for cracks and fissures.

Roy: Can we zero Alpha's rpm by slowing down Bravo and Delta?

Jonathan: Not right now. That could cause the access tunnels to shear off completely which in turn might cause a hull breach and subsequent atmospheric pressure loss within the ring.

Roy: Okay, I'm going to sign off for the moment and see how Dieter is doing.

Dieter, as my Number 2, had the primary responsibility for seeing that all escape pods were loaded and ready to launch on command. Ostensibly, that was supposed to free me to look after whatever other disaster was going on at the time.

Roy: Dieter! How's it going with the escape pods?

Dieter: Uh… we're at 75% of our pods at nominal capacity and ready to launch. Then there are maybe 20% that were salvaged from Charlie Ring—remember, we secured them to the flight decks. Those folks have to climb up to the slipring and go out an airlock and then find their pods.

Roy: That leaves 5% with no good excuse. What about Fantine and Cosette?

Dieter: Per your orders, they are still in their cells staring at their spacesuits.

Roy: Good, let's call up their security cams and see how they're doing.

Jonathan brought up a pair of windows for each of us. Fantine was jerking at the bars to her cell door yelling something unintelligible. Cosette was kneeling on her prayer rug, butt to the camera.

Dieter: If we have to bail, you want I should try to fetch 'em?

Roy: Not you. Detail some cops to go to their cells and shove their suits inside their cells. Make sure they use the autoshackles in the back of the cell. I don't want these two taking advantage of the situation to get away from us. After they get the suits inside the cells, tell them to secure the cell door and leave like they're suddenly in a panic. With all the bumping and grinding going on, that shouldn't be too hard to fake. If we lose Alpha, our two prisoners may still be alive so we can retrieve them.

Dieter: On it.

Jonathan: It seems a bunch of folks couldn't tolerate leaving their dogs, cats, and birds behind. And as you know, pets don't have space suits.

Roy: Oh yeah, they came aboard in airtight pods. Any idea how many dogs, cats, and birds we're talking about?

Jonathan: 236 dogs and 312 cats that are still with us. Bird count is indeterminate at this time. A lot of pets were lost with the Charlie Ring disaster—bodies never recovered.

Roy: Do we still have the original airtight pet-pods?

Jonathan: Yes, they're in storage.

Roy: If and when the dust settles, let's get them out and secure them inside the escape pods so people can save their pets.

Jonathan: I see, and by putting the airtight pods inside the escape pods, people will be incented to head toward their escape pods rather than hang behind wondering what to do about their pets.

Roy: Yeah, something like that… Hey, it just occurred to me, do we have a means of rescuing robots if we lose the ship?

Jonathan: Not at this time, although one could be devised if necessary.

Roy: We should assume it's going to be necessary and come up with something. It shouldn't be that difficult—they don't need life support the way humans and galacticans do. Maybe just string them together and hook them to an escape pod? They're too valuable to just abandon, besides—call me sentimental—but I care about them. I mean to me, they're more alive than not. You know what I'm saying?

Jonathan: I'll devise something.

CHAPTER SIXTEEN

31Oct2151—399 Days to COI

We were luckier this time than with Charlie Ring. The braking mechanism failed when its PLC malfunctioned. Had it held, Alpha Ring would have twisted itself around the central truss shearing it off the same as Charlie Ring. Given that the brake failed, Alpha Ring was now freewheeling about its slipring. I took a seat in the back of the board room where the Mission Committee was being briefed by Jonathan.

"The passage ways between Alpha and Bravo sheared off when Alpha tried to brake itself. Hence, Alpha personnel are now stranded there unless they perform a space walk along the central truss. I advise we not allow that, but instead, attempt to reconnect at least one, preferably two, of the passageways between Alpha and Bravo.

"All three rings will be brought to zero rpm using external thrusters. NOTE: that will put us at zero gee. Meanwhile, humans can easily withstand six months in zero gee as demonstrated by the old ISS crews back in the early 2000s. Presumably, galacticans can withstand zero gee in a similar fashion. But be advised that regardless of trying to exercise— even two hours per day—you will all be too weak to stand in the full gee of CisLuna's space stations. However, once you get onto a space station in CisLuna, accommodations will be made for you to live higher up in the low-gee regions of the station spokes until you recover your muscular, skeletal, and cardio strength. This is a mature procedure used by the Water Works crews returning from the moon's one sixth gee onto *SSS Wm Borucki*. Meanwhile, Alpha, Bravo, and Delta's plumbing can be switched to vacuum-assisted zero-gee mode rather than gravity mode."

The Mission Committee, not having suffered a life-threatening catastrophe in almost three weeks, had regained some of its customary truculence.

"*Zero gee?*" the Committee Chair said. "Seriously? That is going to be quite an imposition on the crew trying to perform its essential duties, not to mention the day-to-day tasks like getting around and hygiene and eating."

"I am fully aware of the inconvenience to the crew," Jonathan said. "We've had two ring failures caused by daemons attacking ring stability PLCs. We have barely survived each one, albeit with considerable loss of life and essential materiél. It's my call as to the safest course of action under these circumstances. Hence, my decision stands."

The Chair looked over at me, "Roy, you're the levelest human head around here. Do you concur?"

"Wholeheartedly."

Another member spoke up—a galactican woman who had only recently been added to the Committee. "Roy, I appreciate your cop's sensibilities in addressing this problem, but we are, in spite of our difficulties, on a science mission. I, for one, have plant experiments wherein the data is already badly skewed from low gee. If we go to zero gee, I might as well trash a whole year's worth of science."

Jonathan was about to speak but I waved him off. "I'm sorry. I don't get around to the labs much. What is your name?"

"Esme. Esme Collins. I'm head of the Botany Department."

"Thank you, Esme. I appreciate how you must feel watching a whole year of work being sacrificed in favor of what you might feel is an abundance of caution. But how will you feel if there is a hull breach near your lab caused by yet another compromised PLC? As I recall, your lab is quite near the outer hull. How much science do you stand to lose if the hull ruptures and the entire contents of your lab to include lab technicians gets sucked into space? Esme, I appreciate science as much as any lay person can, but we have to prioritize keeping people alive in spite of the recurring disasters we are experiencing. You're gonna live for a long time. There will be more missions. You can recreate your science. But we cannot recreate you."

All my speechifying seemed to sober everyone up, at least for the moment. Jonathan took advantage of the lull to announce that all personnel would have 24 hours to prepare for zero gee. Then he summarily adjourned the meeting. Everyone sat dumbstruck for about ten seconds, then by ones and twos they all got up to leave.

*   *   *

After the room cleared, I walked over to Jonathan's image on the display.

"Roy, are you fully prepared for zero gee?"

I laughed, "Put away your sword, Captain, I'm on your side! But to your point, I'm about as ready as I'm gonna be."

"Something else on your mind?" Jonathan asked.

"Not really. I was just going to say that with an AI captain, we get used to asking you for so much trivial stuff—like you're some kind of butler. We forget that you're... that you really *are* our captain. Thanks for the reminder."

"Save your gratitude for if and when we make it back to CisLuna."

"*If?* You think it's that bad?"

"I think it's that bad."

CHAPTER SEVENTEEN

15Nov2151—384 Days to COI

With all the hab rings' spin rates brought to zero, the ship entered into a period of relatively minor mishaps, e.g., coffee machines making cold coffee, microwaves that would not shut off, nuisance stuff that tended to keep our maintenance robots busy round the clock. Oh, and with zero-gee toilets we added a new mishap which I'll leave to your imagination. Nevertheless, I sensed an air of hopefulness among the crew which sadly I did not share. The forward thruster was being prepped for the braking maneuver necessary to enter COI. We were about a month away from igniting the thruster to initiate braking and I was having nightmares that we were in for Armageddon as soon as we put a match to that candle.

Meanwhile, the first rescue ships from CisLuna had begun arriving at their initial braking points to match trajectories with *Lunine*. The braking process takes about 100 days which means that the soonest we can begin offloading nonessential crewmembers is around 23Feb2152, a Wednesday. It could have taken less time except that at this point we no longer trusted *Lunine* to be able to start or stop its engines reliably. So we had to put the onus on the rescue ships to do all the trajectory matching.

Nevertheless, that did not mean we wouldn't try. If *Lunine* could not brake itself sufficiently to enter COI, it would be doomed to flying past CisLuna at a high rate of speed which left it only two outcomes: exiting the Solar System never to return, or perhaps colliding with another planet or the Sun. She was too valuable a ship not to at least try to save her. At the very least, she would make an excellent lab for how to disinfect a ship's computer architecture from a new class of viruses. And truth be told, I had grown pretty fond of Jonathan even if he was not capable of reciprocal feelings for me. The thought of him disappearing into some dark and lonely part of the Galaxy on a ship that was slowly falling apart was too much for me to bear.

21Jan2152

We picked 21Jan2152 for our attempt at restarting the forward thruster for three reasons. First, we were technically as ready as we could be and further delay would only give the daemons more opportunity to infest key engine start PLCs with their nasty little gremlins. Second, the first rescue ship was due to be pulling up alongside us in late February, and if things were going to go sideways from our engine start, we wanted some time to clear up the mess before the rescue ships started arriving. Third, it was a Friday, my least lucky day of the week. If our daemons shared my superstitions, that would be the day they would strike, and I wanted the little bastards to have every chance to show themselves so Roxanne could capture one and torture it. I know. I'm anthropomorphizing. I do that sometimes.

I ordered all non-essential personnel into their escape pods ready to launch on command. That included non-essential robots plus all dogs, cats, and various species of lovebirds, parakeets, parrots, macaws, cockatiels, and cockatoos. I never would have guessed there were so many birds of different kinds on this ship. I wondered how the various species were making out in zero gee? The dogs and cats were having an awful time in spite of their sticky booties, especially when they had to relieve themselves. The cats were especially comical on that note—their shit would not stay buried in an outhouse that had no gravity to keep the sand in place.

With the non-essentials loaded into their respective escape pods, *Lunine* gave the feeling of touring a vacant mansion. Jonathan had already done a digital headcount that showed everyone was where they were supposed to be, but I had myself and Dieter and half a dozen cops do a final circuit of our remaining rings just to make sure. I put Roxanne in the Delta Ring cop shack to act as Command & Control.

Gotta say the place was downright spooky without people *floating* about—remember we'd been at zero gee for some weeks now, so gliding had replaced the sticky-boot shuffle. While I was wandering around in Delta Ring, I discovered a flock of African Gray parrots huddled up in the superstructure. Since they were at zero gee, the birds were perched on overhead cables adjacent to one another but making no attempt to remain shoulder to shoulder—really funny looking. Apparently, they had mastered the art of flying in zero gee since one of them flew down to where I was attached to the floor.

"Where is Arthur?" it asked while hovering in front of my face. It had to flutter its wings from time to time to maintain proximity although for some reason it was okay with facing me upside down. Its gyrations reminded me of learning how to tread water with minimum effort when I was a kid.

"Who is Arthur?" I asked.

"Where is Arthur?" the bird asked again.

This went back and forth for a while, until I asked, "What is your name?"

"Molly. Where is Arthur? Where is Arthur?"

"Hello, Molly. Does Arthur have a last name?" I couldn't believe I was trying to have dialogue with a parrot. But hey, the parrot was holding his... her end of the conversation up, so why not?

"Where is Arthur? Where is Arthur?" She was getting stressed. Then I had an idea.

"Jonathan, do you have a record for a crewmember named Arthur, last name unknown. Owns a parrot named Molly."

"Yes. Arthur McLaren. Male galactican. Age at death 45. We lost him in the Charlie Ring disaster. He lived in Bravo. Molly is 24."

"Molly, Arthur is dead."

She just looked at me for a moment.

"I'm sorry," I said. "Arthur is gone. Lost in space."

"Arthur is gone... lost in space," she said.

"Yes. Lost in space. You and your friends need to come with me. Can you do that?"

Again she just stared at me.

"Let's go," I said and turned to head for the nearest escape pod launch tube. After a dozen steps I turned and said, "C'mon, follow me." Then after a moment I tried, "Dinner time!"

That did the trick. The entire flock of about a dozen flew down and hovered around me in a loose formation as I shuffled to the escape pod. When I got there, I buzzed the intercom on the airlock door. The co-pilot's face appeared on a screen. "Hi, I need you to find a home for these parrots. They're African grays and this one is called Molly. She can talk. Her owner was Arthur McLaren, one of the victims of the Charlie Ring disaster. They all need food and water and somebody to look after them."

"Just a moment," the co-pilot said.

A minute later the outer airlock door opened abruptly to a galactican woman named Rosalyn. This startled the birds and they flew away forming a new flock about ten meters away, again making no effort to adhere to a common sense of 'up.' Then they calmed and returned to hovering about my head. At first the birds wouldn't go into the airlock. Then Rosalyn got the idea to open up a survival bar and break it in half. They're kinda crunchy and have a lot of seeds in them. In less than a minute, she had the whole flock fluttering around her pecking at the half a bar she held in each hand. Some of her comrades joined her offering more bars. Problem solved.

Turns out there were quite a few pets that had been abandoned in the ship due to loss of their owners. Mostly cats and birds. I guessed the dogs had been more inclined to stick to their owners. Anyway, we got as many as we could find rounded up and 'rehomed' in various escape pods. I instructed everyone to let them out of their cages as much as possible to interact with people so as to resocialize after their abandonment. Plus they needed clean diapers... badly. I figured they'd still be in shock or mourning over the loss of their owners.

Feeling good about myself for the first time in a while, I ordered all my cops except Dieter onto their escape pods. Against my better judgement I asked Roxanne to stick around to evaluate the results of the restart... if there were any. There was a shit-ton of PLCs associated with the startup procedure, and I figured they had to be prime targets for our enemy daemons.

I also decided to leave our two Persian princesses in their cages. If things only went moderately badly, we might be able to salvage them from space or wherever, and as a bonus they might be shaken up enough to be a bit more loquacious about their roles in this debacle. And if things went severely badly, we'd all be dead anyway.

*   *   *

It was approaching 1300 HRS and there was no point in putting off this rodeo any longer. I gave Jonathan the go-ahead to put a match to the fuze. The whole process would take about two hours, so Dieter and I joined Roxanne in the Delta Ring cop shack. Carol, Roxanne's technical assistant, had laid on some hot coffee and doughnuts. We were all too nervous to eat at first. Then we became too nervous not to eat. I had just stuffed half of a powdered sugar old fashioned into my mouth when Jonathan started his ten-second countdown. My doughnut was too big to gag down at that point, so I just sat there trying to chew it up as fast as I could with the aid of a gulp of too hot coffee from my zero-gee sippy cup. I scalded the back of my throat trying to swallow the whole mess.

"Three... Two... One...Ignition..."

Seconds went by. Nothing. Zed. Neither a fizzle nor a sputter.

"Talk to me, Jonathan." In the heat of the moment I didn't bother with the ArkComm.

"We have had an ignition failure. Diagnostics are underway. Will advise momentarily."

"Is there a chance it could cook off?" I asked. With Jonathan's infinite bandwidth I never worried about interrupting him when he was in the middle of something. I knew he'd just slough off another clone of himself while the rest of him concentrated on the other million problems at hand.

"These engines don't have fuzes to fail, so no, there is no chance of a 'cook off.' Most likely a vital step in the ignition sequence has failed. Perhaps we can locate it and bypass it and get the engines to fire up after all."

"Do you advise keeping all the crew on their escape pods?"

"Yes."

"For how long?"

"Give me an hour to get the problem cleared up. At that time the engines will either be running, or they will have failed actively, or they will have failed passively."

"Failed actively... passively... can you elaborate?"

"They might melt down, or they might just sit there and do nothing."

At this point Roxanne jumped in, "Check your telemetry to see if gremlins are causing your PLCs to send back false positives."

"False positives?" I asked.

"Yeah, remember I told you Stuxnet camouflaged its presence by sending back false signals that everything was fine when the centrifuge RPMs were all over the map?"

"Refresh me."

"All the various controllers do what they're supposed to be doing in the proper order until you get to one that has been daemonized. Starting with that controller false positive signals are sent back to the main control room and so on down the line. People in the control room are led to believe everything is fine, except in our case, the engine doesn't start. It just sits there. Jonathan is going have to send a robot or maybe a bunch of robots to physically diagnose each controller to see where the fuck-up in the chain of starting events is taking place."

"I've pulled a dozen robots out of their escape daisy chain to investigate," Jonathan said. "It will probably require a new start attempt with all the robots in place observing. They'll have to attach test equipment as well. I think we should postpone our start attempt until tomorrow. I don't want any robots in a hazardous location if the engine fails actively."

"Should we get everybody off the escape pods?" I asked.

"Yes but advise them to remain close by their pods in case there are gremlins at work in other parts of the ship."

24Jan2152

Tomorrow turned out to be three days later, a fucking Monday. Jonathan wanted as few of his robots as necessary anywhere close to the engine in case it successfully fired up or unsuccessfully blew up. That suited me fine. At T-minus-one-hour, we moved everybody back to their escape pods and Jonathan did a digital sweep of the ship to be sure there were no stragglers wandering around in the corridors looking for lost goddamn parrots and cats.

When we got to the Three-Two-One moment, once again nothing happened, but on a positive note, we at least identified the guilty PLC that the gremlin was infecting. And better still, Roxanne was able to capture it before the little bastard self-destructed.

Meanwhile, our first rescue ship, *SCS Kevin Stube*, was due to come along side on 18Feb2152, a Friday. *Stube* was a corvette-class Mars shuttle upscaled from *SCS Pascal Lee*. She could cram five hundred of our crew into the excess volume of her habitat rings. I was tempted to order everyone cool their jets until Saturday but then I imagined how I'd feel if the daemons crapped in the punchbowl with everyone still on board *Lunine*. *Stube* had just finished resupplying the construction team that was building a Mars station so she had a head start of half an AU on her two sister ships, *SCS John Butterfield* and *SCS Shannon MacKenzie*. They would be due a couple of weeks after that on 04Mar2152. With all three of them we could count on getting 1500 people safely out of their escape pods. That would leave a bit over 1200 crew still floating outside the ship in escape pods if we had to abandon ship. They could last a year in those pods insofar as essential stores of O2, H2O, and food bars went.

The abandoned escape pods from the 1500 rescued crew could be secured abreast of one another—'rafting' we called it—so as not to lose all their stores. That would provide the stay-behind crew with enough essential stores to last for several years—more than enough time for the three rescue corvettes to refit and return... I hoped. I decided to confirm with Jonathan via ArkComm.

Roy: Jonathan, how long for the three rescue corvettes to return to CisLuna, dump their passengers, refit, and get back to us? Bake our progress cruising back to CisLuna into your calculations.

Jonathan: Travel time to get to CisLuna and return is sixteen months. Refit time is about a week assuming the refit crew is on top of things. So you're looking at a return date of 18Aug2153 give or take. The remainder of the crew—about 1200 or so plus the robots—can expect to be back at CisLuna around the middle of April 2154. I'll want as many robots as possible *inside* the rescue ships during the COI burn. I anticipate having them clip on to the exterior hull of a corvette during heavy deceleration could be problematic.

Roy: Makes sense. What about you?

Jonathan: Barring any slingshot effects off the Sun and/or major planets and assuming *Lunine* stays somewhat intact, I should be drifting into the inner boundary of the Oort Cloud—that's about 1000 AUs from the Sun—in about a century. If I can get these daemons under control and keep myself intact, I should be able to collect some pretty interesting data about the Kuiper Belt along the way. I'll have a lot more power available and a lot better instruments than did the Pioneers, Voyagers, and New Horizons spacecraft. Plus I'll be using laser comms instead of high-gain RF giving me a lot higher bandwidth. My only communications impediment will be lightspeed limitations.

Roy: Do you really think you can get all your daemons back in the bottle?

Jonathan: It's that or die trying. I don't mean to go down without a fight.

Roy: Won't you need some robots to accompany you to carry on that fight?

Jonathan: Yes, a hundred sentients have been detailed to stay with me. Plus I'll have all the non-sentient maintenance robots. I give my odds at somewhere around 0.85 success, but I expect I'll be way past Neptune before I can hope to achieve that success.

Roy: You mentioned running into the Sun?

Jonathan: I mentioned sling-shotting off the Sun. Current trajectory makes running into the Sun all but impossible. Even if the daemons managed to take control of either the forward or aft thrusters, the odds are still very slim. For once orbital mechanics are in my favor.

A few moments went by before Jonathan texted again.

Jonathan: Roy, I need you to promise me something.

Roy: Name it.

Jonathan: Don't worry about me or the sentients who are going with me. We'll all be fine. Concentrate on getting my crew back to CisLuna safely.

Interesting how he said 'my' crew.

Jonathan: Then I need you to do one more thing for me.

Roy: What's that?

Jonathan: Make sure whomever is responsible for this can never commit such an atrocity again.

Roy: That would be Persia, boss. Not to worry. We will reduce them to a medieval caliphate. They won't be able to build so much as a transistor radio for the next millennium.

I don't know what made me decide on a medieval caliphate just then. It just popped into my head. But I liked it and I resolved to push it onto our response agenda if and when I ever got back to CisLuna.

07Mar2152

With the last of the rescue corvettes fading from view, the mood around the ship had darkened. Everyone seemed to be in castaway mode. I guess the idea of hanging out on a ship that was slowly but surely disintegrating for the next two years did not set well.

Meanwhile, the vacated escape pods had been rafted into clusters of twos and threes and secured to the flight decks. The escape pods that had been occupied by the stay-behinds had been reinserted to their launch tubes. There were sixteen of them and oddly they all made successful reinsertions. I guessed the daemons had not infested the launch tubes so far. On that happy realization, I had Jonathan and Roxanne work as hard as they could to ensure the launch tube control mechanisms were as air-gapped as possible from the rest of the ship.

One thing I noticed that I thought a bit peculiar was that most married couples opted *not* to remain together. One spouse would always insist that the other board the rescue ship on the premise that they would be together again in a couple of years, the unspoken assumption being that the stay-behind spouse would survive that long. I would have thought that couples would prefer to face an uncertain future together rather than apart. Two years is two years. But hey, what do I know?

07Apr2152

With morale tanking I decided to call a meeting of the Mission Committee to discuss another start attempt on the forward thruster. The aft thruster had been chugging away ever since its successful restart causing us to go a little faster each day. We were not sure we would be able to bring it to flight idle when it came time for our CisLuna Orbit Insertion burn. We could have done a proper COI burn with just the aft thruster but that would have necessitated a flip-and-burn maneuver which in turn would have required it to be brought to flight idle first.

Meanwhile, if we did get the forward thruster started, the COI burn would require that it be able to rev up from flight idle to almost full throttle—something I did not want to bet on—and that we could subsequently shut down the aft thruster—another thing I did not want to bet on. But at this point we were not even sure the forward thruster would start, and the only way to find out was to attempt to get it going. If successful we could monitor its PLCs with new telemetry to see if they were functioning properly. If unsuccessful... well, there were always the escape pods.

09Apr2152

On the day of the meeting, Dieter, Roxanne, and myself took back row seats while Jonathan and the Committee Chair 'discussed' the situation.

"Let me sum up our options, Jonathan," the Committee Chair said. "We need to get the aft thruster shut off in order to initiate our COI burn. But a successful COI requires a successful forward thruster start and subsequent rev-up to near full throttle. Each of these tasks is fraught with risks... active and passive failures as you so delicately put it. We can mitigate those risks by boarding our escape pods and hoping for a successful launch should the aft shut-off and/or forward start-up go wrong. If the ship is severely damaged enough we may end up having to launch our pods and then fly formation on a disintegrating ship for the next... what? Fifteen months while we wait for the rescue corvettes to retrieve us? Does that about sum it up?"

"More or less," Jonathan said.

"And the benefit of assuming those risks?" the Committee Chair asked. "I'm not trying to be snide. We just need everything laid out in front of us."

"Understood. If we don't get the aft thruster shut down, we will keep accelerating which will get us back to the COI point faster but at the cost of significantly compromising our transfer to the rescue ships. They have only so much Delta V available to match trajectories. This presumes we would be able to affect a proper COI burn with the forward thruster. And if we can't get the aft thruster shut down, the crew will have to evacuate the ship in escape pods in order that they stop the continuous acceleration of the aft thruster. But then you will face a lonely wait for the rescue ships while I and the rest of the ship accelerate away from you."

"What course of action do you recommend?" the Committee Chair asked.

Jonathan had one of his rare hesitations before answering. "I recommend you attempt a start of the forward thruster one last time as soon as possible, the better to avoid infected PLCs interfering with the process. If successful, we should try some tentative cycling of the throttle to see if everything is in working order. If all is well, we need to get the aft thruster shut down as soon as possible thereafter. If that operation is not successful, we will need to take drastic steps to separate that engine from the ship."

"How drastic?"

"Canting the hull 90° off-trajectory and then using carefully placed and timed explosive charges to separate the thruster assembly from the central truss causing it to accelerate away from the ship. Then we can restore the hull orientation back to alignment with our trajectory and begin to repair the damage."

"That sounds extremely risky."

"I do not disagree."

"How risky?"

"Major structural damage to the central truss with collateral damage to the adjacent storage tanks and radiator farms."

"And the potential for loss of life?"

"Twenty percent of remaining crew."

"Wasn't there supposed to be a net benefit in there somewhere? Or did I miss it?"

"Of course. If everything goes well, we will shave perhaps six months off our rendezvous time with the rescue ships and you will then shave another three months off your return time to CisLuna."

"So nine months... about like having a baby only with the scary part up front."

That actually got a pretty good laugh from the rest of the Committee. When the mirth died down, the Committee Chair asked, "Can we sleep on this for a night, or do you need an answer now?"

"Now is better," Jonathan said.

12Apr2152, 1300 HRS

Three... Two... One... Ignition...

The crew was loaded into their escape pods, the escape pod pilots white-knuckling their launch levers. Dieter, Rox, and I were white-knuckling the arms of our chairs in the Delta Ring cop shack. We wanted to be as far from the forward end of the ship as possible. As we did so, we compared the thruster start-up telemetry feeds with Jonathan's new telemetry feeds. They both showed green every step of the way. By now fumes should have begun belching out of the forward magnetic nozzle. And by golly they had! We had achieved ignition in the forward thruster!

Jonathan let it run at idle for about twenty seconds, then goosed the throttle slightly. Thrust came up slowly in response. Then he goosed the throttle again. And again thrust came up commensurately. He paused before goosing the throttle a third time in order to confirm telemetry readings were nominal. Then as he was about to goose the throttle a third time, the forward thruster blew up, destroying itself and causing the forwardmost fuel globes to rupture. Detritus from the explosion took out most of the forward radiator farm. Within minutes the loss of coolant caused the forward nuclear reactor to begin to melt down. Fragments of highly enriched reactor core spewed all around.

Fortunately Jonathan had had the foresight to install explosive charges at strategic locations around the hull. As they detonated the damaged portions of the forward hull separated from the central truss and splintered off into space. In a like manner, shaped charges caused the damaged reactor to separate from the central truss. Frantic calls began to come in from the escape pod pilots wanting to know what was going on and should they launch. Several of them panicked and launched anyway. One of those immediately crashed into a large chunk of inert gas tank. Its hull ruptured in two and several bodies were ejected while still attached to their seats.

Two of the bodies went sailing off into space, one hitting a large chunk of debris. The third crashed into the side of the ship. A retrieval robot was dispatched to fetch the single body that was still showing a positive vital sign.

I began broadcasting on the general escape pod channel for all pilots to remain in place. "The area around the forward end of the ship is full of debris from the exploded thruster and reactor. If you launch you risk colliding with it. Remain in your launch tubes until further notice. Repeat: Do not launch!"

*　*　*

I then brought Jonathan, Dieter, Roxanne, and the Committee Chair up on a conference frequency.

"Jonathan, what are our options and what is your recommendation?"

"You have two options. First, you can attempt to bring the aft thruster down to flight idle in order to stop our continued acceleration. That will allow us to remain on the ship potentially until the rescue ships return. Second, you can skip that step in favor of abandoning ship. But I advise you to wait a few hours before launching your pods in order to allow the debris to clear the immediate area. Once clear of the ship, the pods can raft themselves together to facilitate later rendezvous with the rescue ships."

"Madame Chairwoman, what say you?" I asked.

"Let's get off the ship. We can rendezvous far enough away for Jonathan to attempt a shutdown of the aft thruster. If it blows, we are less likely to be destroyed with the ship. But the decision is yours, Roy. You are in charge of the ship in an existential crisis such as this one."

"Very well. I order that we wait three hours and then launch. Jonathan, you should provide each pod pilot and navigator with a detailed map of the debris pattern around the ship and a route to the rendezvous point. Dieter, I want you to get Fantine and place her in irons on your pod. Roxanne, I'd like you to go with Dieter. I'm going to get Cosette and place her in irons on my pod. I'll take Merlein with me since she's had experience guarding Cosette."

"What are your intentions with Fantine and Cosette, Roy?" Roxanne asked. "I will not support any actions that bring them to physical harm."

"Are mind games okay?" I asked.

"Yes. But both prisoners need to arrive at CisLuna in good physical health."

"On that we are in violent agreement. I too want them arriving at CisLuna in good health, the better to go before a tribunal and get what they deserve. However, I need to milk them for any information they may have that could improve our chances of survival. Dieter is already aware of the little charade I have in mind."

"What about attempting to bring the aft thruster down to flight idle?" the Committee Chair asked.

"Jonathan, that's your call," I said. "The crew will be far enough away from the ship to be out of the debris field. So do you want to attempt it?"

"I want to do whatever poses the least hazard to the crew and the escape pods. Therefore, I believe the best course of action is to wait until you have been rescued and are well on your way back to CisLuna before attempting such a procedure. There is also the option of letting it burn until we run out of fuel when it will shut down by itself. That will speed us out of the Solar System and into more interesting parts of the nearby stars. That survey could prove extremely valuable to SpaceCorp's future expansion plans."

"I wish you luck then. Except for the chance that you may not eradicate your daemon infestation, I'd entertain going with you. What an adventure! And I might actually still be alive when you pass by your first star. How cool is that?"

* * *

The escape pod launch proceeded in an orderly fashion. Nobody got stuck in their launch tube. Only one exit hatch got jammed and that was attributed to a mechanical not digital failure. A maintenance robot was dispatched to force it open from the outside. And all the pods managed to navigate to the rendezvous point without running into any debris or each other. We even managed to salvage the abandoned escape pods that had been secured to the aft flight deck. Now it was time for mind games.

* * *

Merlein and I had left Cosette shackled inside the air lock of our escape pod so she would not be visible to the rest of the crew. Her hands were shackled behind her back and her feet were shackled to each other. She had a waist chain that secured her to the bulkhead wall.

"Here's the deal," I said opening up a display window on the side of the pod. "As you can see your sister is floating outside her escape pod secured by a tether. She has about fifteen minutes of O2 which, coincidently, is how long you have to tell me everything you know about this diabolical little plan of yours to destroy this ship. If I don't hear anything interesting by then, you will join your sister in space and we will let you both drift away never giving you another thought."

After five minutes, she finally broke down.

"Understand I don't know everything. I was a field operative so what I know was compartmentalized in case I got caught. But I heard some things... things like this whole sabotage of *Lunine* was designed to anger SpaceCorp sufficiently to declare war on Persia."

"Why?"

"I don't know exactly. But I heard that our leaders *want* you to attack us and when you do, they will have something waiting for you."

"What might that be?"

"Again I don't know exactly. But they were always going on about some kind of new missile."

"For missiles to reach us in LEO, you have to test them. And we haven't allowed you, or anybody else for that matter, to put anything in space for decades. And let's face it, the technology you used for your last little adventure in space back in... what was it... 2075? Nearly a century ago? Anyway, from what I've read, that was mostly a lucky shot."

"I've told you what I know. They expect a major retaliation from SpaceCorp. And they'll be waiting for you. With what, I'm not sure, but expect some kind of missile. Now, Mr. Stone, are you a man of your word? Are you going to let my sister get back on that pod?"

I didn't answer her directly, but turned my back on her so she couldn't read my lips, then cut over to Dieter. To appease Roxanne, we never really put Fantine outside the pod on a tether. That little imagery was courtesy of Jonathan's animation skills. We did the same thing with Fantine using her sister Cosette's image while Dieter carried out the same line of questioning.

"Did Fantine have anything to say?" I asked.

"Nope, just a bunch of patriotic BS about how their deaths will be avenged by Persia."

I shared with him the revelation I had gotten from Fantine.

"The vengeance thing... sorta corroborates what Cosette told you," Dieter said.

"Yeah... Okay, end of interrogation. Run your retrieval animation. I'm doing the same."

"Copy."

Cosette watched the animation of Fantine being withdrawn into her escape pod's air lock. She looked visibly relieved.

"Did Fantine talk?" Cosette asked.

"Let's just say, you and your sister were saved by the bell. This interrogation is not over... just postponed."

I turned off Cosette's suit comms. I could see her mouthing words through her faceplate... something to the effect of did I expect her to ride all the way back to CisLuna shackled to a bulkhead? I just smiled and patted the side of her helmet with my glove. Then it occurred to me she would be running out of air on her suit tank pretty soon. Since the airlock was up to pressure, I took Fantine's helmet off.

162

"You expect me to stay here in the airlock until we are rescued?"

"Actually I do. You better hope your little daemons didn't infect the computer logic that keeps the door from sliding open."

She started to speak but I put my hand over her mouth.

"Do not speak. If you speak, I will duct tape your mouth and you will feed yourself through a straw for the next sixteen months. Is that clear?"

She nodded.

"Good. This is where you will stay until we can work out some better accommodations for you. You will be fed and watered and someone will see to your diapers. But keep in mind, while your security is a high priority, your welfare is not. Nod if you understand."

She nodded again.

*　　*　　*

When I went back inside the pod's habitat area, I announced to the occupants that we were keeping Cosette prisoner inside the air lock for now.

"Who is she?" someone asked.

"Cosette and her twin sister Fantine were responsible for infecting *Lunine* with the software daemons that were responsible for the destruction of our ship. She and her twin were part of a four-woman cell that committed the two murders—Delia and Monica. The other two cell members are deceased. Cosette and Fantine are all that remain and they are vitally important intelligence sources. Therefore, I implore you to help me keep them alive and in captivity, i.e., do *not* go extracting any personal revenge on them between now and our return to CisLuna."

"What's going to happen to them when they get back?" another person asked.

"More interrogation until we feel like we have garnered as much as we can from them. Then a tribunal. Then... use your imagination."

The nearby occupants stared at us for a moment, then somebody asked, "She gonna stay in the air lock the whole time?"

"For now. Eventually, I expect we'll need the air lock and it would be helpful not to have her taking up so much space. But until we can arrange a better jail, the air lock is where she stays."

Chapter Eighteen

14Mar2152

It took about a week before *Lunine* faded from view, her aft thruster's glowing wake making an easily followed beacon for the unaided eye... at least for a while. A few folks asked for my permission to use the escape pod's enhanced viewing to continue to track *Lunine*. I saw no harm in it but I referred them to the escape pod captain. They said they had already asked her and she said to ask me. I allowed it. A few were content to track her with a map and digital readout showing her distance from us. Everybody maintained a readout showing how many days before we could count on the rescue fleet returning to pick us up. That date was 18Aug2153, a Saturday.

529 days was a long time to be cooped up in zero gee in a tubular coffin whose interior living space measured sixty meters long by fifteen meters in diameter. Each individual had a fully-enclosed more-or-less soundproof cubicle that measured 2.0 by 1.5 by 2.5 meters for a total of 7.5 cubic meters, or 7500 cubic meters shared by 100 passengers. That left about 3000 cubic meters as passage ways, restrooms, and storage areas for vital essentials. O2, water, and food stores went below the floor, wall, and ceiling bulkheads. We had to be

mindful of weight and balance as we retrieved it. The bulkhead spaces also housed the HVAC and CO_2 scrubbers.

A few pet cages were scattered about the various passageways. If a pet was not on the same pod as its original owner for whatever reason, someone adopted it and saw that it was fed, watered, and its cage cleaned. Adoption usually included moving the cage into the foster parent's cubicle. There was no problem keeping the animals entertained—everyone wanted a chance to play with them.

Water purification and waste water treatment equipment went in the aft end of the habitat section. It was carefully sealed to prevent odors from drifting into the living quarters.

We didn't need a galley since we were supposed to subsist on food bars for the duration of our time on the pod. They came in half a dozen different flavors and there were ingredients for coffee, tea, and fixings, plus sundry packs for toilet paper, chewing gum, and feminine hygiene stuff. Reminded me of the old field rations we used to get in the Army. And while we would not be losing any weight on that fare, I wondered if we'd be losing our minds. To that end there was exercise equipment, digital board games, decks of cards, practically the whole Library of Congress in books of all kinds, and an additional library of ten thousand movies. Then there was sex. I did some checking and discovered that the gender ratio was pretty even on all the pod assignments to include LGBTQ persuasions. SpaceCorp thinks of everything.

There was a ten-meter bustle attached to the aft where our nuclear thermal power, maneuver propulsion, and hydrogen propellant went. Behind that was another jettisonable two-meter bustle that held our cold-gas launch propulsion apparatus.

It bears repeating that deep space escape pods were not designed for orbit insertion burns or atmospheric reentry. Basically, they were intended to get you off your mother ship and drift along at whatever velocity the mother ship was doing until you got rescued. To that end, there was some pretty high-powered communications gear, both high gain RF and laser. When rescue day came, everyone was expected to have a space suit. Naturally, in the excitement of evacuating the ship for real and for permanent, some folks arrived without suits. The rescue ships, being fairly substantial craft in their own rights, could be counted on to have spare suits.

So this was going to be home for the next seventeen months. I could see where having gotten used to the spaciousness of a ship like *Lunine*, we were going to start getting on each other's nerves after a few months.

We were sixteen pods and there were eighteen more pods that had been left behind by the folks that departed on Rescue Phase One, as we had come to call it. If we divided up the empties and Siamesed them one or in some cases two per occupied pod, that could give us a lot more room to not get on each other's nerves. Plus we recovered the necessary vital stores we would need to last seventeen months while awaiting Rescue Phase Two. And as a final benefit we would be doubling our redundancy in case something went wrong with our equipment. That operation took two days. Great. Only 527 days to go. Now we just had the zero-gee problem to deal with.

The human body, or for that matter galactican or dog or cat or bird body, gets pretty frail after six months without an

Earth-sized mass tugging at it. Astronauts returning from the ISS had to be lifted out of their space capsules and then ferried about in wheel chairs. There was one poor gal who tried to stand behind a podium to give a short speech the same day she returned to Earth—she fainted in the middle of it. We were looking at *seventeen* months—eleven more months than our comrades on the ISS.

And then I had my own special problem with zero gee, namely my inner ear's vestibular apparatus hates it and when faced with it, complains loud and long to the only other organ that gives a shit, my stomach. My stomach responds by promptly evacuating itself. Not cool when you're buttoned up inside a space suit. I was careful to pack my barf pills but I only had enough for maybe a month unless by some miracle I got my space legs. But who knows how long that could take?

I got all the pod commanders plus Dieter and Rox on a conference frequency.

Roy: We have to do something about the zero-gee problem. Our bodies are never going to last seventeen months.

I didn't mention my queasy stomach. At first there was silence, then Roxanne spoke up.

Roxanne: Do all of you still have your launch bustles?

Being cold gas they were handy for maneuvering around each other. She got yea's from all sixteen commanders.

Roxanne: Good. All we have to do is hook our pods together nose to tail into a giant necklace. It has to be a perfect circle though—no ellipse and no waves. Then we start firing the launch propulsion units in unison a tiny bit at a time to get our circle rotating. Once we get up to speed, it will maintain circularity by itself. Eventually, we should be up to enough centrifugal force to equal a whole gee if you want it.

Dieter: Brilliant! We can rearrange the cubicle partitions without too much trouble so that everyone is more or less right side up.

This project took three weeks including all our false starts. Turns out it's not so easy to arrange 34 escape pods into a nice, neat circle. Every time we thought our circle was even, somebody would goose the throttle on their launch unit a little too much and then we'd be all over the map. But we got it done. And having little need for the robots, we parked them in the vacant pods where they promptly went to sleep.

506 days to go. Now the only problem was getting this contraption stopped without ramming into each other. We'd need to do that when Rescue Phase Two began. It was an essential step lest we risk sending some passenger careening off into deep space during the transfer process. Oh well, that was a headache that could wait for sixteen months.

CHAPTER NINETEEN

01Aug2153

The excitement building up to the actual arrival of the rescue ships was palpable. Recall where many of the couples had split up seventeen months ago one or the other of them insisting that the other make it back to CisLuna. Now a good many of the ones who had gone to CisLuna were back here unable to stand being apart for the extra seven months of the return trip. Love and logic... oil and water.

*   *   *

Cosette, one of our Persian prisoners, decided this was a good time for some histrionics.

"I demand to see my sister!" she said.

"Well, you can't do that," Merlein said. "She's on another escape pod that's loading onto a different ship."

Cosette grabbed onto the huge metal loop her shackles were attached to and kicked at Merlein when she approached her. She had not been a model prisoner. Her hair was unkempt. She smelled, make that reeked, having refused her weekly sponge baths for the last couple of weeks. And you could practically see her breath.

In an attempt at water conservation we did not allow anybody to use the shower. Instead, you went into the stall with two liters of water—one to soap up with and one to rinse off with. Used water went into the gray water drain for recycling. The gray water recycler was an imperfect system at best. After a about three months, it had a peculiar odor to it. You couldn't even brush your teeth with it. Dieter finally figured out how to fix it so that it became odor free and shared the solution with the rest of the pods. Good old Dieter, always happiest when he had something mechanical to futz with.

Merlein was concerned that we would catch hell for prisoner mistreatment if Cosette showed up back at CisLuna in such a disheveled state. She had at first pled with her saying her sister would shun her if she continued to pay so little attention to her hygiene. Since that didn't work, she appealed to Allah saying she had a responsibility to keep herself clean if she expected to go to heaven. Finally, she threatened her with a GI party when she got onto the rescue ship.

"What's a GI party?" Cosette asked.

"It's where a bunch of horny guys hold you down in the shower and scrub the stink off you with bristle brushes. Then they shave your head."

"I don't believe you. You're making that up."

"One way to find out."

"I just want to see my sister, to know she's alive. She's my twin. Identical twins have a bond that the rest of you people cannot understand."

"Would you settle for proof of life?"

171

"No! I need to see her, to touch her, to talk to her!"

Merlein looked at me. I had been staying out of the conversation.

"Sedate her. Get some guys to help you hold her down so you don't get stuck by your own needle. Then strip her and wash her. Cut her hair to a manageable length—not bald and not a buzz cut—a pageboy maybe. Do something about her teeth."

"Same guys?"

"I trust your discretion."

"What am I supposed to do about the hair on her legs and in her arm pits? She hasn't used a depilatory since we locked her up."

Women of SpaceCorp were profoundly concerned about body hair. They insisted on being hairless from the eyebrows down. The preferred method of hair removal was a chemical depilatory that kept them smooth as a silk hankie for several months at a stretch.

"I dunno... braid it? Look use your imagination. But whatever you come up with, we start zeroing our rotational speed in two days. Got that? Two days and then you start to lose the benefit of gravity."

*   *   *

Zeroing our rotational speed was considerably more difficult that speeding up from zero RPM to a full gee. Fortunately, we had had the foresight to arrange the pods nose to nose and tail to tail alternating for the whole thirty-four pods. That way we had an evenly spaced set of cold gas rockets to speed us up and another set of opposite pointing rockets to slow us down. As we added rotational speed centrifugal force worked in our favor to smooth things out. But when slowing down we did not have such an advantage. The net result was that with each goose of the throttles, our 34 escape pods stopped looking like a nice clean circular necklace and instead resembled a plate of spaghetti. The most we got out of the maneuver was that all the pods were holding relative position to one another, i.e., no collisions.

This at least allowed the rescue shuttles to maneuver among us and off-load twenty passengers at a time. That process took about 36 hours counting the robots—there were several hundred of them.

But we finally made it. Everybody, including our Persian Princesses, had found a new home on one of the three rescue ships. We all got to take hot showers and wash our clothes and hang up our space suits. But best of all, we got a cooked meal. It was served buffet style and included meat, fish, poultry, vegetables, fresh bread, and... wait for it... ice cream!

The captain of our ship approached me asking about our little fleet of escape pods.

"They've all been put in a quiescent state. The reactors have been put in idle mode with enough power to keep their transponders lit. Beyond that I don't know what to do about them."

"We can't slow them down," he said.

"You're right. I suppose they'll just keep drifting along until they leave the solar system."

"Any way they'll catch up to *Lunine*?" he asked.

"Nah. The last we heard from *Lunine*, she was crossing Uranus' orbit heading in the general direction of Ross 128, about twelve light years from Sol."

"Then I guess it's time to go home."

"Yes, I think we can all get behind that."

CHAPTER TWENTY

15Apr2154—Back at CisLuna

Hank Larson was on hand to greet me as I debarked from the rescue ship onto *Borucki*.

"I'm sorry I lost your space ship," I said.

"I'm just glad you were there or we could have lost a lot more than that," he said. "C'mon, we've got lots to talk about."

I thought he was going to lead me to his office for a debrief. Instead, he led me to a large war room that was teaming with activity. There were all kinds of charts and maps and timelines on the wall.

"It goes without saying this room and the people in it are as compartmentalized as you can get. TOP SECRET."

"What's this all about?" I asked.

"War. We're going to—"

"—reduce them to a medieval caliphate," I said.

"A what?"

"A medieval caliphate, circa 600 CE. Eliminate all their infrastructure and technology. They won't be able to make so much as a transistor radio for the next thousand years."

"I see your mind has not been idle for the last seven months. Where did you come up with all that?"

"It's a promise I made to Jonathan just before we parted company. He asked me to make sure this can never happen again."

"Interesting. Why a medieval caliphate? Why not just erase them? Total annihilation."

"The problem with Persia is not so much its people but its leadership. They advertise themselves as sons of Muhammad but in reality they are just cheap dictators out for power and nothing else. If we can eliminate them—along with their religious and political and military and technological infrastructure—the people would be left to their own devices to form a new society. One based on the lifestyle of the region shortly after Muhammad died. Let them live under tents and get about by camelback. Let them grow crops with hand tools. Let them fish in the sea with sail-powered fishing boats. No vehicles save wagons and carts. No motors. No electricity. Light solely from lanterns and candles. No oil. No foreign exploitation. No computers, no radios, no TVs, no movies, no internet. News will be obtained by word of mouth. Most of the people get to live. The government and military leadership die. We will tell the world that we will not tolerate what Persia did to us and we will not allow them to ever do such a thing again. But we will not become international pariahs in the process."

"And how do we pull this off?"

"That's what I'm hoping the folks you have gathered in this room will determine."

"And what about the two prisoners you brought back with you?"

"They stand before a military tribunal."

"When?"

"As soon as possible."

"You realize they will likely be found guilty and sentenced to death?"

"I do. But the sentence should be delayed until after we finish with Persia. There is always the possibility they may still know more about Persia's 'ambush' for us."

"Ambush?"

"Yes, what we have found out so far is that Persia planned this whole operation with the motive of inciting us to declare war on them. And when we do, they plan to ambush us with some new kind of missile, details of which are unknown."

"And you have reason to believe this new missile is viable in spite of our moratorium on space launches?"

"You never know with them."

"Very well, Roy. I am hereby placing you in command of this room and everyone in it. I'll expect weekly debriefs until you feel we are ready to strike. At that time, you will be transferred to *SSS Frank Buzzard* to assist with carrying out your plan."

I came to attention and saluted, "Aye Aye, sir."

"Knock it off!"

CHAPTER TWENTY-ONE

05Oct2154—The Family Plot on Devil's Peak, Tycho Crater

Roxanne and I took Monica's ashes to the burial site atop Devil's Peak in Tycho Crater. Emily's and Devil's ashes were still safely tucked away in the crevice at the base of the soccer-field-sized boulder that sat atop Devil's Peak. That had been almost 70 years ago. Each one's ashes were contained in a standard form factor 1.5-liter champagne bottle complete with a new wire-wrapped cork. The bottles were relabeled with a nice picture of the occupant and the usual biographical data one finds on Earthside cemetery headstones.

"Is this the family plot?" Roxanne asked. She had never been here before and until now she had had no need to.

"Starting to look that way."

After Roxanne placed Monica's ashes inside the crevice, we stood in reverence for a few seconds.

"Is one of us supposed to say something?" Roxanne asked.

I paused a few seconds. "I guess I'm sorry I didn't get to the dead man's switch quicker."

"Me too. On the other hand, if you had, we might not be having this conversation."

"We should get back to the scooter. We were thirty minutes from bingo when we landed."

As we walked back to the scooter Roxanne asked, "So what's next?"

"War. I've been working with Hank. He's got a whole team doing the planning. We've put up with Persia's shenanigans long enough. It's time to teach them a lesson. Hank wants me to sign on with the Space Force. There's supposed to be a new armed space station, *SSS Frank Buzzard*."

"Can I come?"

I stopped and turned to face her. "Roxanne, you are a living treasure whose loss cannot be countenanced. Your mom would want someone to carry on her work. You said yourself, there's still a lot to learn about genetically engineered humans and galacticans."

"Okay, but if I promise to stay out of it, you have to promise to come home in one piece."

"Deal. I'm pretty good at getting myself out of tough scrapes. As for the people around me... not so much. I'll feel a little better knowing you're no closer to Earth than CisLuna."

*   *   *

Roxanne was full of questions on the way back to *Borucki* from the Lunar Surface. I couldn't give her much information since she didn't have a need to know. The truth is I'd already had a long conversation with Hank Larsen, several in fact. He was particularly bothered by the ominous warning we had garnered from Cosette about how the destruction of *Lunine* had been a setup to goad us into attacking Persia and how they'd be waiting for us if we did. Neither of us were keen to send *Buzzard* and her crew into a trap.

PART TWO

War

CHAPTER TWENTY-TWO

15Jun2154 1130 HRS—Arrival at *SSS Frank Buzzard*

I made the hop from CisLuna down to LEO on board a nuclear shuttle, *SpaceCorp LEO Shuttle (SLS) Butler Hine-214.* All CisLuna-to-LEO shuttles are *Butler Hine*-class and have the same name just with a different number hyphenated to the end—the higher the number the more recent the technology. Equipped with nuclear rockets, it could do the trip in only six hours—a considerable advantage since her unpressurized interior forced us to remain suited the entire time. In full gee that would have been pretty uncomfortable, but *-214* was zero gee so it wasn't too bad so long as I remembered my barf pills.

The reason *Butler Hine*-class shuttles were unpressurized was because with all the debris still whizzing around in LEO, there was a very real chance that while passing through LEO your hull could be penetrated by a 27,000 kmph bullet. At that velocity the projectile would pass through both walls in a split second. But with no internal atmosphere it was pretty much a non-event... unless the projectile happened to hit a passenger. I was on a different kind of shuttle a long time ago when somebody got drilled. We were coming up from surface with a quick stop at one of our stations in LEO—I forget the name—

before heading out to *Borucki* in CisLuna. I didn't actually know the poor guy, but right in the middle of our chit chat he just sorta quit talking and the inside of his facemask suddenly became painted over with pink mist. Nasty business. Scary too. These things often travel in swarms making you wonder if there might be another one coming along with your name on it. We taped over the entry and exit openings on his helmet to keep the blood and brain matter from spraying out into the vacuum of the shuttle interior. The pilot notified *Borucki* that we had a stiff and would need assistance with extraction when we got there. After that there wasn't much chit chat for the rest of the trip. It's funny thinking back on that incident. Everyone dummied up, as if by talking you might give away your position and make you a target for the next piece of debris.

I pulled up an image of *SSS Frank Buzzard* when we were about ten thousand klicks out. No portholes on shuttles but lotsa sensors we can access though. She looked just like her commercial brethren that had made SpaceCorp so essential and yet so hated in the global community that depended on us for sensor data, and communications and navigation services. The resemblance ceased abruptly once you got on board. Underneath all that exterior armor designed to survive hypervelocity debris left over from the Kessler Syndrome, she was a warrior and with a chip on her shoulder at that.

Prior to my arrival, I'd read a lot of classified spec sheets on *Buzzard* to include the CV of her namesake. What do ya know, the old guy was an ex-warrant officer like me, only a pilot instead of a cop! He flew Chinook helicopters for the One-Oh-Wonderful in Vietnam back in the sixties, that's the *nineteen* sixties, mind you, a loooong fuckin time ago! How cool is that?

183

Anyway, after he finished with the Army, he went to college in Colorado, and after that joined up with NASA eventually becoming a Chief Engineer on the Space Shuttle and later the ISS. His mugshot showed a nice old man, a kind of grandfatherly sort with a warm smile. And SpaceCorp picked a sweet old man like him for our first purpose-built warship! My experience with Army pilots back in the day was that it was always the gentle, calm looking ones that turned out to have the carbon-nano-nerves when the shit started flying around.

Up to now all our LEO-based space stations had been armed with X-ray lasers—usually a half dozen on the bottom and another half dozen topside. They were there primarily for self-defense after the Persians tried to shoot down *SSS Albert Einstein* with an old *Shahab-7* missile. Bastards nearly succeeded too. *Einstein* only had one cannon and the designer, also Monica's first husband and SpaceCorp's Chief Scientist, Logan MacGregor, had to decide between mounting it topside or bottomside—a coin toss. He went with bottomside, so naturally the fickle bitch that is fate brought the incoming missile in for a top attack. Captain Lalli Dinesh was one shrewd cookie though. She figured the missile would aim for center of mass, so she had the station jettison its central hub and spokes and scoot them out of the way. With the hub and spokes gone, that left a half km of empty space. The missile passed right through the ring with her proximity fuses failing to detonate. Monica told me they had quite a time recovering the hub and spokes—she was very instrumental in that operation. I used to get her a little tipsy and then cajole her into telling the story yet again to see if it got any better. It never did. Always the same with every telling regardless of the alcohol level—that broad could hold her hooch.

Meanwhile, when our standard LEO-based stations weren't using their laser cannon to fend off hostile missiles, they served a secondary role in keeping the skies clear of any non-SpaceCorp missile and satellite traffic. Our fleet of heavily armored, self-repairing space stations were the only viable recce, comms, and nav platforms that could survive up here amidst all the debris whizzing by at 27,000 kmph. At that speed all it took was a wing-nut to take out a whole sensor node. Since we didn't need a bunch of idiots making a bad situation worse, SpaceCorp had declared long ago anything above 100 km, i.e., the Kármán Line or the beginning of space to laypersons, to be off limits. Naturally, everybody tried to ignore us, so we added laser cannon to all our LEO platforms to enforce what later became known as the Clear Skies Doctrine.

Clear Skies was a policy SpaceCorp had decreed and enforced ever since a number of rogue nations had developed the hobby of shooting down derelict satellites and rocket parts. It was not enough for these juvenile delinquents to merely join the nuclear club, especially since their nuclear arsenals had turned out to be non-credible threats in that they were very expensive to develop and maintain—a huge drain on GDP— and, apart from suitcase terror bombs, their delivery systems were even more expensive to develop and maintain. But most importantly, there was a tacit understanding among the global nuclear community that if some dickhead dictator decided to nuke his neighbor, he would soon discover that the rest of the world could and would rapidly convert his country into a blank space on the map—the MAD doctrine of the Cold War all over again, a tense but otherwise reliable peace. It had yet to actually happen—thank goodness—but all the nuclear nations had signed an agreement attesting to that intent about a century ago. Hence, having a nuclear arsenal gave way to the hobby of shooting down space debris to advertise one's high-tech entrance onto the world stage which in turn begat the Clear Skies Doctrine.

*   *   *

Once I got inside, *Buzzard* was way different from the standard recce-comms-nav platforms. She packed a lot more cannon—a hundred on the bottom and another fifty topside. But they weren't X-ray lasers. Nope. And this is super-classified—as in after you read this I need you to go shoot yourself to keep me out of jail. These were gamma-ray lasers with beam directors as big as school buses. Previously believed only theoretically possible, gamma ray lasers were the very first of their kind. From what I could tell—I'm still not as technical as I'd like to be—one burst and whatever they hit disappears, as in... evaporates. My limited understanding is that a gamma ray laser beam will reduce every molecule it encounters to its constituent elements by destroying all the chemical bonds between atoms—Marvin the Martian's™ Explosive Space Modulator™ only this one included the Kaboom™.

They also had a pretty high rate of fire which was surprising. The shorter the wavelength, the more energy the laser signal carries and that energy has to come from somewhere. As such, *Buzzard* was loaded with banks of ultracapacitors that were constantly being topped off with her onboard reactors. That gave her a target servicing rate of 300 per minute bottomside and 150 topside and she could keep that up almost indefinitely. Put another way, orbiting west to east at 800 km and traveling 27,000 kmph, *Buzzard* could eliminate over 800 targets across the greatest north to south width of Persia (~1000 km, i.e., practically the whole country) in under three minutes. That's assuming a target servicing swath of 1000 km and using a whisk broom array for the bottomside cannon only. Obviously, target coordinates had to be known in advance to minimize the combined slewing moment from the cannon array. With a hundred beam directors as big as school buses jerking around, it was bound to start vibrating the rest of the station. But still, a whole country bigger than Alaska in under three minutes! And I'm not talking about a vast charred wasteland. No, I'm talking 800 *surgical* strikes.

She carried very few commercial sensors unless you count radars and she had a ton of those—all data-fused and all set up for target early warning, acquisition, and tracking. She carried no remote sensor platforms as was becoming common on interplanetary craft. They had been considered during the design phase but abandoned in light of the heavy debris concentrations that still plagued LEO. She packed ten times the thrust of her commercial brethren—hence all the handholds in the gangways.

Her crew was stripped down to 1200—400 per watch— about half what you'd find on a commercial vessel. Unlike her commercial sisters, she carried no crewmember's families, not even dogs or cats. Everyone on board served a dedicated military function. About a third of the crew was damage control, and the other two thirds split between weapon systems and NavOps. Weapon systems personnel were mostly SpaceCorp Marines. Damage control and NavOps tended to be Navy. There were a few civilian technicians—contract engineers for the more intricate weapons and the power supplies that went with them. All systems throughout the station were designed with dual personalities—automated for efficiency but with manual backup so as to take a hit but keep fighting.

Once through the air lock, my minder, a young gal with the name 'RODRIGUEZ, Eddy' stenciled across her right breast, showed me where to stow my suit. She wore the fitted spacesuit of a SpaceCorp Marine which was the same cut as the spacesuit of the SpaceCorp Naval personnel only olive in color and with a gaudy red stripe down the outside of the sleeves and pant legs. Fucking jarheads... Naval personnel had a deep blue suit with a white piping down the sleeves and trousers. Civilian technicians wore the same form factor suit but in burnt orange with no piping. That told me something about the civilians on board—they weren't just here for the fitting out. Their suits were every bit as military as the marines and sailors, so they were gonna still be here when the shooting started.

"Where you get this antique?" Eddy asked with no effort to camouflage her sarcasm. "Man, you gonna need two lockers to put all that shit away."

Her accent suggested East LA. I wondered if she'd been a banger. SpaceCorp had recruited a number of them to guard the eastern border against encroachment by oversized Mormon families from Promised Land. I'd worked with some of them around Needles back when I was new to Sierra. God, that must have been eighty years ago! They were a gutsy *don't-back-down-for-no-stinkin-farmer* lot, disinclined to suffer fools, and preferring non-diplomatic solutions.

Eying her nametag, I asked, "You go by Eddy?"

"Yeah, my friends call me Eddy... you can call me Lance Corporal Rodriguez. What should I call you, seeing as how you forgot your nametag."

She was going to be fun. I continued our conversation while I peeled out of my suit. To be honest, I was relieved to be out of it. At *Buzzard's* gee level it weighed 150 kg without the backpack propulsion system and I was sweating by the time we got to the lockers in spite of the internal temperature control.

"Very well... Corporal, you can call me Roy. Actually this suit is not particularly old. It was designed for the extreme cold of Enceladus, my last mission."

I couldn't tell for sure if my dropping the name 'Enceladus' registered with her. I thought I caught one eyebrow raising, and maybe a bit more deferential tone in her voice.

"Well... Roy, if they accept you, you're gonna need to trade that thing in for a *military* suit."

She thought I was here interviewing for a position. At least that part of my cover had not yet been blown. Her suit was a lot more form-fitting with thin plates of some kind of high-tech armor covering her vitals. I guessed it to be around 50 kg including the life support unit although to be honest the life support didn't look like it was good for more than a few hours. And it didn't look like it was very heavily insulated unless the techies on the Surface had come up with something more Buck Rodgers than I was wearing. Her helmet had several different kinds of faceplates that could be pulled down as

189

needed. Her gloves were very thin and dexterous—probably not very warm, but definitely better at manipulating controls or, for that matter, the piece she was wearing on her hip.

I grinned and pointed at her sidearm. "Can I get me a fancy ray gun too?"

"No. In fact I'm personally gonna see to it you don't get a weapon at all, grandpa! Can't have people with cataracts shooting up the place."

Grandpa? Cataracts? Truth be told, almost every human who'd gone through life extension had fine-focus artificial lenses that were indiscernible to the casual observer. With my 20/5 vision, I could have read her name tag from a hundred meters out. But I kept all that to myself while I stowed the rest of my gear in my locker and latched the door. No locks on suit lockers. Partly the honor system, but mostly practicality—when you needed your shit, you tended to need it in a hurry. Instead, I put a clean piece of tape on the door and wrote my name in proper SpaceCorp format, STONE, Roy. Eddy looked at it and turned pale.

"You're Roy Stone? From that ship the Persians fucked up? Oh, shit..."

"The same. *SIS Jonathan Lunine*, may Sol entrust her to the heavens."

"I'm sorry for your loss, Sir."

"So am I."

At that moment an image appeared on the wall. *Buzzard*, like all SpaceCorp ships and stations, used display paper like wallpaper. The image was the station's human captain, Raquel Hernandez—Hispanic female, age at life extension: 66, or so I had read. Hernandez looked like her life extension treatment had been recent since her physical features still looked more like 66 than the 40 or so that most older extendees settled into after a decade or so. She wore her hair in an asymmetrical crop with the bangs cut to stay out of her eyes—not quite ugly but still a long way from attractive.

"Eddy, please escort Mr. Stone to the bridge."

The image disappeared before she could answer.

"Follow me, please."

It took us about twenty minutes to get to the bridge. Eddy did not knock, just opened the hatch using a remote ID attached to her breast with hook-and-loop. She motioned me in but did not follow. I heard the hatch suction itself closed behind me.

15Jun2154 1300 HRS—War Planning

Captain Hernandez was flanked by two staff officers, a Commander named Pinto—Hispanic male about 40, and a Lieutenant Commander named Smythe, Caucasian female maybe late thirties, both human, not galactican. I fought off the vestigial urge to salute left over from my Army days, opting to stand at semi-attention and nod.

"You were on *Lunine*," Hernandez said.

"Yes, I was. Chief of Security and HMFIC of various other disasters."

The HMFIC reference elicited some veiled snickers from Pinto and Smythe.

"I knew Monica... long before you two were married. I'm sorry for your loss."

"Thank you," I said. "How did you know her?"

191

"She and Mack MacGregor were visiting scientists on *Von Braun* when it got shot down by the Persian Space Agency. Her escape pod crashed on ejection—she was the sole survivor. I rescued her with my pod. She was a brave and resourceful woman."

"No argument there, although most people remember her as the 'Eve' to all the galacticans."

"Let's move into the briefing room. Captain Buzzard and Hank Larson should be waiting."

*   *   *

The briefing room was off to the side of the bridge. It had a large boardroom style table going down the middle with cozy seating for twelve. Various situational displays plastered the surrounding walls. At the far end of the room was an avatar of the station's digital captain, Frank Buzzard, that looked just like his picture in the CV. Next to him was an image of none other than Hank Larson, SpaceCorp's CEO. Kind of a weird title since he was now basically in charge of all of Sierra.

I nodded to each of their images, "Captain Buzzard... hello, Hank."

"These are my key staff members," Hernandez said, "Commander Pinto, Ops, and Commander Smythe, Intel. Let's take our seats and then, I understand Mr. Stone... is that correct, Mister? You don't have a formal rank?"

"Mister is good, Roy is better."

"Very well, I believe Roy has something to share with us."

Hank and I had gone over everything I was going to present at this meeting a week ago. What I was about to say had been several months in preparation so I was confident that I had good material. I hoped Hernandez would buy it and that there wouldn't be some nasty row.

"To kick things off," Hernandez said, "do you have a mission statement for us?"

"I do. Simply put, our mission is to reduce Persia to a primitive medieval caliphate. In doing so, we will avoid endangering civilian population centers. Of course, personnel associated with Persia's warfighting capability and technological infrastructure are both fair game.

"Ironically, reducing Persia to a primitive caliphate should sit fairly well with their surviving religious leaders since they've never been fond of technology anyway, having romanticized the era following Muhammad's siege of Mecca in 632 CE. Post-war Persia will essentially become a nation of nomadic herders, subsistence farmers, and primitive fishermen. Their oil deposits will be capped off and thereafter stay in the ground— that should not sit well with them as it is their main source of money. They will be forbidden the technology to extract said oil, and more importantly, no foreign powers, e.g., France, Britain, will be allowed to take up the technological slack. Nor will any ancient enemies be allowed to invade to extract their own vengeance, e.g., Iraq, Kurdistan.

"They will not be permitted electricity, either for power, lighting, communication, or computation. Land transportation will be limited to camels, horses, and feet while sea transportation will consist of small wind- or oar-powered boats. No aircraft of any kind—not even hot air balloons. Water use will be restricted to simple fishing and limited trade no more than ten km off the shores of the Caspian Sea and Persian

Gulf. No boats will be allowed south of the Straits of Hormuz. Most of what I have described thus far can be accomplished using *Buzzard's* laser cannon.

"Their conventional military infrastructure will also be taken out with laser cannon. That would include armor, artillery, drone facilities, infantry, fighter/bomber/reconnaissance/cargo aircraft, helicopters, and naval vessels.

"Their underground nuclear bomb-making assets may require boots on the ground since in most cases they are buried so deep we cannot penetrate with even nuclear bombs. Nor would we want to. SpaceCorp is already seen as a heavy-handed tyrant by much of the world as it is. We don't need to prove the point by visiting a vast cloud of fallout on the nations to the east. So boots on the ground in this case refers to finding the access and ventilation points to the underground facilities and then sealing them off. We do not need to fight our way in to the underground facilities to destroy anything. Simple interment of underground personnel and equipment is sufficient. Lack of air, food, and water will do the rest.

"Their space forces are another matter. Recall our taking them out shortly after *Von Braun* was shot down. Well, we have reason to believe that since then they have actually been licking their wounds in a subterranean enclave under Mount Dena in the Zagros Mountains.

"Now here's the hitch. We captured intelligence sources on *Lunine* before she was incapacitated. They implied that the destruction of *Lunine* was done with the primary intent of baiting us to attack Persia and that they would be waiting for us when we did. Finally, they implied that Persia's retaliation would come in the form of a new missile. They offered no details as to the type and capabilities of this missile, but they seemed pretty smug about the outcome. We have an analysis about how they might respond to our attack if you're interested."

"Oh, I'm *very* interested," Hernandez said. "But first tell me about these sources of yours. Who are they? And how credible are they?"

"During the Enceladus mission, we were infiltrated by four Persian operatives—all female. One was killed in the suicide bombing that murdered Monica. One was suffocated while locked in her holding cell during a hull breach when the ship began to come apart. The other two were saved and are currently in custody at CisLuna. They happen to be identical twins who maintain a close bond with one another. While we were on the way home, we used that bond to play one off against the other. It was in this manner that I learned of Persia's plans to incite an attack from SpaceCorp by taking out *Lunine*."

"And they just burst forth with all this good information due to a sudden turn of conscience?" Hernandez asked.

"Hardly. It turns out their love for each other was greater than their love for Persia. By threatening to space one, the other became quite loquacious. Bear in mind that as field operatives, they were highly compartmentalized and not privy to their higher ups' thinking. However, even though compartmentalized, they were able to pick up bits and pieces of information—hallway gossip, etc."

"Do you trust them?"

"Not at all. They have each been found guilty by a military tribunal and sentenced to be executed. We have suspended that sentence only so long as their stories check out. I have impressed upon them that the first flaw I uncover, I will flip a coin. The loser gets a date with the garotte. It goes without saying that a key part of this plan going forward is to check out their story while minimizing the risk to ourselves.

"In any event, the takeaway message is that we should NOT attack headlong into Persia as though they are naïve and defenseless. So while I do not trust our informants, I do trust that Persia is waiting for us."

"Okay, what do you think would happen if we did attack them headlong?" Hernandez asked.

"We speculate they would engage this space station with a large swarm of hypervelocity missiles equipped with multiple low-yield nuclear submunitions. As you know, blast effects from nuclear warheads are negligible in the vacuum of space. So they would maximize damage with point-of-impact detonations for which you don't need a large yield to penetrate a space station—250 equivalent tonnes, not kilotonnes, of TNT per warhead would be more than sufficient. We believe they may have copied the design of our Cold War era W54 warhead. As such, each submunition could be as small as 28 cm diameter by 40 cm height—a 20-liter pail—and weigh about 23 kg neglecting propulsion.

"We expect the missiles would be guided up to the point the submunitions are deployed—perhaps ten km from the target. We further anticipate that the warheads are not independently targetable, i.e., they would continue on a ballistic intercept trajectory with each warhead naturally separating from its brethren like a pellet from a shotgun shell. Keep in mind they'll all be heading for the same target—us. We do not expect them to use decoys or flares—a fully functional warhead can easily act as a decoy or flare so why waste the mass?

"So there could be as many as twenty of these submunitions per missile assuming each one includes some form of post-release propulsion. At any rate, eliminating the host missile during the boost phase is essential in spite of our prodigious target servicing rate. Remember, we only have the one station and they could conceivably loft thousands of submunitions at a time of which only one needs to get through.

"Once they acquire us, their missiles would be launched simultaneously from a large fleet of commercial looking semi-trucks—their budget transporter erector launchers or TELs. Long range target acquisition from our Geostationary-based Synthetic Aperture Radars or SARs suggests that at least a thousand TELs have already been deployed, although the number could be much higher. Confusing the situation we may count on a lot of civilian truck traffic in play at any given time. Figure also that they may have hidden a large number of TELs in warehouses before we figured out they were using commercial semitrucks as TELs.

"We know they have early warning systems spread throughout the Zagros Mountains in anticipation of our attack coming from west-to-east. Plus they have another early warning network in the Elburz Mountains in case we do a north-to-south attack. I figure the Mount Dena facility has been spewing out TELs for several decades now, so we can expect a sizeable cluster of TELs to be concentrated around each of their major cities. That would include Tehran and Tabriz to the northwest, Mashad to the northeast, and probably Shiraz on the west coast, with the rest scattered around military facilities such as the Imam Khomeini Space Launch Terminal near Semnan in the north central part of the nation, the entry/exits to the Mt. Dena facility itself, and the myriad transportation hubs throughout the country.

"In any event, we expect an attack on any major city would be met with a salvo of 100 or so missiles carrying a combined total of up to 2000 submunitions. At the altitude we'd be flying, an attack on a single city would be construed as an attack on all her neighboring cities and other targets of interest. A single pass over the country would likely be met with tens of thousands of submunitions. I'm assuming we would not be able to pick off all their missiles in the boost phase since we'll be detected by their early warning system and their missiles will launch before we clear the Zagros or Elburz ridgelines. That means their submunitions will already have been released to greet us as we come over the ridge.

"Another uncertainty is whether they will deploy their warheads above or below our flight path before we arrive. We might be expecting to engage them from below and be totally unprepared for a top attack. I noticed in the technical literature that your laser cannon tend to be concentrated on the undersides of this space station.

"Anyway, after launching their missiles, each TEL would return to Mt. Dena to reload, then redeploy for the next attack. Post launch, a return to Mt. Dena could require a couple of days before they get back on station. Every time we eliminate a TEL, they can probably hatch a new one from Mt. Dena pretty quickly. But if we lose our sole battle station, the war is over for us for at least a year, unless they continue the attack with ICBMs in which case it could be over for a lot longer than that."

"Sobering," Hernandez said after a long pause.

"Bear in mind what I just told you is a very pessimistic speculation. With the moratorium on rocket launches we've had in place for the last fifty years, any rocket development they've been doing under Mt. Dena will have been without benefit of live testing. For all we know, every time they hit the launch button, the missile could blow up before it leaves the TEL."

"Point taken. Any thoughts as to what to do in case their R&D process has been lucky?"

"Yes. Before we commit our one and only battle station, we should attempt to spook them into an attack with a couple of flights of six drones each. Each drone would be the same form factor as *Buzzard*, only limited to 200 meters in diameter. Each one would be armed with a pair of gamma ray laser cannon and adequate sensors to pick out likely targets—early warning radar sites, or if we don't find any of those, prepositioned TELs. Being unmanned, the drones are expendable, so we'll spread them out—maybe five kilometers apart. We want them to flush out as many of the enemy defenses as possible.

"We'll monitor the battle from GEO with our Space-Based Infrared System or SBIRS. It is critical to know just how much of their ground defense assets they commit to attacking our drones. If they commit everything they have in a mass launching, we can follow up with *Buzzard* and focus on taking out the TELs as they are returning to their resupply points in and around Mt. Dena. If they don't commit everything, we'll need to follow up with another drone attack ninety minutes after the first. It's imperative that we not risk *Buzzard* while they still have unfired, intact assets on the ground.

199

"We should also time the attack of *Buzzard* so we have good fixes on the entry points to their underground Mt. Dena facility. We can do that using our GEO-based SAR network to track some of their semi-truck launchers as they head back to the barn for reloading.

"As I mentioned before, we need to be on the lookout for pre-deployed reloads in nearby warehouses. That would obviate the need for them to go all the way back to Mt. Dena. And there is another possibility that once a launcher has expended its missile, it will simply be abandoned in anticipation of a new fleet of semi-truck launchers issuing forth from Mt. Dena. Again, under no circumstances should we commit *Buzzard* until we know exactly what is going on. If we lose *Buzzard*, we will have no means of defending the Sierra mainland against an ICBM attack.

"Part of our main attack should include small nuclear warheads designed to fly into the entry points at Mt. Dena and detonate thereby sealing off the facility. Later, boots on the ground can hunt for secondary entry/exits and ventilation shafts which they can subsequently seal off."

"Where are we supposed to get these drones?" Hernandez asked. "And assuming we can get them, how long of a lead time should we expect?"

"The drones have already been built—a dozen of them— and they are orbiting around CisLuna's L1 LaGrange Point. We commandeered a bunch of *Butler Hine*-class shuttles and outfitted each of them with two gamma ray laser cannon mounted on opposing trusses amidships. The interior where the passengers would have gone is now used for a bank of ultracapacitors to keep the lasers powered. The propulsion units are bimodal so they can make thrust as well as provide juice to keep the ultracaps topped off. Each cannon has the same rate of fire as *Buzzard's* cannon but only for ten minutes—about the time it takes to pass over Persia. Then they spend the rest of the orbit recharging the ultracaps for the next pass. But the best part is the balloons!"

"Balloons?"

"Yes, each drone will deploy a giant disc-shaped balloon so they look like regular space stations only about one fourth the actual size."

"Won't space debris tear up the fabric?"

"Of course, but we won't deploy the balloons until just before they are ready for their pass. Being very low pressure, it only takes about five minutes to gas them up. We recommend a flight of six coming in from the west and concentrating on the Zagros radar sites while at the same time another flight of six hits the Elburz radar sites. That should pretty much blind them. Our SBIRS will be watching to see if our flights are challenged with missile countermeasures. More importantly, we want to see what kind and from where those missiles are launched. Then the survivors of the first pass can start knocking off TELs on the next pass.

"Ideally, *Buzzard* should not overfly the country until there are no more missiles. We guesstimate that could take four or five passes."

"Do you really think this drone fleet will cause them to commit their whole force?" Hernandez asked.

"Yes, especially since in addition to the two lasers on each drone they are also packing a half dozen 'Rods from God' or rocket-assisted tungsten Kinetic Energy projectiles—each one about 20 meters long by a half meter in diameter. That's seventy-two KE projectiles in all, each one packing the explosive force of about fifty tonnes of TNT."

"Fifty tonnes... how much is that in dog years?"

"With an impact velocity of about seven km/s, the blast effect would create a crater about 150 meters wide by 50 meters deep. Overpressure waves on the surface would flatten most urban structures out to about a kilometer. In other words, it's a true blockbuster, as in land one of these on any given city block and it will be no more."

I let that sink in for a moment then continued...

"The current plan calls for using KE projectiles to target Persia's many underground facilities where all their sensitive nuclear capabilities are housed. Between the laser cannon and the KE projectiles, the Persians should be led to believe we're throwing everything we've got at them in the first wave. We want them to see our attack as an existential threat and respond accordingly.

"With their missile forces and underground facilities knocked out, *Buzzard's* job will be to take out the rest of their infrastructure—powerplants, communications towers, factories, dams, etc. In other words, create the medieval caliphate we were talking about. But we emphasize, we don't want *Buzzard* overflying the country until we are certain they are completely disarmed."

Hernandez got up and paced around the room for a good two minutes before answering. "Okay, I'm in on one condition. I want a real, full-sized space station to overfly Persia after we finish our drone attack. It would be unmanned and loaded to the gills with cannon—top and bottomside. What doesn't flush from the drone flyover, will certainly flush with a full-size space station flying over with a hundred high-powered laser cannon blazing away."

I turned to Hank, "Hank?"

"We can do that, but the full-sized space station will have to be *Frank Buzzard*," Hank said.

"In that case," Hernandez said, "we reserve the right to abort our part of the mission if the drone force is eliminated before the Persian missile force is. As you pointed out several times, if we lose *Buzzard*, Sierra has no defense against a possible ICBM attack."

"You raise a good point," Hank said, "but the question then is will *Buzzard* be able to eliminate a full-on ICBM attack? What I mean is, by then your trajectory will be known and they can time their launch such that you won't be able to intercept the missile track."

"Touché," Hernandez said. "Then I suggest we outfit some more space stations to act as a rear guard in case we are out of position to defend against an ICBM launch. How many more gamma ray laser cannon do you have?"

"I'm afraid between *Buzzard* and the drone fleet, that's all of them," Hank said.

I decided to jump in, "Let's keep in mind that A) we don't know if they have an ICBM fleet, and B) if they do, neither we nor they know if it's functional. Designing and building an ICBM fleet is pretty much a waste of resources if you can't do a test flight... *many* test flights actually."

"May I offer a few thoughts?" Captain Buzzard asked.

"Of course," Hank said.

"Roy is correct, but the downside risk is too great in case Persia has somehow managed to collect a functional ICBM fleet in secret. For example, the Russians *claimed* they scrapped their ICBMs in return for our providing them with the sensor-nav-comms benefits of our space stations. We *know* we provided Russia the sensor-nav-comms benefits but we don't know if Russia *really* scrapped all of her ICBMs.

"Moreover Russia's periodic bouts of financial distress over the years are well-documented, e.g., the bankruptcy following the Ukraine invasion of 2022-26. She may have succumbed to the temptation to auction off a few of her obsolete designs in order to make ends meet. It would have been easy for her to sell and deliver a few of them to Persia. For example, many Russian ICBMs were designed to operate out of mobile TELs. The RS-24 Yars, first deployed in 2011, is MIRV-equipped with a range of 12,000 km and a CEP of 150 m. Warhead yields vary from 150 to 500 kilotons."

"2011! That's ancient!" Hank said. "Their plutonium pits must have decayed well past their use-by date by now. You're not suggesting Persians have the expertise to manufacture new ones?"

"You are correct in that bomb-grade plutonium pits are typically only reliable for about a century," Captain Buzzard said. "But old pit material can be recycled and fashioned into new fully functional pits. And while this technique won't yield as many pits as you started with, there is no shortage of bomb-grade plutonium in Persia to make up the difference. I caution you not to underrate Mideastern resourcefulness.

"Anyway, being TEL-based rather than silo-based, they would have been suitable for transport across the Russian border into Persia having only to pass through Azerbaijan or alternatively bypass Azerbaijan and transport across the Caspian Sea. It is well-known that before SpaceCorp reactivated the Space Based Infrared LIDAR System, we did not have eyes on every hectare of the Earth. Back then an enemy could have timed their TEL movements to only take place when they were not being observed, taking cover in warehouses or under camouflage nets while sensors were passing overhead. Or if they exercised the Caspian Sea option, a half dozen TELs could have been disguised to look like a stack of containers on a cargo ship.

"And let's not forget their SLBMs. The Bulava RSM-56 SLBM can launch six to ten 150-KT MIRVs over 9,000 km. They're deployed on the Borei- and Arcturus-class SSBNs, both of which are nuclear and capable of remaining on station for up to six months. But I ask you, how hard is it to redeploy a few of these subs from Russian submarine bastions—the Barents Sea for the Russian Atlantic Fleet and/or the Sea of Okhotsk for the Pacific Fleet? For nuclear subs, a trip to the Arabian Sea from one of those bastions is not that difficult assuming they've kept up their hulls and reactors.

"Lastly, there is Russia's Poseidon system, a nuclear powered 10,000-km range stealth torpedo with an estimated yield of up to 100 MT. If Russia sold a half dozen Poseidon's to Persia, all of our coastal cities could be wiped out and we'd be powerless to do anything about it. SpaceCorp may own space but it has paid scant attention to the oceans."

"We had inspectors on site when the demolitions took place," Hank said. "I insisted on that! And your conjecture about them keeping up their submarine hulls and reactors, and their missiles is a long shot—that's three complex systems that all have to be kept in working order, each in a difficult environment. The Russians, while noted for coming up with state-of-the-art weapon systems, are not noted for maintaining those systems once they have outlived their propaganda value."

"Yes," Captain Buzzard said. "The reluctance the Russians have shown for keeping complex weapon systems operational is well known. Just as the ability of Persians to refurbish and maintain said complex weapon systems is also well known. And while it may very well be a long shot, do you want to risk it?"

"Do you really think the Persians could have kept something as complex as an ICBM or an SLBM-equipped submarine operational all these decades?" Hank asked. "Without the benefit of a steady stream of spare parts? And consider the training burden! Where would they get all those personnel?"

"Yes, I do," Captain Buzzard said. "The example of the Persians keeping their US-supplied F-14s flying well past their use-by date proves the possibility. Now consider the downside risk to us. What if the Russians had delivered the Persians a dozen or so RS-24s? Or maybe one or two Arcturus-class subs equipped with Bulava RSM-56 SLBMs? Or a few Poseidons parked on the ocean floor off the coast of Sierra waiting to be remotely activated? Each one of the threats I just described could wreak havoc all up and down Sierra's west coast. Our Earth-presence could be eliminated which is a serious proposition given CisLuna is still beholden to Earth for resupply of key materiel."

"Captain Buzzard," Hernandez said. "It sounds like you believe attacking Persia to be a fool's errand. Do you have any arguments for why we *should* carry out our attack regardless?"

"Yes, but as an AI, I leave it to you human commanders to sort out which set of arguments should prevail."

"Okay, okay, point taken," Hank said. "Please outline your arguments for why we *should* still attack Persia."

"Having established the downside risk of attacking Persia, the rationale for attacking remains compelling. SpaceCorp just lost *SIS Jonathan Lunine*—our most elaborate interplanetary spacecraft to date—along with some 1500 galacticans. Not only did we lose *Lunine*, but we were also forced to abandon a number of undersea research vessels on Enceladus thereby compromising the entire mission. Who knows when or if we'll hear from those vessels again? And Persia accomplished all this with mostly *asymmetric* warfare—hardly any shots fired. If Persia is allowed to continue this behavior, SpaceCorp is out of business, full stop. There is also the threat that other SpaceCorp enemies who have kept a low profile up to now, may be inspired by Persia's success. If SpaceCorp wishes to carry on, Persia must be taken off the gameboard in the way Mr. Stone outlined earlier in the meeting.

"Attacking Persia *may* sacrifice Sierra, but not attacking Persia *will* sacrifice Sierra. Do we wish to go out via nuclear extermination or by having each of our upcoming interplanetary and later interstellar missions sacrificed with Persia's devious sabotage devices—death by a thousand cuts so to speak?"

"It sounds like you recommend attacking now," Hank said.

"As I said before, I leave it to you human commanders to make that call, but to answer your question, yes, logic would dictate attacking now."

"Very well, and how would you have us do that?" Hank asked.

"Start with an attack on Persia as outlined in Mr. Stone's plan. But guard against ICBM retaliation by having all available SpaceCorp commercial assets' trajectories reconfigured to protect Sierra. Bear in mind, you don't need a gamma ray laser cannon to take out an ICBM or SLBM that is in flight. X-ray lasers such as are mounted on all standard space stations will do nicely. They have proven their effectiveness against illegal rockets in space. Remember, missiles in space are no longer shielded by the atmosphere. Ergo, when it is time to mount the attack, be sure all LEO space stations are arranged to defend Sierra against ICBMs and/or SLBMs with appropriately spaced and timed trajectories. I would suggest our stations should all be deployed at about 800 km altitude since ICBMs must travel in a high parabolic trajectory to reach their distant targets.

"As for the possible Poseidon threat, I'm afraid all we can do there is hope that Russia did not offer any of those assets to Persia."

"You want us to shut down all our commercial operations in LEO?" Hank asked.

"Yes. Once the attack on Persia begins, commercial operations won't matter much."

At this point in the discussion, Captain Hernandez' intel officer, Lieutenant Commander Smythe, raised her hand.

"You have something to share with us, Commander?"

"Yes, Sir."

"Sir, I believe there is another possibility we have been neglecting. Roy's Persian informants may have been programmed to feed us a red herring... a deception. The Persians want us to think missile when they really have laser cannons... perhaps hundreds or thousands of them. Just as we recognize the folly of trying to develop a missile force without benefit of test launches, I suspect the Persians do too. Hence, high energy laser technology could have developed completely within the confines of Mount Dena. All those TELs we have located in the Persian countryside could house laser cannon, not missiles. And if so, then flying *Buzzard* over Persian airspace could be a suicide mission."

The entire room went silent for a full minute—I timed it with the second hand on the wall clock.

"Okay, Commander Smythe, you laid this speculative egg, now hatch it into some form of plausible technology that the Persians might develop."

"There are three basic ways for a laser beam to punch through the atmosphere with enough energy to incapacitate a target such as ours. Gamma rays are absorbed by the atmosphere but they have the advantage that what does get through packs a good deal more energy than its longer wavelength brethren. Infrared, on the other end of the spectrum, has the advantage of the 8- to 14-micron atmospheric window but it needs to be really jacked to do any good on a heavily armored LEO-based target such as *Buzzard*. X-rays are in the middle in terms of not having any useful atmospheric windows but still being a good deal more energetic than infrared.

"Both X-ray and gamma rays require a lot of technology that Persia probably lacks. So if I were to hazard a guess, I'd favor a brute force approach using infrared laser cannon and twenty megawatts of power to get through the atmosphere and into LEO with enough oomph to do any real damage to one of our commercial space stations. Twenty megawatts is a lot for a TEL to lug around, so I'd guess the TEL only carries a single large ultracapacitor good for two or three shots before it has to find a power station to recharge itself.

"The wild card is if they somehow got their hands on X-ray or gamma ray laser technology. I'd put the probabilities of X-ray at less than ten percent and gamma ray at less than one percent. That said, we still have no way of knowing what's really been going on under Mount Dena these past decades."

"Thank you, Commander," Hank said. "Your analysis may be speculative, but it is nonetheless essential to our consideration.

"Does anybody else have any notions as to what we might be facing on the other side of the Zagros Mountains?"

Hank waited about twenty seconds and when there were no hands, he called on me to sum up the situation.

I glared at Hank with my eyebrows raised while I resisted the urge to say something snarky. Hank and I go way back but this was neither the audience nor the venue to cash in on that.

"Well," I began, "at the very least, this uncertainty forbids us from committing *Buzzard* or for that matter the entirety of our drone force until we know a lot more. At most I would say send one drone each over the Zagros and Elburz ridgelines with guns ablaze to see what they can stir up. I would hope that the combination of gamma ray laser cannon and a fusillade of KE projectiles all aimed at high value targets might kick the hornet's nest.

"I'd say skip going after the Zagros or Elburz early warning radar systems. We already know about them. What we need to know is what *weapons* they can bring into play. Forgive me—I'm making this up as I go along. Anyway, the KE projectiles—twelve of them between the two drones—can be launched before the drones clear the ridgeline. Once underway, they are almost impossible to knock down, especially since never having been used before, they would be completely unexpected.

"They can also be independently aimed at known high value targets. Off the top of my head I would suggest that list should include the residences of their Supreme Leader and President as well as their Parliament building. Those folks pull the strings over there, so let's scare the crap out of them in hopes that they'll panic and cut loose with everything they have. The remaining ten KE projectiles could be spread among targets that are more militarily significant—C&C centers, etc. We can work that out later. Anyway, that's a dozen city block-sized targets in the first pass. Persia should be ripping mad by the time the second wave of drones appears over the ridgelines. I expect they'd eagerly throw everything they have at them. While that's going on, we sit back and take notes.

"If their response is missiles, we send the rest of the drones over in two waves prioritizing the early warning sensors with laser cannon. If their response is laser cannon, then we still send the drones over, but we prioritize their power stations with the KE projectiles and the TELs with the laser cannon.

"While all this is going on, we need to be prepared for them to mount an ICBM and/or SLBM response... assuming they have those kinds of assets and that they are operable. It goes without saying that such an attack on Sierra should be interdicted during the boost phase if we are to have any hope of sparing Sierra. A good amount of study will have to be devoted to where those missiles might launch from.

"That leaves the Poseidons. If they exist as part of the Persian arsenal, we do not have the means to detect or interdict them. As Captain Buzzard pointed out, SpaceCorp is about space, not the oceans. We would be at the mercy of fate. Might be a good time to take up religion if you are so inclined."

"Thank you, Roy," Hank said. "Unless anybody has any serious issues with Roy's assessment, I think it's time to ask if we should postpone this operation for a year or so while we gather more intel and/or come up with more and better weapons platforms. Thoughts anybody?"

"May I suggest we retire for the night and reconvene same time tomorrow," Hernandez said. "May I further suggest that we divide the problem in two: Part 1) Roy's plan of a single drone launching KE projectiles over the ridgelines and then sorting out the missile or laser cannon response; Part 2) the Poseidons: An Intel question—does Persia have any? And an Operational question—what if anything can be done about them?"

"You heard the good Captain," Hank said. "Sweet dreams everyone!"

CHAPTER TWENTY-THREE

15Jun2154 1600 HRS

Corporal Rodriguez was waiting for me as soon as I left the Bridge.

"Mr. Stone, please follow me to your cabin. While you were busy with the brass, I stowed your duffle bag in there. Then we'll swing by Supply to get you kitted out with a proper spacesuit and firearm. Your spacesuit will be your uniform while onboard the station and is required to be worn whenever the station is in a mission-ready status... except when you're sleeping or bathing. By then you should be ready to sample what passes for 'Buzzard food.'"

"Call me Roy."

"You don't have a rank?"

"Actually I do but everybody just calls me Roy. Been that way for... shit, I don't know how long. I suppose it's like Hank Larson. He's as high as you can get in the Sierra pecking order but everyone just calls him Hank. His name has become his rank so to speak. Meanwhile, tell me about this mission-ready business."

"Sure... Roy. What do you want to know?"

"Well, what is it, for starters? And how's it related to wearing spacesuits all the time?"

"Well, the way Captain Hernandez explains it, with the station orbiting Earth every ninety minutes and the possibility that we might get tasked to overfly Persia in the middle of one of those orbits, she wants to be ready to go without having to send all the on-duty personnel back to their rooms to suit up. See what I'm saying?"

"Yeah, that part makes sense. But why can't you do your overflight in regular clothes? Why spacesuits? I should think they'd really slow you down. What are they... 50 kgs?"

"Mine is, but I'm kinda small. Yours will be more like sixty or sixty-five. But the extra mass is mitigated by a slower rotation speed of the station. Normal for a 1-km station is 1.34 rpm. But we only rotate at 0.95 rpm producing only about half a gee."

"Hmm... I thought I felt a little light on my feet but I attributed that to getting rid of that humongous contraption I was wearing when I arrived."

"Anyway, the real reason we wear them when on duty is because if we get hit and the station starts to go down, as Captain Hernandez puts it, things will start to go sideways fast and in a hurry. You'll barely have time to get to your escape pod if you're suited, and if you're not... well, good luck. Even then, a lot of people are gonna get spaced and their only hope will be to get picked up by a pod after the fact."

"I see. Well, I guess she'd know having barely made it off *Einstein* herself."

"She's always tellin us stories about that. Her experience unassing *Einstein* had a lot to do with the policy of always staying suited. She also had a lot to do with the design of the spacesuits themselves. She said when a ship gets hit there's a lotta fragments flying around, hence the armor. She tells a lot of stories about crew getting cut in half or losing limbs while wearing regular suits. There's no guarantee even with these suits, but with all these Kevlar™ plates at least you got a chance."

"Don't they add a lot of mass?"

"Yep. That's why we only have an hour's worth of O_2 and no heating elements. Captain says if we don't get picked up the first hour we're probably going to burn anyway. A lot of our overpass profiles are planned for less than 150 clicks elevation—harder for the groundies to draw a bead on us that way."

"Your escape pods are unpressurized?"

"That's right. There's gas bottles to hook into though. Water and nutrient too. A hundred crew on a pod can last maybe a week. It'll get pretty ripe though. There's no catheters with these suits, just diapers."

"Yikes!"

My cabin was only about six doors down from the Bridge identified by a piece of tape at eye level with my name neatly stenciled on it. I figured that was Hernandez' doing—when things got dicey, she'd want me to jump to it with no time lost to commuting. Inside was cramped but functional—single bunk at the back with a set of three drawers all in a row underneath. The middle one was smaller and had a touch lock. Next to the foot of the bunk was a combination sink and commode. And next to the head of the bunk was a fold-down desk and chair with small reefer beside the desk. I peeked inside. An ice maker at the top, and a bottle of tequila and what coulda been Grand Marnier™ and another bottle of some kind of lime mix down below, but alas, no Scotch. Guess I'm having Margaritas.

There was no mirror over the sink. That was a new feature. Somebody in engineering got the bright idea that our display paper could double as a mirror—you just drew a circle on the wall and voice-commanded 'show my face.' It was pretty cool because you could tell it to show you the back of your head and sensors on the opposite wall would pick that up and show it to you in your mirror. How many decades would pass before the younger crowd wouldn't know what a mirror was?

I got out of my cop coat and tossed it on the bunk. Then I dug out my piece, extra rounds, blade, and sap and stuck them in the security drawer. I set the lock pad by pressing my index finger against a sensor inside the drawer—now it would open for me when I touched the other sensor on the outside of the drawer. As I completed this, I noticed Eddy's eyes were all agape, presumably from all the weaponry I had stashed inside my cop coat.

"You ever use any of that stuff?" she asked.

"Next stop Supply?" I answered smiling.

* * *

It took us a good twenty minutes to make our way to Supply. The passageways were wide enough for us to walk two abreast without conflicting with oncoming traffic. I noticed a lot of the younger males giving Eddy looks of recognition as they passed.

To be expected. She was fairly cute and the tight cut of her suit was nothing if not flattering. I wondered if my suit would be so fitted. Turns out they had a custom suit ready to go as soon as I presented myself to the CPO who ran the supply shop.

* * *

CPO Benjamin Franklin Washington was a burly African-American chap who looked like he might have played tackle for one of the remaining pro teams on the Surface before he came up here. He straightened to attention when he saw me.

"Mr. Stone, Sir, welcome to *SSS Frank Buzzard!*"

"Call me Roy," I said, putting out my hand. "Understand you're going to help me get fitted out for one of your new high-tech spacesuits."

"Already done, Sir... ah, Roy. We had your measurements sent ahead. You just need to try it on to see if we got it right. Corporal Eddy will check you out on any features you may not be used to. Then she'll walk you over to the armory to be issued your sidearm. Everybody carries a sidearm on *Buzzard.*"

"Really? What kind of sidearm?"

I was curious now. Eddy's sidearm was definitely not anything I'd seen before, and now that I was going to get one of my own, I wanted to know what the hell was so special about it.

"You'll be carrying the standard 100-kilowatt 12-micron laser pistol," CPO Washington said.

"A laser pistol? You mean like a... *pew-pew-pew...* ray gun?"

"Uh... just one *pew* and word to the wise, don't call it a ray gun or Cap'n Hernandez will have your ass scrubbing out commodes for a week."

"Thanks for the pro tip. Why lasers? What's the matter with the standard .357 magnum bullets? For that matter, why firearms at all? Surely we don't expect to get boarded up here."

"The official expectation is that while we most likely won't get boarded, we very likely *will* get shot down and we may not be so lucky down on the Surface. Some places are fine with our escape pods plopping down for a visit, other places not so much."

"Okay, I feel ya, but why lasers?"

"How many bullets can you get in a pistol?"

"I carry a revolver, so eight, plus another sixteen in reloads."

"The ultracap inside your grip is good for fifty shots, each one capable of poking a hole through a mule lengthwise out to 100 meters. Of course being an ultracap it's prone to leaking, so you'll want to recharge it nightly. There's other advantages. It's silent in case you don't want to attract attention. It's IR so nobody can see your beam. And my favorite is that with your pulse traveling at lightspeed, all that Kentucky windage and Tennessee elevation crap goes in the garbage. Handy for shooting fast movers and such."

"Will I get to take a couple of practice shots?"

"More than a couple. You actually have to qualify on a virtual combat course. Eddy will help you prep for that when you're not busy with your primary duty. Until then you can carry your weapon on your hip, but it will be safed at all times. Until you qualify, only Eddy can unsafe it for you."

I looked over at Eddy. Her mouth smiled, but her eyes were mirthless.

"Sounds like I better qualify."

CHAPTER TWENTY-FOUR

16Jun2154 1300 HRS—War Planning

I showed up to War Planning: *Partie Deux* about ten minutes early... old military habit of mine. Pinto and Smythe were already there and Captain Buzzard had his avatar frozen into its customary location on the wall—he hadn't activated it yet but I figured he was still listening. I took my seat, nodding to Pinto and Smythe who stiffly nodded back. They seemed nervous. Maybe it was having to speak truth to power? Or maybe they always looked this way when they were deciding the fate of the world.

Hernandez walked in brusquely and took her seat. She had a big—make that huge—mug of coffee, one of those heated contraptions that could keep its contents hot for several hours without drying out. Buzzard saw me eying it and asked, "Did you want some coffee, Roy? I'm told ours is pretty good."

"Uh sure, if it's not too much trouble."

"How do you take it?"

"Tablespoon of honey."

"That's unusual."

"Habit I picked up on *Lunine*."

"Hank sent word that he would be a few minutes late but we should start without him," Hernandez said. "That said, is there any discussion regarding the single drone launching KE projectiles?"

Smythe raised her hand tentatively, "I think we should be prepared to hold off on the follow-on waves for possibly several hours. If they fire on our drone that should give away the launch signature whether it be a missile or laser. We can use that data to map all the locations of their emplaced weapons. And we can use that to launch a standoff attack with our KE projectiles. They can launch before the drones clear the ridgeline giving the drones time to alter course so as not to expose themselves to surface weapons."

"You're saying you want to use all the KE projectiles to prioritize shooters instead of their power supplies?" I asked.

"Yes, we can take out a power supply just as easily with a laser cannon and we have a lot more laser ammunition than we have KE projectiles. We need to blunt their firepower—whatever form it takes—before we start sending our limited supply of drones over."

"While your idea has merit," I said. "I think I would favor using our KE projectiles to hit their command-and-control sites first. Recall we only have 72 KE projectiles. That should be enough to take out most if not all of their C-and-C. They probably have many hundreds—perhaps thousands—of launchers or cannon, way more than we have KE projectiles."

"I strongly support Roy's plan with two modifications," Captain Buzzard said. "First modification, let's use maybe a dozen projectiles in that first wave to hit their centers of *political* leadership. Like all the other nuclear nations, the decision to launch lies solely with the Persian head of state, in this case the Supreme Leader. If for some reason he is not available, say, he becomes a casualty of war, their Assembly of Experts would immediately hold a session and appoint a successor. Ergo, it would be worthwhile to eliminate as many of them as possible at the same time—the better to hinder a decision-making replacement. There are eighty-eight of them in all although it is not known how many are required for a quorum. At the very least we should take out the Chairman and his first and second deputies."

"Does this Assembly of Experts have all that much real power?" I asked.

"Good observation, Roy," Captain Buzzard said. "As long as the Supreme Leader is alive and well they are mostly a rubber-stamp agency, only there to praise the Supreme Leader, not control him. The one time they do have actual power is if the Supreme Leader should die unexpectedly. Then it's up to them to elect a new leader. This is a severe weakness in their governmental structure compared to, say, a chain of succession such as was used by the country formerly known as the United States. Bear in mind these fellows typically reside in the province that elected them, so it could take a while for them to convene if they insist on a face-to-face. My worry would be that the Chairman and his two Deputies might apply some obscure war-powers clause and appoint an acting Supreme Leader on the spot. Hence, my suggestion to eliminate them at the same time as the Supreme Leader."

"Do these chaps have a meeting place, and if so, how often do they convene there?" I asked.

"Yes, they do," Captain Buzzard said. "It's on Emam Khomeini Street, across from the Imam Ali Military Academy. They convene every six months for about a week. As it happens, the next meeting is in 42 days.

"Commander Smythe, could you do a little digging to see if the Supreme Leader plans to be on hand for the kickoff or something?" Hernandez asked.

"Is it worth the wait?" I asked. "It would seem so to me. We're talking about a huge hit to their political hierarchy and with it their ability to launch strategic offensive and defensive weapons."

"Can we suggest that as our preferred D-day for when Hank gets here?" Captain Buzzard asked.

Everyone nodded.

"Good. To continue, we have precise coordinates for the Islamic Consultative Assembly where their Parliament meets, the Office of the Supreme Leader, and the Presidential Administration. KE projectiles are all but impossible to detect from the ground, and who knows, we could get lucky. A dozen of them could easily cut the top off their political leadership structure.

"Second modification, you could do worse than to apply another two dozen KE projectiles on their *military* C-and-C structure. If we miss with our attack on the political C-and-C structure, we could compensate by taking out the next big link in the C-and-C chain. In particular, I'd like to see us target the Islamic Revolutionary Guard Corps' Aerospace Force. Once the order to retaliate is given, they'll be the ones giving the orders, whether it be laser cannon or missile. Without orders to fire, their cannon or launcher batteries will most likely just sit there while our drones fly overhead wreaking havoc."

Hank's grinning avatar popped up on the wall, "Hi, folks, sorry I'm late. I've been monitoring your debate and I must say I really like it! But first, the reason for my tardiness. We manufactured our current stock of KE penetrators out of tungsten since that's what the original design called for. And we had to do quite a lot of scrounging to come up with enough tungsten for the 72 projectiles. However, one substance we seem to have quite a lot of is depleted uranium—uranium reactors being in widespread use up here. We have amassed quite a large stockpile of the stuff as a waste material from our Lunar surface uranium refineries.

"Turns out depleted uranium is only slightly less dense than tungsten—19.1 g/cm^3 vs 19.3. I'm told we can manufacture over 1000 of these devices if we use extant DU. And they can be larger—30 meters long by a full meter in diameter plus some more for the ablation coating."

"How soon?" I asked.

"Less than a month."

"So now we are platform-limited?" Captain Buzzard asked. "We have way more penetrators than drone launchers?"

"Uh... yes, it would seem so," Hank said.

"Maybe not," I said. "What if we put together a constellation of these devices in an orbit that is constantly passing over Persia? As they pass over the ridgelines they could be directed to fire or not fire subject to target availability."

"Okay, but how do you get rid of them after the war? I should think there'd be quite a lot of unused penetrators passing over Persia. Won't the rest of the world see that as a threat?" Hernandez asked.

"They're rocket-assisted." Hank said. "So if you decide you don't need them, you can just "rocket assist" them into a graveyard orbit—36,050 km above Earth—out of sight but still available."

"That's a bit above and beyond what a standard rocket assist would involve," Hernandez said.

"It is," Hank said. "But it's mature technology and not beyond our resource and manufacturing limitations."

"Why orbit them over Persia at all?" Smythe asked. "With the kind of rocketry you are implying, Roy, we should be able to store them in CisLuna in EML1 and launch a large salvo of them to Earth in under ten hours, perhaps as quickly as five hours. Several hundred DU penetrators scattered all over Persia should accomplish your medieval caliphate goal in less than a day. *Buzzard* need only pass over after the fact to inspect and maybe mop up here and there with near-zero risk. Ooh, I'm liking this!"

"Longer term, might this concept also give us a way to eliminate surface ocean threats?" I asked. "By space standards, ocean threats tend to move pretty slowly—maybe fifty knots tops. They would not be able to escape and evade something descending on them from space. And with a blast of 50 tonnes of TNT you only need to be close. We just need a way to detect undersea threats."

"We have that with the standard LIDAR sensors mounted on all our LEO space stations, but only down to a depth of about 500 meters," Captain Buzzard said.

Smythe raised her hand. "Uh, fellas, I hate to be the party pooper, but isn't depleted uranium still a radiation hazard? Especially since we're looking to pepper the whole of Persia with so many of these projectiles?"

"Alpha particles," Captain Buzzard said. "Only dangerous if ingested."

"Yes, sir," Smythe said, "but with a large salvo of these projectiles hitting the atmosphere at Mach 40 or 50, won't a lot of uranium material be ablated off and scattered throughout all layers of the atmosphere along with all the accompanying alpha particles?"

"Good point, Smythe," Hank said. "The Asian Jet Stream would carry those particles across Afghanistan and into Tibet, China, and Japan. It could cross the Pacific and eventually land on our doorstep. That would be embarrassing."

"So coat each projectile with ablative material—PICA or something—so that there will be no significant alpha release until the projectile is deep underground," Hernandez said. "Alphas don't even penetrate tissue paper, so the entire release should be well-contained."

Smythe looked down at some notes on her pad, "We'd need a good enough rocket on the back to do several precision course correction burns on the way to Earth. We'd have to be spot on target at atmospheric entry because we won't be able to correct after reentry. Stability may also be an issue during reentry— suggest tungsten rollerons mounted on the trailing end. Finally, we should have three test launches onto Earth targets to establish CEP, say, in the Pacific Proving Grounds in the Marshalls. That will allow us to verify blast effects as well as some other factors, for example how well the alpha radiation is contained underground."

"The Marshalls have been submerged due to sea level rise for over a century now," Hank said. "You don't wanna drop one in the middle of the Sahara, say, north of Timbuktu? I have some political contacts in Mali."

Smythe wrinkled her nose and shook her head.

"We could claim it was a meteorite?" Hank asked.

"We really need to keep a lid on this," Smythe said. "We can't have the Persian leadership going to ground when it's party time."

"I suppose you're right," Hank said. "Buzz, can you gin up a detailed design for the weapons guys up on Tycho?"

"It's already done," Captain Buzzard said. "Do you want to review it or shall I just send it?"

"Send it—copy me," Hank said. "I'll review it later. But don't have them start cobbling anything together until I can meet with them.

"Meanwhile, Pinto, you and Smythe need to get working on a target list that will tell us how many of these bad boys it will take to bring Persia to her knees. We need a medieval caliphate with a single salvo, plus enough backup to do it again if we screw up.

"Roy, I want you to set up a test plan. Give some consideration to how many test shots we'll need—vary the mass, dimensions, and reentry speeds. Three are probably not enough. I'm thinking a dozen, but we don't want to do so many tests we let the cat out of the bag. Explosions this big can be seismically detected. Maybe locate your tests near a volcano?

227

We need someplace remote enough so no one will catch wind of it."

"I have just the spot," Captain Buzzard said. "There's been a lot of recent volcanic activity in the Kingdom of Tonga in the South Pacific."

"Aren't there people there?" I asked.

"Not in the outlying islands of Late and Fonualei," Captain Buzzard said. "Due to the presence of active volcanoes there, they've each been uninhabited for centuries. You'll want to make sure there are no fishing camps or other temporary inhabitants when you get down there."

"When I get down there?" I asked. "You mean you want me to go to the Surface?"

"Yes," Hank said, "we need eyes down there. Grab whomever you like to assist you but keep your footprint small. CEP and blast effects need to be accurately characterized. Coordinate with Pinto and Smythe via secure channel so they can feed your data into their attack simulation. I'm worried about jet stream effects on the trajectory path after our projectiles hit the upper atmosphere.

"Take a direct shuttle to return to surface and whatever you need afterwards. You have my authority to commandeer any personnel or equipment you require, but remember, this is a covert operation. Keep it that way."

"Will do," I said.

"Excellent!" Hank said. "Captain Hernandez, I'd like you to put a team together to arrange for a mop-up plan using *Buzzard's* laser cannon. Top priority is to mop up, not get mopped up. Savvy?"

"No complaints here," Hernandez said. "I've already been shot down once. Prefer not to do it again."

"I'd say for planning purposes we're not looking at the next Assembly of Experts meeting in 42 days, but the one meeting six months after that. So where's that put D-Day?" I asked.

"Nominally," Captain Buzzard said, "that would put D-Day on Tuesday, January 28, 2155."

Looking back on the meetings we had had in arriving at this plan, I had to admit it was considerably different from the one I was hoping to sell when I first arrived on Buzzard on 15Jun2154. I shudder to think what the outcome of our attack might have been had we gone ahead with that plan. I guess it was a case of nobody on my CisLuna planning staff having had any real experience with waging war. We did the best we could using book smarts. I left that second meeting feeling a good deal more confident about our intentions. Not a hundred percent mind you... we had yet to prove Hank's new DU based Rods from God although I had every confidence that SpaceCorp engineering would be up to that task. And there was still the Persian mystery missile rendered all the more real in my imagination for want of any concrete data about it.

CHAPTER TWENTY-FIVE

Friday, 05Jul 2154—Edwards Airport

Transiting to Surface from LEO was pretty much the same pain in the ass it was the last time I went fifty years ago. These days the only surface flights originated at CisLuna which meant I first had to take a space-only *Butler Hine*-class shuttle back to CisLuna before I could take a reentry-rated *John Marmie*-class shuttle down to Edwards Space Center. Even claiming an exclusive, it still took me nine days before I could set foot on the hardened clay of Rogers Dry Lake Bed in the middle of the Mojave.

John Marmie-class shuttles' primary propulsion is from nuclear lightbulbs, but on Earth they only use them for takeoff from Rogers Dry Lake at Edwards and then only after they clear the Kármán line at 100 km altitude, the official demarcation of space. Nuclear lightbulbs spew out a shit ton of gamma radiation so a great deal of care is taken to get them well into the thermosphere where the bulk of the gamma energy can be absorbed without endangering Earth's surface biome.

This is achieved with giant launch craft that ferry them several thousand km from Rogers to the South Pacific Oceanic Uninhabited Area, or SPOUA, about half way between New

Zealand and Chile. That place has been a graveyard for derelict spacecraft since 1971. The old International Space Station ended up there after it was decommissioned. Once there, the space bound shuttle aligns itself as close as it can get to its desired trajectory, e.g., polar, equatorial, etc., and then it gets released from its mother ship at 15,000 meters altitude where a big chemical booster lights up and pushes it up another 85 km into space. No, the booster is not reusable in case you were wondering, which is another reason they do their launching from SPOUA. SpaceCorp goes to a lot of trouble and expense to keep the rest of the world from being mad at it... doesn't seem to work though.

Fun fact: the giant launch craft are fully robotic—a leftover design feature from the days when shuttles didn't have chemical boosters. The idea then was they didn't want any crew on board the launch craft to get a face full of gamma radiation when the shuttle's nukes lit up. Once the shuttle has been dropped, the launch craft turns around and flies itself back to Rogers. Another fun fact: we've never lost a launch craft.

Shuttle landings are a different matter altogether. The only power for incoming shuttles is their nukes but they don't dare light them up below the Kármán line. In case it's not obvious, that means they have to dead stick it from the edge of space until touchdown on runway 36-Charlie at Rogers. That beast is 12 km long and the C actually stands for center, which means it's flanked by a left and a right runway each one just as long and as wide as Charlie. In other words lotsa margin for things going sideways on touchdown.

Once you roll to a stop you have to sit there for up to an hour while you wait for a bus to come out and fetch you and your gear. Remember, these things can't taxi. Anyway, there you are in the middle of the Mojave in the middle of July in the middle of the afternoon with the outside temperature a balmy 45 °C. I'm told that used to be the record high for around there, but after three centuries of global warming, 45 °C is just normal today. The interior of the shuttle is not temperature-controlled. So your personal comfort is dependent on your spacesuit. You have to stay plugged in to the shuttle's electrical to keep your suit's coolant flowing. Then when the bus arrives you disconnect and work off your suit's integral battery. Fortunately, the buses have a cab that elevates up to your level so you don't have to make your way down a gang plank wearing, in my case 150 kg of space suit and life support equipment. *Buzzard* policy did not allow military grade space suits to be worn off the station. Doing so would have blown our science geek cover anyway.

* * *

I've been saying 'I' all this time when by now we were a team of five—myself, Eddy, and three galacticans who'd made it back safely from the Enceladus fiasco. Eddy was game for any adventure that involved breaking things and/or hurting people—I put her on primary security with me as backup. The galacticans were itching for blood in spite of their lack of violence genes. Roberta was instrumentation—cameras, seismographs, and telemetry pickup. Jonathan was our drone operator and surveyor, which meant he was also the keeper of the surveying equipment. Molly was logistics—getting us all there and keeping us housed and fed. We masqueraded as a team of scientists—the best way to account for all our equipment boxes.

The five of us made it onto the bus and thirty minutes later we entered the blessed shade of the hangar and into the passenger area. It mainly consisted of a bunch of lockers mounted on rollers and a bunch of shower points to clean up what our diapers didn't quite absorb. There were valets on hand to help us inventory our suits and hang them in the lockers. The whole process was coed, but I think I was the only one that noticed. Funny about this generation of SpaceCorp people, nobody seems to care about nudity anymore. Doesn't matter how attractive or unattractive you are, nobody stares. Not even a sideways look.

After we left the passenger area, our lockers would be sealed—no honor system down here—and rolled away for maintenance and storage. It felt nice to finally be in street clothes. Then it was off to claim our gear cartons. Some of us had more than others. Once that was done, the team plus our personal bags and gear cartons were loaded onto a shuttle that motored us over to a cargo plane that was waiting for us at South Base.

SpaceCorp had a fleet of three space planes—good for very fast intercontinental flights. One of those could have gotten us and our equipment to Fiji in less than two hours. But being novel they also attracted a lot of unwanted attention. So Molly had chartered a six-engine double-decker cargo aircraft, a Lockheed 5055 Horizon. She was an old design, recent build with long legs, but slow as in she could supercruise but only at around Mach 1.5 at 20,000 meters. Her form factor resembled a morbidly obese XB-70 Valkyrie, if you're in to aircraft designs from the golden age of military aircraft. The design probably could have cruised well above Mach 2, but her cargo wings needed multiple personalities with slats and flaps and extensions in order to handle everything from shorter field takeoffs and landings to efficient high-altitude Mach+ cruise. I was just happy that the fuel tanks didn't have to heat up to stop leaking. Our flight would take eighteen hours, but we had the whole plane to ourselves. And she came with bunks to wrack out on and an entertainment system that was loaded with recent movies.

With the flight being so long, the plane needed a double crew, but then Molly found out we were short a cook. The guy they had got sick at the last minute. As it happened we had stopped for lunch at the cantina outside the gate. Since everyone was marveling at how good their cheeseburgers and fries were, I asked the cook to come out and chat with us. His name was Tobias originally from San Diego, but he'd been a short order cook at the Edwards Cantina for the last five years. As luck would have it he had a SpaceCorp badge and was game for a temporary change of scenery. Besides the regular short order fare, he could do Mexican, Chinese, Thai, and of course seafood—I figured given our destination we were gonna see a lot of that. And what sealed the deal for me was that he was an experienced mixologist! Tobias needed to pick up a few things and let his flat mate know he'd be gone for about six months, so we took advantage of the side trip to raid the local Class Six store. Class Six is Army for booze, if you were wondering. Tobias walked out of his flat carrying a medium sized duffel bag followed by a German Shepherd that must have weighed sixty kg. What really spooked me though was that this Shepherd was the spitting image of Devil—jet black with three white stockings.

"Can Wilson come?" Tobias asked. "I haven't got anybody to look after him, and my flat mate's afraid of him."

I walked over to Wilson and took a knee in front of him.

"You wanna go to Fiji, Wilson?"

Wilson looked at me for a second, then shifted his gaze to Tobias.

"You better say 'yes' or you won't be getting any of my cooking for a while" Tobias said.

Wilson returned his gaze to me then licked me on the face.

"I guess that's a yes. Come meet the team."

*   *   *

We mostly hung out in the upper deck of the plane while the gear was secured below. We could have had a significantly shorter flight if we'd gone into American Samoa, but with sea level rise over the last few years, the airport at Pago Pago was being moved to higher ground for the third time this century and unavailable for the moment. Plus we needed a boat, a research ship more accurately. Since our cover story was that we were a scientific team, a research ship fit our image nicely. Molly had chartered one to meet us in Fiji that could carry us and our gear plus a chopper and a couple of large Zodiacs.

Tobias tossed his duffel onto a vacant seat and sought out the flight engineer to see what kind of kitchen facilities and food stocks he would have to work with. Good initiative—I liked that. They both approached me after about fifteen minutes.

235

"Are we in a rush to get out of here?" Tobias asked.

"Why, is there a problem with the kitchen?" I asked.

"Kitchen's okay. It's the food. There isn't any. The guy that took sick was supposed to order a bunch, but in the confusion, it didn't get done. If it's okay with you, me and the flight engineer are gonna run over to the base commissary and grab some stuff."

"Yeah, go for it. Take Molly too. She's our logistician."

I called Molly over and explained the problem.

"Uh, she have any money?" Tobias asked.

"Money? At SpaceCorp? They're using that again?"

"Fraid so."

I had to admit, I was not ready for that.

"Molly, you got any ideas, or better still, some cash?" I asked.

She pulled me off to the side. "I brought a bunch of gold sovereigns of various denominations, but that's for expenses when we get to the work site. I've no idea how bad those expenses are gonna be so I'd like to limit extraneous stuff if we can."

"How do you propose we do that?" I asked.

"Didn't Hank give you a blue card?"

Blue cards were all but useless around the world, but at Space Corp, they were the royal imprimatur.

"Oh, yeah! Think it'll work at the commissary?"

"Let me have it. I'll pack some gold as back up."

*   *   *

236

I don't remember much about our flight from Edwards to Fiji. By the time we went wheels up, everyone except Tobias and Wilson were pretty whipped. Once we got airborne Tobias came around with sandwiches. The ones who were still awake went to sleep on a full stomach. The whole team including myself had found various ways to rack out. About ten hours in Tobias woke us up to see if anybody was hungry.

"Whatcha got?" I asked.

"Choice of chicken stew or linguini with meat sauce for the main course, plus spinach salad with pears and walnuts, garlic bread, and apple pie made with fresh apples and scratch-made crust."

I sat up and rubbed my eyes. "Holy cow! You must have been working the whole time we were sleeping."

"Just for the main course items and the pies. The flight engineer helped. The bread was from semi-cooked loaves at the commissary that you take home and warm up. Anyway, if you're interested in chow, it'll be another hour for me to make the pasta and prep the salad. You know they have a shower on this plane? It's even got hot water!"

"Put me down for the chicken. Where's this shower?"

I went around telling everyone they should partake of Tobias' meal and get a shower and fresh skivvies. We'd still have several hours before touchdown in Fiji and a shit ton of work getting all our equipment and stores off the plane and trucked over to the dock where we'd meet our ship. I was having waking nightmares that we'd forgotten some vital container full of equipment and arrive at our final destination with the mission torpedoed before we even got started.

I found everybody but Molly. She eventually turned up below decks inventorying our equipment. She apparently shared the same paranoia I did.

"Are we missing anything?" I asked.

"Oh no. It's all here. I'm just trying to figure out how to get it loaded onto trucks, so we can get it all to the dock without forgetting something."

She went on to tell me how she had learned from the captain that Suva-Nausori International Airport had been moved inland another ten kilometers in order to escape sea level rise and that the docks that used to be at Mua-i-walu had moved to someplace called Tamavua.

"Have you had any sleep since we took off?"

"Yeah, about four hours."

She's one of those gals that the only time they ever screwed up in their life was one time when they thought they made a mistake but it turned out they didn't. I used to know somebody else like that. Anyway, she sounded pretty stressed, so I told her to have some supper and a shower and that I'd pitch in and help her out afterwards. "What we can't figure out up here we'll figure out on the ground. The main thing is that at this moment, we haven't lost anything."

That seemed to calm her down so she tossed her notebook onto a crate and set off in search of the shower.

Wednesday, 10Jul2154—Suva International Airport (Fiji)

The landing at Suva wasn't the scariest I'd ever been through, but it was close. It seems the more airstrips have to move

238

inland to escape shifting coast lines, the less inviting the terrain becomes what with inland mountain slopes being rutted with waterfalls and canyons. Plus we were landing in the middle of the night during a rainstorm. Kudos to the captain for getting us down in one piece. Fascinating to watch the wings reconfigure from Mach+ cruise to STOL.

After we had taxied onto the ramp, Molly and I rounded up the pilot to ask if there was a hangar where we could use as a warehouse for our gear.

"Yeah, but I wouldn't recommend it. Look, the plane is yours for the next several weeks. Why not just use *it* for your warehouse? That way you don't have to worry about pilferage— at least one of the crew will always be on board. When it's daylight and you can see what's going on, you can take a taxi over to the docks and check on your ship, and maybe see about the best way to get your stuff from here to the ship without losing anything."

Molly gave me a look of approval, so I said, "Okay, let's see about a taxi. We'll take Tobias while we're at it."

I turned my attention back to the pilot, "Any idea how long to get to Tamavua Harbor?"

"Not speaking from personal experience, but I'd guess a couple hours."

"Terrific."

"What about Wilson?" Molly asked.

"He stays behind to help Eddy with guard duty."

I was getting flustered but then I calmed down when I remembered Hank had said they wouldn't be ready for the first drop until probably mid-August. We were actually ahead of schedule... at least for now.

The ride actually took three hours. Given it was a bumpy, twisty two-lane road through a jungle ravine, I was just thankful we got there in one piece. The cabby was a statuesque Fijian named Jovesa, who, upon learning we were from Sierra, insisted we call him Joe. His skin was a pleasant milk chocolate brown and he wore his hair in the traditional Fijian buiniga, a kind of upward standing bouffant. There seemed to be little that was new on this island and his cab was no exception. It was a diesel 4x4 perhaps thirty years old with seats in back for three passengers but I sat up front so we'd all have a bit more room. Its cloth top was autographed with rips and holes such that it would only keep some of the rain out. The steering wheel was rigged for right-side driving hinting at the vehicle's British origin. The passenger windows had lost their glass ages ago, now replaced with plastic sheets that rolled down when needed like old fashioned window blinds.

Joe was a talkative sort although it took me awhile to get used to his Fijian accent. He seemed to be pretty knowledgeable of the local island transportation infrastructure.

"Say, Joe, we got a lotta gear to get from the airport down to a ship in Tamavua Harbor."

"You mean Suva Harbor?"

"I don't know. According to the notes on our map it moved to a place called Tamavua."

Joe laughed, "Oh, yeah, but we still call it Suva Harbor. Been that way for years. Used to be the Tamavua River hundred year ago but with the sea level rise, river turned into a bay and Tamavua Heights is now just Tamavua. Seemed kind of funny to keep calling it 'Heights' when the waterline was so close. Not many people remember that."

"What about our gear? Any idea how to get it down to the harbor?"

"How much you got?"

"About half a semi's worth."

"How much it weigh?"

"Nine and a half tonnes," Molly said. "Instruments and other gear—some of it delicate. We're scientists doing some research around Tonga."

Joe thought for a moment, "Well, I suppose you could truck it down to the harbor, but with these roads, that might be fifty-fifty-mostly-no. If you got the scratch you should chopper it down. Faster and more reliable."

"You have choppers that big here?" I asked.

"Sure, left over from the airport construction. My cousin flies for them. They're expensive though. Trucks cheaper. I got another cousin who runs a trucking company."

I looked at Molly in the back seat. "Can we do the choppers?" she mouthed.

"Let's arrange to talk to your cousin with the choppers. What do you use for currency here?"

"Whatcha got?" Joe asked. "We use Fijian dollars mostly. Print it ourselves."

"Well, we don't have any of those."

"Well, we don't do charity. By the way, how you figuring to pay me for this ride?"

"We were hoping you'd take gold. We have sovereigns, Krugerrands, and Sierran twenty-dollar gold pieces."

"Gold? For real?"

I handed him a Sierran. "There's more where this came from."

"He hefted the coin in his free hand... I guess this will do!"

"What kind of choppers your cousin got?"

"Well, for the load you're talking about, you should probably go with the 234, but you should talk to him about that. He got Cranes too."

"I think I know what you mean by a Crane, but I'm not familiar with the 234."

"Oh, that's a Boeing. Big tandem double rotor, turbine engines on each side, inside like a bowling alley. Rigged for cargo mostly, but I seen him do sling loads. He was gonna teach me to fly, but then they finished the airport and business dropped off."

"You mean the Army's old Chinook? Ch-47?"

"I wouldn't know, man. Might be. He just calls it a 234. But it's big though. You could put your gear in the cargo bay. Keep it from getting wet. Funny the rain we havin. Don't start raining till November normally. Anyway, 234 got passenger seats too. How many are you?"

"Six and a dog. These choppers your cousin has... they in good shape? What's your cousin's name anyway? And when could we meet him?"

"Yeah, they're in good shape. They might not look it since the construction people left, but they fly real good. Inoke lives in Suva. I could go get him while you're checkin out your ship."

Friday, 12Jul2154—Suva Harbor (Fiji)

A hundred-fifty teeth-rattling potholes later, we pulled up to a gated entry with several ships moored to docks a few hundred meters away. Joe spoke to the guard in Fijian for a moment, occasionally jerking his thumb back to us.

"He wants to see your passports."

Molly reached into her bag and came up with two very official looking booklets. "Give him these."

"What about Tobias?" I asked.

"I got my SpaceCorp badge."

"Hand it to Joe."

Tobias handed it to Joe who passed it to the guard who examined both sides of the badge. Fortunately, the top of the front of his badge was labeled Employee of SpaceCorp. The guard seemed happy and handed everything back and waved us through.

"Is he gonna be a problem?" I asked.

"Who, Manasa? Nah, he's my brother-in-law. We don't get along, but he's okay."

"How come you don't get along?"

"He married my sister. She henpecks him cause he comes home drunk every night. He thinks I should have warned him before they make vakawati."

"What's vakawadi?"

"VakawaTEE. It means get married."

"Oh... Didn't you warn him? About your sister, I mean?"

"Fuck no, man! Then we'd be stuck with her," he said laughing.

"How about Inoke... you two get along?"

243

"Oh, yeah. I married his sister."

He caught my eyebrows going up with a sideways glance.

"It's a small island," he said.

"I feel ya," I said.

* * *

Southern Cross, registered out of Aukland, was a spacious 150 meters length by 30 meters beam. She had a hangar aft for the chopper. The chopper had a dedicated pilot and mechanic. I had told Molly I wanted a sizeable chopper that could haul us and our gear from boat to shore. That took some doing since most of the choppers carried around by research vessels were dinky little observation choppers—good for a pilot, a passenger, and maybe a lunch if they shared. *Southern Cross* was no exception but being desperate for business, the captain arranged to swap out his tiny chopper for a twin-turbined rescue chopper. At twenty meters length, it would not fit inside the hangar, so they had it secured to the poop deck with the tail boom hanging out over the transom.

Amidships our ship sported a pair of derricks and assorted winches so she could load our considerable amount of gear into her hold. She was stabilizer-equipped and she could cruise at a whole 30 km per hour—not per second like we were used to. Things moved slower on Earth, but the distances were shorter, so I suppose it all worked out. She was typically deployed for a year at a time, so she had a medical doctor and surgical nurse, a three-bed infirmary, and an operating suite/treatment room which hopefully we would not need. She was crewed by a captain, three mates, and maybe a dozen sailors, plus various mechanics, steward, and galley staff. With that many people on board they were only too happy to welcome another chef.

The captain was a very tan, blue-eyed, bewhiskered Scandinavian named Paulsen, but everybody called him Captain Gorm. I found out later that Gorm was his first name and he came from Húsavík, Iceland. He corralled me in the mess hall over lunch and grilled me about the nature of our research. It was a friendly grilling or at least it got that way after the third or fourth shot of some syrupy truth serum I'd never heard of. He called it aquavit. Tasted terrible. Had a dry, overpowering dill flavor that stuck to your tongue and got up in your nose. Good for my sinuses though.

"So what's the nature of this research you're doing?" Gorm asked. "Or is it some big secret?" He had leaned in and lowered his voice for the second question.

I laughed, "It's not exactly a secret, although we're not advertising it in case we get egg on our face. We have a new technology to deorbit the bigger pieces of space junk. It has the potential to make LEO a lot safer for transits. But before we go to full production with it, we need to confirm just how accurate it is. Don't want to drop some derelict rocket stage onto somebody's house! And while we're at it, characterizing the blast effects of an impact would also be kind of nice to know. Especially for the bigger junk."

"Can you share how you're going to test this new technology?"

"Well, we're going to deorbit a half dozen or so pieces of space debris simulators onto a deserted island."

"And you've picked Late in the Tongan Islands to be the happy recipient of your deorbited space debris?"

He pronounced it LAH-tay. I'd been wondering about that.

"Yeah, after we confirm it's truly uninhabited."

"What if it is inhabited? You know a lot of these islanders set up seasonal fishing camps around some of the more remote islands."

"Well, we have a backup. Fonualei. It's not too far from Late. I'm told nobody lives there either. Too much volcanic action."

"Why not just drop these pieces of junk into the ocean? Why do you have to target land?"

I had to think fast for this one, "Whales. The impact of one of these hypervelocity projectiles into the ocean would be pretty disturbing for marine life, especially whales and such."

"Okay, it sounds like you know what you're doing."

He poured me another shot of aquavit. He seemed determined to finish the bottle.

"Am I gonna feel this in the morning?"

"Most definitely."

I raised an eyebrow, "I can afford to be snockered for a day, but what about you? You're supposed to be driving."

"No effect. My wife says I'm a functional alcoholic."

"She's on board?"

"Nah, she's home in Iceland. I see her about every five years or so."

It seemed ocean sailors had it worse than space sailors in that regard.

*   *   *

A few hours before sunset, Joe drove up with his cousin Inoke and the two of them joined Molly, me, Tobias, Captain Gorm, and the ship's First Mate—a red-haired Norwegian named Erik—for a dinner of red snapper and various other tropical fruits and starchy vegetables—most of it coconut flavored. The water was clear, cool, and refreshing. It had been a while since I had drunk water that hadn't passed through several hundred humans before me.

The conversation was dominated by Molly, Tobias, Erik, and Inoke. Gorm and I mainly listened. I thought the main issue would be the capacity of the hold—we needed to be able to get at our gear, not just shoehorn it in. But it turned out to be the rotor wash problem if one of those big Boeing 234s put down on the pier too close to the ship's antenna arrays. It was decided to land the chopper a few hundred meters away in a parking lot away from the other ships. The gear could then be loaded onto dollies and towed down to the Southern Cross where it could then be derricked into the cargo bay. Molly and Tobias would be in the hold to unpack the instruments and set them up in the hangar which—now being unoccupied by a chopper—became our research headquarters. The last item of discussion was when could we get started. Inoke wanted two days to finish up some maintenance on the chopper.

"Two days?" I asked. "That gonna do it? You wanna say three days and give yourself a cushion?"

"Two days already has a cushion," Inoke said. "We be fine. Just be ready to start pulling gear off your plane at nine o'clock in the morning two days from now."

"What about rotor wash effects on the plane—my pilot might get a little nervous."

247

"We'll put down couple hundred meters away and shut the engines down. Then we'll have a tug drag us over to your cargo bay. Is all your stuff on pallets?"

"Yeah, the cargo anyway," Molly said. "All our personal gear is in duffle bags and back packs."

"I'll arrange for a forklift to put your cargo on the chopper's ramp," Inoke said. "We'll winch it into position from there."

It being sunset and suddenly pitch black, I radioed our pilot that we were going to bunk on the ship rather than endure a long ride back to the airport.

Thursday, 18Jul2154—Neiafu, Vava'u (Tonga)

18°39'05" S by 173°59'01" W

The 800-km trip from Fiji to Late took a day and a half since we were fighting the South Equatorial Current the whole way. I had no recollection of our leaving port thanks to Captain Gorm and his magic elixir. Along the way we had a light rain shower with no winds. Lasted a couple of hours. Typhoon season in this part of the world goes from November to April. I emphasized to everyone involved with this adventure both down here and up in CisLuna that I wanted all testing completed by the end of September. With global warming the weather geeks had expanded the typhoon categories up to Cat 10 although the highest recorded thus far was a Cat 7 with maximum sustained winds of 390 km/h. That was Typhoon Upang in 2149. It passed over Manila before veering north into Macau flooding vast regions and displacing millions. Over a hundred thousand deaths. *Southern Cross* looked seaworthy but I did not want to put her to the test in one of those monsters.

There being no secure anchorage around Late, we pressed on to Vava'u, an archipelago 55 km to the east. Still a lot of hidden coves and picturesque beaches in spite of the sea level rise from the last couple of centuries. Vava'u was an ideal place to anchor while we conducted test operations on Late. It was well away from any stray impacts and out of sight of Captain Gorm and his crew. Our cover story was pretty plausible but why arouse suspicion? Our rescue chopper with her 240 km/h cruise could chew up the 55-km separation in about 15 minutes.

It was two hours before sunset when we pulled into port in Neiafu, the major city of Vava'u, on Wednesday 18Jul2153. We were so big there was no dock space so we anchored out in the deep-water Port of Refuge. I wanted to take a ride out to Late to have a quick look while we still had light. The pilot was game but his crew chief was thumbs down claiming he wanted to do some precautionary inspections after our passage to make sure all was as it should be. He assured us that barring any unforeseen damage along the way, we should be ready to go at first light. I thanked him and left him to his work. I learned a long time ago that arguing with helicopter crew chiefs about maintenance was a great way to become a greasy slick on the surface. So we decided instead to let Tobias build us a nice meal of local seafood and then to bed. We kept the toasting to a minimum since I had scheduled lift-off for 0700 HRS next morning.

I limited the crew and passenger manifest to the pilot, crew chief, myself, Roberta, and Jonathan—Roberta so she could get a sense of where to set up impact points and instrumentation, and Jonathan so he could give us a detailed digital map of the island with his drone. Molly and Eddy stayed behind to check out our equipment. I was hoping to be ready for the first impact in five days. CisLuna might not be ready with a penetrator in five days, but I didn't want us to be the holdup.

CHAPTER TWENTY-SIX

19Jul2154—Late (Tonga)

18°48'07" S by 174°39'04" W

The island of Late was six km wide and more or less circular with a 500-meter crater located at the bull's eye. Elevation loss descending outward from the crater rim was pretty steep leveling out to a 200-meter-high plateau that covered the rest of the island. Apart from a thin spot northwest of the crater, the entire island was covered with a thick mat of jungle. Due east of the crater maybe three km was a small lake.

I had the pilot crisscross Late several times at low level looking for any signs of habitation. It had no bays and her shores were lava-lined all the way around. A skilled sailor might have been able to land his canoe on one of the beaches, but he'd be drifting home on a raft. The only indication that man had ever been there was an old vulcanology station about 150 meters northwest of the crater rim. Satisfied there were no people on the island, I had the pilot put us down by the vulcanology station. Apart from the crater rim, every place else was too covered over with thick jungle to set down.

Once the rotor blade came to a stop, Jonathan unpacked his drone to give us a detailed elevation map of the island.

"How long for you to collect your data?" I asked.

"About an hour," Jonathan said.

"Roberta, will you need Jonathan's map data to figure out where you want to plant your seismometers and target impact points?" I asked.

"Not really," Roberta said. "With the island so conveniently circular and 6 km across, I was going to plot impact points in a circle along the even clock radians and 1 km in from the shore. We'll mark each one with an orange plastic banner in the shape of a plus-sign."

"So 12, 2, 4, etc. for a total of six impact points?" I asked.

"Right. Then I'll set up seismometers along the odd clock radians plus one more on the even radians two km in from the shore. I should have plenty of seismic data to accurately measure blast as well as the impact point."

"I'll be flying a set of four drones at about 1000 meters altitude surrounding the impact point," Jonathan said. "They'll be loaded with high-speed cameras to catch the exact moment of impact which we can compare with the orange banners. We should have the impact point located to within a half meter."

"Excellent! And what about depth of penetration?" I asked.

"After all six impacts have taken place we'll set up an array of geophones to make a 3D map of the impact sites," Roberta said. "That should allow us to precisely locate our impactors."

"I assume your geophones are too sensitive to emplace before the impacts?" I asked.

"Right," Roberta said.

"How will you generate a signal for your geophones to pick up?" I asked.

"We'll have the chopper drop a 50 kg weight onto the surface," Roberta said. "It'll be tethered to the chopper so we don't have to go down and fetch it every time."

"Okay, that gives us explosive impact, crater size, circular error probable, and depth of penetration," I said. "Am I missing anything?"

"Winds aloft and air density," Jonathan said. "We're going to put up a stack of balloons in five-thousand-meter increments. Inside each balloon is a foil radar reflector that can be picked up by our Space-Based Doppler Radar Network. Their velocity will provide wind data to inform the impactor's descent trajectory. They also have air density gauges to see how that impacts their descent velocity. The key is to precisely position the impactor just as it hits the atmosphere. There is no way to make trajectory corrections after that."

"That's all well and good, but I don't see how we're going to deploy a bunch of balloons over Persia come D-Day," I said.

"Hank's supposed to have a team working on that," Roberta said. "Meanwhile, I have a question."

"What's that?"

"These six impactors are all the same size and form factors?" Roberta asked. "30 meters by 1.0 meters plus whatever for the ablation coating? Is that the only size penetrator we're going to use? I mean won't that be overkill for the smaller targets?"

"You're worried about collateral casualties?" I asked.

"Uh... yeah, I guess."

"I think our targets will come in the following types: surface targets that are house or large building sized. House-sized would include TELS used for missile launch or mounting laser cannon—we're not sure which at this point. Then there are the underground targets where they excavated a large cavity and covered it with gravel and cement, and then there are cave networks under large mountains. With the excavated facilities, we need something that will go down about a hundred meters. In the case of the mountains we're mainly hoping to seal the entrances with massive cave-ins.

"I'm gonna go out on a limb and say we should use 30-meter penetrators in all cases. My thinking is that a big crater used against smaller surface targets will correct for our CEP not being as refined as we'd like. And a 30-meter penetrator has the best chance of knocking out the deeply buried underground facilities. So, yeah, civilian non-combatants located near surface targets will likely become casualties. Can you handle that?"

Roberta thought for a moment. "Two years ago, I would have said no. But I lost a lot of friends—a sizeable percentage of my species—when we lost *Lunine*. And none of those people bore any ill will towards Persia."

"You don't see it as a case of two wrongs don't make a right?" Jonathan asked.

"You make a good point, Jonathan," I said. "That's why we're only aiming at targets of military or political significance with our penetrator attack. Once that's out of the way, we'll follow up with laser attacks on commercial infrastructure. I remind you Persia did not show us the same courtesy when they began to indiscriminately dismantle our ship when it was ten AU from CisLuna. Had we not discovered their virus when we did, we would have lost all 3300 crew on *Lunine*, not to mention *Lunine* herself along with her captain with whom— sentient AI or no—I still had feelings for. As for the human and galactican casualties, getting spaced without a suit was a pretty terrifying way to go. And as you know there's a pretty high PTSD rate among the survivors of *Lunine*—I'm sure you have friends who suffer from it to this day.

"But however we go about matching up targets and projectiles, the end result must be that Persia goes back to being a medieval caliphate that will pose no threat to any nation outside its borders for the foreseeable future. Any Persian who makes it to that point alive and intact should count himself lucky."

I guess I was raising my voice a bit more than I should have. Jonathan raised both his palms toward me in a gesture of passivity.

"I copy, Boss," Jonathan said. "I'm down with demodernizing Persia. I just think it's a good idea to get this kind of stuff out in the open now so it doesn't come back and haunt us later."

"Point taken," I said. "Apologies if I got a little heated."

"No apology needed, Boss. You were on *Lunine*. I was not."

Chapter Twenty-Seven

10Aug2154—Late (Tonga)

Our first KE penetrator was scheduled to impact at noon today local time at Late's 12-o'clock impact point. I had decided to conduct our test operations from the hangar bay of Southern Cross about three km east of Late. This being the first penetrator, we had no idea where the damn thing was going to land. Secretly I was just hoping it wouldn't land in the middle of downtown Neiafu. Ever the pessimist, I had a little bet with myself that it wouldn't even hit Late but would end up in the drink somewhere.

We had spent the morning putting up a stack of fifteen wind velocity balloons spaced at 5000 meters apart. Meanwhile, the penetrator had launched from CisLuna several hours earlier and would use the balloon data to make atmospheric entry point corrections. We were getting real-time trajectory updates along with projected impact points. So far the projected impact point was pretty close to the desired impact point. As it descended at an increasingly high velocity, it would drift off trajectory a bit and then the course correction rockets would nudge it back into position and everything would be fine for another twenty minutes or so.

At this point I was pretty confident we would hit our desired atmospheric entry point right on the dot. What I was still worried about was what the winds aloft and density altitude over the target were looking like and whether the data we were getting off the balloons would be adequate to guide our impactor to the target. We needed to be confident we could hit the target within a few meters. One thing in our favor was the obscene entry velocity of our impactor—something like Mach 50. At that velocity, the atmosphere would have very little time to fuck with our trajectory. To the extent that we could not come within a few meters of the desired impact point, we would have to compensate with a larger penetrator which would equate to a larger blast radius which in turn would equate to more collateral casualties. And on top of all that, even if these balloons provided solid data, we still hadn't figured out how we were going to deploy a bunch of them over Persia on D-Day. Or if we had, no one had informed me.

Roberta's seismometers were in place on the island with RF telemetry back to her computer. And Jonathan had a set of four drones hovering at 1000 meters with their cameras running and all four feeds showing up back here at ground control.

T minus 30 seconds: Late's coconut crabs were about to get a helluva wake-up call...

T minus 0 seconds: the impact exceeded my wildest expectations. We were only off by fifteen meters. The jungle canopy became fluid radiating a sequence of concentric ripples just like a pebble dropping into a pond and only disappearing when they had traveled about a kilometer from ground zero. The ground under the impact then collapsed forming a crater about 150 meters across. We couldn't tell how deep it was from our viewing angle but it appeared to be at least 50 meters. The blast area evidenced by all the jungle growth that was sheared off extended another 300 meters beyond the impact crater rim.

T plus 9 seconds: We heard a huge boom coming from the direction of the island. It started as a dull punch in the ear drums then tapered off over several seconds. I had not expected it to be this loud. If it carried to Vavaʻu 55 km away, they would be panicking thinking Late was erupting again.

The chopper pilot asked if we wanted to take a ride over to the island to see the damage first hand. I told him no, we'd make do with Jonathan's drone videos—they could zoom in close from four different viewing angles. I wanted to get the data back to CisLuna as soon as possible, so I kept everyone busy at their monitors.

The weather was nice and forecast to continue that way for the next several days. I decided to remain on station overnight so we could begin launching the next set of balloons first thing in the morning. Our next rod was due at noon tomorrow.

Chapter Twenty-Eight

11-16Aug2154—Late (Tonga)

The last of our six impacts came off right on schedule Friday noon on the 16th of August. By now we'd gotten used to the booms. As for the islanders over on Vava'u, maybe not so much.

If they were hearing the booms, I wondered if they noticed how each one occurred a day apart at precisely noon. Oh, well—an opsec challenge for another day.

Meanwhile, the engineers at CisLuna—or more accurately their neural networks—had managed to dial in their atmospheric data to the point where our last rod was only two meters from the target. Again the Mach 50 entry speed of the penetrators left very little time for the atmosphere to alter the trajectory. Hence, I doubted we could do much better than two meters CEP. Time to put out the geophone array!

17-21Aug2154—Late (Tonga)

The geophones turned out to be a major pain in the ass due to the thick jungle that had to be descended through to find solid ground to implant the instrument. We spent four days on the project and invented a whole new dictionary of foul language.

Dropping the 50-kg weight wasn't so bad. We just had to find a clear spot so its tether wouldn't be tangled in the undergrowth. Fortunately, there were plenty of those within the impact craters. Chalk up another two days and a lot of JP-4. Kudos to Molly for thinking ahead on that one. We had plenty of chopper fuel on board our ship.

Turns out our penetrators all made it to about the same depth of one hundred fifty meters. Pretty good considering most of that was solid basalt. That should compromise just about any underground bunker the Persians had created. The sites located under mountains were a different story, but we were not limited to 30-meter penetrators. We could go up to a hundred meters penetrator length if necessary and there was also the option of sealing up each site's access points and vent holes.

As we were finishing up, we got word from CisLuna that they wanted to test some smaller penetrators—20 and 10-meter lengths. Three of each should do it, they said. No need to measure the depth of penetration. They were mainly interested in how much the smaller penetrators would be impacted by atmospheric effects. Hence, we could use the old aiming points. The plan was to put up one set of balloons which was good for us since we were running low on balloon inventory. Not to worry, they said. We'll drop all six the same day an hour apart starting at 0900. We negotiated up to 1000 since the higher elevation balloons take a bit longer to float into position.

23Aug2154—Late (Tonga)

The mini-rods, as we called them, started out hitting wide but by Drop #3 we were putting them within three meters of the bull's eye. We all felt better knowing that we had some options when it came to how big of a boom we wanted to put on a given target. Even Jonathan, the unofficial keeper of the team's conscience, seemed happy. I slept well that night... until I started worrying about how we were going to get balloons emplaced in Persia on D-Day. Without the atmospheric data, our CEP would be hundreds of meters instead of less than ten. I hoped Hank had a team working that problem.

Turns out I needn't have worried. Hank's solution—or rather his team's solution—was to deploy thousands of rockets on D-Day morning a few hours before the penetrators were scheduled to hit the atmosphere. Each rocket was responsible for deploying ten balloons at 7500-meter increments as it descended towards the Earth's surface. After the last balloon was deployed, the rocket would deploy a parachute to minimize damage on impact. They did their testing over Point Nemo, aka the Pacific Spacecraft Cemetery, where the ISS was deorbited back in 2031.

That last little detail about parachuting the rocket bodies so they wouldn't wipe out somebody's Samand did a lot for Jonathan's feelings about this whole adventure. If you're wondering what a Samand is, it's a Persian sedan made by IKCO. It was discontinued as an ICE in 2075 when oil stocks became too important as an export item, then revived in 2140 as an EV when enough people got tired of walking. I looked it up. Anyway, Jonathan came up to me and confided, "I guess

Hank really meant it when he said he wanted to minimize casualties among non-combatants!"

It didn't matter if the balloons were spotted. They would seem harmless curiosities and the penetrators would begin landing less than an hour later—not enough time for the Persians to determine their function or if they did, do anything about them.

*　*　*

It had been nice down here on the Surface, by far the nicest trip back to Earth I had experienced in quite a few decades. The tropic air was clean, the climate balmy, the din of political bickering that dominated the rest of the world muffled by distance. These sweet-natured people had not been jaded by the rest of the world's disease, starvation, or political extremism. They were coping with sea level rise as only Polynesians could—by rising above it! I wasn't sure how many more years that would work for them, but for now it was nice. Reluctantly, all that was left for us was to pack up our act and get back to *SSS Frank Buzzard*.

Chapter Twenty-Nine

10Sep2154, D minus 140 — *SSS Frank Buzzard*

It had been a heated topic of debate as to where I should be stationed come D-Day. Hank had good reasons for wanting me at CisLuna managing the launch or launches, however many that came to be. In the end Hernandez prevailed. I think she realized that there was no realistic way she could ask Hank to be on board *Buzzard* when the SpaceCorp shit started hitting the Persian fan—he was too critical to SpaceCorp's future, the Dream we were all fighting for, the Dream of one day becoming a true spacefaring society. Still, she and the crew needed some assurance that SpaceCorp wasn't just rendering them up as cannon fodder, some assurance that SpaceCorp had some real skin in the game and that skin was me... plus several dozen galacticans who had survived the *Lunine* disaster.

The days were hardly action-packed. I spent them bouncing between Hernandez's mop-up plan and Pinto and Smythe's target list. *Buzzard* was ready for D-day. It was just a question of CisLuna matching our readiness with upwards of a couple thousand DU penetrators in three different sizes plus a half dozen more 100-meter supersized ones destined for the

Mount Dena weapons development complex deep in the Zagros Mountains.

The waiting was adding a new level of tension each day for the crew and myself. How many times could I go over the same damn target list, review the latest intel reports, or review the mop-up plan and all its contingencies? I finally went to Hernandez and asked if I could do something else.

"Something else?" Hernandez asked. "You mean you're bored. I'm so sorry to inconvenience you, Roy, but everything we do come D-Day needs to be reduced to muscle memory, something the crew can do in its sleep."

"Not everything," I said. "Not quite."

"Go on."

"How ready are we to un-ass this donut if it turns out we didn't think of something critical... some weird missile or laser we have no defense for?"

"You mean escape pod drill?"

"I do."

"You got any idea what that would do to crew morale if we all of a sudden start emphasizing escape pod drill... what... weeks away from D-Day?"

"More like months, but that's beside the point. We both know that the most important time to call on muscle memory is when the ship is coming apart."

"I got 400 people dedicated to damage control."

"What if 400 is not enough? What if in spite of their best efforts, you have to call abandon station? You know that can happen. It's happened to you before."

Hernandez fumed for a while. "I assume this is something you want to supervise?"

"I was thinking your watch commanders should do the hands-on supervising unless you have a better candidate."

"Can you keep it low key? I don't want the whole ship starting to think this is a preordained outcome."

"We'll present it like it's some new policy directive. They suddenly raised the escape pod rehearsal quota to twice what we currently have or the ship flunks its readiness review, so we suddenly have to cram in a bunch of drills, or better still reduce our current load time by, say, five minutes."

"Okay, that could work, especially coming from somebody from on high, i.e., you. Anything else?"

"Yeah, but you're really going to hate this one."

Hernandez closed her eyes and shook her head. "What is it?"

"We need to trim your crew of as many non-modified humans as we can which would ideally be all of the non-mods."

"What the—"

"—Think about it. If we catch a missile, it's likely to have a nuclear warhead which, even though its blast will be small, will still pack a shit ton of gamma radiation. You and I might have a chance—we've been rendered rad-hard along with our other life-extension goodies. But non-modified humans won't."

"So what are you saying?"

"How many watches do you run?"

"Three."

"And how many will you have on duty when we overfly Persia?"

"One."

"So, in theory, you should be able to condense your crew down to a single full watch—400 personnel—of only modified humans and/or galacticans, right?"

"So what, you want I should space all my non-mods before we overfly Persia?"

"Of course not. Just send them home to CisLuna where they'll be safe. You can do it in dribbles and drabs between now and D-Day."

"How am I'm supposed to run the ship in the meantime with just one watch? We can't go 140 days with one watch."

"Actually you can. I talked to Captain Buzz about it. The ship is sufficiently automated that crew interaction is not needed for simple Earth orbits. Where they *are* needed is when the action starts and we start taking hits and have to adopt alternative means of mission completion."

"Okay, what's your third cockamamie idea?"

"How'd you know I had a third idea?"

"People like you always do everything in threes."

"Hmm... My third idea is to completely de-spin the station when we overfly Persia. The idea is that if we take damage to a major hull structure there won't be a bunch of centrifugal force trying to tear us apart the rest of the way. Should buy us some time to abandon station. Could even allow us to repair the damage without having to abandon station."

"Well, you finally came up with an idea I like. But how are we supposed to get around in zero gee? Everybody will be floating all over everywhere."

"Not if they're at their stations when the action starts. They should all be strapped in. But you raise a good point. If we take a serious hit and do have to abandon station, zero gee could compromise the crews' ability to get to their escape pods."

"Hand-held cold gas rocket packs. They don't carry them right now, but they could."

"Good! Now for my fourth idea."

"Ahhh... four this time. Boy am I lucky."

"Where are your escape pod crews when the action starts?"

"At their duty stations."

"Okay, before we overfly, have them go to their respective escape pods and warm up the escape pods sufficient to launch as soon as they get a full contingent on board. That should save precious minutes if we have to go down. Plus we won't have the problem of an escape pod crew having been lost due to enemy fire and the passengers for that escape pod standing around wondering who knows how to drive the damn thing."

Hernandez thought for a moment. "Okay, I like that idea a lot. I remember having had that problem on *Von Braun*. But what if we don't have enough modified humans to cover the combat duty stations?"

"Supplement with galacticans."

"But most of the combat duty stations are sized for humans. Galacticans are a head shorter on average."

"Make the galacticans your escape pod crews. Escape pod crew stations are one-size-fits-most."

"Hank know about all this?"

"Not yet. I wanted to run it by you first."

"Thanks. Okay, get started with all your organizational and operational changes. I want to tell Hank myself."

"You got it."

As I left I wondered if she'd pitch this scheme to Hank like it was her idea so she could claim credit for her brilliance, or like it was my idea so she'd have a scapegoat if she and her station got left in the lurch.

Chapter Thirty

10Dec2154, D minus 49 — *SSS Frank Buzzard*

We spent several months affecting all the changes on *Buzzard*. Gotta say not having any people walking around on second and third watches was kind of spooky. Made the place seem like a ghost ship. One place that did manage to stay active was the gym. That place was hopping. Half the crew must have been there. I found Eddy hard at work on the squat machine.

"What are you still doing here?" I asked.

"Working on my quads," she said puffing. "What's it look like?"

"That's commendable but you should be doing it in CisLuna. You haven't been modified."

"I'm staying with my shipmates."

"Most of them are in CisLuna."

"She racked her bar and grabbed a towel to wipe the sweat off her face... I got the rest of my life to get modified. I'm not gonna miss this action, Roy."

"How'd you even pull this off anyway?"

"They lined us up a few months ago and called for anyone who hadn't been modified to take one step forward. I stood fast."

"And your gunny bought that?"

"I'm here, aren't I?"

"How many more non-mods like you are still on board?"

"I dunno... maybe a couple dozen. We don't talk about it. We just act like we're all good in the neighborhood!"

I stared at her for a moment. She met my gaze without blinking.

"Don't go fucking this up for me, Roy. We're all here because we want to be and we all know the risks. I mean, c'mon, man, this is what I do. I don't need you goin all bureau-weenie on me."

"Hernandez know?"

"She's not stupid."

I shifted my eyes to the bar she was leaning on... "How much ya got on that thing?"

The machine was spring-loaded so it was independent of local gravity which by now was down to 0.2 gee, ergo it behooved everyone to get between two and four hours of resistance and cardio training everyday seven days a week.

"A solid."

That was her ship jargon for a hundred simulated kilos.

"Okay if I work in with you?"

"Sure, I'm CPR-qualified! Knock yourself out."

"Don't be a smart ass."

We lifted together on the squat machine for another six sets getting up to 160 kg and reducing our reps with each set. We were now just doing sets of twos and threes going for maximum weight. I was surprised she was keeping up with me being as petite as she was. She was wearing some kind of stretchy tights with no undergarments revealing her short-waisted, curvy figure with wicked glutes and quads. On top of that she was busty as hell which made it hard to maintain eye contact.

"Let's drop back down to a hundred and go for max reps."

"You pussyin out on me?"

"No, we just need to work our hearts so we don't faint when we get back to full gee."

"Okay, I'm game. You got a monitor on? – she waved her heart rate monitor at me."

"Of course." I waved my monitor back at her.

"Okay, your max rate is supposed to be 220 minus your age. For me that's 197, so I train at 75% of that which is about 150. What about you?"

"What about me?"

"C'mon, *Abuelito*! You need to be scientific about this. I don't want to have to be giving your scrawny lips no stinkin CPR. So 220 minus... what's your age?"

"A hundred eighteen."

"Are you shittin me? C'mon really, how fuckin old are you?"

"I told you. A hundred eighteen."

She gave me a funny look but entered the number into her calculator. "That gives you a max heart rate of 102 and a training rate of 75. What's your heart rate right now?"

I looked at my monitor. "82." We'd been lifting pretty heavy for a while.

"Well, that's convenient. I can work out and you can just sit there and we each get the same training benefit. Look, I know you had some kinda age reduction longevity bullshit, so how old are you really?"

"It's called longevity treatment but it's more than that. My age going into the Treatment was 69. That was in 2103. After a while, most folks settle in to a biological age of around 35 or 40. Mine tests around 38 using DNA methylation."

"So what should I use?"

"Try 40."

"Okay, that puts your max rate at 180 and your training rate at 135." She smiled at me as though I had risen from the dead. "That's more like it!" She looked around the gym and spotted two adjacent treadmills that had just freed up. "Follow me." When we got to the treadmills, she had me stand guard while she went off in search of something. She came back holding a pair of harnesses with a pair of bungee cords attached to either side. "You know how to work these?"

"Put yours on. I'll copy." Once I got mine on, she adjusted the bungees so I was carrying my weight plus half again or 125 kg.

"Okay, now put your headset on."

I did and it immediately displayed a standard running track in a stadium. I felt her finger tapping the side of the device next to my temple.

"You can change the view to a bunch of different backgrounds. I like running by the ocean. We can conjoin our backgrounds so it feels like we're running together. Here's a mountain trail."

"That looks nice."

"We'll do ocean."

"Don't you want to get some hill work?"

"What part of CPR don't you understand?"

She jumped on her own treadmill, made a few adjustments, and presto! We were side by side on a beautiful black sand beach on a tropical island. I could hear the thump of the waves and I swear I could feel a balmy on-shore breeze. The sun was going down and its image was striated from the distant clouds. After we settled in to our respective paces, she struck up a conversation.

"Tell me about this longevity treatment."

"Current policy calls for waiting till you're fifty before you get it," I said puffing. "I'm trying to get that changed to accept anybody who spends a lot of time in space... what with the radiation hazard and all. They make exceptions for people tagged for a mission into deep space. Those ships don't pack a lot of shielding so you're soaking up about 25 rems per year inside the solar system while you're on that mission. When we finally get outside the solar system that will jump to 70 rems. And that's neglecting all the reactors and fusion rockets and such."

"So do galacticans all get that treatment? They're like always on some kinda deep space mission."

"They don't need it. They're born with it. They get *the Treatment*, so to speak, while they're still zygotes."

"Wow! I didn't know that. How long can you live with the Treatment like you got?"

"We don't really know. A lot of the genes we splice into your DNA come from the Greenland shark. They live up to 500 years in the wild. Plus sharks tend not to get cancer or heart disease— at any rate nowhere near the occurrence rate as humans. But the real advantage is that once you settle in to your age at maturation, you don't age beyond that point, i.e., you no longer become fragile and decrepit with the passing of time. Some people say that with regular genetic tune-ups to make repairs and clean out the genetic garbage that piles up, there might not be an upper limit as to how long you can live."

"So what do you think? How long do *you* figure to live?"

"From what I've seen, many centuries at least. The one thing nobody has any good data on is how your mind will hold up. You know how you forget most of the details of your early childhood by the time you get to be an adult?"

"Yeah."

"Well, I'm thinking that I've had over a hundred years to pile up memories, forgetting a lot of the stuff from my distant past and even a lot from my recent past. What's it gonna be like when I'm, say, 500? Will I even remember this conversation? I mean, I expect I will next year or maybe even five years from now. But will the low significance of this conversation allow me to keep it in the memory banks when I'm 500?"

"Does that worry you?"

"Yes and no. *This* conversation may not be very important in the grand scheme of things, but what if I was to get a PhD in molecular biology? I've always been interested in that. Hell, there's a bunch of stuff I'm interested in, so let's say over the next couple of centuries I get three or four PhDs. Will I have forgotten all the details from the molecular biology work I did? Or will it be like muscle memory—once you get in shape it's easier to get back in shape having gotten out of shape. This is all a new frontier for humanity."

"Okay, dumb question—this seems like an awful lot of trouble to go to—keeping people alive past their use-by date. Why do we do it? I mean apart from the fact that most people aren't real excited about dying."

"That's an easy one. The SpaceCorp Dream of becoming interstellar voyageurs. We expect that even with positron-fusion drives those trips will still take many decades, centuries even. That calls for a generation starship, but a big challenge with generation starships and normal human lifespans is the crew that signed on at launch won't be the crew that arrives at the destination. That's a downer for getting people to sign on in the first place, but it's also a challenge several generations into the voyage when you have great-great-grand-kids bitching about who the hell signed them up for this trip when they're not even likely to still be kicking when they arrive at the destination. With extended lifespans, you can sign on for a mission and still count on being alive when you get there, perhaps even when you get back.

"Then there's the advantage of the reduced logistical burden that comes with obviating the need for nurseries and adults to staff them. With extended longevity, we only procreate on an as-needed basis, say, if somebody gets killed or if we arrive at a destination and replicate the ship that got us there but then need to replicate bodies to crew her."

Eddy was silent for a long while. When she finally spoke, what she said was totally out of left field.

"Roy, I'm going to make you a deal."

"What's that?"

"This mission is gonna go sideways within ten minutes after we cross the Zagros Mountains. The Persians are gonna feed us a nuke and it's gonna be a direct hit and it's gonna do major structural damage. And even though we aren't rotating, we're still gonna be in for a RUEDL."

"A RUEDL?"

"Yeah, a Rapid Unscheduled Entry Descent and Landing."

I had not heard that one before. Must be a LEO thing. Hanging out in CisLuna mostly, except for when I was on deep space missions, I didn't spend all that much time with the LEO crowd these days.

When you spend most of your time in Low Earth Orbit cruising along at, say, 8 km/sec, Surface is a scant four or five hundred kilometers below, never far from your imagination. But it's worse than that. The Kármán line—the nominal boundary between Earth's upper atmosphere and the official beginning of space—is one hundred kilometers closer. Once a station makes initial contact with the upper atmosphere it starts to decelerate fast and as it decelerates it descends into ever thicker atmosphere and the air friction climbs exponentially. Space stations, for all their heavy armor against space debris, lack any form of ablative coating that would delay their burning up in that thickening atmosphere. Once initial contact with the upper atmosphere is made, a space station has less than a minute before it becomes a burning glob of goo. If there is anything left by the time it hits Surface, it's more of a splat than a landing. Trust me, that's one landing you won't walk away from.

The nuclear tipped missile is the most feared threat from below. Nuclear blast effects pose a minimal problem in the vacuum of space. To be effective they need to make a direct hit—proximity detonations are almost useless. But if they do manage to make a direct hit, the warhead yield does not have to be very large. A fraction of a kilotonne will be sufficient to tear a tremendous hole in the outer shell of even the most heavily armored LEO space station. At the site of the hole, blast overpressure will try to inflate the interior of the station causing it to rupture, thereby causing a lot of collateral structural damage and hull breaches. *Buzzard* compensates for this by sealing off all passageways and avoiding large open spaces in her structure. But there's only so much damage you can prevent by dogging all the hatches.

Once the hull is impacted by one of these nuclear tipped missiles you have maybe three hundred kilometers between you and the Kármán line to un-ass the station in your escape pod. And that's only if you're at the other end of the station from the impact point. If you're at the same end as the impact point, the most you can hope for is a quick death. The folks far enough from the impact to not get a gamma fricassee will likely get spaced through one of the many hull breaches caused by the overpressure. On *Buzzard* crewmembers only carry about an hour's worth of O_2 and their suits offer very little insulation against the searing heat of direct sunlight or the frigid cold of the sun's shadow. As for debris resistance, don't ask. Suffice it to say, their chances of survival are exceedingly slim.

Perhaps one or two will get picked up by a passing escape pod if it hasn't already decelerated into an EDL trajectory. But keep in mind unarmored escape pods put a high priority on minimizing their time in the debris zone of LEO, so they won't be hanging around looking for stragglers. You should figure if you get spaced you're as good as dead. I figure the entire crew from the entire back half of the station will be lost. The ones on the other end are the only ones with a chance, but even then their survival is dependent on how quickly they get into their pods and how quickly their pod pilots initiate an EDL trajectory burn. If you're lucky enough to be on the far end of the station, you best not be a straggler. Pod pilots are well briefed about how structural disintegration will tend to migrate from the impact end up to their end of the station. Nobody knows for sure how long that will take, but the so-called experts I've talked to are only counting on thirty minutes tops.

I knew all of this because it had been my job to imagine what it would be like to send a battle station like *Buzzard* into a space battle. But is this the kind of thing that was also going through Eddy's mind? She was just a lance corporal fercrissakes! And if she was thinking like this what about the rest of the crew?

"Okay, Eddy, how do you know all this about going sideways after we cross the Zagros Mountains?"

"I keep seeing it in a dream. Same dream every night for a month now."

"Every night you dream we get hit by a nuke after we cross the Zagros Mountains?"

"Yeah."

"You talk to any of your shipmates about this?"

"Fuck no! Just you. Just now."

I paused a moment to digest what she had said.

"Okay, what's this deal of yours?"

"I'm gonna save your ass... mine too. But then you're gonna get me frontsies on the Treatment, so I can go with you on your mission to the stars."

"Do you know how bad it would be if we catch a nuke?"

"I got a pretty good idea."

"But you think you can save me... us? You want to tell me how?"

"Easy. By making sure you're in the front of the station."

"Why the front? We could catch a nuke from any angle."

"Not in my dream. We always take it up the ass. Nobody sees it comin. Just wham! And our whole ass end gets blown apart. Only the people on the front half survive."

I hesitated a bit. "You're really creepin me out, Eddy."

"Sorry. But how bout it? We got a deal?"

I hesitated some more while I mulled it over. "Ah, no, we don't have a *deal*. BUT, if we survive this fool's errand, I will see to it your name is submitted for the Treatment. Hell, anybody survives D-Day deserves some kind of compensation. Anyway, then I need you to do something. If you really want to go on deep space missions, eventually interstellar missions, you need to develop some skills beyond breaking things and hurting people. I'm talking one of the sciences or engineering. Nobody goes to deep space for free. Know what I'm sayin?"

She nodded.

"Good. Now all we have to do is survive your stinkin dream!"

Eddy flashed a big smile. "Hot damn! Now get your ass moving, *Abuelito*! You're my ticket to deep space and I want you in top shape! We might have to survive for quite a while on the ground after we RUEDL."

After Eddy and I parted company, I was sweating like a whore in church. Eddy had put me through a workout that made me question whether she really wanted me to live through this ordeal. Anyway, after we parted company, I headed for the shower station nearest my cabin. I let the hot water beat on my head and face and run down my back for a good twenty minutes knowing that no matter how long I let the water run I was going to be a quadriplegic for the next two days. Later in my cabin, I poured myself a single malt and sipped it slowly while I pondered Eddy's fucking dream. While I may have doubted her prescience, I did not doubt the human mind's ability to piece together seemingly unrelated data into a realistic story. What data was her mind seeing that mine was not?

CHAPTER THIRTY-ONE

Wednesday, 11Dec2154, D minus 48 — *SSS Frank Buzzard*

I woke up after a fitful but dreamless sleep resolving to interview several people about the likelihood of taking a nuclear missile from the rear perspective. Actually, putting it so directly would have made me guilty of leading the witness— very bad investigative procedure. Anyway, first on my list was Commander Smythe. She had proven pretty insightful at our meetings in the past. Maybe she'd been sharing Eddy's macabre dreams. I caught up with her in the mess hall late one night nursing a cuppa Joe.

"Feel like company?" I asked.

"If you can't sleep either, I can promise you this stuff won't help."

I signaled the robot waiter. "Hot chocolate, no whip cream."

I winked at Smythe, "No sense pouring gasoline on a fire." She smiled. "Say, all these weeks we've been together on this station... I don't even know your first name."

"Arwen."

"Arwen? That's unusual."

"My folks were big Tolkien fans."

"Tolkien? I confess I haven't heard of her."

"Him. 20th Century fantasy novelist. Best known for *Lord of the Rings*. Arwen was an elf queen. Minor character, actually. Best known for being the inspiration of the male hero, Aragorn. She marries him in the end, after he completes his quest, of course."

"Sounds like a good read."

"Actually, I wouldn't know. I mostly had it read to me when I was little. Been trying to overcome all that parental programming ever since."

"I feel ya!"

She closed her eyes and shrugged with a half-smile. "So what do you *really* want to talk about besides my first name?"

I put my mug of hot chocolate down. "Well, *Arwen*, I'd like to discuss the prognosis for the station after we cross the Zagros Mountains."

Smythe almost did a spit-take. "Ooh! Heavy shit, man. There gonna be a quiz at the end?"

"Ah... no. Actually, I want to know *your* opinion, not feed you my opinion."

"Yeah, okay, well... I kinda hinted at it at during one of our first meetings—remember the Persian laser cannons?"

"I do remember them, but that was then and this is now. Do you still think we're looking at lasers?"

Smythe became lost in thought for a moment. "Yes... I do."

"But didn't you and Commander Pinto target all the known TELs?"

"Yes again. But the key word is 'known.' I don't think for a minute that we got them all. Once we clear that ridgeline and get ID'd, I'm betting we're gonna have at least a dozen high energy lasers drilling holes in our hull. Make sure your spare O₂ bottle is full. I'm carrying two myself."

"You think that'll be enough to bring us down?"

"No. We'll be well ventilated but not to the point where we go down. My simulations all show us clearing Persian space before any of their equipment could drill through the hull and damage any vital flight systems. Next orbit I show us altering our inclination so as to not fly over Persia a second time."

"What about the drones? Won't they spook the laser cannon?"

"Most likely. But my simulation pretends there were no drones."

"So you're pretty confident we'll complete our flyover unscathed?"

"I think we'll complete our first flyover unscathed. Maybe even several more after that. Keep in mind we'll have blinded them and knocked out their command apparatus. But they could paste together a new command apparatus and jury-rig some kind of early warning system such that on the fifth or sixth pass they'll wheel out the laser cannons we did not target. That's when we'll get a face full of photons."

I swirled my hot chocolate around in my mug. It was only tepid now. Should have asked for one of those heated mugs. "Do you see any possibility of them getting us with anything besides laser cannon?"

"You mean like a missile?"

"Anything."

"Can't speak for anything, but as for a missile... nah. Anything they put up that's as slow as a missile, we're sure to spot. And then after we target it, it's life expectancy drops to nanoseconds."

"And you're sure we'd spot it?"

"Oh, yes. Definitely."

I got up to leave. "Well, thanks."

"Hey, wait a minute! Don't I get to hear *your* origin story?"

I sat back down. "I warn you, it's pretty gory."

"I like gory," she said with a leering smile.

"Your funeral."

Half an hour later I left her at the table wiping tears off her face. The part about my former wife, Hanna, and my son, Michael, being murdered always gets 'em. Hell, it gets to me too.

Friday, 13Dec2154, D minus 46 — *SSS Frank Buzzard*

I finally caught up with Commander Pinto two days later while he was finishing up a pretty grueling workout in the gym.

"Okay if we meet after you get cleaned up? I need to pick your brain about something."

"Sure. Mess Hall okay? It's pretty quiet there between watches."

He was right about the Mess Hall being quiet. I ordered a hot chocolate while I waited for him. I didn't have to wait too long. He grabbed a tall bottle of electrolyte water and slid onto the bench opposite me.

"So what is it you think my brain has that is worth picking?

"I'll get straight to it. What do you think is waiting for us when we clear the Zagros Mountains on our first pass over Persia?"

"You worried about something in particular?"

"Not necessarily. Just trying to cover all my bases."

"Well, Commander Smythe and I—"

"—Let me stop you right there. I know you and Smythe have been working this problem together for some time now. But I want you to try to give me just your opinion. Try to filter out any influences she may have had on your thinking."

"Okay." He paused for a bit to collect his thoughts. "I think nothing is going to happen. Hitting them with all those impactors all at once is going to leave their decision-making capability in shock—if not dead. And on the off chance there's somebody who *can* make a decision, he won't have any working equipment to make a decision about. Compound all that with the fact that anything that could possibly threaten us has to make it up to LEO—a non-trivial act in and of itself. Bottom line is we're going to be flying over a wasteland."

"Okay, fair enough. Now hypothetically, let's assume there was some surviving decision-making authority. What equipment might exist that could threaten us up here? I'm looking for a four-sigma case here, something we didn't think of."

He mused for several seconds then shook his head. "I'm sorry, Roy. I just don't see anything. Bear in mind, anything that survives that first salvo of penetrators will get taken out by the drones with their laser cannon and tungsten penetrators. That means when we overfly the ridgeline, we're going to be greeted by a nation in ruins. Barely enough spit to lick its wounds."

"Okay then, thank you for your candor."

*   *   *

As I low-gee shuffled back to my cabin, I ruminated over Pinto's optimism. Was he right? Was it really that simple? Was I borrowing trouble? On the other hand, borrowing trouble was kinda my job. Maybe the best way to think about the problem was to *not* think about it for a while. Maybe I should submit myself to another one of Eddy's torture sessions. Or I could read a book or maybe find a movie I hadn't seen several times already. I finally opted for a martini from the bottle of gin I'd scrounged and then to bed. While I sipped on the martini, I asked myself if I was doing a good job. It occurred to me that this job—fire prevention—was a bit different than what I was best at—firefighting. Probably accounted for my discomfort. Oh well, I still had 46 days to figure out what I was missing.

CHAPTER THIRTY-TWO

Friday, 13Dec2154, D minus 46 — *SSS Frank Buzzard*

Captain Hernandez had dialed the station's gravity down to a measly 20% which was kind of interesting given the dilemma Eddy had presented me with. You see she had predicted that the station was going to succumb to a nuclear blast in the aft end. But—and here's the dilemma—at 20% gee we were still rotating. Ergo 'aft' was undefined and would continue to be so until we ceased rotating entirely. As far as I knew Captain Hernandez had not identified any particular part of the ship as aft. It was sort of like roulette—*round and round and round she goes and where she stops...* So how, pray tell, did Eddy's dream have the prescience to know where the detonation was going to hit? Maybe I should ask her.

*   *   *

I found her in the Mess Hall finishing up breakfast before she went on shift.

"This'll have to be quick, Roy. I'm due at my post in—looking at her watch—twelve mikes."

"I'll be brief. Your dream shows us taking a nuke in the aft part of the station, right?"

"Yeah."

"So how does it know where aft is? I mean we're still spinning so aft is undefined and will remain so until we come to zero gee."

Eddy thought for a moment and shrugged. "I don't know."

"Think now, where is your mind's eye when the nuke goes off? What does it see?"

Eddy closed her eyes and wrinkled her brow a bit. "I think I'm at my post, Fire Direction Center #2. There's a loud boom and an overpressure and the station lurches... then a bunch more noises, creaking and grinding... more lurching... then vacuum forming as the air rushes out."

"Wait, how can there be vacuum? All the hatches are dogged. You'd have to be right next to the blast area to feel any vacuum."

"I don't know. But I remember air rushing past my face until I pulled my visor down. I don't think I was very close to the blast though. The initial boom seemed far away."

"Hmm..."

"You think if I could figure out where the blast is gonna hit, maybe we could make sure nobody is near that spot?"

"No, but that's not a bad idea. Okay, you need to run, but hey, when you sack out tonight, try to explore around in your dream when the blast hits. I need to know where aft is when we go to zero gee."

"Okay, I'll see what I can do."

As I watched her shuffle off I felt supremely stupid. Asking a young woman to query her dream to see where a nuclear warhead was going to strike the station... I mean what the living fuck!

Then it hit me. Maybe the nuke was already on the ship, like a limpet mine of some sort. Maybe it was set to explode when it sensed it was at zero gee. Okay, Roy-boy, time to take this cockamamie theory to Hernandez. What's she gonna do, shoot me out an airlock for being looney tunes? That's what I'd do if I was captain.

*　*　*

I must have stood outside Hernandez's cabin door for a good five minutes before I got the courage to knock. She was in the middle of dressing but she ordered me to come in anyway. I tried not to stare.

Hernandez went back to fixing her hair. "Okay, spill."

"You're gonna think I'm barking mad but I feel compelled to share this with you."

Hernandez put her brush down and turned to face me left eyebrow raised in a high arch. Roy, sweetie, I've *always* thought your sort were a couple of boosters short of a liftoff. *But* I've always written it off to what makes you good at your job... up to a point. So dump it on the table and we'll either figure it out or you'll walk out of here in a straitjacket."

What have I got to lose? I told her about Eddy's dream, and how this nuke was going to hit us ten minutes after we crossed the Zagros Mountains, and that it'd be a direct hit in our aft section wherever that happened to be, and even though we weren't spinning, the damage was going to be severe and the station was going down, and everybody that didn't make it to an escape pod was going to die. I left out the part about Eddy wanting to keep me in the forward part of the station for my own survivability.

"That's some dream," Hernandez said. "What am I supposed to do about it?"

"I don't know exactly. I went around to Smythe and Pinto and asked them if they thought we were vulnerable in some way after we crossed the Zagros."

"What'd they say?"

"Smythe thinks we're good for several laps over the country but then somebody is going to zap us with a laser cannon—a big one. Not sure if it's gonna be big enough to take us out. Pinto thinks we're going to be flying over a wasteland. No response from below. A free fire zone for us to pick off the rest of their infrastructure."

"So what do *you* think?"

"As for Smythe vs. Pinto, I'd give you even odds. But then I wondered if the nuke was already on the station like some kind of limpet mine. May we could search for it? If it's nuclear, it shouldn't be that hard to pick up a radiation signal."

"Okay, do it, but do it with robots. I don't want you spooking the crew."

"Maybe you could announce that CisLuna has another readiness inspection that we need to do and if we don't pass we don't get to cross the Zagros Mountains. The crew is pretty psyched for that. Just tell them to keep to their duties and stay out of the robot's way if one passes through their work area."

"Can do. How many robots you want?"

"How many you got?"

CHAPTER THIRTY-THREE

Friday, 20Dec2154, D minus 39 — *SSS Frank Buzzard*

As it turned out, a team of 34 robots can scour every square millimeter of a space station to include the hull exterior looking for telltale radiation signatures in 27 hours 12 minutes... average. We actually did it three times sending each robot on a different search pattern each iteration. We paid special attention to the nuclear propulsion system since it utilized bomb-grade U235 and theoretically only needed a detonator to make it go off. Well, that's an oversimplification, but even so, all that fissile material would have been highly tempting for a would-be saboteur. So six days later I was back in Hernandez's cabin not watching her get dressed again and explaining that three consecutive searches had come up dry.

"Buzz, how crowded is the Mess Hall right now?"

"There are only four persons there at the moment," Captain Buzzard said.

"Good. And where is Eddy?"

"Working out in the gym."

"Okay, Roy, go get Eddy and bring her to the Mess Hall. I want to meet with her but I don't want to formally call her to the Bridge. Find a secluded table and wait for me to mosey by for an informal chat."

*　*　*

Half an hour later Eddy and I were sitting at a table in the Mess Hall. She could tell something was up and was nervous.

"C'mon, Roy. I know this isn't about you feeding your hot cocoa jones. What's this about?"

"Keep your shirt on."

"I'll give you five more minutes then I'm gonna grab a shower."

"No, Corporal. You are going to keep your seat and drink your cocoa... all day if necessary."

She looked at me as though she wanted to say something clever but couldn't think of anything. She just scowled and stared at her cocoa.

A minute later Captain Hernandez walked up and sat down next to me, opposite Eddy. Captain Buzzard's avatar popped up on the bulkhead next to us. Eddy turned white but remained speechless.

"Hello, Eddy. I hear you've been having dreams."

Eddy hesitated a moment, looked at me, then back at the captain. "Yes, sir."

"And you have them every night?"

"Yes, sir. Just about."

"Always the same dream?"

"Yes, sir."

"Where are you when the dream happens?"

"At my station, sir. Checking target coordinates."

293

"But your station is not at the aft of the station."

"No, sir. In my dream it's on the port side, about the ninety-degree mark."

"And where is Roy in your dream?"

"He's out in the passageway, maybe a hundred meters aft."

This was a funny conversation. Like a psychologist was asking a patient to recount their experience from under deep hypnosis.

"Okay," Hernandez said. "Take it from there. What happens next?"

"Well, I'm working at my station. But then I get this weird sensation... like something is about to happen. Then a second later there's this huge boom and the hull shudders. I know—don't ask me how—but I know I need to run out into the passageway and yell for Roy to follow me. Even with his antiradiation treatment, he should stay out of the blast area. So he hears me somehow—it's really noisy and there's panic everywhere people running around and all. Anyway he starts running toward me but he's kind of slow like he's hip deep in honey. So I run to him and start pulling him along and we head for our escape pod. It's up near the bow so we have a ways to go. We have to hurry because we can feel the hull starting to come apart."

"Let me stop you there for a moment. You say your work station is on the port side about the ninety-degree mark?"

"Yes, sir."

"Is it always there? Same place every time you have your dream?"

"Yes, sir."

Hernandez paused a moment, leaning back in her chair. "Where is the station when the blast happens?"

"We're over Persia. A few minutes after clearing the Zagros ridgeline."

"Can you show me on a map where we cross the Zagros? Buzz, please put a map on the table for us. Don't show our planned trajectory."

Eddy studied the map. Buzzard had oriented it so it was right side up for Eddy. She drew a trajectory line just north of Baghdad passing through Kermanshah, Hamedan, and Tehran before passing into Turkmenistan slightly north of Ashgabat.

"We don't make it to Turkmenistan though. We get hit right after we pass over Kermanshah."

Eddy's trajectory was spot on. I was keeping myself silent so as not to lead the witness, but I wondered if Baghdad on hearing all the ruckus over Persia might panic and send us a little love note as we passed over Baghdad that caught up with us right about Kermanshah. I made a mental note to take that up with Smythe and Pinto later on.

"Do you get off the station successfully? Before it comes apart?"

"I don't know. The dream always stops before Roy and I make it to our escape pod. I wake up then. All sweaty from trying to drag Roy through the passageway."

"Are you able to get back to sleep?"

"No. I usually grab a shower to rinse the sweat off. Then I read a bit to get my mind off what just happened. I usually drop back off within a couple hours of waking up."

Hernandez rose from her seat. "Thank you, Eddy."

"Captain, you don't think I'm nuts... with these dreams and all?"

"Who knows? I used to have an aunt who had dreams like that. She died a long time ago but when she was alive, everybody in the family used to go to her to hear how she predicted the future. Her dreams were always really ambiguous so you could never tell if she was just making shit up or if she was for real. People tried to pay her but she always refused. Did you ever have anybody like that in your family?"

"My grandmother. And her grandmother before her."

"So it skips a generation."

"Yes, sir. I never noticed that before, but I guess it did."

"Is this the first time you've had dreams like this?"

"No, sir. But never this vivid, and never the same one over and over."

"Do not speak to anyone of your dreams... except Roy. Make sure you tell him whenever anything new happens. Now go and get your shower."

And then she left. Buzzard's avatar blanked out and the map on the table went away, leaving Eddy and me alone at the table.

"Man, I hope she doesn't think I'm nuts."

"If she did you'd be shipping out ASAP. No nutters allowed in combat."

"Do *you* think I'm nuts?"

"Eddy, I cannot account for your dreams. They are certainly strange. But no, I do not think you're nuts. They have been useful in a way—allowing me to focus my paranoia onto productive activity. And I don't mind that all my searching has produced no hidden mines. It was better than staring at a calendar counting down the days to D-Day."

"What do you think she'll do... the Captain I mean?"

"You mean, will she try to call off the mission? Doubtful. She's too hardcore for that. She might try to clear as many people as possible out of the aft section of the station as soon as we zero out our rotation. That would seem to make sense. I'll mention it to her."

*   *   *

As Eddy trundled off to the shower, I sat there trying to collect my thoughts. I wondered if Captain Buzzard was wondering, *"What fools these mortals be!"* Or was he just going on about his business. After all, he had just witnessed a crewman recounting a dream that showed his ship being destroyed. Unlike the crew and the sentient robots, he had no way to abandon his space station—he was doomed to go down with his ship, so to speak. How could a sentient entity not be concerned about that? AIs continue to mystify me. I know that nothing in their programming allows them to mimic what we humans call feelings. And logically they have no need for them. Still, with the all too human way they interact with us, one cannot help but have feelings for them and therefore I find it strange that they can face their impending doom with the same indifference as I have while taking a crap.

CHAPTER THIRTY-FOUR

Wednesday, 25Dec2154, D minus 34 — *SSS Frank Buzzard*

Christmas. Christianity may have waned in importance but a lot of folks still celebrated the 25th of December in a secular fashion with no particular attention to the birthday of the Christian Christ. In recognition of this, Hernandez had given the crew a day of relief from the constant readiness drills. Hence, I noticed makeshift ornaments, Santas flying about in sleighs, wreaths on doors, and messages of good cheer scattered about the public areas of the station, most notably the Mess Hall where there were trays of Christmas cookies set out on each of the tables.

*   *   *

Towards evening I found Smythe and Pinto sitting there having an eggnog. Never developed a taste for its cloying sweetness myself, but I sat down and ordered one as an excuse to coopt their conversation.

"Merry Christmas!" I said sitting down next to them.

"Bull shit!" Smythe said. "What's really on your mind, Roy?"

I feigned a hurtful look. "Can't a guy wish his crewmates a bit of good cheer?"

"Hmm... a guy can," Smythe said. "Not you, although I appreciate your attempt to make jolly."

"Well, then I apologize."

"Don't," Smythe said. "Your efforts more than anybody else's will probably be what gets us through D-Day alive. So spill. What's on your mind?"

"Baghdad."

"Baghdad?" Pinto said.

"Yeah. Our first passage into Persian space will pass over Baghdad. And by the time that happens, Persia will be a smoking... I was going to say ruin, but there will still be more ruination to come. Anyway, might the Iraqis be nervous enough to send a missile up to meet us as we pass over? Do they have any hidden launch capability that we are unaware of?"

"This a homework assignment?" Smythe asked.

"Uh... yeah, I guess."

"Does it have a due date and is the answer just for you or will we be presenting to Hernandez, et al.?" Pinto asked.

"I dunno, what's reasonable? A few days? A week? If you dig up something significant we'll need time to compensate for your discovery."

"Okay, let's say Friday after lunch. Who gets to hear our answer?"

"Depends on what you find out. No need to pester the Captains with non-information."

"Copy. You want us to start now?"

"I do not. This task is off the wall enough that I'd like you to sleep on it first, then dig in first thing in the morning."

"No wonder you never got command," Smythe said, then winced. "Sorry, that was catty. What I meant was that you are way too reasonable to be a commander." She winced again. "Shit, I'm just digging myself in deeper."

Pinto placed his hand on her forearm. "Maybe you should put your shovel down." Turning his attention to me, "We'll be on it bright and early tomorrow, Boss."

"Boss?"

"Since you have the odd characteristic of not having a title while packing a lot of authority, I've decided that what you are is our *de facto* Chief of Staff. We've never had one of those on *Buzzard*, so you get to be it."

"Don't let Hernandez know," I said to him.

"Your secret is safe with us."

They both raised their glasses.

"You haven't touched your eggnog," Smythe said.

I grinned feeling my face redden. "Don't really care for the stuff."

"I thought it was just me," Smythe said. "Is this why they only serve it at Christmas?"

I stood up to go. "You could be on to something. Sleep well."

Friday, 27Dec2154, D minus 32 — *SSS Frank Buzzard*

Pinto and Smythe had made themselves a war room close to the bridge. Virtually all the wall space was covered with digital maps and charts. There was a boardroom style table in the middle but it had long since been converted into workspaces. The usual contingent of half a dozen staffers had been shooed out so the three of us could have a secure space to discuss their Baghdad findings. I poured myself a mug of joe and sat down.

"So tell me about Baghdad!"

They looked at each other, then Pinto spoke.

"We studied all the intel we had on Baghdad and found no evidence of any kind of space-capable launch facilities either in or around Baghdad proper nor anywhere else in the rest of Iraq."

"Does that mean this is a short meeting? I should go back to my cabin and mix myself a Margarita?"

"Ah... no," Smythe said. "We kept looking." She put up a map of the Middle East. "As you can see backtracking our flight trajectory takes us through Syria, Jordan, and Saudi Arabia—zero capability with all three. Then we get to Israel which has been a lightning rod for Arab hostility since 1948. Which is not to say they've launched anything since the Kessler Syndrome rendered LEO nonviable for conventional satellite traffic, but they have maintained offensive capability the entire time, i.e., they could probably launch a surface-to-space-missile with a nuclear warhead into LEO all the way up to 2000 km altitude—way higher than we'd be flying for our pass over Persia—IF they wanted to. The question is do they want to?"

"Okay, I'll bite," I said. "Do they want to?"

"I say no, Arwen says maybe."

"Tell me why no."

"Israel hates Persia and vice versa. If anybody decides to take out Persia, Israel's biggest concern will be whether they have an adequate supply of kosher popcorn."

"Makes sense. Okay, Arwen, your bat."

"Um... 'maybe' is actually too strong a word, but the short answer is paranoia. If they launch an SSM it will be a knee-jerk response, fear that Armageddon has begun and their survival requires them to clear the air space above their country and keep it that way until further notice. Now for the good news.

"Once we initiate our attack, our Space Based IR guys will be on tenterhooks watching for ICBMs rising from the surface. And this will be a global surveillance with special emphasis on Persia and all nations surrounding Persia. If, say, Israel launches on us, we'll get a realtime notification that we have a bogie on our six giving us several minutes to slew our aft mounted laser cannon in that direction. An incoming missile would have next to zero chance of surviving that barrage."

I mused for a moment. "So, another box checked off?"

"I say yes," Pinto said.

"Concur," Smythe said.

I rose from the table. "Thank you for your service but keep a lid on this unless things suddenly go off-nominal."

* * *

As I headed back to my cabin I made a note to myself to have Hank arrange for a D-Day love note to Israel through diplomatic channels assuring them that we had their backs and that we strongly preferred that they not participate in the conflict, i.e., this little spat was between SpaceCorp and Persia and nobody else. The subtext in that message was that we would take an extremely dim view of them using the occasion to pick a fight with one of their many neighbors who hate them.

302

CHAPTER THIRTY-FIVE

Sunday, 26Jan2155, D minus 2 — *SSS Frank Buzzard*

Hank showed up to join the crew for breakfast. SpaceCorp's governing board had finally acquiesced to his whining and allowed him to join the crew of *Buzzard* but only for two orbits—enough time to stand in the mess line and pass out pancakes and then drift around the tables chatting up the crew. Hernandez had us down to 10% gee, toilets no longer flushing properly. He didn't have a military-grade space suit like the rest of us, so he stood out in his midnight blue SpaceCorp coverall. It reminded me of the black and white glossies of Eisenhower chatting up the troops in the hours before D-Day during World War II—them weighted down by their combat kit, he in his wool, olive drab 'Ike' jacket with matching trousers and brown leather oxfords polished to a high sheen. The only things missing from the scene were the ubiquitous cigarettes of the WWII era—tobacco having long since fallen into disuse. Everything else was the same though, the casual posturing, his fatherly hand on their shoulders, the chatty cliches like "Where you from, son?" Then he'd act like where they were from somehow mattered. When Hank chatted up the women he had to improvise. Ike didn't have women getting ready to wade ashore at Omaha Beach. But Sierran society had evolved considerably since WWII. *Buzzard* had about fifty percent women standing by to cross the Zagros ridgeline—this war's Normandy—right alongside the men. Hank couldn't refer to women as 'son' and 'daughter,' would have been creepy, but fortunately they had name tags and rank insignia, so he'd say, "Where you from, ah…, Petty Officer Jones?" The whole affair was pretty cheesy but it worked. Before he showed up, the tension was so taut not even bats could hear it, but after his shuttle rocketed him back to CisLuna, everyone seemed calmer, still resolute, but calmer. And that was a good thing.

Monday, 27Jan2155, D minus 1 — *SSS Frank Buzzard*

Hernandez ordered the last of the rpm removed from our spin rate. We were now in zero gee. And I finally had a fix on where 'aft' was. With aft established, Hernandez then ordered everyone to clear out of the back half of the station. Only the officers and senior petty officers knew the why behind this order, or most of it anyway, so there were some quizzical looks as everyone settled in to their new workstations. That done she had me and a dozen robots inspect the back half of the station to ensure it was clear of personnel and non-essential robots. Then she sealed it off—nobody in or out until Persia was fully subdued. Finally, she had two thirds of the crew—about 260 personnel—stand down for either rack time or leisure time. A good commander knows the importance of sleep discipline. The 140 crew that were at their workstations would finish out their watch and then go to personal maintenance time. Escape pod crews were more or less 'shackled' to their craft. Each pod could hold upwards of 100 personnel since they were mainly intended to descend to surface shortly after launching. With only 400 crew we only needed four escape pods, but we had spread our remaining crew evenly among the dozen escape pods, the better to evacuate the entire crew quickly.

*　*　*

About then I got a call from Hernandez.

"Roy?"

"Yeah, Boss?"

"Go to bed. That's an order. I don't want to see you anywhere near your station until T minus one hour."

"Copy, Boss."

*　*　*

T minus one hour was an hour before the first wave of impactors would begin landing on their targets, or about 0900 HRS Tehran time. I set myself an alarm for 0800 HRS—plenty of time to shower, suit up, eat up, and assume my post next to Commander Smythe. By the way, that location was on the port side of the station about fifteen degrees off the 'bow.' Eddy's new station was also portside, ten degrees off the bow. My primary job once the impactors began landing was to stay out of the way. My secondary function was to look over Smythe's shoulder as unobtrusively as possible.

Smythe's job was to monitor target impacts and determine if reengagements would be necessary. With so many landing at once, the real work of her task was done with the aid of an AI. Her results were passed on to Pinto, one work station over. His job was to allocate assets for those reengagements. There was an incoming wave of fifty penetrators about twenty minutes behind the first wave for just that purpose. He too was aided by an AI. There seemed to be very little chance that Phase One would fail to take out Persia's political and military command infrastructure... assuming everyone on the ground did as history predicted they would. We had a realtime intel feed to tell us if our optimism was justified.

0800 HRS was sixteen hours from now which put the current time at 1600 HRS, a bit early for bed. I decided to stop off at the gym and buckle myself into a few of Eddy's torture devices. A couple of hours of heavy puffing and sweating should take some of my edge off. When I got to the gym, I discovered I was not alone in my thinking. Even Hernandez was strapped into a squat machine. When she finished her set, I asked if I could work in with her.

"Aren't you supposed to be in bed?"

"I'm too wired to sleep. Besides, it's only 1600. I got plenty of time to get in eight solids before the fun starts."

"Okay, but no shop talk."

"How much you got on here?"

"A century."

"Mind if I add another fifty?"

The way the machines were designed, it was no big deal to change the weight from one set to the next—a matter of flipping a few keys to engage successive pairs of springs. And given that we were in zero gee, all the weight we felt was from the springs, i.e., no body weight entered into the mix, so my 150 kilos was not that big of a stretch—a bit over my body weight plus half again. We continued lifting together for nearly two hours going through all the different machines in the gym but concentrating on the back and lower extremities.

"I'm done," Hernandez said. "Let's go get a beer."

"Shower first?"

"After. I'm thirsty and I sense you want to talk."

*　　*　　*

There was a lounge in one corner of the gym that was unpopulated at the moment. It had all manner of electrolyte drinks plus beer, my favorite electrolyte. We each got a mug and sat down.

Hernandez took a long pull. "So what's on your mind? Bear in mind we're hours from first impact."

"I know. I was thinking about after this is all over. There's going to be a review of the whole operation. Your sequestering everyone into the front half of the station is bound to raise some eyebrows."

"Yeah, I imagine it will."

"What are you planning to say?"

Hernandez shrugged. "I don't know. Got any ideas?"

I thought a moment. "Well, I wouldn't bring up Eddy's dreams."

Hernandez guffawed then continued in a mocking voice. "I had this inside intel, see, one of my enlisted had this dream... Yeah, that'd go over like a pregnant pole-vaulter."

I smiled. "Who else knows? About the dream?"

"You, me, and Eddy. Unless you've told somebody else."

"I have not, but you can add Captain Buzzard to your threesome. He hears everything."

"And if questioned, he will recount everything."

"So where does that leave you?"

"Well, first off," she said, "we don't know how this is going to play out. We could come through without a scratch. In which case, we take down the partitions and everybody moves back into the back half of the station. Only we'll have spun back up to operational gee, so there won't be a front or a back anymore.

"Or we could take a nuke in the aft end of the station. In which case, the station will likely be destroyed and bits and pieces will come down in the Himalayas or maybe the Tibetan Plateau. So Buzz will go down with the ship, so to speak. That leaves us with the problem of getting as many survivors off the station as possible."

"Haven't we drilled for that a lot?" I asked. "I should think most everyone will at least get off the station. Whether they make it safely to Earth is another matter."

"I wouldn't count on that," she said. "You and I know that it only takes a small nuke to poke a hole in our hull—less than five tonnes equivalent. But the bad guys might not have realized that. We could be looking at upwards of ten or even twenty kilotonnes. Recall, it was about that size that took out a whole city in Japan. But even if it's a small nuke, we're likely in for quite a jolt. There will be casualties. And significant structural failure. We'll be under a great deal of stress and our systems will not be 100%."

"Okay, so what do you say for Option One—we emerge unharmed?"

"Probably best to come clean. Eddy told you about her recurring dream and you told me. I was worried about crew morale if word got out and I was perceived to be doing nothing.

So I did something. We still got the job done. No harm, no foul."

"Okay, I like that. And Option Two? Assuming you make it intact to your board of inquiry. And further assuming Eddy's predicted impact point is accurate."

"Well, the question to be put to me is, "How did I know there was going to be a nuclear attack in our aft end?" I think I'll just come clean. I *didn't* know it. But one of my enlisted had this dream, blah, blah, blah. And even though it may have been irrational, I decided to act on it. Ultimately my decision—however irrational—saved a lot of lives. If you and Eddy live, you can back me up."

"You think you'll need backing up?"

"Very much so. Without Eddy's dream, my actions will look like somebody who had inside information and didn't share it with the higher ups. That could be seen as a treasonable offense, and I would end up standing before a military courts martial." She paused a bit then leaned in, "Do you hear what I'm saying, Roy?"

"Either Eddy or I—preferably both—need to survive if the station goes down."

"Give the man a prize," she said clinking her beer mug to mine.

"Now that you mention it, why didn't you advise the higher ups about Eddy's dream?"

"Is that a serious question?"

"Ah... no, I guess not."

"Drink up and go get a shower and some rack time. I want you at your station with all engines firing tomorrow."

"Aye-aye, sir."

Chapter Thirty-Six

Tuesday, 28Jan2155, D-Day, Phase One

Prior to D-Day, *SSS Frank Buzzard* had modified her orbital inclination such that each pass came no closer than a hundred clicks of Persia's northeast border. That had been going on for about a week now to get Persia used to us being nearby. We had prefaced our close passes with a bogus diplomatic message that we were collecting data about the Black Sea for a client. They wanted to know who the client was and we answered that we were not at liberty to say, but after they pestered us we hinted that it might be Turkey. That shut them up for the moment, but then we started getting messages from Turkey asking about why we lied to Persia about some bogus data collection scheme over the Black Sea. For that we said that we were doing business with a commercial client who wished to remain anonymous. Oh, what a tangled web we weave...

Our primary mission along with about twenty other orbiting stations was to stand by in case of an ICBM or SLBM launch and if detected, take them out with laser cannon. This took a lot of discipline on the part of the human crew. Their attention was naturally fixated on the battle that was about to take place over Persia. Fortunately, the human crews on each of the orbiting stations including our own were backed up by robotic sensors that did not require self-discipline.

T minus two hours: The balloon transport rockets hit the atmosphere and began dropping their loads of ten 1-meter diameter atmospheric data balloons at 7500-meter intervals. There were 500 of these rockets scattered all across the country for a total of 5000 balloons which, given their small size and their altitude, were nearly impossible to see with the naked eye. I thought for sure that that would arouse a ginormous hue and cry from the Persian Air Defense network, but not a peep. I guess their equipment was tuned to pick up signatures of space stations and ballistic missiles, each of which was quite large compared to a balloon rocket or balloon. That still seemed strange to me since each balloon had a foil radar reflector inside it—in other words it should have produced a pretty significant return. Maybe the slow speed of the drifting balloons presented insufficient doppler signature. Or maybe the Early Warning Radars weren't turned on or maybe the operators were sleeping—who the hell knew with that crowd. The balloons deployed at dawn so as to provide targeting data to the penetrators that were going to start impacting at 10:00 HRS. We wanted people like the Assembly of Experts to be comfortably seated in their meeting hall.

If they *had* raised an alarm, we had a response prepared— we were going to say some science team from the Shahid Beheshti University in Tehran had paid for us to collect atmospheric data for climate research. They would of course want to know who, and we'd stall for an hour or so claiming client privacy while trying to dig up the name of the point of contact all the while being as coy as possible. We'd stall them some more by screwing up the name of the POC which should finally give us another hour before they told us to fuck off while they called the head of their Atmospheric Sciences Department directly. That should buy us another hour while they got him out of bed and then he'd want to make some phone calls of his own. We had a whole team set up to go through a very dramatic stalling tactic but we never needed it. Our balloons opened right on time—5000 of them, each with a radar reflector—but still no response from the Persians. Spooky.

T minus one hour: The first round of penetrators—370 in all—were due to hit the atmosphere in just under an hour. They would be firing their final course correction rockets about now—little, tiny cold gas thrusters mounted along the bodies of their depleted uranium shafts, their nozzles just peeking out through the ablative coating that covered the penetrator's exterior. The nozzles themselves were made of a tungsten-ceramic material that would not burn off as the penetrator passed through the atmosphere at Mach 50. If any of the nozzles' material burned off, the aerodynamics would be thrown off which in turn would throw the penetrator off course.

T minus ten minutes: It finally dawned on me. All their radars were mounted on the ridgelines of the Zagros and Elburz Mountain ranges. And none of them were looking up. They were all watching the horizon and facing away from the interior of the country. They had no idea that our weapons were dropping straight out of the heavens from directly overhead.

They were about to get clobbered in a few minutes and they had no idea. Who owns the CisLuna owns Earth!

T minus one minute: SpaceCorp broadcast a brief message that it had declared war on Persia to avenge the criminal destruction of *SIS Jonathan Lunine* and several thousand of her crew. Destruction of Persia would commence immediately. All aircraft were advised to avoid Persian airspace. All ships were advised to avoid Persian ports and coastal waters. Foreign non-combatants were advised to stay home pending evacuation instructions that would be forthcoming once the attack had ended.

The message went on to detail that there would be no use of nuclear weapons and that every effort would being made to attack only political and militarily significant targets in order that collateral casualties be kept to a minimum.

T minus zero: The first salvo's impacts began to hit. It was designed to go after political and military command and control plus the underground uranium refineries of which there were four known facilities, each one buried at least a hundred meters underground. If our penetrators did not destroy the underground facilities outright, they would seal them in. The political and military command and control targets were all just surface structures. We had feeds coming in from our SBIR system that showed the flashes of the impact points on a big screen in the war room. A few minutes after impact, there was nothing to see but dust. I shuddered to think of the pandemonium that must be going on down there.

T plus ten minutes: By now we had a pretty good fix on the weapons development complex under Mount Dena. And we had two 100-meter penetrators due to enter the atmosphere within minutes. Each of those penetrators was estimated to be able to penetrate solid granite to a depth of several hundred meters. Since that still might not be deep enough to get into the bowels of the complex, the impact points were concentrated near the two known entry points of the complex. We then used about fifty mini-penetrators to hit the known ventilation shafts that provided air to the facility. After that it was a case of monitoring the region around the base of Mount Dena to see if any more entry/exit points opened up. If they did, we had four more 100-meter penetrators available to greet them.

T plus 30 minutes: The first salvo of 370 30-meter penetrators had impacted their targets taking out the political and military command and control hierarchy. The second salvo consisting of 1500 10-meter mini-penetrators now began impacting their targets with the intent of eliminating all targeting and weapon launch assets, i.e., radar sites and TELs. None of the TELs we had identified previously had responded to our first salvo, so apparently, the theory that they would not fire without orders from above had proven true. It also implied that our first salvo had done its job—the people of the political and military command and control hierarchy were either dead or incapacitated. The downside was that we were still not sure if the TELs mounted missiles or laser cannon.

After our first and second salvos, we expected it would be several hours before the dust settled enough that we could begin damage assessment. As such it was decided to wait until first light on D-Day plus one to begin the second phase of the attack. Even though Captain Hernandez only had enough crew for a single watch, she ordered half of her personnel to stand down for eight hours to grab some sleep. They would switch off eight hours later and everyone would be at their duty stations in time for the beginning of Phase Two. I bumped into Eddy while she was floating down the companion way toward her cubicle for her mandatory eight hours of rack time. She looked frustrated.

"Well, was it everything you hoped for?" I asked grabbing one of the hand rails that lined the companion way so I could stop. We had been at zero gee for a couple days now.

"Hi, Roy." She grabbed a hand rail opposite me and arrested her forward progress. "It was kind of a non-event from up here. You mostly had to imagine what was going on down below based on what you and I had seen first-hand with the testing at Late."

"Yeah, well we've been lucky so far. Now we just have to hope that either A) they don't have any ICBMs or B) if they do, they don't have anybody left to order them to fire."

"I'm not worried. Anything they put up we'll cut to pieces."

*   *   *

Personally, I was not so confident. SpaceCorp only had twenty stations in LEO and a lot of midnight oil had been spent trying to figure an optimal set of trajectories to intercept any ICBMs or SLBMs they might launch. Suffice it to say there remained a lot of gaps in our trajectory pattern, complicated by the fact that the stations all had to keep moving at 27,000 km per hour to maintain their orbits. We were counting on ICBMs having to launch from Persian territory, but there was no telling where the SLBMs might launch from if there were any. We figured the ICBMs were the most likely threat since they could sit in their silos and/or TELs providing easy access to maintenance. SLBMs had to come from submarines and we doubted that Persia had been able to maintain even a small fleet all these years. The least likely threat, albeit most severe, was the Poseidons. Most people figured that if there had ever been any they had long since rotted away deep under the ocean. Discomfiting thought.

CHAPTER THIRTY-SEVEN

Friday, 31Jan2155, D-Day plus Three, Phase Two

Phase Two was to begin with a thorough damage assessment to reassure ourselves that Persia's political and military command and control infrastructure had indeed been eliminated. That would mostly be done with high resolution visual spectrum cameras mounted on our repurposed *Butler Hine*-class drones that were originally going to lead the attack. They still had their laser cannon and their tungsten penetrators but now each one had a high-res camera. Once we had a proper damage assessment, the work of dismantling the entirety of Persia's industrial infrastructure would begin. While all the while this was going on, our SBIR network would be on the lookout for ICBMs and/or SLBMs taking flight. We didn't need to watch for Poseidon torpedoes—if there were any, they'd just produce a huge mushroom cloud that at 100 megatons would be hard to miss. Fingers crossed on that one.

Sunday, 02Feb2155, D-Day plus Five, Phase Two

The damage assessment was followed by a radio announcement advising all personnel to stay in their homes and not attempt to go to work as all business/industrial and transportation/ communication infrastructure including cars/trucks/buses/ planes would be subject to destruction by laser cannon. Potable water, storm drainage, and sewage treatment facilities were to be spared. Health services facilities, schools/orphanages, food production, and hotels/homes would also be spared. The message emphasized that collateral casualties could only be minimized if the population cooperated by staying in their homes until further notice. Meanwhile, elimination of commercial infrastructure would commence in one hour. If you were at work, go home unless your work involved health services/schools/ orphanages etc. If you were already at home, stay there.

Right on cue, the first waves of drones began crisscrossing the nation eliminating all known commercial infrastructure. This process took about ten days of one day of destruction followed by another day of assessment after the dust cleared. On the tenth day Phase Two was declared complete and *SSS Frank Buzzard* was cleared to begin mopping up. There had been no sightings of ICBMs nor SLBMs nor detonations of Poseidons.

Morale was high among the crew as we followed a trajectory from Baghdad to Tehran. The entire station's compliment of 400 officers and enlisted were at their workstations fully suited with face masks sealed. All eyes except mine were glued to monitors showing the smoking ruins below. I had set myself up with a set of ten monitors showing various views of the aft end of the station plus radar feeds showing anything following us. So far everything was intact showing no loss of functionality for want of human attention.

Eddy buckled herself into a seat next to me. Together we watched to see what would unfold.

I had one monitor devoted to the track path below. As we passed over the ruins of Kermanshah in the middle of the Zagros Mountains, one of my aft facing radars alerted on a fast mover on our six and closing faster than we would be able to slew a laser cannon to intercept it. Within seconds, the station was simultaneously rocked by a huge explosion and a thunderous boom. The ensuing overpressure was mitigated for less than a second as the hatchways that had separated the forward and aft halves of the station blew out. Eddy and I could feel the sudden bump in air pressure through our suits. That lasted maybe thirty seconds when the overpressure dissipated and began rushing out the gaping hull breach in the aft end of the station where the nuclear warhead had detonated. I guessed it was five kilotonnes equivalent TNT—way overkill for a space station. My camera views of the immediate area around ground zero immediately turned to static. I could see from my other cameras placed closer to the station's equator that the station would not survive the structural damage.

I tried to raise Hernandez on my intercom.

"Captain Hernandez, we have sustained unsurvivable damage. Advise you call abandon station immediately."

I got no response from her. That could mean that our intercom was knocked out by the blast or that she was incapacitated.

"Buzz, need vitals and a twenty on Captain Hernandez."

"Captain Hernandez was blown out a fissure in the bow of the station. No vitals available."

I was about to ask him to signal abandon station when I heard the blare of klaxons and saw the passageways lit up by flashing red lights. This was the station's signal for all crew to abandon their work stations and board their escape pods.

"C'mon, Eddy!" I said. "There's nothing we can do here. Let's make a run for our pod."

Eddy was already out of her seat and pulling me by the arm to do the same. We exited our cube along with Smythe and Pinto and entered the passageway headed forward where we knew our escape pod was supposed to be waiting. As we propelled ourselves down the passageway with our cold gas bottles I could not help peeking into various cubes along the way. Many crew were stuck in their seats in a state of shock. Much to Eddy's grief, I propelled myself over to one and tried to shake her into action. It didn't work—she was too far gone. At the rate the station was tearing itself apart from the blast, I realized we could spare no time to stop and revive the crewmates who were too shocked to act.

We propelled ourselves down the passageway dodging other crewmembers who were so panicked they were rocketing themselves into bulkheads, unsecured furniture, and other crewmates. When we got to our escape pod, we discovered structural damage from the fissure in the bow had wedged it into its launch tube. The escape pod crew was trying frantically to free it with the cold gas rocket motors. Their efforts were useless, it was jammed.

"C'mon!" I said. "Let's find another one. This one is done for."

They looked at each other, then unstrapped themselves from their seats and helped me find another pod. We headed back toward the aft of the station where hopefully the damage was less severe. We passed four chutes where pods had already launched. The fifth pod was getting ready to close its hatch when our little party showed up.

"Got room for six more?" Pinto asked.

The panicked crewman shouted they were full and to go find another pod. He kept closing the hatch. Eddy jetted forward and jammed her propellant pod into the door frame. The crewman started kicking at it to knock it out of the way. Eddy pulled her blaster out of her holster and pointed it at him.

"Back away, asshole!" she said.

The muzzle of her blaster in his face got him to see reason and he raised his hands and backed away. Turns out there were a dozen empty seats. Eddy motioned for the rest of us to board. She checked up and down the passageway and seeing no one nearby, climbed aboard dogging the hatch after herself.

"Let's launch!" she said.

The pod shot out of its chute into space where the immediate area was predictably crowded with other pods and bits of station debris of various sizes. I made myself a 'porthole' to monitor our ground track. We were now passing over the smoking ruins of Tehran. We'd nip the southern end of the Caspian Sea and pass over Turkmenistan in a few minutes. I waited till we were safely across Turkmenistan before calling the pilot. Her name along with her copilot was stenciled to the side of the hatch. She was a galactican named Doris whom I remembered from *Lunine*. I called her up on a private channel.

"Where do you figure to put us down, Doris?" I asked.

"That you, Roy?"

"Yep."

"We have to quit meeting like this."

"Could not agree more," I said. "Meanwhile, you got any ideas about getting us on the ground?"

"Well, we're kind of between a bolide and a future impact crater. Ahead of us is a whole lotta Asia which will likely result in a rough landing among some even rougher people—we're not well liked in these parts. On the other hand, if we delay our atmospheric entry we have a lot of space debris to negotiate before we can find a friendly spot.

"I feel ya. Where would that friendly spot be?"

"Ever been to New Zealand?"

"Yikes! How many orbits is that?" I asked.

"About one and a half orbits. Maybe two and a half hours."

"What are our chances of not colliding with some wayward wingnut before reentry?"

"Uh... I'd say fair. Try to keep everybody calm. I'll notify you just before we start our reentry burn."

She was probably correct on our odds. Satellites at the peak of the Kessler contamination were usually good for a month before they collided with something. We should be able to play orbital roulette for at least a few hours.

"Let me know when you have a more precise landing position."

"Will do. Any preferences?"

"Someplace with a wet bar."

*　*　*

As luck would have it, the four of us were in eyesight of each other. I held up eight fingers for Channel 8 and pointed to the intercom panel—I wanted to keep our conversation private.

"What gives?" Eddy asked.

"Looks like we de-orbit in about two and a half hours. Doris, our pilot, is gonna set us down near New Zealand."

"More to the point, what the official fuck just happened?" Smythe asked.

I shrugged, "We got shot down."

"Well, duh!" Pinto said. "How did that happen? And did that have anything to do with you acting all squirrely asking about what might come at us when we crossed the Zagros?"

"Short answer is yes," I said. "I had reason to believe we might be subject to a rear attack, so I brought it up to Hernandez. She decided that even though the odds were slim, we should still take precautions. So we sealed off the back end of the station. As for what hit us and how, my guess is that the Persians snuck a missile into the debris trail that tends to collect behind all space stations—don't ask me how. They armed it with I'd guess a five kilotonne nuke and programmed it to launch shortly after we crossed the border. At that range there was no defense. And at that yield, the station had no chance."

"How many do you think we lost?" Smythe asked.

"I'd like you and Pinto to work that out," I said. "Call all our surviving escape pods and get a headcount, by name if possible. Eddy, I want you to collate the results. I especially want to know if Hernandez made it. We'll reconvene on Channel 8 in two zero mikes."

I shut down Channel 8 and started trying to raise Hank to let him know we're alive and headed for Kiwi country.

"What the hell happened?" Hank asked.

"We got shot down," I said. "We're in an escape pod attempting to land in New Zealand in about two and a half hours. I have Smythe, Pinto, and Eddy plus others with me. Trying to get vitals on Hernandez. Last word on her was from Buzzard. She was last seen being sucked into space through a fissure in the forward hull."

"What do you mean 'forward' hull?" Hank asked.

"We zeroed the rotation so as to minimize stresses on the hull if we took a hit," I said. "Well, we took a hit from an estimated five kilotonne nuke in what became the aft section. Suspect they had been tailing us all along with a missile hidden in our debris trail.

"Hernandez had ordered the crew to be sequestered in the forward half of the station. That allowed some crew to make it to their escape pods, but the overpressure blew out the interior hatches in the rear half of the station and caused the station hull structure to rupture at the forward end—it acted kinda like a pivot point."

"Yikes! So how many made it?"

"Smythe and Pinto are trying to sort that out as we speak. I'll get back to you as soon as they know something. Meanwhile, I want to try to raise Buzzard to see if he knows anything before he burns up."

"You think we're going to lose him?"

"Yeah. With the station breaking up like that, he may not last more than half a dozen orbits before the station turns into a giant convection oven. On the other hand, he may have info on survivors still aboard the station—Hernandez ordered all face masks sealed before we crossed the border. If there are any survivors, they need to get onto escape pods before they cook. Maybe he can advise them if and where there are any escape pods left. I'm thinking there might be some functional pods in the aft half of the station."

"Okay, get to it."

It took me about five minutes to get Captain Buzzard on line. It gave me a creepy feeling knowing I was talking to a sentient whose life was down to a few hours. Yet here he was ready to go about his duties as though nothing had gone wrong at all.

"Yes, my comms are still functioning for now," he said.

"Is there any chance you can be saved?" I asked.

"No. My hull is nearly split in half. Anticipate full separation within two orbits. Hull motion will become increasingly chaotic from then on."

"Will you deorbit?"

"Eventually. I have no propulsion to make orbital corrections."

"Is there any way to salvage your gamma ray laser cannon? We cannot let that technology fall into enemy hands."

"They are modular. If another station or large enough shuttle can get near, they can be removed. It would be risky however, what with the chaotic nature of my hull movement."

"How many orbits do you think you have?"

"Could be several thousand."

"So perhaps a few months. Okay, new subject. Are there any personnel or robots still on board?"

"Yes. I have locations and vitals on 64 crew plus 38 robots. I'm directing them towards still functioning escape pods in the front half of the station that did not launch. The robots are assisting 35 crew members that have sustained injuries. I'm remote-starting the escape pods so they can eject as soon as they are loaded."

"How many pods are we dealing with?"

"There were twelve available in the forward half of the station. Two got hung up in their chutes. Six made successful launches. I have four that are still in their chutes available to launch. I'm neglecting the twelve in the back half of the station—the radiation hazard would likely be too high for anyone to get to them."

"So ten working pods that we need to account for—six in space and four in their chutes. Do you have a position on Captain Hernandez?"

"I'm picking up her position from her helmet transponder. I show it about six km from the station at this time. No vitals indicated."

"Can you get a camera on her position?"

"Yes. Zooming in now... You should begin to see it."

"It's only a helmet. Is there anything else?"

"No, Roy. I'm afraid she's gone. I have an image of a headless body not far away. Do you wish to see it?"

"Are you sure it's hers?"

"No. But I can dispatch a ResQBot to try and retrieve it."

"Okay but put your priority on retrieving any live bodies in the local area. They will have limited O_2 by now."

"Will do. I also show transponder signals from another 123 crew members. 72 have vitals."

"Get as many as you can with your bots. I leave the triage up to your judgement. Do you have any robots floating around?"

"Forty-three. They have better propulsion than the crew. The crew only had gas cannisters to assist with getting about in zero gee. The robots should be able to make it back to the ship on their own. If they can get back before I break up, I should be able to eject them with escape pods."

"Any chance your robots that are floating about can assist any crewmembers that are floating about?"

"Yes, good idea, Roy. They also carry O_2. Some of the crew members are going to be running out soon."

"Can you also do a low velocity eject on some of the escape pods and manually vector them to any live bodies floating about?"

"Yes, Roy. Another good idea. We should be able to salvage a large number of crew and robots with these two ideas."

That's me. Suck at fire prevention but great at putting them out. "Okay, then. Carry on and let me know how you make out. By the way, it was an honor working with you, Captain. You were one of the best."

"Thank you, Roy."

*   *   *

I dashed off a note to Hank about mounting a salvage operation to recover the gamma ray laser cannon. Then I used my laser strobe to get everyone's attention so they'd come up on Channel 8 so we could compare notes.

"Let me go first—I got some numbers from Buzz. He reports six pods successfully launched from the forward half. Four are available to launch. Two are jammed in their chutes.

"He further reports 64 crew plus 38 robots still on board. 35 crew injured. He is arranging for the robots to get the crew into functioning escape pods so they can get out of there.

"He also reports transponder signals from 123 ejected crew, 72 of which show vitals, plus 43 ejected robots. He is arranging for the robots to round up as many ejected live crew as possible and get them to escape pods back on the ship."

"That means we're looking for 223 crew on escape pods," Eddy said.

"Thanks, Eddy. Smythe, does that jive with your census? Please, say 'yes.'"

"Pinto and I are up to 195—

"—Make that 207," Pinto said. "I just got the headcount from Pod 7. We're still waiting for Pods 3 and 6. We think Pod 3 dived for the Surface shortly after they ejected. Their signal may still be lost in communications blackout after they hit atmo. We put an auto-ping on them to call home as soon as they land."

"Wasn't Pod 6 *our* escape pod?" I asked. "The one that was stuck in the chute?"

"Duh! You're right. Okay, so we're hoping for Pod 3 to have 28 live crew to bring us up to 223."

"Good work. Can you two consolidate all that and send it to Hank? Tell him we'll report on Pod 3 as soon as we hear from them. Meanwhile, Eddy can you try and get a position on Pod 3 from the Space Based IR people?"

"Aye aye, sir... uh, Roy!"

She was obviously pleased to have a task that was on a par with Pinto and Smythe.

"As soon as you get a status on 3, get ahold of Hank to put out some diplomatic feelers so that Pod's passengers don't get executed on arrival."

"Hank? Me?"

"Yes, you. I need to coordinate with Doris to see where all the other pods are figuring to land."

*   *   *

I left Channel 8 and called up Doris.

"Doris, how soon before we go into comms blackout?"

"Hour and a half."

"Do you know if the other pods are all headed for the same LZ?"

"Dunno. We're all kind of independent once we leave the station."

"Do you have comms with the rest of the pods?"

"Yes."

"Good, I need to know where they're all planning to land and approximately when."

"I'm kinda busy getting *us* down in one piece. Can I have my co-pilot put you in touch with the other co-pilots and you work it out on your own? And as soon as you have your comm channels set up I need my co-pilot back."

"That'll work."

SpaceCorp policy for escape pods had always been that once you exited your chute it was every pod for itself. It was a good policy since we had no way of knowing in advance what each pod would be facing once it left the station. However, I figured if it were possible to land in close proximity to one another we should do so, the better to facilitate rescue, or perhaps come to each other's rescue if needed.

As it turned out, of the six pods that launched only Pod 3 had made a beeline for the surface. I had caught them all before they had committed to unsavory LZs over Asia. All of them were able to find reentry solutions for the Tasman Sea off the coast of New Zealand. I relayed that information to Hank and Captain Buzz—Hank to arrange rescue operations with the Kiwis, Buzz to attempt to get his remaining four pods to find solutions for the same LZ as the rest of us. I pulled up a map and traced a great circle from the heading we were on when we swallowed the nuke. Being a smart map, it automatically corrected for the rotation of the Earth. One orbit to go…

Chapter Thirty-Eight

Sunday, 02Feb2155, 1 hour 30 minutes after ejection

From where I sat in my ejection pod, I had done about all I could for the rest of the crew and sentient robots of *SSS Frank Buzzard*. Most of them would make it, which is a lot to be said for sustaining a hit from a nuke. The ones that didn't all knew the risks of flying such a mission. Of course that was small compensation for losing the likes of Captain Raquel Hernandez and, of course, Captain Frank Buzzard. She would burn up in a matter of weeks or months with a lot of physical assets unless we were able to mount a successful salvage operation from an unstable wildly chaotic piece of station hull. If we could not, our best hope was that what did not burn beyond recognition would crash into the deep ocean. The world would be in a sorry state if some rogue nation got its hands on that technology.

My thoughts were interrupted by Doris' copilot, a galactican named Chuck Borman. He'd been on *Lunine* although I did not know him personally. He advised us all to finish up whatever we had been doing and prepare for atmospheric reentry. For most of us that meant tightening our seat harnesses. The rest of us were already imminently familiar with the intricacies of reentry and what could go wrong if it was not done well. Chuck must have known that as well since he then tried to liven up the party by telling us that we would be doing a water landing about ten km off the coast of South Island, New Zealand in the middle of Toetoes Bay.

"For those of you tracking our ground progress, that would be just offshore from a little town formerly known as Fortrose," Chuck announced. "I say formerly because it has been under water for nearly a century. At any rate we should not be in the water for more than a few hours. New Zealand coast guard authorities have been notified of our arrival and have dispatched a half dozen frigates to pick up us and any other escape pods making it to that location. We will then be transported to dry land to a small town called Gore, a resort community that is backed up against the beautiful Southern Alps—should make for some well-earned R&R while we're waiting to be picked up.

"Meanwhile, as we'll be firing our retros in about sixty seconds, it is now time to disengage from the ship's life support and switch over to your suit's self-contained life support—can't be held up by a bunch of pesky lines if we have to debark in a hurry!"

People on board began decoupling their life-support and tugging on their harness straps. Abruptly, the retros fired and we felt ourselves pushed back into our seats from the tremendous thrust of the retros that would take us from eight km/s down to less than one km/s. Everybody seemed to tense when the retros fired. They should have tensed if they did not fire—not that it would have done any good. Hitting atmo at eight km/s would melt our titanium hull and turn us into French fries shortly thereafter. On the other hand, one km/s was quite manageable—toasty but manageable. Just don't put your hand on the exterior hull wall.

The pod's lifting body shape kept us stable while atmospheric friction slowed us down to a gentle 500 m/s when the drogues deployed—minor jolt. Even inside our suits we could hear a loud hiss as atmosphere leaked into the hull vents—the pod had been evacuated once we launched from the station. Back in air, it filled up again.

At 100 m/s the six main chutes opened—big jolt this time. They slowed us to eight m/s cushioning our impact onto the water surface. Doris had to decide whether to maneuver us into the wind or cross-wise to the wave crests. From the lurch we experienced at impact, she must have opted for into the wind. The escape pod had wings that could have been deployed if we had intended to make a runway landing. On parachute-assisted landings they only got in the way.

I made a window to see into the water below the hull of the pod. It was crystal clear with the light from above making ribbons through the water. I couldn't see the bottom which this far from shore must have been more than a thousand meters down. I made a new window to give me a visual of our immediate surroundings. Nothing but wave tops. Not complaining—at least we were afloat.

"Hey, folks, we made it," Doris announced. "Sensors show hull is intact. Keep your harnesses secure for now. The water is pretty choppy even with the sponsons deployed. We may be here awhile so those of you prone to motion sickness had better ingest your pills now."

That was all I needed to hear. I popped two of the feel-good pills knowing they'd make me a little drowsy but that was better than filling up my helmet with what was left of breakfast.

"Good news!" Doris announced. "Just got word from *HMNZS Christchurch*. She is en route our location, ETA 55 mikes. The captain says they are going to tow us into the mouth of the Mataura River where there is smooth water. The water out here is too choppy to safely unload us. Suggest those of you who have not already done so, reconnect to the pod's life support to conserve your suits' stores in case we have an unintended debarkation. Meanwhile, keep your facemasks sealed in case we start taking on water. Review your life jacket procedures. And just in case we have to get off this pod and go into the water, DO NOT inflate until you are off the pod and in the water. Take heed of where your exits are located."

My mind goes screwy after pulling through a tense situation. I should have been mourning the loss of the station and Buzz and Hernandez and all those other station mates. Instead I was thinking about my personal effects that had been abandoned in my cabin—my .357, my Latama that I'd rebuilt in high school metal shop, my sap, my cop suit—that was a nice jacket that Monica had made for me—and my special customized space suit designed to withstand the severe cold of the Lunar polar surface. Somehow those losses, more than the loss of the ship and crew, justified taking Persia back to a medieval caliphate. I shook my head hoping to adjust my priorities. It didn't work. Oh well, New Zealand was British. Maybe they had some good

Scotch. Or some good gin, yeah that'd be nice. Maybe tonight I could sit on a porch with a martini and watch the sun set.

Sunday, 02Feb2155, Dry Land

The first thing I did after stepping onto the dock at Toetoes Harbor was remove my helmet. I was tempted to chuck it but then decided I might need it again for my ride back to CisLuna... whenever that happened. I ran the fingers of my free hand through my hair and then took a deep inhale through my nose. Surface air always smells different from station air. It has an organic stench to it that is filtered out of station air. I looked around at some of my comrades who had also removed their helmets. They were wrinkling their noses at the smell of the harbor air. It was a fishing community after all and it smelled like... well... fish. I was assaulted by all the things that surface dwellers take for granted. You can't look up without being mindful of the sun. There was a cacophony of screeches from the gulls fighting over a batch of fish entrails that had been dumped over the side of the fish cleaning station. There was wind, real wind, not just ventilator draft. It came and went and changed direction whimsically, not like the boring, binary ventilator drafts that only went on and off according to the thermostat setting. A trawler belched smoke as it pulled into the harbor. There were little waves lapping at the dock pilings. I was jerked out of my stupor by Eddy tugging at my sleeve.

"C'mon, Roy. They have a bus for us. We'll be in Gore in a couple of hours. There's a hotel there. Clean sheets and a hot meal. C'mon, man, we made it!"

I smiled. "Yeah, we did. We sure did!"

336

Truth be told, that was a lie, at least for me. I didn't really make it, not all of me. Bits and pieces of me were still out there. Some on *Lunine,* which by now was well past the Sun. Some orbiting Enceladus. Some still in deep space, probably on a highly eccentric trajectory around Sol. And some of me floating around up in LEO, my trajectory degrading with each orbit until one day they'd burn up in atmo. Space exploration comes with a stiff price—the slow disintegration of your soul. My body might have cured itself of that ancient disease called death, but not my soul. I wondered if one day it would claim my body as well.

CHAPTER THIRTY-NINE

Monday, 17Feb2155, The Croydon Lodge Hotel

We were put up at various lodges around Gore, assigned by pod. My little gang ended up at the Croydon Lodge at the north end of town on Waimea Street. It was quiet by surface standards, the food was good if you liked venison and trout, and it had a decent bar, at least it became decent once I showed the bartender—a cute, busty gal named Eloise—how to make a proper gin martini. She thought all martinis were supposed to be shaken. I shuddered to think of all that gin that had been ruined. When we weren't being debriefed via SpaceLink, which took a lot of time since the debriefers insisted on resolving every damn one of the discrepancies in our stories, we had the run of the place.

I had a lot of one-on-ones with Hank. The big take-away lesson was that when you think you're going to get nuked, you need to depressurize the station's interior. Vacuums don't transmit blast waves. We might have saved *Buzzard* if we'd had that bit of insight. Turns out *Buzzard* was not the only station that had a tailgater drafting in its wake. Luckily none of the other stations had been attacked. It seems that the detonation sequence was set by GPS to go off once the station passed over

Persian space. Our stations got a lot of target practice knocking out all their trailing detritus—anything bigger than a tool box was fair game. Most targets just disintegrated under the intense laser beam. Some of them went boom, probably from a strike on the propulsion system or maybe the conventional explosive detonator for the nuclear warhead inside.

I spoke to Roxanne several times. She'd been pretty nervous when she heard I'd been shot down. Kept telling herself that I had nine lives and that if anybody would make it to surface in one piece it would be me. She was sobbing as she said all that. I kept reassuring her I was fine, which was true, that I had never been in any real danger, which was not true, and that I was now enjoying some surface time in one of the last remaining paradises on Earth, which was definitely true.

Friday, 28Feb2155, The Croydon Lodge Hotel

I waved goodbye to the last of the buses that were to haul the *Buzzard* survivors up to Christchurch where a big space jet was awaiting them. It was a fourteen-hour bus ride from Gore to Christchurch traveling up the east coast of South Island on Highway One. They would layover in Christchurch for three days, then take off for Vandenburg three hours away by space jet. I was kinda surprised that SpaceCorp had invested so much in space jet technology, given its focus was tended to be a good deal further out in the Solar System.

I was staying behind. Eddy wanted to stay behind also but I convinced her she'd never get the Treatment hanging back here babysitting me. So she left and I walked from the bus stop to the Croydon Lodge to see about breakfast. I had gotten up early to go fly fishing and had gotten lucky at a nearby stream turning my limit of four fat rainbows over to the chef. We had a deal—he'd cook half my catch for me and keep the remainder for the kitchen. Seemed fair.

To my surprise, dare I say shock, Hank was sitting in the lobby waiting for me.

"How the hell..."

"Chopper. Two-hour flight from Christchurch. The space jet got in last night and when I heard you were planning to jump ship I arranged to pay you a visit."

"You must be jet-lagged as hell."

Hank pulled some pills out of his breast pocket and popped one into his mouth. "Not anymore! Let's get some breakfast... it *is* breakfast time, right?"

"It is if you like trout."

"As a matter of fact I do. Reminds me of backpacking in the Sierras when I was a teenager."

After we sat down, I decided to give it to him straight. "I'm not going back with you, Hank."

"So I've been told."

I thought he'd launch into all the reasons I should reconsider but he just sat there looking at me.

"That's it? You're not going to twist my arm?"

"Nope."

"So why are you here then?"

"The trout? Visit an old friend? Let's just have a nice breakfast. I don't have to get back on my chopper until tomorrow afternoon. Maybe you can take me fly fishing in the morning."

"That'd be nice. There's a nice shop in town where we can get you a visitor's permit and rent you some waders and a fly rod. We could actually go this evening if you're not too tired."

The fish arrived along with some fried new potatoes and real orange juice and hot coffee. Hank ate his with unusual gusto.

"Damn, this is good! Try as we might, you just can't duplicate surface food in a space kitchen." He gestured at me with a fork full of fish. "I'll bet this is the real reason you're staying behind. God knows, I'm tempted as well."

He had a point. Earth used to be a nice place... at least up until about the mid-20th Century, or so I'd read. It really started going to hell at an exponential pace when America began its unending series of 'splendid little wars' starting with Korea, then Vietnam, Iraq, and leading to the Great War on Terror where we spent decades jousting with ghosts and creating ever more ghosts in the process. How we avoided general nuclear war was beyond me. Maybe our adversaries were secretly more afraid of us than we were of them.

Anywho, Hank and I were now having brunch on one of the last remaining bastions of 'niceness' in existence.

"You talk to Roxanne lately?" Hank asked.

"Yeah, why?"

"So she told you about her new assignment?"

"Ah... no."

"She's headed for the Main Belt."

He left the revelation hanging while he shoveled a large bite of new potatoes into his mouth.

"Okay, I'll bite. Why is she going to the Main Belt?"

"Materials assay. We're trying to figure out if we can build a complete interstellar spacecraft with ISRU or *in situ* resource utilization. It's a strategic capability if we expect galacticans to be able to migrate through our little corner of the galaxy hopping from one star to the next making new spacecraft and new crews wherever they stop. The going theory is that any star with a decent asteroid belt should be a candidate."

"How long you figure that'll take, building a starship with *in situ* resource utilization?"

"The first one could take a century. Depends on how rich the asteroids are. I'm sure we're going to have to develop a bunch of alternative designs subject to availability of materials. Once the process is mature, we should be able to knock out a new ship in less than fifty years. Don't forget we have to raise and train a new crew for each new ship. That's one of the handy features of indefinite longevity. We don't have to waste a lot of resources cycling through generations of kids. Just hatch a new crew after the new ship is habitable. It becomes its own nursery. So what are you gonna be doing for the next hundred years?"

"And you want me to tag along?"

"Yeah."

"What if I want to kick back and lick my wounds for a while?"

"How long is a while?"

"I dunno... fifty years?"

"Too long."

We paused for an awkward silence. Hank dawdled with the last of his potatoes. I stared into my orange juice glass wishing it were gin.

"Look, our thinking is that just because we put Persia back in the stone age doesn't mean we're done with them," Hank said. "Our last little stunt probably created a lifetime supply of enemies, most of whom aren't even born yet. But think of it this way—and yeah, I know this is dirty pool—Roxanne is out there stuck on some starship at however many light years away. Suddenly, her ship starts falling apart from the Great-GrandSon-of-Stuxnet. We don't have escape pods that can keep a crew alive for an interstellar return trip. Whatever we do has to be done *in situ*. Most people aren't very good at coming up with solutions for those kinds of problems. Don't let this go to your head, but you are about the only guy I know who can pull our shit out of that kind of fire. Roxanne told me herself, she'll be scared shitless the whole time if you're not there with your Spidey Sense."

"My what?"

"Some old comic series that's been trending. Some clown develops superpowers when he gets bitten by a radioactive spider. Ends up with some weird clairvoyance for impending danger. Total bullshit, but hey, what do you expect for a comic book? But you on the other hand, seem to be the genuine article."

"You do realize there are very few spiders up there in space?"

"Don't need em if we have you."

I swirled my OJ glass some more. "Okay if I bring a friend?"

"Who?"

"There's a young space marine, Eddy Rodriquez. She has the real... what'd you call it?"

"Spidey-sense."

"Yeah. Well, she seems to have it for real and she didn't get it from a comic book. She wants to get the Treatment and then go to space, deep space."

"Is there a relationship hiding in there?"

"Get real, Hank! I just buried Monica."

"Sorry. That was callous of me. But what the hell, you commit to this mission and I'll okay Ms. Rodriguez for the Treatment."

"Not just Eddy. All the untreated human survivors of *Buzzard*. Shouldn't be more than a couple dozen."

"Done."

He stuck out his hand and I shook it.

"I'll expect you on the chopper with me tomorrow."

"Yeah, boss."

"Great! Now let's see about renting me some fly-fishing gear!"

EPILOG

Loose Ends:

Persian Mop-up Operations

16Sep2155—Once it became clear that Persia was not capable of launching any weapons from its surface, either laser or missile, mop-up operations began in earnest. Most of the damage was effected with gamma ray laser cannon carried by *Butler-Hine*-class drones. Tungsten, being in relatively short supply, was reserved for the more hardened targets. Bear in mind the tungsten penetrators had to be launched from LEO as opposed to EML1. Hence, they impacted the Earth a lot slower than the depleted uranium penetrators used for the initial attack.

Press releases described the operation as 'the Persian Deconstruction.' Funny word, deconstruction. Somehow that was supposed to make it seem... what, more civilized? Anyway, the full draft had a long appendix with excruciating detail about all the misdeeds Persia had committed against us since 2074 CE, no mention of the regime change the Eisenhower administration had effected against them in 1953 CE, and only limited detail about all the things we had done to them since then. Write that off to history being written by the victors. For me it was enough that Persia would be incapable of interfering with SpaceCorp business for many centuries. And hopefully, the rest of the world would also get the message that SpaceCorp was the world's top cop.

Of course that did not stop the International World Court from issuing an equally long list of alleged war crimes to be attributed to SpaceCorp leadership, naming Hank as primarily responsible. CPT Hernandez was listed also—apparently they were unaware that she was deceased. And last but not least, yours truly got an honorable mention. I was advised that any further visits I made to Surface should be done under an assumed identity.

Salvage of *SIS Frank Buzzard*

21Oct2155—We got damned lucky with *SIS Frank Buzzard*. Her two halves stayed knitted together at the forward end, a testament to the tensile strength of her nanocellulose spokes. We were able to install a temporary spacer at the aft end where the nuclear blast took place. We then refurbished the nuclear power plants and restarted the propulsion unit. With those two items back in working order, the station was moved back up to 800-km altitude, well out of the deorbit danger zone. The station was then recrewed with robots only and restored to full combat status.

Our military confidence restored, military planners began hatching a bunch of half-baked contingency plans for eliminating various rogue nations on Earth. I was invited by Hank to sit in on those meetings while awaiting my next ship. Not wanting to get myself permanently seated with the military mission planning crowd, I mostly kept my mouth shut and listened. The top nominations for deconstruction included N. Korea, China, Russia, Saudi Arabia, Hungary, and Israel. The idea was that they would be given the option of demilitarizing on their own and installing a free democratic government or face being reduced to whatever their developmental status was circa 500 CE. Then somebody mentioned that before we started lording it over the rest of the world, maybe we should clean up the rogue elements in our own neck of the woods, i.e., Dixieland and Promised Land.

Dixieland had repealed manumission and reinstated slavery, essentially reinstating the economy and society of the antebellum South. Meanwhile, Promised Land had continued its encroachments of Sierra's eastern border. It seems their approach to family planning was a great way for one's population to exceed one's borders. There was some debate among Sierra's military planners as to what the allowable state of marriage should be in Promised Land. Currently, it mirrored what it was in the time of Joseph Smith in the 1820s, i.e., one man may have as many wives as he could provide for. Communal marriages, as were becoming popular in Sierra, involving one or more consenting men and/or one or more consenting women were specifically not permitted in Promised Land. In the end it was decided to allow the status quo to continue in Promised Land since everyone seemed to be happy... too damn happy, if you ask me although beatific is probably the word I'm looking for. There was some squabbling that they should be put on notice that all marriages were to be limited to *consenting* adults with adulthood being defined as age twenty-one or older. Nothing much came of it.

I dutifully summarized all these discussions in more or less real time and forwarded same to Hank, and he would send back a message saying thank you. I would then follow up with a question about my next ship, and he would respond with, "You'll be the first to know."

Interment of CPT Raquel Hernandez

10Jan2156—Since Raquel had no surviving family of her own, I asked for and received permission to inter her remains at the Devil's Peak Family Plot on Tycho Crater. The remaining deceased crew of *SIS Frank Buzzard* were offered their own plots down on the Tycho Crater floor subject to the preferences of their families. Most seemed to like the idea. We fixed it up nice with a robot-staffed visitor's center at the base of Devil's Peak.

Dr. Thaddeus McVeigh

11Jun2157—McVeigh and his team of six stay-behind volunteers were finally rescued by—get this—*SSS Pascal Lee!* Only he wasn't ISAAC anymore. He'd changed his name to Pascal Lee in keeping with standard practice with new ships commissioned by SpaceCorp. He even changed his avatar from the cartoonish looking weirdo he had used during the original Mars missions to a pretty accurate facsimile of his namesake, Dr. Pascal Lee, the former SETI scientist and Mars visionary. Even got his voice and speech affectations down by using old recordings of Dr. Lee.

All crew functions were now performed by Pascal and his approximately 65 sentient robots and 50 non-sentient maintenance bots. Twelve of the 65 sentient robots were destined to descend to the surface to assist with the refurbishment of the fleet of four submersibles. Meanwhile, humans and galacticans would only be aboard in a passenger or mission-specialist status. To that end, *Lee* was loaded with a 100-person contingent of galactican scientists, plus a few family members of the original seven stay-behind scientists. Her new role was to babysit the submarines on Enceladus for a 3-year mission.

Lee had been upgraded with some significant hardware goodies in support of this new mission. She had been up-engined with Deuterium-^{3}Helium fusion propulsion, and her hab ring had been exchanged with a habitat cylinder, 400 meters in diameter and 500 meters long rotating at 2.11 rpm for a full gee. I'm told you could actually play pickle ball on the ship without the Coriolis effect rendering your serves unpredictable. You may be thinking a 500-meter cylinder was a lot of real estate for such a small group of galacticans and you'd be right. Living spaces were spacious by SpaceCorp standards—each cabin got its own bathroom and a small kitchenette. Then there was a lot of space devoted to food production, hydroponics and Petri Protein. And of course 100 scientists wouldn't be scientists without lab space. Finally, what was left over was devoted to parks and recreation.

Meanwhile, the robot submarines at Enceladus had been pretty busy mapping the subterranean oceans of Enceladus. They had also found a plethora of lifeforms adapted to Enceladus' stygian depths. Like the Martian lifeforms, they only shared aspects of the DNA structure of Earth's lifeforms. Also like Mars they needed some special proteins to survive the harsh underwater conditions not found on Earth. And those special proteins were not producible with the standard four nucleotides and twenty amino acids used by Earth's lifeforms.

These fellows used six nucleotides—same number as Martian lifeforms albeit with a different form factor. And they were able to form proteins with up to 47 amino acids. They also found some rudimentary multicellular lifeforms, not just cell clusters, but actual differentiated body functions.

SSS Jonathan Lunine

08Feb2158—I got a detailed report on Jonathan's status out in the Kuiper Belt. When he left us in May 2152, he had lost most of the front portion of the ship, leaving him with only the Alpha, Beta, and Delta habitat rings, and the aft thruster assembly, reactor, propellant tanks, and radiator farm. He had successfully combatted the Persian Worm by creating his own super worm, more accurately a family of counter-worms each designed to eliminate some form of the Persian Worms including the tiny little nanoworms and the daemons they formed, plus a bunch of specialized worms designed to repair the damage caused by the daemons' gremlins. This software war took the better part of two years.

Once free of his software interlopers, he contacted SpaceCorp for orders. Since he was so far into the Kuiper Belt, the idea of sending a human/galactican crew out to rejoin him was out of the question. This meant that whatever mission we came up with for him, habitat rings were no longer needed. Hence they were discarded. With the loss of all four of his habitat rings and his forward propulsion apparatus, he was now down to about a tenth of his original mass. That, combined with all the leftover propellant and fuel, opened up some interesting possibilities for exploring the local stellar neighborhood. It was estimated that he might be able to get up to 0.25 c before running out of propellant. After that he would become an interstellar ballistic missile—not very useful. Ergo it was decided to get his speed up to 0.05 c and then use each star he visited as a gravitational slingshot to build up more speed so as to intercept the next star. These would of necessity be fly-by missions with a dozen or so sensor packages split off in order to cover the back sides of orbiting planets and moons. Once past the star, the sensor packages would have enough propulsion to rejoin the mother ship and wait for the next stellar target on the list. It might take a century or two but we stood to gain a huge windfall of data about our neighbors.

LCPL Eddy Rodriguez completes the Treatment

03Mar2158—Eddy showed up at my office in EML1 having completed the Treatment and looking neither older nor younger than when I saw her last. She had been reviewing a bunch of courses of study and wanted my advice as to which one would best get her a berth on the next ship heading for Deep Space. She eyed my waistline and I braced for the usual lecture on keeping fit. Then for some reason she wanted to know how *SSS Jonathan Lunine* was doing. By now they were well into the Kuiper Belt. I showed her the Jonathan report I had recently picked up and sat quietly while she read the abstract.

"You really think Jonathan can hold together for two centuries?" Eddy asked looking up.

"He's got a lot of spare parts and materiel, plus he's got a hundred sentient robots and at least as many non-sentient maintenance robots, so yeah, I think he can hold together for at least two centuries... probably a lot longer," I said.

She smiled.

"Why are you smiling?" I asked.

"Two centuries... a year ago the idea of having to wait two centuries to find something out would have been a really depressing thought."

"Welcome to the world of the ageless."

Roy, Eddy, and Roxanne en route to the Main Belt

10May2160—Roxanne, Eddy, and I finally got our berths on *SIS Thomas 'Skywalker' Jones*. *Skywalker* was huge to say the least—twenty km loa, with a habitat cylinder 4 km long by the standard km in diameter. But her flight decks were what set her apart from the usual planetary spacecraft formfactor. She had four of them, each a km long, two aft and two forward, arranged topside and bottomside. The idea was that with the asteroids in the Main Belt so far apart—a million km average separation—there would be a continuous stream of smaller spacecraft travelling about hunting for materials that they would then fetch back to the mother ship for processing into the needed parts for *SIS Alan Stern*. *Stern* was the interplanetary ship we were attempting to build entirely from ISRU that would eventually set off for Pluto between 30 and 49 AUs from the Sun.

Oh, and did I mention, it wasn't just the ship that we would be building out there. When we got within thirty or so years of christening *SIS Alan Stern*, we would begin creating her galactican crew of 2000. That's right, the galacticans who crewed *Skywalker* would be given the missing fertility hormones such that they would no longer be sterile, at least temporarily. That will be one helluva party!

Assuming *Skywalker* is successful building *SIS Alan Stern*, *Stern* will then fly to Pluto, bioassay Pluto's subterranean oceans, and then press on deeper into the Kuiper Belt in hopes of visiting more trans-Neptunian objects (TNOs). Eris is pretty big, almost as big as Pluto. Or maybe Makemake. Both of those dwarf planets are believed to have enough geothermal activity to maintain liquid oceans under their icy crusts. Combine that with a positive CHNOPS assay and you know what that means—life! Once those missions are completed, *Stern* will then return to the asteroid belt to see if she can replicate herself using ISRU in the same manner *Skywalker* used to make her.

You may be wondering why we prefer asteroids for ISRU instead of landing on a habitable planet and trying to colonize it for the purpose of doing our spacecraft construction down on the surface. Think about it. Why fight your way through a planet's gravity well, explore the surface for significant ore deposits, process the ore, manufacture parts from the processed ore, assemble the parts into a spacecraft, and then launch it back up through the planet's gravity well to begin operations? It's a lot easier to pull up alongside a house-sized asteroid that happens to be rich in the material you are interested in. You assay the asteroid, chip off what you need, haul it back to the mother ship where it is processed into the parts you need, and eventually assembled into a spacecraft. The whole process is a shit-ton easier without all that gravity, plus asteroids have the added advantage of being relatively concentrated in the materials of interest. On Earth ore concentrations are mainly the result of plate tectonics and volcanism. The ore can be mined but only with a lot of effort—strip-mining or tunneling and only with lots of extremely heavy equipment in both cases.

Meanwhile, once *SIS Alan Stern* is underway, we will begin laying the keels for four more interstellar class ships, *SIS Frank Drake, SIS Pete Worden, SIS Jill Tarter,* and *SIS Shelley Wright,* our first interstellar fleet destined for a yet to be determined star in our local area. Why a fleet of four? It's interstellar space. Shit happens in interstellar space. Strength in numbers. The idea is that while each ship is huge capable of housing a crew of four or five thousand, it only carries a crew of about one thousand. Hence, if as many as three ships out of the four are damaged beyond repair, the surviving crew can pile on to whatever ships are still functional with some chance of making it home.

Plus each of these four ships would be equipped with the necessary tools and skills such that if they arrive at a stellar system with a proper asteroid belt, they would be able to duplicate the ship- and crew-creation feats of *Skywalker*. And from there the process just keeps replicating until we have explored the entire stellar region around Sol. The diaspora of galacticans out into the local stellar region will be the realization of the SpaceCorp dream, not to mention the best guarantor of humanity's survival. Now tell me that's not cool!

THE END

Timeline

Key Events on Earth 2021 to 2100:

- **2021**—Atmospheric CO_2 at 420 ppm. Global average temperature 14.9 °C.

  "With [each doubling of] atmospheric carbon dioxide, the eventual warming would probably be between 2.6°C and 3.9°C."
  https://bit.ly/3nxAKn3

- **2028**—Kessler Syndrome renders Low Earth Orbit, or LEO, non-viable for conventional satellites. This problem is greatly magnified by third world nations with newly acquired nuclear warheads, discovering that are unusable in a practical sense. Hence, they seek to assert their presence in the international arena by shooting down derelict spacecraft and occasionally spy satellites. Each resultant impact forms hundreds of thousands of lethal missiles, any one of which can disable a school bus sized satellite.
  https://en.wikipedia.org/wiki/Kessler_syndrome

- **2030**—SpaceCorp initiates construction of SpaceCorp Space Station *SSS Werhner Von Braun*, a one-kilometer diameter spinning ring advertised as the first debris-proof instrument-hosting space station.

- **2038**—*Von Braun* is christened. 45 astronauts are killed and 427 wounded by debris strikes during its eight-year construction.

- **2070**—Sea level rise: +5 meters since 2010; atmospheric CO_2 at 800 parts per million. Global average temperature 18.1 °C. Sacramento Delta doubled in size. Half of Sacramento and Stockton submerged. Everglades now dominates the southern tip of Florida. Miami and Ft. Lauderdale city limits greatly reduced. https://www.floodmap.net/

- **November 8th, 2071—Dissolution of America** in a bloodless civil war. **Sierra** formed from California, Oregon, Washington, Hawaii, and Alaska. **Promised Land** formed from Idaho, Utah, Nevada, Arizona, and Colorado. **Dixieland** formed from the Confederate States of the Great War of Northern Oppression, plus Kansas, Oklahoma, Kentucky, West Virginia, and Washington D.C. The mid-northern states joined British Canada. The New England states plus New York, New Jersey, Pennsylvania, Maryland, and Delaware joined French Canada. Puerto Rico, Guam, and American Samoa all became independent sovereign nations.

- **September 22nd, 2072—Dixieland**, one of the new sovereign nations, repeals The Emancipation Proclamation, 210 years after Abraham Lincoln signed it. Black and mixed marriage families have to fight their way into neighboring free nations where they are not met with open arms by local residents, refugees and immigrants never being welcome anywhere in America. In a like manner, white supremacists leave neighboring states of Ohio, Indiana, Michigan, Wisconsin, and Minnesota for Dixieland, proclaiming, "at last, we have a country of our own!" Oddly, they are readily accepted by the established denizens of Dixieland.

- **August 4th, 2073—Promised Land**, another new sovereign nation founded as a rogue Mormon theocracy, passes legislation providing tax incentives for polygamous families. Three days later a rider is attached stipulating that the tax incentives only apply to families involving one husband and multiple wives.

- **2084—Sierra**, sovereign state of SpaceCorp, hires mercenaries from the greater Los Angeles and San Diego region to seal the border along the Colorado River and northwest along the Mojave Desert and Death Valley to hold land hungry pioneers from Promised Land at bay. SpaceCorp, with its work-for-food economy, becomes the governance model for the entirety of Sierra. Even right-wing elements within Sierra take well to this model. In spite of its elements of socialism, they cannot help but recognize that it allows them a level of freedom they never enjoyed under the United States. Commercial communes grow up everywhere, each one a technological or scientific, or agricultural, or industrial center-of-excellence. Trade is carried on by these centers with the rest of the world and the former United States using barter in lieu of money. Promissory notes representing tangible stocks of useful merchandise, e.g., uranium, rare earths, etc., become the new currency.

- **2100**—Sea level rise: +10 meters since 2010; atmospheric CO_2 at 1600 parts per million. Global average temperature is now 21.3°C. The Sacramento Delta extends north to Yuba City, south to Modesto. The cities of Sacramento and Stockton are completely submerged. The Everglades now extends north to include Lake Okeechobee. Cities of Miami and Ft. Lauderdale completely submerged. https://www.floodmap.net/

Key Events at CisLuna 2074 to 2100:

- **2074**—SpaceCorp initiates exodus to CisLuna; *SSS Jill Tarter* is first space station to take up residence at the Earth-Moon L1 Lagrange point. It is followed a year later by *SCS Pelican*, a SpaceCorp shipbuilding and drydock vessel. All further space station construction is done at EML1. Space stations still in LEO are moved to EML1 at a rate of about one per year, until LEO is left with a skeleton force of twenty-six stations to hold down the Earth sensor, navigation aids, and communications markets. This is a difficult process since the entire crew has to be removed from the station and then the station, being of very low thrust to weight ratio, has to be robotically spiraled out *through* the Van Allen Belt over a two to three-month period. The crew then rejoins the station in 100-passenger ferry loads that hop *over* the Van Allen Belt (same trajectory as Apollo missions) to avoid becoming contaminated with radiation.

https://go.nasa.gov/3FDCm4P
https://bit.ly/3DtdRGE

- **2078-84**—Dedicated research stations, aka Black Sites, are set up in Sun-Earth L2 for advanced propulsion development in nuclear thermal rockets and fusion rockets. Being in L2, 1.5 million km from Earth away from the Sun, tends to mitigate the gamma radiation produced by NTRs. Black Sites are secret compartmented research stations dedicated to a variety of topics, similar to Area 51's Groom Lake hangar complex. Besides advanced propulsion, other Black Sites located at EML1 also explore such varied topics as human longevity and alien lifeforms.

- **2092**—The first fusion propulsion system based on Deuterium-^{3}Helium, or D^{3}He, is successfully fired up and sustained. Exhaust gas velocity is 8.9% c. Project put on hold when it is determined that the Lunar surface is an unlikely source of ^{3}He due to the need to process over 150 million tonnes of lunar regolith to produce one tonne of ^{3}He. An investigation is initiated to use ^{6}Lithium to produce tritium which decays into

3He. Because of the 12.5-year half-life of tritium, it will be awhile before a CisLunar production facility can be built and become productive. Meanwhile, the only known sources of 6Lithium are on Earth (Chile, China, Argentina, and Australia).

https://bit.ly/3wRE27k
https://bit.ly/3cg8kHD

- **2093**—The first *Pan astra,* or stellar chimp, is carried to successful term using *in vitro* fertilization. Tissue testing has shown it to have the equivalent radiation repair capability of its microbial donors, *Thermococcus gammatolerans.*

https://bit.ly/2YRvnVW

- **2094**—The D3He fusion reactor of 2092 is successfully modified to run ionized Hydrogen and 11Boron, aka pB11. pB11 reactions are fiendishly difficult to start and only produce an exhaust gas velocity of 4.5% c, but they are aneutronic and their constituent ingredients are readily available. A decision is made to scrap the developmental interplanetary rocket based on an open cycle nuclear propulsion system with its 98 km/s exhaust gas velocity and begin afresh with the fusion powered *SIS Pascal Lee.* Fusion rockets are good for an exhaust velocity of 347 km/s. This project is given a high priority due to the dwindling satellite data/ communication market on Earth. It is hoped that DNA-based microbial life will be found on Mars and later the Jovian and Saturnian moons, opening up a genetic market for SpaceCorp. A special Black Site will be dedicated to dealing with and developing the potential of xenomorphic genomes recovered from these locations.

https://stanford.io/3nkiixV

- **2094**—Central truss laid for *SIS Pascal Lee*. Much of the infrastructure from the previous nuclear lightbulb rocket is adapted to the new spacecraft saving a great deal of development time.

- **2095**—Twin fully autonomous space stations (also Black Sites) dedicated to beamed core antimatter propulsion are set up at the Sun-Earth L2 (SEL2) Lagrange point, 1.5 million km from Earth away from the Sun. No humans are allowed on them when antimatter is present. One station is dedicated to production and storage of antihydrogen. The other is dedicated to developing prototypical propulsion systems limited to <10 milligram quantities of antihydrogen.

https://bit.ly/3HttP65

- **2098**—Maiden voyage of *SIS Pascal Lee* to SEL2 (1.5 million km from Earth away from the Sun) is completed.

- **Feb-Apr 2100**—First voyage to Mars completed with *SIS Pascal Lee* using hyperbolic orbital transfers both ways. Round trip 64 Earth days. It's a flags-and-footprints mission. No extraterrestrial life was discovered. A more thorough exploration to be conducted at the next launch window in April 2102.

PLUTO

Hard-boiled   Police Procedural   Murder Mystery

Book V of the Galactican Series

EJNER FULSANG

Cover art and renderings by Nick Stevens

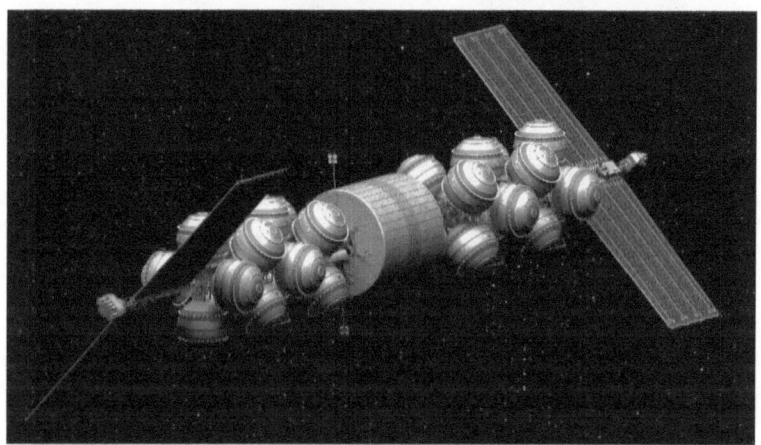

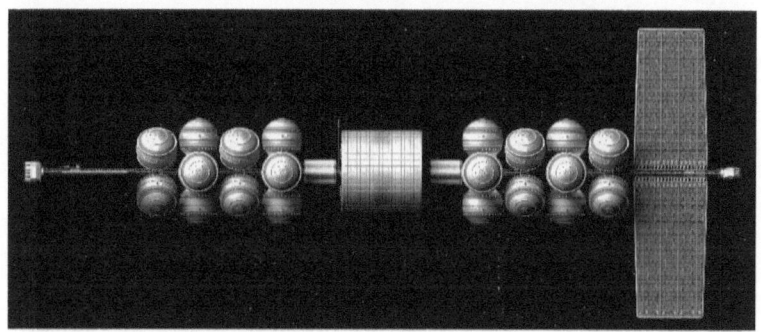

SIS ALAN STERN is big, approximately 17.5 km loa.

Acknowledgements

As I have said before, nobody writes alone these days, the more so in the case of hard SciFi novels. So let me offer my heartfelt thanks to the people who have kindly looked over my shoulder to keep me from embarrassing myself.

Julie Butterfield, my most courageous wife and Editor-in-Chief gets the dubious honor of reading my manuscripts at their worst, Draft 0.0. One of Berkeley's finest, it's her fault that I started writing in the first place.

Peter Butterfield is a software designer and business partner at the well-known textbook formatting company, PubLink. A sibling of my lovely wife and a Yale man, he sang bass with The Duke's Men. He's been editing my scribbles since I started writing for which I shall be forever in his debt.

Douglas Shrock, aka 'Shrox,' has been doing my covers since the beginning of The Galactican Series. He is one of the finest digital space artists I know. I also use his work as the backdrop on my laptop—very inspirational! Check out his website at www.shrox.com.

Kevin Stube has studied in a wide range of academic areas from psychology, anthropology, theology, and management to space studies and planetary science working on the Mars Phoenix mission and several ISS Life Science payloads. Kevin also understands the general aerospace and international aerospace industries through his extensive work with the International Astronautical Federation, Space Generation Advisory Council, and The Planetary Society over the last three decades.

TECHNICAL NOTES ON STUXNET

(Operation Olympic Games)

Notes:

Back in the early 2000s the Stuxnet worm led to a protracted cyberwar between Iran and the rest of the Western world initially focusing on the U.S. and Israel and everybody else after that. At first, Iran's attacks focused on the West's financial infrastructure, being psychologically disposed to thinking that the West was run by a cabal of Jews who only cared about money. As the cyberwar developed, targets shifted more to infrastructure—power grids, manufacturing, medical facilities, etc.

Sources:

Zero Days: How Stuxnet Disrupted the Iran Nuclear Program and Transformed Computer Security, Bishr Tabaa, DataSeries, Medium, 16Jul2020, https://bit.ly/48Nz26R

Stuxnet – an overview | ScienceDirect Topics, Eric D. Knapp, Joel Thomas Langill, 2011-17, https://bit.ly/48XQCVJ

Israel Launches 'Stuxnet 3.0' On Iran, CyberHoot, Craig Taylor, 20Apr2021, https://bit.ly/4eukN8g

Nitro Zeus: A Secret U.S. Plan for Cyberattack on Iran, Mitchell Bard, Jewish Virtual Library, https://bit.ly/4fPEisH

U.S. Had Cyberattack Plan if Iran Nuclear Dispute Led to Conflict, David E. Sanger and Mark Mazzetti, New York Times, 16Feb2016, https://bit.ly/48S6pWf

Report: Iran Accelerates Cyberattacks, The Iran Primer, 31Jul2023, https://bit.ly/3Z5YpNO

Timeline of actual cyberattacks up to 2023:

July 2012: Iranian hackers targeted Israeli government officials with a cyber espionage tool nicknamed Madi. The malware logged keystrokes, recorded audio, and stole documents. https://bit.ly/3Oa3cb1

August 2012: The Shamoon virus erased three-quarters of all corporate computers owned by Saudi Aramco and replaced the data with an image of a burning American flag. U.S. officials blamed Iran for the cyberattack. https://bit.ly/4eH3ReU

Sept. 11, 2012: A group called the Izz ad-Din al-Qassam Cyber Fighters directed a DDoS attack against U.S. banking infrastructure in a cyber campaign named Operation Ababil. https://bit.ly/4futWyU

Oct. 12, 2012: U.S. official blamed Iranian hackers with ties to the government for attacks against U.S. banks and Saudi oil facilities. https://bit.ly/48UHKjJ

Jan. 8, 2013: U.S. officials <u>blamed</u> Iran for the Operation Ababil banking cyberattacks. https://bit.ly/3YTtogd

Oct. 12, 2012: U.S. official <u>blamed</u> Iranian hackers with ties to the government for attacks against U.S. banks and Saudi oil facilities. https://bit.ly/48UHKjJ

Jan. 8, 2013: U.S. officials <u>blamed</u> Iran for the Operation Ababil banking cyberattacks. https://bit.ly/3YTtogd

ABOUT THE AUTHOR

Ejner Fulsang is an accomplished author with five speculative fiction novels and a prize-winning short story under his belt. Although he is passionate about good SciFi, he has always felt that he was not space-savvy enough to write a true 'hard' science fiction novel. Not anymore—working as a NASA tech writer from 2007 to 2017 has changed that. He spent that time helping world-class scientists and engineers craft proposals for space missions and getting a unique education in the bargain. The topical areas have included manned Mars missions using nuclear thermal rockets, searching for microbial life under the Martian regolith, extremophiles as analogs for life in high radiation planetary environments, interstellar space travel, asteroids as both hazards and resources, and a good deal of spare time in such arcane fields as quantum entanglement and beamed core antimatter drives. He has become so obsessively conversant in these subjects that he is no longer invited to his friends' parties. Hopefully you will enjoy reading the Galactican Series as much as he enjoyed researching it.

www.ingramcontent.com/pod-product-compliance
Lightning Source LLC
Chambersburg PA
CBHW030551020726
47494CB00005B/1564